DARK TIME

Other fiction by the author:

Northward (2018)
Flood Moon (2017)
Absolute Truth (2015)

DARK TIME

CHUCK RADDA

lefora
PUBLISHING LLC

Note: This revised edition of *Dark Time* has been reformatted for readability. The text remains the same.

Author's photo by Lindsay Vigue Photography

Published by Lefora Publishing

Author's website: chuckradda.net

Email: chuck@chuckradda.net

For Deanie

Fear

ɔm her bedroom window Keira Eason stares at unusual activity across the street: ɪrge green truck has backed into the driveway and two men stand leaning on it, ɪking from paper cups and grinding out cigarettes on the grass. It's Saturday ɪrning, and though Keira is too young to understand what qualities a perfect day ɪ June is supposed to possess—what the air is supposed to feel like, smell like, ɪn look like through sun-squinting eyes—some inherent awareness prompts her ɪaise the window a few inches.

ɪhrough the screen she can hear them swearing, using language she isn't ɪposed to use. They yell the f-word over and over and one of them shrieks about ɪ shitty job. She silently admonishes them. She's ten, but she knows better than ɪay words like that. Moments later some other grown-ups come out of the house, ɪ conversation quiets, and the two men remove something heavy from the back ɪ the truck—something large and soft and colorful, mostly green but with flecks ɪ yellow. They lug it around back, out of sight. They're big men but they struggle ɪh it, then return and carry more items, less appealing and less colorful. ɪchinery maybe, something on wheels. Another trip and another, and Keira ɪtches until some time later the truck pulls away and rumbles down the street, ɪrlson's Inflatables, in yellow, painted on its side.

ɪ"Those trucks shake the whole house," Keira's mother says. Keira has not heard ɪyone enter the room and doesn't know when she arrived.

ɪ"The men were swearing, Mom."

ɪ"Yes. I heard them. Looks like a party," she says, and points out the balloons ɪd to the porch lights, the fence posts, even the branches of a newly-leafed red ɪple in the front yard. Keira had been so taken by the truck, she didn't notice.

ɪ"Are we going to the party, Mom?"

ɪ"We don't really know the Reed family that well."

ɪ"But on Halloween I went there to trick or treat. You let me go by myself."

ɪ"Because it was close by, but they're just neighbors," her mother says. "I'll bet ɪu don't even know the little girl's name."

ɪ"It's Sylvy. The men brought something in that truck. Something big."

ɪ"A dinosaur," her mother says, ignoring her daughter's correct answer. "You ɔw it up and bounce on it, or in it. It's something new."

ɪ"You bounce on it?"

"Like the trampoline at cousin Cathy's party. Remember how you ha
headache afterwards?"

Keira remembers the headache, but remembers also how her cousin laughed a
told her it was a small price to pay for fun. Of course her sister Hayley fell a
bent her finger back and cried for an hour. She's only seven and cries all the ti
anyway. But that was a while ago. What Keira wants now is an explanation of w
there'd be a dinosaur across the street when she won't be bouncing on it. She
see one daffodil-yellow corner of it sticking out from behind the garage. It's ri
there, practically within reach.

"Too hot for that kind of thing anyway," her mother says, her voice flat a
unconvincing. She wipes her forehead with her sleeve to confirm the stateme
"Everyone will be sweating and hot, overheated."

Keira barely registers the comment.

"Can I go over there and play?"

"That would be party-crashing," her mother says, then carefully explains w
such a thing is not to be done, how parties are planned with a certain number
guests expected, and how if there are too many there won't be enough cake, enou
ice cream, enough anything. She races through the litany of reasons, precludi
the opportunity for questions or objections. Keira listens attentively. She alwa
does, just like in school when a teacher is explaining something in arithmetic. S
even, at some level, understands that she is not entitled to be at this party.

"I guess," her mom says as she leaves the room, "you should have gone w
your father and sister."

To the library? On a Saturday? Why? Keira had no stupid second-gra
assignment about birds to do, so she didn't need to be looking through pictu
books on some long table writing down notes about feathers and nests. She'd rath
have the morning to herself and play with Hayley in the afternoon. But Ke
doesn't sulk, doesn't dwell on disappointment. Not ever. By noon she has forgott
the party entirely, immersed as she always is in some fantastical drama in t
backyard playhouse her father built and in which she keeps the characters of h
little plays.

Then the music begins.

It's awful music, tinny, blaring, the same series of notes again and again, bu
sounds like the merry-go-round at the carnival her father always claims is dirty a
horrid yet takes the family to every April when it comes to town. She walks arou
to the front of the house and stands on the sidewalk. She hears voices, high-pitch

d screaming, voices she has heard on a spinning carnival ride where some kids
rew up but she begged to ride again and did.

She is beginning to understand why people crash parties.

A blue station wagon pulls up. It's Laura Marin's mom. Laura is her best school
end and yet, here she is, across the street, walking up the very same sidewalk
here Keira walked on Halloween…by herself. She shouts Laura's name and
oves closer to the curb, stopping just short of the street. The mother proffers a
lfhearted wave but Laura herself, carrying a gift in both hands, lays it on the
ound and gestures wildly.

"Come to the party!" she yells, but her mother picks up the gift—Keira can see
yellow bow on it—and quickly pulls Laura around back.

It takes Keira only seconds to realize that playing with her best school friend is
fferent from crashing a party. And this best school friend has actually invited
er. *Come to the party*, she said. Keira doesn't doubt she has heard her correctly.

She steps off the curb and dutifully looks both ways. There aren't many cars on
aple Drive, not ever, but she has learned to be careful. During a bicentennial
rade, three years before, a little boy in her class was struck by a car and taken to
e hospital. Keira was only seven but she remembers.

Now she's ten. She knows very little about deceit and subterfuge. She doesn't
now how to look as if she belongs. She's just suddenly there, in those drab green
orts and that simple gray t-shirt, standing amidst the booming music and the
lden streamers and the girls in the colorful jerseys. She considers going home to
ange into something pretty when a voice stops her.

"I know you. You live across the street."

It's Sylvy.

"I came on Halloween," Keira says. She is about to explain her presence when
ylvy cuts her off.

"I thought you couldn't come. Do you want to bounce with me?"

"I think I can do that," Keira says, carefully parsing her mother's concerns. "But
can't have cake and ice cream because there won't be enough. And I think I can
ay with Laura."

"Laura Marin? She's fat," Sylvy says. "Why do you want to play with her?"

"She's my friend."

"I'll be your friend if you want to bounce. Come on."

Keira sees a line of kids and, for the first time, sees this inflated dinosaur up
ose: that heap of plastic those men dragged from the truck has been transformed

into something wondrous and huge, higher than the porch of the house, spewi
out that music which now, so close to the source, seems slightly less awful. Lau
is in line talking with other kids she recognizes, though most are strangers to h
And Laura doesn't look fat even though she does have breasts that are bigger th
everyone else's. That doesn't make her fat. That's what Keira's mother sa
anyway, and she's always right.

Almost always.

"I guess we should get in line," Keira says.

"We don't have to. Come on. Bouncing is more fun when you sneak in."

Keira follows her new friend through a yard festooned with flags and balloo
whipping about almost to the horizontal in the suddenly freshening breeze. Grow
ups linger on the edges of the group, holding glasses that drip condensation. Son
of the men drink from bottles; a few of them smoke cigarettes. At the front of t
line a large man stands, the father from across the street—Sylvy's father—the o
who dropped candy into Keira's plastic Halloween pumpkin the previous fall.
one hand, he holds a can of soda and in the other a cigarette that he occasional
puffs on, aiming the smoke downwind away from the children. Keira eyes hi
warily.

"If your father sees me...."

Sylvy pulls her along. "I'll show you a secret, but you can't tell anyone."

Keira follows the girl onto the back porch and into the house, passing a bo
coming the other way. He holds a wad of bloodstained tissue to his nose and look
ashen while a woman, his mother maybe, leads him back into the yard. He look
straight at Keira, there's a moment of recognition and his right hand goes up in
near-wave, but in that same instant he seems to remember his own embarrassmer
and humiliation. She knows him from school, but she isn't supposed to be ther
and tries to hide behind Sylvy. It doesn't matter. The boy doesn't want to be see
either, his bouncing fun apparently over. The girls pass a gray-haired woman wi
tiny glasses who seems busy with something in the sink as water splashe
everywhere. She never sees them.

Sylvy leads the way down some steps. The basement is dark, but Sylvy insis
that they not turn on a light, that they might be seen. Enough midday sunlig
streams through the undersized windows to allow them to see where they're goin
but Keira feels unsure that she should be there. It was one thing to be standing i
the yard looking for Laura, but it's something else to be sneaking around i

meone's cellar. If she could leave…but Sylvy has a tight grip on Keira's hand
d leads the way across the concrete floor toward a sliver of light.

"Up those stairs," Sylvy says, "is the dinosaur. There's a slanted door that goes
tside. If we push it open a little bit and squeeze through, we won't have to wait
line. I'll go first."

"But your father…."

"It's my birthday and Daddy says I can do whatever I want. I told him to get the
inosaur so it's really mine."

"To keep?"

"No, stupid."

Even without the condescension in Sylvy's voice, Keira knows her question
ade no sense. Still, just for that moment Keira envisions it: an amusement park
ght across the street. She and Sylvy, and Hayley too if she's not too young—
very day, all summer once school got out. Maybe not Laura, but so what? Still,
e question was stupid and she's embarrassed to have asked it; besides, Sylvy is
lready pushing open the door and Keira sees a widening band of light under it,
ke the sky in the evening when the sun has set and a thin strip of daytime remains
nd she knows it's time to go into the house.

Then something bangs on the metal door and Sylvy laughs.

"Someone jumped on it," she says.

"What if you open it and someone jumps on it then?"

"Then they'll crack their head open," she says, laughing even harder.

Keira sees it differently…sees the door landing on Sylvy and cracking *her* head
pen. Maybe she should warn her, but then what? Have herself be called stupid
gain? Besides, they're this close….

So she chooses instead to watch her new friend open the door by inches until
ere is almost enough room to squeeze through. At that instant the girl turns
round and Keira can see her face. Sylvy isn't scared at all. She is laughing and
er mouth shows the randomness of her teeth and the spaces where there will be
ore. There's a look of triumph and accomplishment, maybe the same look Keira
as when one of her playhouse dramas has turned out well, when all the characters
ave behaved and the ending has left everyone feeling satisfied. So it's okay after
ll to crash a party and make a new friend. She won't even be punished.

And then just like that there is no light and no smile and no sound except a door
mashing shut and the softer sound of something striking the cold concrete floor
t her feet.

For a moment Keira says nothing. Waiting. Sylvy will have to push that do[or]
open again. Just a delay. In a minute or two they'll be on the dinosaur.

"Get up," Keira says. "Come on."

Sylvy doesn't answer.

Keira bends down and feels around. It's really dark. If she pushes that do[or]
open—but she can't. She'll be caught for sure.

"Come on, Sylvy, get up."

She sounds like her own mother awakening the girls for school. She and h[er]
sister always obey quickly, but this girl....

Keira's voice became louder, each plea more demanding and more desperat[e]
her shouts swallowed by the motorized roar of the machinery and the music blari[ng]
alongside it.

"Come on, we're gonna get in trouble."

She nudges Sylvy once, then again. Maybe the girl is ticklish. She feels arou[nd]
some more, finds her knees, and squeezes the skin just above the kneecap. Nothin[g]

Maybe she's hurt? In school the nurse has given them a first-aid lesson on wh[at]
to do if that happens. Call somebody: that's most important, but who? Her mothe[r]
who had specifically told her not to go? Sylvy's mom, who had specifically n[ot]
invited her? She could tell her own father maybe—at least he didn't know abo[ut]
any of this—and even though there might be punishment later, he had never raise[d]
his voice to her and she was sure he wouldn't this time either.

But her father isn't home and she can't leave the girl there. She squints in th[e]
darkness. There are parts of Keira's own cellar that she avoids—corners wit[h]
spider webs and beetles and oversized bugs too ugly for names—dark areas wher[e]
the light barely reaches. If this is one of those places, she has to make sure the gi[rl]
is awake before she leaves her there.

And so she sits, the tops of her legs recoiling against the cold concrete. Abov[e]
her the loudspeaker continues to pump out music at the same monotonous, b[ut]
almost comforting, level. As long as the music plays…. Occasionally a screa[m]
interrupts, someone has been knocked down or has jumped too high or is ju[st]
thrilled to be part of such an extraordinary event. Maybe the boy with the blood[y]
nose has smashed his face again.

And then the machine stops and she hears more adult voices than children's.

At first they are calm and inquisitive, like her own mother entering Keira'[s]
bedroom and calling her although they both know she's there. Not so much [a]
question as a greeting.

hen the voices grow more demanding.

Come on, now, Sylvy, stop hiding."

's a man's voice. Then a woman shouts something about presents.

nd cake.

nd ice cream.

orbidden items.

nippets of sentences resonate above the metal door in the suddenly quiet yard

Keira nudges the girl again.

I can't have cake," she says. "My mother said not to. There won't be enough."

ut it isn't her mother who proclaimed the rule: it's Keira herself. That had been

deal. No cake or ice cream or anything else meted out to guests. Just playing

h a friend. And now she hasn't even done that and she's angry. Sylvy has ruined

whole day.

I can't stay here now," she says, then lifts herself off the step and walks slowly

oss the cellar. She can hear footsteps above her, water running, voices with

re urgency.

he is ready to run out of the house and across the street, without looking both

ys if necessary. But when she steps into the light of the kitchen, the house is

et. At the sink the same woman is struggling with a pile of paper plates, trying

ear off the cellophane.

Did you find the bathroom okay, little girl?"

Keira mumbles a yes and sidesteps the puddle of water on the floor. The woman

nts without ever having looked at her.

As soon as we find out where my niece is hiding," she says, "we'll have cake."

Jp until that point the idea that Sylvy is merely hiding never occurred to her.

de-and-go-seek was fun, of course, but people usually hid alone. They didn't

g a friend along and hide with her. But the Reeds, well, maybe they played the

ne differently. Or maybe there was a new variation that hadn't gotten around

schoolyard yet. Or maybe Sylvy was playing a trick on Keira, pretending to be

eep, sort of like hiding. It wasn't a very nice trick, and it meant there would be

bouncing on the dinosaur. Maybe Sylvy didn't like her after all.

"She's down there," Keira says, and points to the cellar door, slightly ajar as she

t it. She is angry now. It was bad enough not to be invited, but to be cheated like

s?

"Why in the world…?" the woman begins but lets the thought go, takes a sharp

ife, and pokes the blade into the packet of dishes. "They wrap these so damn

tight," she says, then leans toward the window in front of her and yelled outs
"I have the dishes. Anyone find her yet?"

Before there's an answer, Keira is gone. She recrosses Maple Drive and sits
the big rock outside her play house watching some bees hovering near the salv
Such a strange name for a plant, gross like saliva, but pretty to look at. And alw
covered with bees, their hum filling the space between the afternoon silence a
the shrill scream of the police sirens that begins a short time later.

Sometime after that a policewoman comes to the Eason house. The lady in
kitchen struggling with the paper plates remembers a little girl but has no idea w
she looked like or what she was wearing. The officer's questions are innocu
and humane; nobody is accusing anyone but everyone wants to know how
happened. Keira admits to having peeked into the yard but nothing more. F
parents, both home now, confirm it.

On the TV someone calls it a freak accident, says that ten-year-old Sylvia R
had become the innocent victim of childhood mischief, the desire to play
harmless trick. But (the reporter says) at the moment she pushed open that ce
hatch, someone else at the party jumped on it, someone who had been running a
chose that split second to land full force, to knock her backwards, to cause her he
to hit the concrete steps and end her life.

A freak accident.

Keira doesn't know what the term even means, but something about it seems
erase all responsibility: hers, Sylvy's, the boy who jumped on the door. No one
to blame.

That night she tells her parents the whole story. Her mother looks wary but h
father seems pleased.

"You should always tell the truth," he says.

Keira nods.

"But sometimes," he says. "The truth makes it worse and people need
hear…nicer things."

"I don't know what you mean."

"See," her mom says, "If you tell Sylvy's mom and dad what happened, they
be even sadder. It's better to say that you weren't there and it was just an acciden

"But it *was* an accident."

"Yes, and that's why nobody is responsible."

"I don't think Sylvy liked me anyway. She said I was stupid."

'Well you're not stupid," her father says with exaggerated incredulity. "We all know that."

Her mother nods. "She isn't a very nice girl."

She isn't. Just like that the conversation slips into the present tense, and just like that there has been no death—just Sylvy who *doesn't* like Keira. Sylvy who *isn't* a very nice girl.

Keira, anticipating some sort of punishment and finding none in the offing, accepts the argument. But it's a strange conversation: her father always makes jokes, but tonight there are none. He doesn't smile or laugh. And Keira still doesn't understand how the truth can make someone sadder, but she has occasionally been sent to her room for little bits of misbehavior, and this escape seems too good to question.

Besides, some of the story really is true.

She never bounced on the dinosaur.

She never ate any cake.

Sylvy did, in fact, ruin the day.

That night it snows so hard and so heavily that Keira can hear the flakes striking the roof above her bed. Her play house is buried and the street is blocked by drifts taller than she. Now no one can cross, and anyway there's nothing to cross to: the Reeds' house has vanished and bits of daffodil-yellow plastic whip across the white landscape, occasionally striking her bedroom window before disappearing in the riotous squall. A policeman stands in the street as the snow rises and covers him. Keira should tell somebody, but then she hears her mother awakening her for school. On Sunday? On Sunday? Keira repeats it as loudly as she can but her mother doesn't seem to hear: how can she with the snow crashing on the roof like that? Keira pulls the sheet over her head but it does no good. Her mother will not relent. Angrily the girl jumps up to confront this woman who refuses to let her sleep, who can't figure out that there's no school on Sunday, who can't stop the terrible, deafening snow.

"You were having a nightmare, Keira."

"But it's Sunday," she answers, half mumbling. "There's no school anyway."

"Of course there isn't. You're sweating, honey. Do you want some water?"

Keira shakes her head, steals a glance at the window. The shade is drawn but ruffles slightly in the nighttime breezes. There's no snow slanting by, not tonight. Across the street it's perfectly quiet, though cars lined the curb when she went to sleep and every light was blazing.

"I thought it was snowing…."
"Not on the longest day of the year."
"It was making so much noise."
"Nightmares are never real," her mother says.
"I remember the street filling up and a policeman...."
"Most of what you think you remember isn't even true."
"Like Sylvy?"
"Like Sylvy."
Years later when Keira Eason considered the events of that Saturday afternoo
she could not say with any certainty that she had ever crossed the street, descend
those stairs, been with Sylvy at all. And her parents, from the beginning, agreed

om the Manhattan shoreline, it's a child's beach toy, maybe abandoned for a
ore interesting one and casually left to drift away.

From the Manhattan shoreline, where chattering teeth and rapid breathing and
hispers of imminent death cannot be heard, the anomaly is jarring: aircraft are
tended to fly, not float. Yet this afternoon a plane, languid and tranquil, pivots
ently counterclockwise downstream.

Then other movement disturbs the serenity. Shapes appear on both wings, human
apes that appear to be standing on the river itself, creating a symmetry on either
de of the fuselage. Then the boats: commuter ferries and private craft racing west
om the New York docks, east from the Jersey moorings, speeding toward the
rcraft like an impromptu winter regatta. On the frozen riverbanks emergency
ehicle lights flash as triage units appear. Hospitals on both sides have been
erted; emergency staffs hustled in. Everything quickens, and along the river's
lge people sense panic and mortality. The havoc, for that's what it is despite the
rlier appearance of calm, races along from all sides. The boats encircle the plane,
convergence of small and large vessels, and begin to unburden the wings as the
ane continues its slow turn downriver.

No one knows what to make of it: a plane crash without wreckage or casualties.
he survivors, if that's what they're called, huddle on the wings chatting on cell
hones or waving to ferry operators who jockey for rescue positions. Within
inutes newsmen will attach the word "miracle" to the event, but while the plane
ill drifts toward the open Atlantic, there is little time to classify anything, or to
elebrate. A machine designed to fly six miles above rivers cannot long float on
em, and there are survivors to rescue before the thirty tons of aircraft sinks
evitably to the bottom.

On the starboard wing Keira Wilkes remains essentially silent while she and her
vo sons await rescue. They are among the last out of the cabin and they will be
mong the last into a boat, but she says little while the boys jabber to each other
bout wet shoes and a lost video game. They don't seem frightened, perhaps as a
eflection of her. She has been calm throughout, sauntering down the aisle of the
rippled airliner with an air of indifference, as if choosing a seat for a sightseeing
our. Thirty years before she had been less tranquil in the face of an accident and a
fe had ended. She will not let that happen again. Today's approach is measured,

restrained. No one will die, least of all the two children entrusted to her, tl children she had carried inside her, had nurtured, had dressed and fed and loved

Survivors clamber onto the rescue boat while Keira waits, holds the boys' han loosely as boats pull away across the wind-chopped current. Like the others, all tl others, they've been saved, their elation tempered only by the fact that they hard knew they were in danger. Some warnings followed seconds later by a perfe landing, a few commands, and there they were, standing in the middle of tl Hudson staring at the New York skyline, waiting for a ride like children peerir down the street for the school bus.

They end up on a small ferry from Jersey. The three of them stand all the way the Manhattan shore, wrapped in thick orange blankets, the color of rescue. The in quick succession, questions as to their condition, responses that they're oka then a more measured walk toward some idling buses waiting to return them LaGuardia. Keira Wilkes lets Brett lead—he is older—but she rests a hand on h shoulder while she holds James's hand with the other. A man in a uniform wav them toward an idling coach where another man with a clipboard takes names. F smiles at them as they ascend the steps and Keira tells the older boy to take tl first empty row. Brett peers ahead, a scout in wartime, past the occupied seats the emptier ones near the back.

"Here?" he asks, turning around and pointing, and his mother nods somberly, a if any choice is the wrong one, the way she nodded when he lit the fireplace withou permission and didn't open the damper and the house reeked of unseasoned hal burned wood for a month. This time, though, he has done nothing wrong. The boy take a seat.

"What about you?" James asks.

Six years old but he has done the math: three into two don't go withou squeezing. He slides closer to Brett who grudgingly pushes closer to the window either out of the desire not to be touched, or less likely, out of consideration for h brother.

No, their mother says. She will sit across the aisle, but first she must tell th driver something. She drapes her scarf over the seat back as if it will somehow have the efficacy of a police barrier or crime-scene tape, as if no one would dar cross it or move it, or under any circumstances, steal it.

"If anyone asks," she says, "just say it's your mother's scarf."

Then she hesitates.

No, that's not right. If someone wants to sit there, let them. You're big boys. If
n't come back right away, if I have to sit somewhere else, you'll be fine, right?"
mes shakes his head. It makes no sense to find a seat then walk away and tell
eone you'll take it later. It won't be there. He frowns at her.
Don't worry. The driver needs to know how many kids are here and who the
ents are," she says in the same unusual monotone. "He's afraid some kids might
separated and wind up getting lost. We can't let that happen, right?"
mes can. He doesn't care about the other kids, hasn't even seen any: he has
d his attention on finding a seat, not taking inventory of the other passengers.
l, he isn't going to win this argument, and Brett seems to accept the situation.
here is something weird or untoward about his mother checking in with the
ver and insuring the fact that kids have their parents nearby, he certainly can't
it. He can say that to his brother, and it might be comforting, but he's nine
rs old and not interested in comforting others just yet. He hardly even
nowledges his mother, and when he does, it's unkind. Go ahead, Mom, he says
imself, don't just stand there like an asshole and tell us what you're going to
..do it.
eira Wilkes pats James on the head as Brett pulls his iPod out of his pocket.
glares at it. How did that survive when they were ordered to leave everything
ind, to evacuate immediately. He deserves a reprimand, but not by her, not
ay.
he backs away and bumps into a man searching for a seat, a man in a sport coat
tie who is not dressed properly for such a bitterly cold day. They share a glance,
ordless non-greeting between survivors headed in opposite directions. Excuse
, she says, but by that time he has pushed past and cannot possibly have heard
.
wo, three rows up she turns around again and smiles, as if the trip were
denly more wearisome than she had anticipated. Then she returns to the boys.
Your father will be very proud of you," she says. "Be sure to tell him how brave
were."
ames starts to stand: Brett holds him down.
Don't ever be afraid of things," she says.
rett sloughs off the comment. He isn't afraid of things. He pushes
perceptibly closer to the window. Keira kisses James on the forehead, then
ds Brett a small piece of paper, like a business card with a number on it.
Your father will need this," she says. "Watch your brother."

She takes a few steps back, not removing her eyes from the boys. Not yet. B
peers out the window, proof that he is old enough not to have to gawk at his mo
anymore when she leaves him for a moment or two. He has been in school f
years, has gotten well past the anxiety of being left with a strange adult in a stra
room with strange children. Even in first grade he shunted her aside at the do
confident that he could withstand the next six hours alone, and did. She kno
him, knows he would never trade away that perceived independence by follow
her down the aisle. No, Brett will check the window, maybe get a glimpse of
river, stare it down, establish that final victory.

But James: he stands to peer over the seat in front of him.

"You should sit," Brett says. "You can't stand up when the bus is moving."

"It's not a school bus. Mom wouldn't be on a school bus. And we're not mov
yet."

"It's a rule on all buses, don't you know? It's a law," he adds, making it up as
goes along. Keira hears him, recoils at his bullying authority but can do nothin

"It's a stupid law," James says.

The older boy glares at him but James remains standing, retaining eye cont
with his mother who has backed away a few steps more.

Two women, one weeping, stumble down the aisle past her, then sit across
aisle. The calm one lays her head against Keira's scarf and holds the other's ha
like a boy with his girlfriend. James watches them for a while. The shaking wom
relaxes, sits back, then leans forward and cries some more. The cycle becon
fascinating to James who, between glances up the aisle, watches the closer dra
unfold.

Brett leans across the aisle. "That's my mother's scarf," he says, pointing.

The woman hands it to him. The lights dim. The bus begins to move.

"Mom!"

James starts to rise but Brett pulls him back down.

"Stay in your seat," he says, glancing past him as the bus picks up speed. "I
the law."

Martin Wilkes had been able to move things around a bit, his family would not
ve been at the airport without him. Instead he sits in his office preparing to cajole
e Robert K. Blackmoor, whose portfolio, like just about everyone else's, has
ploded in flames in the first inglorious, sputtering decade of the millennium.
en in prosperous times Blackmoor is a consummate pain in the ass; but the sheer
lume of his holdings means that when he doesn't like market behavior, stock
rformance, dividend reinvestment, a board of directors vote, or any number of
er criteria he uses to judge the worth of an investment firm, he demands and
ceives a personal audience.

At Tolliver & Byrne that invariably means Martin Wilkes, and that necessitates
hange of plans: instead of driving in together from Connecticut, he'll meet Keira
d the boys at the airport.

"At least we'll take off together," he told them the previous evening, and the
ilkes family, seemingly inured to last-minute changes, hardly reacted. James still
aimed they were flying south like the robins in winter; and Brett, who was in
urth grade and knew that robins didn't go south or anywhere else, again
minded his brother that he was too stupid to live—an assessment that earned him
nild reprimand.

"I'll take the train in and work until noon," Martin said, "keep my eleven o'clock,
ke the limo to LaGuardia, meet you in the terminal. Of course that means you'll
ve to drive in. And they're talking about some snow. Nothing big, but—"

"I've driven in snow," Keira said, then laughed. "Such a complicated plan," and
e winked at James "just to fly south."

Brett glared at her.

By ten the following morning the snow had fizzled, but even the new and
mplicated plan exploded when Tolliver himself strode into Wilkes's office and
gged him to stay into the afternoon and deal with "that goddamn Blackmoor."

"I can slough him off to an assistant," Tolliver said, "but he won't be happy."

"He can't come in before 11:00?"

"The snow held him up."

"But I'm meeting my family at LaGuardia."

"Say the word, Martin. I'll send him to Lasher."

Wilkes bristled at the suggestion.

"Lasher? What's he been here, a week?"

"It's almost a year, Martin."

"Has he begun to shave yet?"

"You were that young too when you started. Maybe if he worked with someo
like Blackmoor once in a while—"

Wilkes didn't need to hear the end of the sentence. The implication was clear.
young hotshot can always supplant an aging superstar: it's a dictum of the financ
world but one that Wilkes didn't have to accept. First off he's only forty; secor
Todd Lasher is an asshole. The problem, however, is there are other, better To
Lashers lurking on the sidewalks and inside personnel offices all over low
Manhattan.

"No, no, fuck it, I'll do it."

"I can get Blackmoor here at noon, if that's any help."

"It would be, yes."

"And it's Savannah, right, where you're going?"

"Through Charlotte. U.S. Air."

"Done," Tolliver says with the authority only money can radiate. "And forg
the tickets. You'll be first class all the way through."

"My family is leaving on time. I'm catching up with them in Charlotte," he say

"Then you're all first class from Charlotte on in, and back. That's it."

That it's probably as close as Tolliver will ever come to thank you, but Wilk
phones Keira immediately. She hasn't left the house yet.

"People like Blackmoor pay the bills, our bills too," he says, but she stops hi
short. She has never required explanations when it came to his work, not when h
salary has allowed them to live in a beautiful home in a desirable town wi
excellent schools and the best of everything—and not when he's the commut
leaving the house in darkness these winter mornings and returning in the san
darkness at night. She has encouraged him to go out somewhere to lunc
occasionally—get out of the building, experience sunlight. Invariably he settles c
something from the cafeteria and eats at his desk.

"If you worked at the North Pole," she told him, not two days earlier, "you'd l
no worse off."

"Overrated," he answered. "Nobody needs sunlight. Maybe some warmth on
in a while, but that's why we have summer."

"Don't you think the cold holds some magic, too?"

"Not to anyone in his right mind."

She scoffs at the so-called upgrade, of flying first class.

"Charlotte all the way to Savannah? What's that, five minutes?"

"We'll arrive together, though, and first class is still first class. The kids will be impressed."

"They're not old enough for the free cocktails."

"But we are. Pick up a DVD in the airport and let them watch a movie while we get drunk."

"It'll have to be a very short movie," she says.

Maybe so, but for Martin Wilkes there's another upside to this, one he doesn't share: Keira Wilkes is a bore to travel with, always sitting with a book in her face or working some cretinoid crossword puzzle from an in-flight magazine. Or even worse, pulling a sketch pad and pencils from her carry-on and wasting an entire flight drawing. Eventually he broke her of that habit, reminding her that other passengers found it disconcerting—thought she was sketching them. It wasn't true, but she did draw attention to herself, even mild adulation at times, from people who wouldn't know good art if it fell off an easel and hit them. No one compliments her on the crosswords.

So the three of them can bore each other to Charlotte where Wilkes can rescue them with first class seats, a glass of wine for Keira, maybe a a gin for himself. Or two. Everybody wins.

Keira Eason is, despite his occasional carping, a significant upgrade from the girls and women who preceded her, and even after fifteen years of marriage he marvels sometimes at how he found her, at why she agreed even to go out with him, let alone marry him. He doesn't have killer good looks—never did—and his grandmother who assured him when he was twelve that he would grow into a handsome man has been proven, if not wrong, at least overly optimistic. But Keira loves him, and he knows the absurdity of trying to objectify an emotion. Unfortunately today her reward will be an airplane flight alone with their children while he sits on the fourteenth floor and placates a client who earns more money in a year than Wilkes will earn in his lifetime.

Robert K. Blackmoor has been a T&B client since the Carter administration, and his father even before that, when Tolliver Byrne Snyder and Wells reigned as a giant of Wall Street—back before Snyder sold off his share and Wells decided he had earned enough money in his lifetime and quietly killed himself. None of this affected Blackmoor, a survivor of two heart attacks and enough surgeries to fill a spreadsheet. He speaks of death in oblique terms—he wants his fortune "dispensed

when the time comes" by someone who knows the ins and outs—someone li
Wilkes. Blackmoor has already dispensed part of it, seeding a college fund wi
$100,000 for Brett and James: he doesn't want them to "scrounge for scholarship
or "kiss some committee member's ass." It's probably a good thing: neither bo
has shown any remarkable scholastic prowess so far. Ethically, legally, Wilk
cannot accept such largesse or sign off on it or even know about it. On paper it
an annuity, but both Wilkes and Blackmoor have a tacit understanding of what it
for. With all the shenanigans discrediting Wall Street, Wilkes stays within the rul
and Blackmoor, always scheming, admires that.

But today, even the promise of free college for the boys seems insufficier
Eleven o'clock comes and goes. Noon. Twelve-fifteen—no Blackmoor. Wilke
buzzes the receptionist.

"Anything yet, Sandy?"

"Just checked in downstairs," Sandy Qualling says. "If he trusts the elevator n
to fail, he should be here in a minute or two."

"And if not?"

"We'll find him dead in the stairwell. It's a win either way."

Sandy Qualling is the most indiscreet person Wilkes has ever met, but she keep
her job by picking and choosing her indiscretions and, at times like this, by sayin
just the right thing. She's married with rumors, but doesn't appear interested
expanding them with Wilkes or anyone else at T&B. Still, she deems it proper
discuss all manner of bedroom diversions she and her husband have created
freshen up their seemingly continuous sex lives. It may not be her intention
titillate, but when she starts spinning a tale of the latest debauch, Wilkes can't b
the only man who feels some movement between his legs, or the only man whos
later fantasies center on her. Qualling probably earns a third of what Wilkes doe
and Wilkes sometimes thinks her relative impoverishment has led to more person
risk-taking and sexual experimentation. At other times he knows she's just horn
and fortunate enough to have latched on to an equally lascivious man whom sh
can spend her multiple-orgasmic life with—or on top of—or under. Wilkes doesn
find her particularly attractive, but he is fascinated by (yet skeptical of) he
husband's ability to, as Qualling puts it, keep going all night. If it's true, Wilke
would be a most unsuitable sex partner, always sated by the one orgasm Keira ha
been content to provide on occasion. Sandy Qualling is the stuff of adolescer
fantasy, and Wilkes is about to lapse into one when the intercom interrupts

onds later the fantasy stands before him, then steps aside so that Blackmoor
fill the entryway.

Mr. Blackmoor," he says, as Qualling gently pulls the door closed. "Good to
you."

This isn't social," he says, his eyes following the receptionist out the door.

Beautiful woman," Blackmoor says. "But that blazer—it covers her tits."

Wilkes smiles as he tries and fails to recall a visit when Blackmoor hasn't made
milar comment. No tits—good, he thinks, that's your penance for keeping me
e.

Blackmoor throws his gray topcoat on the table and reveals a pair of jeans and a
nel shirt. Even dressed like a tenant farmer, he looks formal and foreboding as
slides into his accustomed chair.

So tell me, you...uh... getting anything from that woman?"

Very good work."

I wouldn't mind," Blackmoor says. "I can still get it up pretty good."

It's important to stay healthy," Wilkes says. He blushes faintly, not because
ckmoor has embarrassed him with his locker room banter, but because Wilkes
s so recently considered the same scenario. Time to reset the conversation.

So, Mr. Blackmoor," he says, "what can we do for you today?"

The predictable responses spew out.

He's losing his shirt.

He's going to invest elsewhere.

Tolliver & Byrne is fucking him over.

And today he's added a new complaint.

He doesn't like the new president.

He hasn't actually been inaugurated yet," Wilkes says, choosing not to agree
though he feels the same way.

People like us—he's gonna shut us down."

Wilkes smiles. Us? People like Us? Blackmoor owns homes in Greenwich, Park
y, and some island off the west coast of Florida. He maintains an apartment on
Upper East Side and spends most of the summer living on an eighty-foot yacht
keeps moored at Montauk—a yacht that has never known the open sea but
tead floats comfortably tethered at a sheltered, gated marina with armed guards
d a phalanx of security cameras. Martin Wilkes, the other "us" in the room pays
trangling mortgage on an extended Cape in a pricey southwestern Connecticut
bdivision and rents a summer place for two weeks on the New Jersey shore. He

doesn't know where his boat is anchored because he's pretty sure he doesn't own one. He is far from indigent—two cars and a wife who does not need to work a house cleaner twice a month and kids who will ride out the public educat system for another year or two before going private. Yet he's several promoti away from those obscene Wall Street bonuses that seem rife, at least in the ne No, he is not in any way part of the us that includes Robert K. Blackmoor, instead of demurring, he dutifully hits a few buttons on his laptop, takes a rem from off his desk, and seconds later watches as a list of holdings spreads acro forty-two-inch flat-screen monitor on the wall next to them.

"Impressive," Blackmoor says. "I have one too. I'm so fucking blind I nee screen that big just to read the game scores. Now if you could just switch or ju or move or whatever to the bottom line—"

Wilkes clicks. Blackmoor is down three million dollars.

"Jesus Christ," the man says.

Wilkes buzzes his assistant Andy who, seconds later, arrives with a tray, bottles of spring water, some glasses, and ice.

"Thanks," Wilkes says. "Mr. Blackmoor, you know Andy Campanella, dc you?"

"We've met," Blackmoor responds with some annoyance. "Whenever you busy with an important client, I wind up talking with Handy Andy here. offense, boy."

"None taken," Andy says with a smile, then closes the door behind him.

Andy is young, black, just out of Columbia by way of city schools—more c New Yorker than Wilkes will ever be. A brilliant kid, but in a company l Tolliver & Byrne, just a kid. He'll struggle to gain a position like Wilkes's, or m likely, catch on with another firm. Wilkes hopes that doesn't happen too soon.

"Kind of hard to insult that boy, isn't it?" Blackmoor asks. "Must be happy have a black president."

"Andy and I don't talk politics."

"And how does a black guy get an Italian name?"

"Roy Campanella had an Italian name," he says, and Blackmoor, old enough remember not only the Brooklyn Dodgers but the uniform numbers of th players—including Campanella's 39—is impressed.

"You know your history," he says, but without stopping for a breath, moves his next talking point.

"And this fucking Madoff. How do I know you're not doing that to me?"

"You've been with us for a long time, Mr. Blackmoor. I think you know our reputation for integrity."

"Madoff had a reputation too. He made lots of money for his clients until he didn't."

More charts on the screen. More indications of integrity. More stroking. For this he's missing a flight? Not even watching Keira work a crossword could be this tedious.

Finally Blackmoor gets to the point.

"When is the turnaround? Just tell me that."

Wilkes frowns slightly. "It may be a while."

"I don't have a while," Blackmoor says. "I've had twenty heart attacks and I've got a prostate the size of a fucking Mercedes. What kind of while are we talking about?"

"Couple years maybe. Maybe 2011."

"Fuck me. I could die twice by then."

"Mr. Blackmoor, I wish I were as healthy as you were."

"Really? Want to trade? I'll try a go 'round with your receptionist there. How is she in that area? You didn't say."

"You'll have to ask her husband."

"Oh, don't be so fucking discreet, Wilkes."

"I could be a little more daring if you'd like, maybe throw your money around some untested areas. Just say the word."

"Yeah, I get it. Truth is," Blackmoor says, "my wife is taking this financial mess worse than I am. She's the one wanted me to come down here and get some answers."

"With all due respect," Wilkes says, risking a smile. "You already know the answers."

"Yeah, but if I get home and say 'that asshole at T&B doesn't know shit,' then I'm off the hook for a while, especially if I can bring home a printout."

"And I'm the asshole."

"It isn't personal—so get me a printout."

He buzzes Andy and relays the request.

"Hell," Blackmoor says, sounding almost contrite, "I don't blame you for this mess, but Jesus, my wife gets a statement like the last one and she goes nuts."

"Get an e-statement."

"Can I do that?"

"And save paper. Technically I'm required to send it only to the pers
requesting it. It would forgo all mailings."

Wilkes arranges for the change, fails to convince Blackmoor not to u
Blackmoor as his password, and logs off the account. The screen defaults to a W
Street ticker filled with red numbers. Bad timing.

Blackmoor glowers at it. Wilkes assures him that things will turn around.

"And I can tell my wife that?" Blackmoor says. "She doesn't respond well
bullshit."

"She probably gets that from you. If I'm wrong, blame it on me."

"Oh I plan to. She'll tell me to dump you again and I'll tell her you're doing t
best you can. Come on, I'll buy you lunch."

"I can't today," Wilkes says. "My wife's at LaGuardia..." he looks at his watc
"Hopefully she's in the air by now. My family's flying out and I'm going to cat
up with them later."

"So you stayed here to meet with me?"

"Mr. Byrne had a lot going on and he needed me to handle some of it. Yo
appointment was just one more thing."

"Bullshit. Where're you headed?"

"Savannah."

"Nice place, still cold there this time of year."

"It's family. We—"

"Went down there once in February. Froze my ass off. Your wife won't like i

"She likes the cold. She finds winter charming."

"I do, too, looking north at it from Florida. That receptionist," Blackmoor say
reverting to Miss Qualling again. "I don't want to see her covered up with a blaz
next time."

"I'm not sure if she takes requests."

"Then I'll ask her myself—next time. Or I'll come back when the weather
warmer and the clothes are not so...."

"Numerous?"

"Annoying."

It's almost one by the time Blackmoor leaves, and at this point Wilkes no long
needs to rush. The altered schedule allows him plenty of time to make th
connecting flight, and rather than leave a mess to deal with when he returns, l
leisurely tends to Blackmoor's data, marks a few changes, even checks oth
clients' accounts before his door opens and Sandy Qualling leans in, exposing

1ooth triangle of ruddy skin at her throat. The blazer is off—Blackmoor's bad
ck.

"You have a call. It's Mrs. Wilkes."

"She didn't leave yet?"

"I didn't ask."

He punches a button on his console.

"Everything all right, Keir?"

"We're just boarding now."

"Are the boys okay?"

"Yeah."

The pitch of her voice isn't quite right. Unless something has gone wrong, there's
) reason to call.

"You sound—are you sure everything is okay?"

"Yes, The boys are right here. Want to talk to them?"

Wilkes laughs.

"No. Unless—are they afraid? They've flown before."

"I think they're fine. Do you know what, though? So weird."

The pitch rises further and her pace quickens.

"I met someone in the airport that I haven't seen since grade school maybe, I
an't even remember when, it was so long ago."

"A friend?"

"A guy. A kid. I mean he was a kid. We knew each other. He was a grade behind
1e. Or else the same grade—I don't even remember. He was flying to Chicago.
e remembers all these things from school, from town, I mean things that nobody
ould remember, stupid stuff."

She repeats the last two words, then stops, her breath coming fast as if she has
ıst stepped off the treadmill or returned from a long run. He waits. Nothing.

"Keir?"

"I mean you see someone after thirty years and all they talk about is...is
hildhood crap? I don't think he ever asked if I had a family, or if I was married,
r...."

It was that voice. Wilkes knew it well. He had heard it just before Christmas
vhen a furniture delivery man, maneuvering a table through the front door,
cratched both the table and the door. It took hours for the voice to normalize that
ay.

That voice.

"Keira?"

"What?"

"Maybe, you know, the kids were with you so he probably figured—"

"It's polite to ask, isn't it? Don't you ask? Wouldn't that be normal? Are the your boys? How old are they? What does your husband do? Even if they dor care, it's sort of...of...what we do."

The words are hurtling off her tongue, gaining momentum like an avalanch Wilkes envisions her in a line moving forward, almost at the skyway. It's alwa a little hectic in an airport—not a good place to be upset.

"You're right. I'd have asked," he says. He waits a beat. "You have the boardir passes and all?"

"Such a jerk, and all these people around. It's just embarrassing to kno someone like that."

"Who was it?"

"Brett stop that," she says. Her son is undoubtedly making himself a pain. H voice has still not leveled off and he fears she might cry. But before he's eve aware, his sympathy becomes frustration—he can't be there to make things rig so he removes himself from the situation. After all, he faces this kind insensitivity every day and doesn't come crying to her, to anybody. So the wor sucks—it isn't new information.

"Listen," he says, trying to sound sympathetic, "the world is full of people lik that. Self-centered, narrow—I just spent an hour with one. Just forget it."

There's some chatter at the other end—no indication that she has heard him.

"I'll see you in a little while," he says.

"Yes, self-centered..." then something unintelligible. Then "...a few hours."

"And forget that guy. What was—?"

He can hear voices in the background, some announcement being made, the nothing.

He considers calling her back, but he knows he would hardly be able to calm he in person, let alone on a cell phone. He smiles. An old boyfriend, no doub dredging up some night they spent fumbling with each other's clothes in a parke car somewhere. Grade school? Not likely. Older. Some guy remembers that fir round of high school sex—stupid, yes—but what does it matter now? Then agai maybe she's uncomfortable with the memory, maybe it was better than she wan to remember, better than sex with her husband has ever been. No matter: he ha

dy Qualling to fill in the gaps of his sexual fantasy life—it's only fair that Keira
e someone too.

hey have seldom spoken of their childhoods. She told him once she was too
ng for nostalgia and he agreed: his own bland upbringing inspired little need
reminiscence. It's as if they had both sprung full grown upon each other and
an living as one—a situation he finds not at all uncomfortable, one that spares
the tedium of high school reunions and dreary searches through old yearbooks
ind out whatever happened to—

e straightens his desktop, chats with Andy for a while and drops some folders
he assistant's desk, informs Byrne of Blackmoor's intentions to remain a client,
eventually finds his way to the elevator. His driver—a woman named Caroline
has worked there longer than he has—waits in the lobby and, minutes later,
Lincoln Town Car crawls through Manhattan traffic toward the tunnel and the
E.

fucked-up day—that's all it is, but tonight they'll be wolfing down pecan pie
River Street and laughing about Blackmoor and Byrne and maybe even the old
friend who probably couldn't unhook her bra thirty years ago and wanted to
logize. Once the kids are asleep tonight, Wilkes will have no similar difficulty.
the quiet cocoon of the limo he watches the blur of buildings and people as it
sses from avenue to avenue and beyond, the stops becoming less frequent as
y move eastward to another borough. A siren interrupts the quiet. Then another
. He dismisses them both. It's New York, for God's sake: sirens and taxi
ns—they're part of the soundscape.

hen more sirens—even for Manhattan an inordinate number. He remembers
l and rolls down the window divider.

What's going on, Caroline?"

A boat in the Hudson," she says, swerving to pass a slow-moving van. "It hit a
ry or something. I don't know. Some kind of rescue on the river. I can get the
vs if you'd like."

That's okay."

e doesn't want the news. Or the weather. Or the sports. Or the latest catastrophe
m Wall Street. Most of all he doesn't want yet another call from the office, but
cell chirps and the readout says Campanella, A.

 fucked up day already.

e shouldn't answer, but he does.

this one of those times I should have shut off my phone?"

"Martin. This is Byrne. I'm on Andy's cell. Where are you?"

"Over the bridge," he answers. "What did I forget?"

"Listen, I think they're okay, everyone on the plane. Your family is okay."

"What are you talking about?"

"The plane. It's down, but everyone got off."

"Down! What do you mean down? It crashed?"

"It's intact and floating. It's on the river—"

"What river?"

"The Hudson—it's just floating there. I'm watching on your monitor—they're
tting people off. Everyone is getting off. Everyone seems okay."

Wilkes is listening and processing, but the words are crowded out by image and
rmise. He knows what happens when planes hit the water—the accepted joke of
 flight attendants advising the passengers that "in case of a water landing..."
ere is no water landing—planes spiral into the sea and smash apart and everyone
es. Or if somehow a pilot manages to ease the plane onto the surface of the water,
en everyone lives long enough to drown. Or today, with temperatures in the 20s,
rviving the impact means freezing to death before there's time to drown.

An image flashes through his mind—a highjacked airliner in Africa—big, a
ide-body that tried to land in shallow water. One of the wings dipped, caught the
ean surface, spun away, leaving the fuselage and the passengers to somersault
ross the waves like a tumbling race car in one of those track accidents where the
iver should have been dead a dozen times over but somehow crawls out with a
rained wrist. People walked away from that plane crash too. Literally walked,
e water was so shallow. But that wasn't January, and even in those friendlier
ements, many people died.

"What kind of plane?" Wilkes yells.

"What? I don't know."

"Where are the engines?"

"Jesus, Martin, how the hell—"

"Just look. Are the engines on the tail?"

He might regret this badgering later, but at the moment he doesn't see any other
ay to get a simple question answered.

"I don't see any," Byrne says. If he's insulted, his voice doesn't indicate it. "I not really the clearest picture. It's far away, like from shore."

Engines below the wing then. Not good. A deft pilot could aim his plane towa shore, maybe come to rest in shallow water where the passengers could sit a await rescue, or maybe wade to safety. But he would have to be piloting a pla with the engines on the tail where they couldn't catch the water and rip the win from the fuselage and leave nothing but a long cylinder open to the elemen Without wings the fuselage would roll like a log in a stream, but wouldn't flc like one—not for long.

Caroline is staring at him in the rearview mirror. They make brief eye cont before she looks away.

Now Andy is on the phone.

"It's an Airbus 320," he says. "I'm watching it now. People are standing on t wing."

"There are wings?"

"It's a plane, Mr. Wilkes."

"I know that. The wings are...are still there?"

"The people are standing on something—both sides."

"How many people?"

"I can't tell. Lots of them. Maybe a hundred."

"Survivors?"

"Yes—they're standing on the wing of the plane. I'm watching it. There are boa around and they're filling up with...passengers."

"Can you see engines on the wing?"

"I can't see the wing—I can just see the people. They're just standing there the water."

"How about on the tail? Are the engines up there?"

"Mr. Wilkes, please. I don't know about any engines. If it can't land and car float then it doesn't know that. People are standing around and waiting to get in boats. Are you at the airport yet?"

Wilkes tries to process the information, but he can't catch up. He knows planes- how in the world had this one not broken apart?

"What? What did you ask me?"

"Are you at La Guardia yet?"

"Another ten minutes."

"There are no details," Andy says, "about where the passengers are being taken

"Can you see faces?"

"It's too far away."

"Are there people in the water? Can you see that?"

"I can't tell. I don't think so."

"Jesus, should I go back to the river?"

"If it were me, I'd check in with the airline. They're cut out for this. If you go back to midtown, there's nothing you can do. You can't rescue anybody."

"But I can be there."

"I don't even know what side they're taking the people to. Maybe Jersey. People with injuries will end up in the hospital; the others I'm sure will be taken back to LaGuardia. At the very least the airline would give you transport to the hospital afterward."

Wilkes taps on the glass to get Caroline's attention, then rolls down the glass.

"Hurry," Wilkes says. "Something's happened."

"Yes sir," she says. She's known Wilkes forever and if she asked him to explain, he would do so without hesitation. Instead she does what she does best: screeches down the expressway past cars already exceeding the speed limit. Wilkes hears Byrne's voice again.

"Martin, the crawl says everyone got out of the plane alive."

"They couldn't possibly know at this point..."

Byrne is insistent. "Everyone. The captain was the last one out."

"Are they all in boats?"

"Not yet. I can still...."

The signal disappears and Wilkes returns the phone to his pocket. He doesn't want to talk to anyone getting his facts from a telephoto lens.

At the U.S. Airways terminal he grips his carry-on and tips Caroline the twenty he stuck in his shirt pocket when he left the city. Then he deliberately slows his pace, for even at this moment he understands that running helter-skelter through an airport building is likely to get him tackled and arrested, if not shot. He will gather himself and walk to a counter where he will be mentally prepared for what certainly awaits: distraught relatives, weeping family members, harried and confused agents. He will not contribute to the hysteria. His phone chirps. It's Campanella again. He declines the call. Enough Andy, or Byrne, whoever. Leave a message.

At the counter he finds four somewhat serene agents, two of them involved in quiet but earnest conversations. One is on the phone. One gestures for him to approach. She appears to be Wilkes's age, and her oval, angular face reveas concern, maybe even anxiety. But there is no panic, not even after Wilkes inforn her that his wife is on 1549. There are no meaningless questions: And your nam sir? Are you sure? Do you have identification? This woman is past all th bullshit—quick and methodical. She picks up a phone and asks that someor named Jasmine come to her counter. In less than a minute Wilkes is being led dov a well-lit corridor by a black woman in a charcoal-grey pencil skirt and a cri white blouse.

He takes a few steps with her, then turns around to thank the woman at t counter and realizes he never looked at her name tag. He seldom fails to do that— bank tellers, waitresses, clothing store employees—he learned in his youth to ca people by name, until today.

"Thank you," he yells back, and she returns a cordial wave.

"That's Connie," his new guide tells him. "She's very good."

"And you're Jasmine," he says quickly, as if to atone for his recent gaffe.

"Yes, Mr. Wilkes. I'm taking you to a waiting room, but you won't be waitir long."

Did she just wink? That can't be. Not here. Not now. There's a fucking plar full of people in the Hudson River and this woman is winking? He sneaks a glanc at her face while they walk: she looks like a child who has found the closet whe her Christmas presents have been hidden and maybe peeked at a few but mu remain nonchalant while harboring the wonderful secret.

"Everything is unofficial," she whispers, her dark eyes masking strong emotions, "and you'll hear more as we learn more. But right now—and I'm almo afraid to say this—we think everyone is fine."

She gasps, as if the information overwhelms even her, as if she were stiflir tears. She holds his elbow, not so much to lead him but to share some of h positive energy. And then she winks again—this time he is certain of it. He asl her what happened, but she doesn't know. By then they have reached the somewh stark but not inhospitable waiting room where he hears the same story again— officially. A television is blaring and a small group has gathered around to watc as passengers are being guided on to, as the commentator says, "anything th floats—ferries, police and fire boats, even private craft in the area." Slowly they' being removed from the stricken aircraft, which remains, inexplicably, afloat.

Finally Wilkes gets a good look at the plane. It doesn't look stricken at al Gleaming white in the angled January sun with the Hudson a remarkable azur intact, undamaged—like a tableau in a history museum but life-size and mesmerizing. Not even Jasmine or the rest of the airline employees seem able to wrt their eyes from the broadcast.

Live.

The word seems to radiate from the lower right hand corner of the screen, and Wilkes considers that it can almost be a shout to the passengers—a verb, a command, an order. Live, everybody, live!

Jasmine slides to a position near the TV.

"You folks continue to watch," she says, lowering the sound, making the sporadic chirping of cell phones more noticeable, "but we are starting to get reports where the passengers are being taken. No one is unaccounted for." She stops. Laughs. "That was a stupid sentence. I mean everyone is accounted for. There are no reports of anyone missing."

Hesitant cheers rise from the group and there is some applause. Jasmine acknowledges it, but accepting praise apparently isn't in her job description: delineating the facts is.

"There is probably going to be some hypothermia, maybe some bumps and bruises, but some passengers..." As she pauses to control her emotions, Wilkes is certain she's a breath away from tears again. "...some passengers are standing around waiting for a cab." Then despite herself, she laughs out loud. "I'm sorry," she says, tears finally breaking the surface, "but I'm so relieved!"

"You're relieved," a woman near her says, and then everyone laughs...or cries. It's hard to make the distinction. He isn't even sure what he's doing, though his eyes feel damp and unfocused. The bizarre transition from Byrne's first terrifying words some ten minutes earlier to this scene of near-giddiness is difficult to reconcile. So Keira is all right. And Brett, James, all right too. They could have been dead—just like that in an instant—taken from him. Instead they're somewhere in that montage of plane and boats and currents.

Jasmine runs both hands over her severely pulled-back hair and waits for the room to quiet—and for herself to regain some equanimity.

"As we get more information on individuals," she says, "we'll tell you exactly where they are. And we'll get you where you need to be. We have cars and vans ready."

"My husband just called," a woman shouts, waving her cell phone. She is fifty, maybe a little past that with blond hair in a ponytail and a voice like a schoolgirl. She says his feet are freezing and it was slippery on the wing. He tossed the shoes in the river for a better grip. Now he's barefoot on some boat. He can be such jerk sometimes."

She laughs at her own pretended outrage.

"What about the others?" someone asks her. A polite tone. Not a demand b question.

"He says everyone's okay. There are divers in wetsuits but no one else is in water. They're all getting into boats or they already did."

More questions pepper her.

"Everyone? Everyone's all right?"

"Is he sure?"

"My mother is almost 80. Did he see an old woman?"

The schoolgirl voice stops them.

"All I know is he says everyone's out of the plane. He sounded a little scar think."

"Maybe it was the cold," someone else says, as if to explain away even slightest negative aspect.

"Maybe, yes, it could be. But I think what Jasmine said is true. They're all oka

Wilkes sits down. He can't remember having breathed much since Byrne's c and now he is sucking in volumes of air while he continues to fix his stare on TV monitor. When Jasmine walks near him. He jumps to his feet.

"Thank you," he says.

"Believe me—it's my pleasure."

"Nobody..." he hesitates, but he must ask... "nobody asked the obvi question."

"Pardon?"

"How long before the plane sinks?"

"Hours. I should have mentioned that."

"What!"

The glow returns to her eyes. "Someone was on the horn with Airbus. T designed that thing to float. There's some kind of plug—like in a bathtub. Ther more to it than that, but...can you imagine?"

"Keira—Keira Wilkes—that's my wife's name. And we have two kids—B and James—they're with her. When you learn something about them, I'll just here."

'The first names coming in seem to be the people who need medical treatment. e others, well we'll get them as they reach shore. Maybe she'll call. Oh, that ninds me..."

She excuses herself and races over to a whiteboard, then scribbles a phone mber in comically large numbers ending with a nine filled with curlicues and urishes.

"That's my cell," she says loudly enough to be heard, though every time she aks the room goes silent—as if she holds their fortunes in her hands. Then she ds, "If I get stuck somewhere and you can't find me, call."

She waits a moment to see if there are any more concerns, then, with a smile, ns to leave. Wilkes intercepted her again.

"And they're being put into cabs? Buses? What's the plan to get them back e?"

'Buses mostly—they're playing that by ear—nothing like this has ever ppened."

A hint of uncertainty, but he understands—there is work to do, other passengers care for. This Jasmine will not be spending the evening at home with her family, it's a certainty. Whatever they're paying her, today at least, is not enough.

'Thank you, Jasmine," he says again.

'Jazz," she says, then throws her arms around his neck and squeezed him so hard nearly loses his balance.

'Sorry, Mr. Wilkes," she says, "but this is a miracle!"

She hurries off while he tries to steady himself.

ke most metropolitan airports, LaGuardia isn't part of any metropolis. If anyone
quires an understanding of just how massive New York City actually is, all he
ed do is drive from Manhattan to a major airport, any one, Newark included.
'ilkes has done it often enough to know—has cursed the Mid-Town Tunnel or
e the L.I.E. as an eight-miles-as-the-crow-flies jaunt stretched into a forty-five
inute expedition. One time, in a pinch, T&B flew him to JFK in a helicopter—
00 for ten minutes' flying time not including its own catalog of security checks
d luggage limitations.

The point is, and Wilkes knows it, nobody shoots back and forth between
aGuardia and downtown; and even on a day like this, he does not plan a trip to
e West Side based on hearsay or whim or panic. Jasmine has said the uninjured
ssengers will be returning to the airport and she knows more than he does.

He tries Keira's cell, but he knows the result even before it immediately engages
r voice mail. She isn't married to the device, never has been, is more likely to
ave it home or shut it off or zip it into her carry-on and stow it. But there's always
chance she might borrow someone else's for a quick "I'm okay." He'll stay off
e line, just in case. He checks the battery indicator and is relieved to find the
one almost fully charged.

This room, he thinks, scanning the unremarkable furniture and bland wall
ngings, this is where people come for the bad news. Every airport must have
e, and he wonders if U.S. Air has ever incurred a major crash from LaGuardia,
to LaGuardia, and if this is where the distraught family members have been told
e worst. Or do all the airlines share this space, and do they have a name for it—
mething they call it when no one was listening? Death Lounge? The Suite of
ternal Rest? How about the Crash Chamber? It's all in bad taste, but he smiles
cause, today at least, it's none of those. A miracle is still a miracle.

He waits. Occasionally he paces.

He hasn't eaten since forcing down a few bites of a bagel many hours before, but
finds a pretzel stand in the pre-security area and buys one that's suffocating in
nnamon sugar, then adds a coffee from another concession. Within seconds he's
usting the powdery detritus off his suit, and seconds after that the pretzel, with a
te or two missing, lies in a trash barrel. He finishes the coffee and heads off for
e bathroom to wash his sticky hands.

He takes his time—lets the blower dry every vestige of moisture. The longer he waits, the better the chance something will occur while he's gone; but when he enters the concourse again, nothing has changed. Travelers are headed for the gates, apparently undeterred by the fact that one of those things on which they plan to fly somewhere is, at this moment, floating in a river ten miles west. Then again, maybe it's a good day to fly: he can't remember ever hearing of two planes going down in the same day.

He risks some battery drain and phones Keira's parents in nearby Westchester, then his own folks with whom, since they uprooted to Phoenix, he has only sporadic contact. Finally he leaves a message for Keira's sister Hayley. There's some disconnect between the two, and even though Keira blames it on Hayley running off to live with her boyfriend in Salt Lake, Wilkes is sure it goes beyond that. Keira doesn't talk about it and Wilkes doesn't care that much about her family politics. All the calls are essentially superfluous, since the news outlets already have more information than he does.

The waiting room seems devoid of fear, but he can sense anxiety. The euphoria has diminished to a warm, not unwelcome, tranquility; though an impatience is beginning to settle in: everyone wants it over with. He sits again, this time a few places down from a woman in boots and a black sweater long enough to serve as a skirt had she not been wearing jeans as well. She leans forward, elbows on her knees, her gloved hands supporting her head. She looks at him and shrugs. He does the same. She inches closer to him.

"So we wait, huh?" she asks.

"I guess. I wish they'd tell us something."

She shakes her head. "I know it's better than the alternative, but I wish they'd just, you know, keep us apprised. Who do you know on the plane?"

"My wife and our two boys."

"God," the woman says. "You must have been—I don't know, I can't even imagine." She shifts a lock of unruly hair off her forehead and takes out a cigarette. She can't smoke it, but she wants to.

"I'm embarrassed to admit," he says, "I wasn't really anything. The first I heard of it, they were already rescued. I probably didn't have time to be worried. How about you?"

"My brother's on it. Stupid ass. He just got a divorce and now he's going to do all those things he couldn't do when he was married, like play golf in January. Wonder how that'll work out with his clubs at the bottom of the Hudson."

ilkes smiles. It's the first time he has thought about something as mundane as
gage.
Maybe they're just wet. Maybe the cargo is salvageable."
he looks dubious, flips the cigarette between her fingers. "I don't know, hitting
water that way...I'm Sarah."
Martin," he says.
actually live around the corner," she says, "right off Northern Boulevard. I
ld have walked here, for God's sake."
Your brother called you?"
From some ferry. I wish to hell he had stayed married. His wife could have
ked him up. Of course that would have meant being sober enough to drive and
would have been a stretch for her. Who am I kidding? I'd have picked him up
way."
How old is your brother?"
ot that he cares, but it's his roundabout way of ascertaining Susan's age. She's
active, or would be had she not thrown on old clothes and left the house without
ke-up. Emergencies will do that to a person, he says to himself, enjoying the
of his observation.
Thirty-two. Got married when he was nineteen. That worked out pretty well,
n't it?"
Kids?"
Thank God, no. They say God watches over babies and drunks. This time he
k care of both at once."
he smiles but she isn't joking. She has been put out by this. Sister and brother:
bably at each other's throats since childhood. But now they'll both have stories
ell at family gatherings. His near-death experience and her ruined afternoon
cuing the stupid ass while he wept over his lost clubs.
ut Sarah, then. Maybe thirty? He doesn't want to flirt with some kid and become
deviant of the waiting room, but if she's Sandy Qualling's age...
Kind of young for marriage, I guess."
Not to the right person."
Vilkes ponders a response. If he agrees, she knows he's not interested. But
nething noncommittal may move the conversation a step forward. Maybe she'll
ice his failure to agree and ask why he seems unsure and he'll tell her it's a long
ry. And Jesus, if she lives right on Northern and he's forever flying out of

LaGuardia, he can offer to meet her at one of the terminal lounges someti
maybe continue the long story.

Fantasy. Nothing more. They play out in his mind all the time, always arriv
at some point where they no longer make sense. He doesn't know if such acti
is normal—doesn't broach the issue with friends and colleagues. He never act
any of them and he won't today either.

"You're right," he says, immediately, regretfully, putting an end to a plea
daydream. "You gotta marry the right person. Did your brother say anything al
a woman with two kids?"

"Sorry. His teeth were chattering so much I could hardly understand him. He
said he was all right and needed a ride from the airport. It was like being in h
school all over again, except then he'd call and beg for a ride when all his frie
found some bimbo to make out with and he didn't. How old are your kids?"

"Nine and six."

"Good, good, old enough to handle themselves. I wouldn't want to be a mo
with an infant in that situation, especially...."

She stops. There is activity near the door, a murmur, a sense of excitement. Sa
stands up.

"There he is," she says. "Madras shorts, flip-flops, ear muffs. What an assho

She races over, hugs him briefly, then stands back and shakes her head.
brother smiles, shrugs. Sarah turns around, gets Wilkes's attention and point
the survivor as if to say, See? Asshole.

In seconds the two of them are gone.

Throughout the room blankets abound, wrapped around people's shoulders
draped behind them, some dragging on the floor. Maybe beneath them are busir
suits and jeans, but now the throng looks like so many monks being herded b
to the monastery after some abortive escape attempt.

A few kids straggle in, but the arrivals are mostly adults, business types like
on a midday flight. Many of them seem dazed and nearly all of them quiet.
Sarah said, they'll have stories to tell in years to come, but right now the tales
bottled up by fear and relief, and when they talk the words come out in stacc
outbursts. One survivor says this is the first bus, that more are coming. Anot
complains blandly about the cold. Another is weeping, the blanket parti
shielding his face. A white-haired woman tosses a blanket on a chair and ligh
cigarette, takes a few puffs, then without apology grinds it out with her foot
Wilkes didn't know it before, he knows it now: this has not been some glori

racle to the survivors; instead it has been an afternoon of horror and trauma amid specter of a cold and watery death. In a day or two they may very well celebrate ir good fortune, but at the moment they do not feel the least bit euphoric.

He will have to remember this when dealing with Keira, provide her with enough overy time. And if it takes a day or two or a week, then he can certainly accede her wishes. Maybe it will put in perspective the annoying childhood friend at airport, teach her not to lose her composure that way. The kids, of course, that ll be different. Kids are resilient—they rocket from dejection to joy in seconds, ving the trauma for their parents to sort through. Still, he will keep an eye on em too, make sure there is no emotional residue.

But those are concerns for later. When the next bus does arrive and his family unds into the terminal, he will welcome their safe return before dealing with ch minutiae.

A few seats to the left a man in a gray suit is holding court.

"They overloaded the plane," he says, "trying to save a buck."

Others hear him, look up, move closer. The suit is custom made; Wilkes cognizes the quality.

"See what happens is," the man says, holding his right hand flat in the air mulating a plane, "you need lift to keep flying—air under the wings—and you ve to go fast. If you can't go fast enough because the plane is too heavy, the gines stall. That's what happened."

"Like a car," someone nearby says. "And then you can't start it."

Some nod their heads in agreement; others who have paid only casual attention asp the logic. Wilkes knows better.

"That's not what a stall is," he says barely loud enough to be heard. There's just mething annoying about a guy in a $1,500 suit spouting off about things he esn't know, survivor or not.

The man glances at Wilkes.

"What?"

"That's not what a stall is. It's not the engine dying like a car. It's really the ngs that stall."

"Yeah, the engines on the wings."

"Not the engines."

The man shakes his head, a condescending motion that tells Wilkes—that tells eryone—that the debate is beneath the dignity of a man in a bespoke suit.

"It doesn't matter," Wilkes says and looks away. His first inclination—to s‌
out of it—would have been the wiser choice. Now it's too late.

"What doesn't matter?" the man yells. "That we almost died out there? T‌
doesn't matter?"

No one else says anything—but everyone is ringside, waiting for the next bl‌
to land. They yearn to welcome their loved ones, but as a diversion, this will‌
nicely. Wilkes doesn't disappoint them.

"I mean it doesn't matter because there'll be an investigation and we'll all kno‌
The important thing is that nobody was killed."

He hopes his fatuous call for unity and gratitude will end things. And it mig‌
have, except for a woman nearby who leans toward him.

"They didn't give you a blanket?"

"I wasn't on the plane," he mumbles, the admission obliterating whate‌
remains of his credibility. He sees a few smirks. Already he has invested too mu‌
time and energy into this discussion to capitulate so quickly. Maybe he can recla‌
some self-respect.

"I was just trying to tell you what a stall is. It happens to the wing, not t‌
engine."

"We don't care what it happens to," another man says. "Why should you?"

"Because if the plane was too heavy—"

"I doesn't matter," a woman says. She glares at Wilkes and pulls the blank‌
around her neck. "You've been sitting in this nice warm room while we've be‌
freezing. We all thought we were going to die. The plane was on fire! Try‌
imagine that!"

This is the first he's heard of a fire and he dismisses it without comment, thou‌
his first inclination is to tell her they're lucky to have landed in the water a‌
doused the flames. Instead, he lowers his voice.

"All I'm saying is if the plane went into a stall...."

He sounds more and more like a whining child and he knows he should stc‌
Hardly anyone is listening, but the pontificating man in the tailored suit remai‌
engaged and Wilkes wants one more shot.

"...then it was caused by engine failure, not too much weight."

The man smiles. "Do you work for the airline?"

"I'm a financial advisor."

"I see. You haven't been planted here to relieve the airline of responsibility,‌
negligence."

"I don't know if anyone was negligent. I just know...."

"What a stall is. And everyone else here—" he is whispering now, has taken a new tack. "Would it have mattered if they were wrong about it for a while, if they had someone to blame? People like to have someone to blame. Whatever your theory is...."

"I don't have a theory. And I didn't know you were arguing on their behalf. Are you a lawyer?" Wilkes asked.

The man shakes his head. "Fuck you. When I don't have a theory I keep my mouth shut."

"I don't keep my mouth shut when someone is blatantly wrong, and you...."

"Mr. Wilkes?"

He looks up. It's Jasmine. The giddy young woman has arrived to do the job she was hired for. Wilkes is a customer who is screwing up relations. She has probably heard only snippets of the argument, but she's come to stop it.

"Maybe we can continue this discussion later when everyone has calmed down? We're all on edge right now."

He looks at her and nods, but he refuses even to glance at his adversary. Life is too short to deal with idiots. Undoubtedly the self-appointed aviation expert feels the same. Jasmine backs away and resurrects her official voice.

"A few announcements for the passengers here," she says. "We're matching your names against the manifest. This way when we salvage what we can from the plane, we'll arrange for you to retrieve it and file a claim for the rest."

"Did everything float away?" someone yells. It sounds like a kid and Wilkes whips his head around. Have the boys arrived without his knowing? He scans the room again and finds the source of the question—a teenager in a Mets hat.

Jasmine shakes her head. "There's almost no debris in the water. It's not likely everything sank so...maybe the plane held together and the luggage is still inside. We just don't know."

"But it would be all wet."

"Right now, sir, we can't say for sure, but we will be in contact with each of you. At the moment we need to arrange for you all to, well, to get where you want to go. We've called in some emergency staff and opened more gates for those of you flying home. If you'll come with me, I'll set you up with an agent who will make arrangements for transport home, or to a local hotel, or to Charlotte on a later flight."

"What about food?" It's that kid again, and everyone laughs.

"I almost forgot," Jasmine says and waves a sheaf of papers. "I have vouche[rs]
and so do the other agents. Now I don't want to rush you, but another bus will [be]
arriving soon and we would like to get some processing done. So if you are able [to]
stand and walk, please follow me. Does anyone require assistance?"

Nobody does, and slowly the survivors rise and leave the room. Some of the[m]
stumble slightly, and a few seem unsure of where they are going. Again Mart[in]
Wilkes finds himself practically alone in a large room, waiting.

Jasmine's promise of another busload takes the edge off his anger, though [he]
hasn't forgotten. He wishes he had that man's name—maybe he can find out-
send him some information on the principles of flight. Win in absentia, but st[ill a]
win.

The "soon" Jasmine promised becomes ten, then fifteen minutes. Wilkes leav[es]
for the main concourse and finds her again, bouncing back and forth betwe[en]
agents.

"Any word on the second bus?"

"Oh, Mr. Wilkes isn't it? Yes, I mean, let me check."

She takes out a cellphone and punches in a number, looks at her watch.

"Fifteen minutes more. Late-day traffic and a fender bender on the L.I.E. I'[m]
very sorry."

"Not your fault," he says, and though he is annoyed that they just couldn't li[ne]
up a bunch of buses all at once and get them all back here at the same tim[e,]
complaining to Jasmine seems not only fruitless but almost sadistic. On his wa[y]
back to the waiting room he spies the self-appointed aviation expert involved in [an]
animated discussion with a TSA agent.

So he really is an asshole, Wilkes says to himself. To barely survive an accide[nt]
and then argue with someone who's trying to help. Not being able to explain a sta[ll]
is the least of that guy's problems.

But when he takes one more look back: the man is mimicking a plane in flig[ht]
and the agent is laughing—they're both laughing. It doesn't take a genius to kno[w]
why, or for that matter who they're laughing at. He slams himself down into [a]
chair. Where the hell is his family?

5

es appears first, shoved from behind as usual by his older brother. Wilkes
ht have to reprimand Brett later, but not in front of Keira. Not now. No doubt
boys are tired, scared, maybe disoriented and confused. And Keira is probably
austed from having to deal with them. Wilkes hurries toward the pair, all the
 glancing beyond them. He holds the shoulders of the more easily accessible
es, but he talks directly to Brett.

Where's Mom?"

he older boy shrugs.

She isn't with you?"

She was on the wing—I saw her. She took off her shoes and—"

I don't mean the plane. Wasn't she on the bus?"

Yes."

Then where is she?"

She went to talk to the bus driver."

What, just now?"

e looks past the boys—maybe she's right behind.

No," James says. "Before."

Why would...did she know him?"

ames's mouth scrunches up and his eyes began fluttering like some underage
uette. The tears will come next but Wilkes doesn't want them, not until he's
red out what the hell is going on.

James, tell me what happened after you landed."

It was a woman," James says.

Who?"

The bus driver."

Okay then."

Wilkes pulls back a little. He is treading lightly here. James will not hold together
 feels he's being badgered. He turns to Brett instead.

Tell me about the landing."

It was okay, I guess," Brett mumbles. "Then they opened the doors and some
er came in. Then one of the airplane crew, she started telling people what to
 to walk out onto the wing so we did that."

Mom too?"

"Everybody."

"But I mean, definitely Mom. She was actually standing with you."

He nods.

"What row were you in?"

"Twenty. I remember because—"

"Did you all go out the same side?"

Wilkes doesn't even know why he asks the question, but he wants details
Brett says yes, the same side.

Now Wilkes has her out of the plane, but it doesn't make a lot of sense that
would allow herself to be separated from the boys. For the first time he thinks th
may be casualty figures after all, that this initial euphoria will be diluted s
enough by the awful facts. Still, if the boys are right—

"And you saw her on the bus—"

"Yes," Brett says, then looks to his younger brother for authentication. Ja
doesn't see him: he's scanning the crowd. Searching. Wilkes takes the boys' ha
and tells them to come with him. He's been blaming the boys when it's Keira
left her children to go chat with the bus driver. It wasn't as if she were takir
sightseeing tour and needed some attractions pointed out; she was crossing
fucking East River for Christ's sake. In the dark. In a city she'd visited count
times. He locates Jasmine nearby and explains the situation. She looks quizzi
but only momentarily. Then she's on her phone and seconds later he hears a pag
*U.S. Airways flight 1549 passenger Keira Wilkes to the U.S. Airways cou
please*. Amidst all the chaos, Jasmine tells him, sometimes the simplest things
screwed up and the most obvious solution is best.

Not this time. Minutes go by: Keira doesn't appear.

"Keep an eye on these kids," Jasmine directs a young man behind the coun
then turns to Wilkes. "They'll be fine."

It's more of a question, but he gets it. He tells the boys to wait with this nice r
while Jasmine stands off to the side.

"Come with me please," she says, her tone so authoritative that he expects
to take his hand and drag him along. She doesn't, but she walks purposefu
looking for all the world like any other harried passenger trying to mak
connection. He does the same. Outside the terminal in a restricted zone a city
is idling, its headlights cutting through the clear dusk. A uniformed woman v
an ID badge that reads Almeda stands nearby holding a lit cigarette. Jasmin

dial, non-threatening, as she inquires: a woman and two kids, she says, were
y on the bus?

The driver flicks away the cigarette and shrugs. "Maybe. They tell me to drive,
ive."

"We know she got on, we just don't know if she stayed on."

"The kids are okay? 'Cause once I start driving—"

"They're inside. They're fine. They said that their mother went up to talk to you
fore they left the city. Do you remember anyone doing that?"

"Yeah. Some woman said her husband was supposed to be right behind her but
sn't—she seemed kind of panicky, had to go find him. I thought she got back
."

"She left her kids on the bus."

"I didn't know she had kids. Didn't say nothin' about that. It was a mess down
re, names checked off and crossed off and...shit, I don't know if she got back on
not. I kinda lost track. All's I know was she was alone and everyone's trying to
ve us...."

Jasmine inches closer to her, puts a hand on her shoulder. "Ms. Almeda, no one's
ming you in any way."

"Blaming me? Now listen—"

"I know things were a mess, but do you remember what the woman looked like?"

"A woman in a blanket like everybody else. Glasses, though—she was wearing
isses. I remember the frames—kind of a nice purplish shade."

Wilkes nods. Keira's reading glasses.

"The names that were checked off, who has that list?"

"No idea," the woman says, taking out another cigarette. She is wavering
tween relief at not being held culpable and anger at being associated with the
aos. "Could have been Port Authority, might have been a cop, someone from the
line. First I was told to wait, then I was told to drive."

"Okay, thanks, Ms. Almeda."

"You think something happened to this woman? Like she was abducted or
mething?"

Jasmine's voice is soothing, consoling.

"Nothing like that. You're right, it was a mess. We don't know much more than
at. Now get in out of the cold before you catch pneumonia."

The driver lights the new cigarette and takes two deep, rapid drags. "Once I got
e signal to leave, I pulled out. Did I do something wrong?"

"Absolutely not," Jasmine says, and she smiles. "You're part of one of greatest rescues in history. You'll have a story to tell your grandkids. You sho stop smoking, though, make sure you get the chance."

Wilkes remains silent. Jasmine knows how to talk to people, even has the ner to suggest to a stranger that she quit smoking. He nods to the bus driver, Jasmine is already leading him back inside, cell phone in hand.

"We'll find out who was working the other end of this," she says. "Let's get y back to your kids. See if Port Authority knows something."

Inside the waiting room Jasmine's ersatz assistant stands stiffly next to Brett a James. In terms of people skills, he is Jasmine's antithesis, but as a sentry he perfect: stony, stiff, silent, cemented in place, though a bit too boyish to lo threatening. To his visible relief Jasmine dismisses him.

"It's okay, kids," Wilkes says. "Everything will be fine. Just have to wait a whi Are you hungry?"

"What if she drowned," James says, his eyes teary. The battle to control emotions has been lost and logic has gone with it.

"What? Mom? No, of course not. You just got separated, that's all. Like t time at Disney World, the parade when we had to look for her and she was looki for us? It's the same thing, except this time she has to find us."

Brett seems calmer and more contemplative. Maybe he understands what h just happened, how close they have come to sudden death. James wants his moth He always wants his mother, but that isn't so abnormal. One kid for each of the That's the way it went in families.

"Maybe a hamburger," Brett says, responding to the question his father has but forgotten. "I saw a Five-Guys before."

"Something light for now, we'll eat when Mommy shows up. Want a donut o pretzel?"

Brett wants a hamburger but he acquiesces.

"And you Jamesy, pretzel?"

The younger boy presses his lips together and shakes his head. There is no e contact.

"All right then," Wilkes says, feigning an absurd cheeriness. It's always eas to conceal anger than fear, and his anger is building. For Keira to leave the ki like that? He peels a five out of his wallet and hands it to Brett.

"Here. The pretzel place is just outside that door. Get whatever one you want

The boy takes the money and practically catapults out of his seat. Martin leans ose to James.

"Want to go with him? Get a pretzel?"

The younger boy shakes his head as Brett rushes away. Martin put his arm und James.

"Don't worry about Mom," he said. "She can take care of herself pretty well."

"The water—it was really cold."

"But she wasn't in the water."

"I could feel it."

"That's why you shouldn't wear sneakers in the winter."

James accepts the suggestion, unaware of how abysmally lame the comment is. en Wilkes realizes that there is no lesson here, that people don't select footwear sed on the river on which their plane will touch down.

He feels the sneakers.

"They seem pretty dry."

"Yeah. Now."

"We'll get some new ones tomorrow, maybe even on the way home. We can p at the mall. What's that store Mom likes?"

James doesn't answer.

"What about the birthday party, Dad?"

"The what?"

"The birthday party. We're supposed to be there."

Wilkes has forgotten it already. He calls Savannah and lets them know the uation, or most of it anyway. As for continuing the trip—without luggage and sentials Keira would be lost. The clothes aren't an issue, but she has pills in her rry-on, and an accumulated panoply of make-up painstakingly assembled over e months and years. It will take her days to replenish everything, and she won't avel without it.

"We'll see what Mom says. We'll leave it up to her."

"When is she going to be here?"

"You know what? Let's find out. As soon as Brett comes back, let's find out why ey're keeping Mom from getting here."

The older boy returns with an oversized pretzel in a laughably enormous white g, but before he can take a seat, Wilkes waves him away.

"Eat while you're walking," he says. "We have to see somebody."

He's had enough of planes and buses and experts on aviation and—if Keira c
leave those kids on the bus—with her too. Even perky customer relations peop
have begun to wear thin. Jasmine needs to know that the airline, the rescuers, a
she herself have failed.

"Let's find your mother," he says. His tone is that of a father involved in a fam
game of hide-and-go-seek. Inside, though, he is seething.

rest of the evening evolves into an escalating series of interviews, each one
e frustrating and more desperate. When the last bus from the city arrives
out Keira Wilkes aboard, all pretense of optimism and normality vanishes.
nine checks area hospitals from Bridgeport to Newark, even a few on the Island
walk-in centers as far as Islip. Nothing.
Sometimes," she says when she separates herself from other airline officials
speaks to Wilkes, "people in shock can become disoriented."
So she's wandering around Manhattan?"
Or she's home. Does she have friends in the city?"
Acquaintances. Mostly mine. No real friends."
Then home," she says, checking her clipboard. "You said Fairfield?"
Fairfield County. Wilton. How would she get there?"
Trains run to Connecticut all the time."
take one every day," he says. A curt response, but this is not the time for this
man to overstate the obvious. "What I mean," he adds, trying to soften the tone,
how does she get from a rescue scene to her home without telling anyone?"
Have you tried calling your house?"
Of course not."
e takes out his cell. Four rings then straight to voice mail.
There you go," he says. "Any other ideas?"
e has become satiated of Jasmine's upbeat responses to what appears to be an
easingly grim issue, but her approach remains unchanged.
There was a forced landing in Albuquerque a few years back," she says, still
ffling through hospital reports. "Passengers slid out the chute. There were a few
and scratches but everyone was okay—except one of the men disappeared.
wife couldn't find him anywhere. Turns out he took a cab downtown and went
movie."
Keira doesn't care for movies."
But what I'm saying—"
know what you're saying. It's that post-traumatic disorder bullshit that
liers get."
It's an actual condition and it's always possible that—"

"Keira isn't a soldier. She's not wandering around Little Italy looking for car
And she certainly wouldn't leave her kids."

He points to them, sitting somewhat apart, probably wanting to get out of
terminal every bit as much as they want to see their mother.

"Thank God they're okay," Jasmine says.

"Well she fucking didn't know that when they rescued her. If they ever did. H
you called the police?"

Jasmine's expression is losing its sparkle: she's readjusting to a less favor:
reality.

"Yes, sir, we did."

"But of course she hasn't been missing long enough. Great fucking system
have."

"You're right, Mr. Wilkes." The anger, the vulgarity. She seems okay with b
She has probably heard her share dealing with a flying public bitching at
reduced schedules and lousy food and uncomfortable planes. "All I can tell yo
that we've accounted for all passengers and crew..." she hesitates here, not wan
to belabor the obvious... "and your kids place her on the bus, safe."

"But in that chaos," Wilkes says, "when everyone is trying to save their own
would anyone have noticed a victim in the water? And it's so cold, someone co
have fallen in, gone into shock, just sunk quietly and died. Who would know?"

"But—"

"Yeah, I get it. No one saw anything bad, just a fucking airplane in the mic
of the river—just that bad thing."

He has chosen to ignore the boys' story. Accepting it would disallow him fr
attacking this underling whose patience and composure apparently mask a bla
incompetence. Of course if he continues pressing her, someone will accuse him
either racism or sexism. He wishes Jasmine were a white male, someone he co
confront as he did that self-appointed expert on aeronautics hours earlier.

Instead he backs off, raising both hands as a kind of tacit apology because
can't bring himself to make one.

"These situations," she says, her eyes fixing on James, who seems slightly
worse for wear, "they have a way of working out. I have your cell number and
have mine. I'm not going home."

Hiring practices, he whispers as she walks away. A person like that applying
work at Tolliver & Byrne wouldn't even make it past security. And yet here sh

rking for a major airline in customer relations. She probably can't spell her job e.

"Spell what?" Brett says.

"What?"

"You said she couldn't spell something."

"I was just...I didn't know if she could spell mommy's name."

He'll have to be more careful about what thoughts he allows himself to verbalize, pecially with the kids around. And he can't swear in front of them either. But if did say it aloud, too bad. Too fucking bad. He'll make sure to fill out the next stomer satisfaction questionnaire and specifically mention a black woman med Jasmine Pierce, or just to be safe, a person named Jasmine, who was unable provide any help.

The waiting room has emptied out save for a young couple in the opposite corner, the TV coverage blares on. Some sort of tethering lines have been attached to plane and it seems to have been towed to a dock. Floodlights illuminate a oreline filled with apparatus to pluck it from the water. The camera focuses on a rker, his breath visible from twenty yards. Wilkes worries about an derdressed Keira wandering the streets somewhere, having escaped a plane sh to die of exposure in New York City.

The young couple in the corner exchange a passionless kiss before the man nds, picks up a red-and-white-striped cane, and limps toward Martin.

"My mother-in-law was on the plane. She called from the hospital. They had to eck her because she's old, poor circulation, some frostbite. She's fine. They're nging her back here. Maybe the person you're waiting for—"

"Don't count on it. They're supposed to be bringing back my wife, too. I've been re all afternoon and all night."

"They got my mother-in-law a limo. With the money they're going to save in vsuits from nobody dying, they'll be able to buy everyone a limo. Maybe your fe is on one too. Those your kids?"

Wilkes nods. He isn't going to bother introducing them to some guy they'll never again.

"I'm Paul," the man says. "If you're wondering about the cane, sprained my kle playing rugby."

He waves the proof of his injury; apparently this is intended to impress people.

"Rough game," Wilkes says. It may not be the expected response, but it's all he n muster.

"I never got hurt before. Getting older I guess." He leans down to James's lev
"It'll be good to have your mother back, huh? Scary day."

James nods. Brett looks away. On the TV is emblazoned a phrase, Miracle
the Hudson, along with the picture of a mustachioed man in a captain's hat. Will
can't make out the rest of the caption, probably the pilot's name or something, a
if it is, it's a long one.

"Miracle on the Hudson," Paul says, then tries to engage the boys aga
"Imagine, almost losing their mother that way, and you—"

"They were on the flight with her."

"What? Really?"

"They got separated somehow."

"Holy shit," Paul says, then covers his mouth as Brett snickers. "Sorry for 1
language, little man. How the...how did that happen?"

"That's what we're waiting to find out. No one here knows anything."

Paul nods and gestures toward his wife. "She heard the plane was overload
and couldn't get enough speed to climb. If they can prove that...." He stops m
sentence: he has no particular thoughts on completing it. But Wilkes knows wl
he means. If they can prove that, lots of smart NYC lawyers will be queuing up
make their fortunes. And if negligent baggage handlers lost track of the weig
overloaded or failed to balance the compartment, and made it impossible for t
aircraft to climb, then there is a buck to be made, many bucks. A decade earl
Flight 800 put TWA out of business. Could this do the same for U.S. Airways?

"Can't believe they separated a mother and her kids," Paul says. "Talk abc
stupidity."

"Have you talked to Jasmine? That'll give you some idea what we're deali
with."

"She the black chick?"

Wilkes nods, the motion almost surreptitious, conspiratorial.

"Pretty girl. Between you and me," Paul whispers, "with that ass she does
have to know anything."

"I didn't notice."

"I wouldn't mind, you know?" and he makes some obscene mimicry with I
fist, "but I got to get back to my wife, see if maybe she heard from her motl
again. If I hear anything more about the overloaded baggage and all, I'll let y
know. Hey, maybe they'll be in the same limo."

Paul limps back to his wife for another passionless kiss. Wilkes, having already forgotten his flirtation with the woman from Northern Boulevard, feels sorry for the woman, sharing her husband's affections with Jasmine and, probably, a lot of others. Still, it's a kiss. Somewhere along the way he and Keira have cut back on those, using them primarily as a prelude to sex which then, itself, proceeds mostly by rote—that tentative touching, some little maneuvers, and on, and on. He joked with Keira once that it would be easier if he arrived home from work and they both neatly piled up their clothes and had at it. They could be done before dinner, and the boys, busy with their video games, wouldn't even hear them. She didn't find the suggestion particularly amusing. To her the preliminaries, apparently, were important. He doubted if Sandy Qualling at work wasted her time with them. Work.

Everyone would have left by now, but he has Andy's home number, Byrne's too. They probably aren't worried, survivors of so-called miracles couldn't possibly be suffering, and his colleagues probably envision Wilkes and his wife in the throes of some wild, post-apocalyptic drunken debauch—or enjoying a mild evening in Savannah, having caught a later flight.

Then again Byrne is well-connected, and he may know people in the airline industry, too. If there were a problem, or if this one continues, Byrne is the man to rectify it. He takes out his cell, then decides against the call; he'll do it later from home.

He's more concerned with the boys who have transformed into zoo animals exploring the limits of their cages. Occasionally they stop pacing and dart between chairs or construct a rudimentary game of tag. They may very well be frightened for their mother, but they have been cooped up long enough to suppress some of that concern. And the limping man has taken his fantasies of the black chick and left. Apparently that limo has arrived; if so, Keira was not in it. The room, the terminal, the whole airport it seems belongs to Martin, James, and Brett Wilkes.

Wilkes lets them be until Brett changes course and darts over to him.

"I forgot," he says, pulling a card out of his pocket. "Mom gave me this."

It's a ticket, bent and wrinkled, but there's no question as to what it is: a claim check for an off-site parking service.

"When did she give you this?"

"On the bus."

"Why didn't you tell me right away?"

"I forgot."

Wilkes stares at the card as if it were a cryptogram that, examined the right wa
will divulge Keira's whereabouts and allow all of them to go home. He thinks
dialing the phone number, retrieving the car, and searching it for clues; but he is
an investigator, and unless she left a note of explanation, chances are the eff
would be wasted. He considers telling the airport people, but he's afraid they w
dismiss her as a runaway. He may be angry with her, but he's not ready to lab
her a criminal. He slips the ticket it into his jacket pocket.

When Jasmine returns, her ebullience and optimism have given way
exhaustion. If Paul the injured rugby player could see her now, he might be le
excited about the prospects of getting inside that skirt.

"Mr. Wilkes," she says. He stops her in mid-sentence.

"I understand the plane was overloaded. That's why it went down."

"What? No. It was apparently a bird strike. The plane collided with a flock
birds just before the crash."

"What kind of birds?"

"Gulls, maybe, or geese. We're not sure."

"Are you sure of anything?"

"Sir," she says. She takes a deep breath. This same woman who threw her arr
around him not long before now seems ready to collapse. But it isn't Wilkes's jc
to coddle some airline employee. She's earning a salary; let her do her fucking jc

"Sir," she repeats, and she looks directly at him. "I understand your frustratio
but—"

"I'm not frustrated. I just want to know if you're sure of anything."

"Nobody is leaving here until we resolve this."

"You're wrong there, Jazz." He pulls the claim check out of his pocket. "We'
going home. Have one of your associates get our car. We're not riding in a van
some parking lot, not at this time of night."

Jasmine studies the card.

"How did you get this?"

"My son had it. He forgot."

"Your wife gave it to him?"

"We always let him carry it," he says, fabricating the tale on the fly. "It teach
responsibility. We all need to learn that."

Jasmine quietly absorbs that barb also, then punches a number on her cell ar
another employee rushes over, takes the card, and rushes off.

'll take you to the pickup spot," she says, her voice cooler now, less ommodating. She has been servile and compliant and, in her own way, diligent; she appears to have grown as tired of Wilkes as he has of her. Or maybe he sn't care to face the obvious: the claim check has changed things. o longer are they looking for some victim of mischance. Keira Wilkes is a way.

lkes will keep the boys out of school the following day. They were supposed to in Savannah anyway; their absence from classes will not be noticed. Overtired d manic as midnight approaches, they continually seek assurances that this is all ng to work out somehow and Wilkes does his best to be convincing.

'Tomorrow will be better," he says, falling back on the empty mantra several es before the boys finally fall asleep. He does too, or at least he remembers a v dreams.

The phone calls from the airline begin early in the morning and continue radically until they're interrupted by one from a Sergeant Hagan at NYPD. He's king at a report on a missing passenger, and though he stops short of claiming wants to hear Wilkes's side of the story, that is exactly what he wants to hear. lkes obliges. He isn't sure yet he wants the cops involved, though each passing ur (it's now coming up on twenty-four of them) makes it less likely that he can olve this on his own. Hagan listens, grunts a few times, and at the end pauses long that Wilkes asks if he's still there.

'It doesn't sound like an abduction," Hagan says. "You haven't received any som calls?"

'It's not the kind of thing I'd forget to mention."

'Little details sometimes escape us," Hagan says, returning the sarcasm. "Of rse sometimes kidnappers don't like cops involved. Is that what's happening e? Because when a kidnaper says he's gonna hurt the victim if you call the cops, 's gonna hurt the victim anyway. You know that, right?"

'I do now. I haven't received any calls."

'Well of course if you had—"

'I haven't."

Another long pause. Wilkes hears tapping on a keyboard.

'Has anyone else seen her?"

'Not as far as I know."

'If you do, let us know."

'Because then you wouldn't look for her?"

'She's an adult. She can go wherever she wants. I'll be in touch."

When they hang up Wilkes knows that neither of them will ever hear from the er again, and that's fine. It isn't that Wilkes doubts the cops' willingness to do

their job. More than 30,000 of them on the payroll should be able to find a w
educated, intelligent, attractive young woman meandering about Manhattan. I
the police are brought in to solve crimes, and it seems more and more unlikely t
one has been committed.

Early in the afternoon he opens his laptop and begins another letter (he l
already trashed a few of them) concerning the incompetence and "snippiness" c
U.S. Airways employee named Jasmine Pierce. Nowhere does he use the wc
woman or black: he will not let sex or race play a part in this. He prints out
diatribe and leaves it to fester on his desk next to an unaddressed envelope, but
continuing onslaught of phone calls from the airline keeps him from followi
through. Jasmine herself calls several times with updates, concerns, and follo
ups. He knows she's merely covering her ass and he's suitably polite. S
enumerates specifics: each passenger will receive $5,000 to cover prelimina
expenses and hardships. Whatever her previous level of exhaustion, she's on t
of everything today, though she sounds less confident when she mentions t
incipient investigation into a passenger's disappearance. Even in his current st
of disgust Wilkes knows how that works. He knows that the airline would,
course, like to find his wife but that Jasmine herself will be the subject of t
probe. The pilot and crew are heroes and immune to censure, and the corpor
hierarchy remain shielded and unscathed, but those farther down the food cha
never enjoy such privilege: Jasmine. Even that hapless bus driver.

Maybe then he shouldn't pile on: he takes the letter he has carefully compose
folds it in half, and runs it through a crosscut shredder.

His motives are not completely altruistic. Jasmine will draw instant sympat
from all the bleeding hearts, and Wilkes will end up the villain: the misogynist, t
racist. In a country with a newly elected black President, pointing out the imagin
inadequacies of someone like Jasmine can only cause trouble. Keira once cal
him a bigot—only half in jest—when he refused to patronize a gas station af
9/11 because the owners spoke with some sort of Middle-Eastern accent. Witho
her there to modify his views, he would have to do a better job of policing himse
And merely touting his broad-mindedness by pointing out his black assistant is
going to cut it anymore, not as long as Andy remains merely another assistant w
a white boss.

Better to have shredded that letter, though he retains the original on his ha
drive.

Sandy Qualling calls him to reset his schedule for the following week. Wilkes assures her he'll be back by then, that the situation will certainly be resolved. She tells him that Robert Blackmoor has called and wants Wilkes's home number. It has something to do with the disappearance.

"How does he know?"

"Everyone knows," she says.

She apologizes for disturbing him, but moments later when Blackmoor calls his cell, there is no small talk.

"Tell me what you need, Wilkes."

"I don't need anything, sir."

"I'm giving you a name," Blackmoor says. "Use it if you want to."

"Whose name?"

"Frankie Mac, that's the name he goes by. He's a bit of a shit but thorough, discreet, reasonably priced. If he doesn't come through, you don't pay."

"Wait a minute—"

"He's a private investigator. Least I can do," Blackmoor says. "I emailed you his business card info."

"I don't know if I want to go that route."

"Byrne and I will split expenses."

"Byrne?"

"He's richer than I am. You should have been with your wife yesterday. My fault. And his."

When the line goes dead Wilkes assumes Blackmoor has hung up. He checks the mail, opens the attachment.

Francis McNally
Investigator
Discreet. Reasonable.

The decision not to go that route lasts a very short time, but when he calls the PI he learns that the business card is less than accurate, especially the reasonable part. Frankie Mac wants a hefty retainer paid up front for a week's work. A prorated refund is available, he assures Wilkes, should Keira turn up for dinner some night before the seven days have passed. Then there's an hourly rate and charges for background checks; the PI doesn't think Keira will require any. All video recording and written reports will be included, unless they become excessive. He speaks

quickly, as if he were reading from prepared notes, and only at the end does Wilk[es]
get a word in.

"What would be excessive?" he asks.

"If you want the sound man from *Lawrence of Arabia*," Frankie says, "it'll c[ost]
you."

"From where?"

"It's a movie. How about *Jaws*?"

Wilkes recognizes the second reference, but wonders if this failure [to]
communicate will become ongoing, or if he should hire a younger man. He ca[n't]
ask McNally's age unless he wants to add age discrimination to his list of gaffe[s].

"I'll get back to you," Wilkes says.

Silence. Has he said the wrong thing? He adds a quick addendum.

"Tomorrow, the latest."

"You're not buying a car, Mr. Wilkes, and I'm not some salesman trying [to]
convince you that it'll be gone from the lot tomorrow when it won't. With missi[ng]
persons time is of the vital. I live in White Plains. There's a Chili's in Stamfo[rd].
Meet me in one hour. Does that work for you?"

Wilkes doesn't hear much after *of the vital* and needs the rest repeate[d].
Chili's. Stamford. An hour.

"It's closer for me than for you," Wilkes says.

"I'll itemize your first bill and charge you mileage. Get someone to watch t[he]
kids or bring them. I'll be in the bar; good-looking older guy with hair."

"Blackmoor told you I had kids?"

"Is it a secret?"

"No, but—"

"I don't have kids. Now we're even. One hour."

As soon as Wilkes hangs up, he regrets his decision. A bit of a shit may ha[ve]
been an understatement, and a day to think it over, and find someone else, was n[ot]
an unreasonable request. Still, his in-laws are there, having arrived before Wilk[es]
had even finished his first cup of coffee, and they're entertaining the boys a[nd]
trying to stay out of the way. He has always gotten along with the Easons, thou[gh]
he has found them, at times, secretive, reticent. Often their reserve has bother[ed]
him; at other times, their intolerance. Earlier Keira's sister Hayley called, a[nd]
though she and Keira have never been close, Wilkes spent a good deal of tim[e]
assuaging her concerns, even sugarcoating some of what had happened. But wh[en]
he handed the phone to Mrs. Eason, the conversation deteriorated in secon[ds]

ing with entrenched recriminations and raised voices. Afterwards Mrs. Eason
the phone gently on the counter.

Iayley," she said, shaking her head in apparent disbelief. "Good thing she and
n't talk much."

ioments later it was as if Hayley had never called.

ow it's his turn to be secretive. He tells the Easons he's meeting with an airline
cial, tells the boys to be good, and punches the restaurant into his GPS. He
ves after the weekday lunch crowd has returned to work, and the restaurant is
rly as quiet as Wilkes's home. At the bar there are three men: only one of them
hair, lots of it, a tangled mass of graying curls appropriate on an aging 80s rock
, maybe. In front of the man is a nearly empty beer mug. Appearances are
ortant in the business world, and if this is McNally, maybe it's already time to
e.

he only private investigator he has ever met before works for Tolliver & Byrne,
oman named Reeves who does background checks, observes spending habits,
traces loans, all within the confines and comfort of her perfect Saks wardrobe.
's good, but her assignments require business suits and heels and a professional
ieanor. Frankie Mac's apparently require modified work boots into which some
/ denims are half-tucked. Ascertaining how this man and Robert K. Blackmoor
r crossed paths is more than an adequate reason to stay.

Mr. McNally?"

e turns around. He's wearing a madras tie.

Wilkes, you made good time. Any word on Keira?"

Wilkes bristles at the familiarity.

Mrs. Wilkes is still missing."

Mrs. Wilkes? Did I have the name wrong, Isn't it Keira?"

That's it."

Sit then. First, I need a list of old boyfriends. Hers, not yours. What are you
king?"

Boodles...rocks."

What are boodles?"

t's a brand of gin."

Never heard of it. I'll try one too. How much is it?"

Wilkes laughs. "There's a question you seldom hear. I'll buy."

Then I'll try. How about those old boyfriends?"

That's your first question? Before anything else?"

"I did ask if she was still missing. If you didn't have such a goddamn great a
it would have been my second. So again—"

"Just seems weird."

"But I know everything else. Want me to ask something I already know
answer to? I can do that. Do you have kids?"

"I already told you...."

"Good, that's out of the way. Boyfriends?"

"I just don't know why you need that information."

"Tell you what, Mr. Wilkes. You lay out the investigation for me and I'll fol
your paradigm."

"I don't have one."

"Then let's say we use mine. I've earned a decent living from it. Old boyfrie
first, unless she was married before."

"She wasn't."

"I knew that. You've made me waste time. Engaged?"

"No."

"That's good. I didn't know that. Who was the first guy she slept with?"

"I think I was."

"No, seriously, you can just say you don't know. I'm okay with that. I d
know the first guy my wife slept with either."

"To the best of my knowledge...."

"Okay, okay," McNally says wearily, "you were the first one in. Jeez, it's
sex. Are your kids adopted?"

"Of course not. Why?"

"When I told you my rates before, did you understand what hourly meant
you're going to ask me a question every time I ask you one, I'm going to be re
wealthy really soon."

"They're not adopted."

"And they're yours—I mean biologically. Not some intro vitro stuff. Not th
care but—"

"In vitro."

"Keep running up that bill."

"The kids are mine. We had them, normally, when we slept together."

"I still enjoy that normally stuff myself. Reason I ask, I heard a story once wh
this woman had a turkey baster baby and everything—"

"That's a little insensitive, don't you think?"

McNally frowns. It's the look of a man who has just read a mathematical theorem
 can make no sense of it.
 Like I said, everything was going well until she became obsessed with finding
 donor and left her husband on this search and never came back. You don't think
 ira did this, do you?"
 That's some story. It's not true, is it?"
 I'm pretty sure some of it is. So it was real intercourse then. That word
 ercourse, I hope that's not insensitive too. What about the wife, is she adopted?"
 Keira? No."
 So no sudden mania to find her roots after her life flashes before her. Sometimes
 en a person barely escapes death, they like to go back and fix all the things they
 ked up. That's not gonna happen with me. I don't fuck up."
 Neither does Keira."
 Let's get to it then," McNally says, pushing back some of the curls that have
 pped over his forehead. "Got anything going on the side she might have caught
 d of?"
 No."
 Two ice-filled glasses of clear liquid appear on the polished mahogany bar.
 Nally picks his up first.
 Here's to a successful resolution," he says. "You sip this stuff, right? I mean
 not like a shot and a beer, without the beer?"
 You sip it."
 McNally tries some, then holds the glass away from him, peering at the clear
 uid.
 No wonder they mix this with tonic," he says.
 You'll develop a taste for good gin."
 McNally shakes his head. "Remember your first ice cream cone? Did you have
 endure the agony while your mom said don't worry, you'll develop a taste for
 I'm fifty—well, I was fifty ten years ago—so I don't have to develop a taste for
 ything. Now what about this Qualling chick at work? I hear she's pretty hot."
 She's attractive."
 That's what Bobby Blackmoor says when his wife's not listening, though not
 those words."
 Bobby? You call him Bobby?"
 McNally shrugs.

"Unfortunately we're not judging a beauty contest, Wilkes. Attractive won
don't interest me until they jump in the sack with someone else's husband
boyfriend or lover. Then I want to know about them. Ms. Qualling has had
share of one-nighters with some of your very own colleagues. I just want to kn
if your dick was one of her diversions."

"No, I... It wasn't. Are you sure about her?"

"Pisses you off a bit, doesn't it? Bet you wanted to hit that yourself but thou
she was out of reach. She's not."

"Blackmoor may drool over her; I don't."

"Bobby's 120 years old. He drools on everything. But if you say you're
screwing her, I guess I'll believe you. I mean, why would you lie to the man wh
trying to help you find your wife? How about before Qualling? Or after?
during? Any other little side trips for Mr. Johnson or are you really a one-wom
guy? 'Cause see I don't think you are. I think you slept with Millie Hendrickson
least once, maybe more. Now if I'm wrong here, you gotta tell me, because th
dead-ends are going to cost you money."

"How do you even know Millie Hendrickson?"

"I know she lives next door and I always start close to home. Maybe she s
you every day, wants you, hires someone to abduct your wife, waits for the dust
settle, shitcans her husband—her second husband, I might add—and bang, you a
Millie, happily ever after. Bang. I threw that in for humor."

Wilkes shakes his head. Millie Hendrickson is definitely appealing, and h
caught a few glimpses of her in various stages of neighborly undress, a houseco
a bathrobe maybe. But his fleeting fantasies have been only that.

"Sorry," Wilkes says. "Nothing going on with her."

"I'd be sorry too."

The PI pulls out his phone and produces a photo of a woman in a bikini top a
a towel covering her from the waist down. Her back is to the camera and her he
is turned, apparently looking around to see who called her name. It's Millie,
long wet hair clinging to her neck and her sunglasses low on her nose.

"You gotta wanna hit that, Wilkes. A c-note says there's nothing under t
towel."

"Where'd you get that picture?"

"Sorry, trade secrets, though hacking into a personal website is as easy as..
making this drink. I'm just trying to impress you with my pre-investigati
investigation."

"I only talked to you an hour ago."

"I talked to Bobby before that, sort of laid the groundwork. How am I doing?"

"If all you're going to do is list women you think I'd like to, as you put it, hit, then I'm not impressed."

"But look at this. What kind of woman puts a picture like this on the Internet? Oh never mind, I know the answer: an attractive one. Who else besides Hendrickson?"

"Going back how far?"

"Going back to when it became adultery. Let's use that paradigm."

"You like that word, don't you?"

"It was big in the nineties, made people sound important. By the time I caught on, it was obsolete, but if it comes back I'll be ready. How many others?"

"None."

"None? Seriously? It really doesn't do any good to make shit up. If I work for you, I don't go telling people your private life, least of all your wife. How many others?"

One. There is one. A few summers back Keira invited a college friend to one of their picnics and Wilkes found her rummaging for a beer in the garage where, both of them already drunk, they spent the next five minutes with their hands slithering around inside each others' shorts. Satisfying as it had been for both of them, they never spoke of it again or made any secretive plans to relive the moment. No one ever knew, and no one needs to know, especially this surly PI Wilkes already dislikes.

"None," he says again.

"Blackmoor thinks, I mean he's an old man and all so I wouldn't give him any credence, Bobby thinks he's seen you checking out that Qualling many times, watching her ass leave the room, watching her tits enter. Do you ever look at her face?"

"That's Blackmoor's autobiography. I see that woman every day. It's no big thrill. Sandy Qualling is not responsible for this."

"A flock of birds was responsible. I can't talk to them but I can talk to you—and I want to know if you've ever been unfaithful to your wife and if she could have known. I don't need names or locations or individual sexual positions. Yes or no?"

"I already told you."

"Tell me again. And listen, I'm really good. I find out things that even the people who hire me don't want me to find out. Yes or no?"

"All right, listen," he says, and details the garage incident, leaving out t
woman's name not so much out of discretion but because he isn't sure
remembers it. McNally is plainly disappointed.

"And that's it?"

"Isn't that enough?"

"What's that now, remorse? I'm just asking because I don't give a shit abc
remorse. It's a phony emotion."

"Apologizing? Feeling bad? What's wrong with that?"

"How about you don't do things you have to apologize for? Wouldn't that
better?"

"Maybe, if we lived in a perfect world."

"See, that's what guys like you tell themselves when they slip their fingers dov
some other woman's pants. But shouldn't we be at least perfect enough not to
that?"

"Are you passing moral judgments?"

"We're debating human nature."

"If we were all as perfect as you'd like us to be, you'd be out of work."

"Maybe, but people would still keep blaming themselves for whatever go
wrong."

"I don't blame myself."

"I think you do. If you hadn't traded your family for work—Bobby told me hc
you stayed that morning—so now you got that karma thing working for you. (
against you. I never quite got that. And then there's God. He's queued up to ki
your ass too. Except, now listen to me 'cause this is important, you aren't bei
punished. God doesn't give a rat's ass about drunken indiscretions or some tip
chick in the garage or some family going to Savannah. And I gotta tell you, I do
like that college friend as a kidnapping suspect, do you? Unless the two of yc
want to relive that little climax on a daily basis. Five minutes? Really? You g
each other off in five minutes? And drunk? I'm impressed."

"You don't really think—"

"I doubt if she told your wife. Women talk but they don't call to chat abc
screwing each other's husbands. Not in my experience."

"We didn't—"

"Yeah, yeah, poetic license. Either way, there's no kidnaping here. You're on
a second-rate womanizer. I can't imagine you'd be a first-rate criminal. No offens
Do you gamble?"

No."

No horses, slots, online poker? How about alcohol? Do you drink a lot?"

I like the occasional beer, wine with dinner."

And this Boodles, which is sort of growing on me. Ever been treated for alcoholism or mental illness? Ever been in a drug program?"

Jesus, don't you want to know if I'm a sex offender?"

Already checked—you aren't on the register. What about your clients? Lost any of them a fortune lately?"

We're all taking the same bath."

Blackmoor says you're good. A few awards from your peers. And you haven't been arrested yet. How long before the Feds shut your place down?"

Wilkes detests the question, but once he has admitted to his little drunken dalliance, the door is open. Drunk or not, he was dishonest with his wife to whom he was legally and emotionally bound to be true: cheating a client would be a walk in the park by comparison.

They're not going to. We're clean."

Then it's you. Thing is," McNally says, adopting the tone of a philosopher, "husbands, men in general, we're pains in the ass. Most wives probably have a good reason to run off. Mine too. Another Boogles?"

With a d. Boodles. Yeah."

I'm pretty good at what I do, Wilkes. I will find your wife."

Tell me the truth," Wilkes says as two new glasses arrive. "Do you think she's alright?"

I don't think she's dead. Is that what you mean?"

Jesus, don't pull any punches on my account."

You've considered that. I know it. Problem is, there are lots of bad things that happen while we're alive. I've found people working in prostitution to support a drug habit. Some guy was peddling kiddie porn and a woman—"

I get the point."

So that alive stuff, it's not the be-all and end. But I just have a feel for these things and I think she'll turn up all right."

End-all. Be-all and end-all."

Like I said. Talk to the cops?"

Yes."

But you aren't hounding them."

I didn't think it was worth it."

"Good for you. Why burden them with a possible crime? I mean, they're b
enough, aren't they?"

Wilkes smiles.

"So you can take a joke," McNally says. "I'm just busting balls, Wilkes. I kn
you don't want your kids to see their mother's name all over the TV. I
understand that. I still don't understand this drink. What the hell is gin, anywa

"It's made from juniper berries."

"Thanks for clarifying."

He gulps down the rest and flips over the tab.

"Thirty-two dollars? Jesus Christ, where do they get these juniper ber
Mars?"

"You had that beer too."

"I already paid for that."

Wilkes reaches for the check. "I told you I was getting this."

"No, no," McNally says. "I'm making the big bucks. You're gonna pay one
or the other."

He waves over the bartender and hands him a fifty, asks for a ten in return,
leads Wilkes to the door. McNally pulls out a pair of sunglasses, puts an arm
Wilkes's shoulder.

"You didn't kill her, did you? I mean really, your alibi is airtight, but you co
have hired somebody."

"One of my kids?"

"Their alibis are good too. Anyway, I had to ask one more time. If I had
suspicion, I'm not as effective."

"You're a PI. Don't you thrive on suspicion?"

"Of the other guy, not my client. Trust is of the vital."

Wilkes allows himself another smile, wonders if these little malapropisms
intentional.

"Look, if you're as good as Blackmoor says, won't you eventually catch
anyway? Or aren't you that good?"

McNally laughs a bit too loudly. A waitress looks over.

"I'm certainly good enough to catch someone like you."

"Then maybe it's time to stop with the bullshit questions and really deal with
problem?"

"But it's my idiom, Wilkes. I'm the hard-nosed, sarcastic PI."

"Not in that madras tie you're not."

The wife thinks the whole act is pretty amusing 'cause I'm such a pussy at
ne, but it plays and pays well. Still," and he pauses and looks around, "I guess
n taper it back a little. From here on, I'm on the clock. And you. Do your part.
ep out of your garage when you're drunk."

mes, three years younger than his brother, is easier to deal with on an objective
vel. Most of the time he seems content to sit by the living room window and stare
t, as if it will make perfect sense for his mother suddenly to appear, walk in,
ake dinner, and carry on as she did before they boarded that plane.

"You know how Mom hates the cold," Wilkes says to interrupt his gaze. "I'll bet
e comes back when all this snow melts...."

James nods, but it's another lie. If anything the opposite is true. Keira has always
en the one to reject terms like "heavy snow warning" as ludicrous: why did
ople need to be warned of something so beautiful? The January trip to Savannah
ld no charm for her, at least no climatological one; in fact, Wilkes might just as
uthfully have said to James "I'll bet she comes back before all this snow melts...."

Brett is more analytical. He wants to know what the cops are doing. When they
ll make an arrest? If there's a kidnapper will he be put to death? Will Mom have
testify? Will he and his brother? Brett relishes the idea of a PI working the case,
ough Wilkes continues to squelch the idea that a crime has occurred.

Brett wants a time frame. A week? A month? Longer?

"I'll tell you what," Wilkes says, and takes out his Blackberry. "On Monday, if
om's not back here, we'll both go to the police station. That gives her the whole
eekend. That's long enough for anyone to act weird."

The boy doesn't buy into this any more than Wilkes does: Brett's mother isn't
me snotty-nosed kid with a makeshift backpack bolting to a life of freedom
cause her parents won't let her get a piercing like the other girls. Keira Wilkes
a woman of steady habits and an earned reputation for stability. Even so, the boy
ems willing to accept the remote possibility that there are forces and emotions
doesn't quite grasp, that the adult world comprises enigmas and mysteries that
ight elude the uncomplicated perceptions of a fourth-grader.

Regardless of their differences, the boys are Wilkes's to deal with until Keira
turns, his and their reliable babysitter. Danielle Gomez does not pursue enigmas
require details, she simply works when asked and accepts her ten dollars an hour
thout quibbling. Her only foible is a continuing obsession with the Laci Peterson
urder, and Wilkes wonders if she envisions him as the reincarnation of Laci's
sband. But the upsides to Danielle outweigh everything: she's competent and
stworthy, and the house is always spotless after her visits. Not only that, but she

somehow enlists Brett and James to help her clean. The older boy probably thin
she's cute though to Wilkes she appears scrawny, swimming in clothes far too b
As for James, he's probably following the older boy's lead, nothing more. T
extra work has netted the girl several tips, none of which ever bothered Keira
him—it was almost like having an interim housecleaner. And again, on sh
notice, Danielle agrees to be there when the boys come home from school Mond
afternoon. She can even do Friday, she says, but Wilkes declines: he'll keep t
boys home one more day.

The evening degenerates into a constant skein of phone calls: Byrne, th
Tolliver, then Andy, then the Easons, then some relatives Hayley seems to ha
alerted, then Andy again. By eleven he has told the same story so many times th
he begins to bore himself with it. The gin helps though, and by the time he flips
the news at eleven to find that the Miracle on the Hudson remains the lead stor
he is hardly able to comprehend much of anything. He doesn't want to go to be
though, not alone.

Outside the wind is rippling the canvas awning, the one he shouldn't leave up
winter but does because the ratcheting mechanism has become balky. Now
wonders if it's merely rusted, and he troops off to the garage for some WD-40. I
can actually reach the crank from a side window which, when he forces it ope
allows a gush of January air to whip into the room. He quickly slathers the gea
with a continuous spray until the wind, deflected by some construction angle, shi
slightly and sends it back into his face.

He curses loudly and wonders if he will lose his eyesight to some caustic spra
He can't read the label because he can't focus on anything, but he feels his way
the kitchen for some paper towels and wipes his eyes. He can see after all. He c
also feel the living room chilling from the open window. He hurls the can of W
40 onto the lawn where it bounces and rolls off an encrusted snow bank, then
closes the window. Maybe, he thinks, he's had enough gin.

The boys are upstairs where he should be. His expressed certitude about Keira
return will lose its credibility when Brett and James discover their father hidi
downstairs on the couch. But sleeping alone in a bed where he once made love
his wife unnerves him, and though he tries not to think about the sex because
reduces Keira's absence to something crude, he remembers the little scenarios th
would play out, the little variations they would sometimes try, and sometimes (
he learned one day in a Nordstrom dressing room) even the venue.

ut now this is the venue, and now his responsibilities as a husband have been ended. He is a father only and it's his job to make the house a sanctuary, a en of solace and quiet where homework will get done and school projects will ompleted and clothes will be washed and folded and put away and bills will be , and, eventually, Keira will return—Keira who has said goodbye to her dren in the dim lights of a motor coach and left without looking back. How in world does a woman do that? And how does he not hate her for it?

ne next six hours are divided into periods of restless sleep and wakeful cipation of some horrible phone call. At sunrise, when it is barely bright enough iscern objects in the living room, he calls McNally.

m not a doctor," the PI says though he doesn't sound groggy. "You can't just any time."

igured you were up."

And now I am. What have you got?"

What have I got? Shouldn't I be asking you?"

You called me. And you didn't ask."

ilkes waits a beat. "I had trouble sleeping."

Well there's something we can share."

know it's early, but you said yesterday that your gut told you she was alive. at else?"

..and well. Alive and well."

mean what else do you think?"

know what you mean. Listen, Wilkes, you seem like a decent guy, and at this t—"

Do you think she's with somebody? A man?"

t's the 21st century pal, maybe it's a woman. Look, I hate to start your day on wrong foot, but I think she's planned this for a while."

So that's your approach? Infidelity?"

nfidelity isn't an approach; it's one way I make my living. But it's early on, while I have you on the phone—"

You had information on my neighbor and Miss Qualling instantly."

Your neighbor's picture is on the Internet, and Miss Qualling is in Wikipedia er promiscuity, or should be. That was the easy part. That was to impress you. t was free. The real investigative work is a hell of a lot harder, and slower. ile I have you here, I need a list of places you've been with her, just in case she ted to go back and have a good time without dragging you along."

Wilkes lists a few: Atlantic City, San Antonio, Las Vegas, Sun Valley, D.C
McNally laughs.

"Well at least we know she hasn't run away to some place she fell in love v
Did you ever take her anywhere good? Rome? Paris? London?"

"We got passports last year, but she wanted to see the boardwalk."

"Jesus, buy a Monopoly board. Atlantic City? I thought you didn't gamble.'

"We played a few slots there, just for fun."

"That's a waste of a passport. You're lucky she didn't have it with her that
She might be in one of those places people really go on vacation. Gonna sue
airline?"

"Should I?"

"Emotional distress. People will do it. I'd retain a lawyer just in case. Are
going into work?"

"I'm keeping the kids home."

"Get a sitter and meet me for lunch in the city. You can put in an hour or tw
the office. People will want to commiserate. It'll make them feel better. Ma
you too. I don't do that."

"Do what?"

"Commiseration. Solace. Empathy."

McNally suggests a deli a block and a half from Wilkes's office. One o'cl
He puts down the phone, wakes up his laptop, then lists the places the
vacationed. He can easily defend those destinations: Keira was the trip-plan
She spent entire evenings flitting from one travel site to the next, booking fli
and hotels and attractions. And when she would finally present the finished pro
to him in the form of several print-outs and confirmations, he just asked her w
and what to pack. If she had wanted Rome or Paris, she'd have chosen it.

But the passport was his idea. A conversation about the Vancouver Olym
had evolved into a discussion of the changes in travel and a colleague's compl
that "you can't even go to Montreal anymore." Wilkes had no desire to see Can
but Tolliver & Byrne did some business in Toronto, and he could envision a
when he'd be part of some meeting and maybe be able to turn it into a week
getaway. Keira would enjoy Toronto, he thought at the time. People spoke Engl
the city itself carried a reputation for being cosmopolitan, the flight was sin
and direct, and he was sure he could talk her into it. Of course now he'd hav
find her first.

n mid-morning with the boys still asleep he phones Danielle Gomez. He needs
after all. No worries, she says, because she may in fact have none. She'll be by
10:00. He brews some coffee and picks the morning paper off the lawn, then
aks his house-shoe rule by tramping through the newly fallen dusting of snow
retrieve the WD-40 can. He doesn't read the paper: another article on airplane
racles carries little appeal, especially when this recent miracle has somehow
luded him. He carries the coffee mug into his study and places it atop a two-
wer file cabinet, then slides open the top drawer—the one with the important
uments—car titles, mortgage papers, marriage license, birth certificates. With
Nally's words still fresh, he lifts out the folder labeled passports and opens it.
side there is only his.

or a moment he stares, as if the reappearance of objects is perfectly natural and
other passport will soon materialize. It doesn't. He tries the folders on either
e, then a few more. He is, after all, prone to misfile things at home. Then he
cks to see if it's in no folder—just lying in the bottom of the cabinet where he
e found (he's embarrassed to admit) their marriage license.

's not loose. It's not anywhere. His stomach begins to hurt and he spends the
t ten minutes in the bathroom trying to negate the cramps that have almost
bled him over. Nerves. The missing passport leaves him feeling like the
hteen-year-old Martin Wilkes at a college interview, or the graduate
erviewing for his first real job. In those days the anxiety was paralyzing. He
ught he had gotten past it. He hasn't, not entirely.

When Danielle arrives she asks if there are any more vacuum cleaner bags—the
t time she babysat she used the last one. He assures her there are plenty, makes
ne quick goodbyes, then races to the train station—and past it. He doesn't want
e a slave to the Amtrak schedule, choosing instead to drive all the way in, show
face at T&B, hand off some responsibilities to Andy, maybe assuage some
cerns. Once inside the offices, though, he can almost hear the eggshells
ckling underfoot. Only Sandy Qualling seems to have remembered her role,
king with him about upcoming appointments, a conference in Baltimore he
bably won't be attending, calls she has shunted away. He half expects her to
ale him with some new sexual exploits, and since talking with McNally he can't
p wondering how many of his colleagues have participated, but today at least
 has provided some normality and he's grateful for that.

He isn't quite so grateful to McNally, who has selected a noisy, crowded
where each table practically abuts the next. It's conducive to nothing, especia
conversation.

"Up before dawn," McNally says, leaning across the table to be heard. He we
a tan flannel, but he's added a down vest of an indeterminate green shade. An
different madras tie.

"Couldn't sleep."

"Understandable." McNally studies him like a captured insect. "Looks like y
know something. Come on. You show me yours; I'll show you mine."

Wilkes waves away the approaching waiter.

"Keira's passport is gone."

"Well, she flew to Toronto the morning after so that's kind of a given. That v
our waiter by the way. Don't you want to order?"

Wilkes is unsure how much of McNally's statement has been absorbed by
noise around them.

"Say that again?"

"Keira, your wife, she flew to Toronto on Thursday morning."

"Jesus, if I hadn't called you wouldn't have told me?"

"I don't call to chat. I call when I have some real information, but," and he
out a sigh of exasperation "since you went through all the trouble of driving in,
least I can do is put your mind at ease."

"How does that put my mind at ease?"

"She's alive," he says, cupping his hands as if he's shouting across some chas
"She's not in the fucking river or held in an abandoned mine shaft by kidnappe
I know how crime victims think, they get these wild ideas...."

Wilkes is furious.

"The morning after? What did she do that night?"

"I'd take a gander at credit card receipts, maybe on line, rather than wait for
bill."

"Why didn't you just hack into my account while you were at it."

"Encrypted passwords are a bitch—though I do have some people. Anywa
don't care what she bought or where she stayed. I want to know where she enc
up. Are we going to order or not?"

"This is some game for you. But for me—"

"It's what? Life and death? 'Cause I gotta tell you—you can act like you
pissed at me, but you're really pissed at her. She's gone and I'm here finding

ngs faster than you can comprehend. You may not like it, but I'm earning my
ep."

"Bullshit!"

Wilkes's voice rises almost to the din of the clashing plates and shouted kitchen
ders. McNally leans back and says nothing for a moment, before nodding.

"We should order or they'll make us leave. Of course since you snubbed the
aiter, there's not much chance he'll come back anytime this year."

The PI stands up and makes eye contact and the young man returns.

"Coffee," Wilkes spits out. "Just—coffee."

McNally orders egg salad on whole wheat and cajoles the waiter into adding a
w jalapeños to the mix.

"Gotta eat," he says. "Still pissed off? You've had a minute."

Wilkes isn't so much breathing as gasping. He wants to call Blackmoor, who
commended this fuck-up, and tell him to find another financial advisor, another
mpany; but he isn't sure he can cobble together a comprehensible sentence.

"That's better," the PI says, responding to the silence. "Now listen. JFK has a
mber of hotels on site and—"

"She flew out of Kennedy? The bus—"

"She couldn't have taken the car if you took the car, remember?"

"So?"

"She took a cab from one to the other. It happens all the time. People put together
ing itineraries that involve two nearby airports. As I was saying, she probably
t a room under her own name—and why not? Nobody was really looking for her
cept you and some panicky U.S. Air people, and they were at the other airport.
ou have to admit that's ballsy."

Wilkes doesn't, nor does he return McNally's grin.

"All right maybe it isn't. Next morning she boarded a CRJ and that was it. Now
u're not going door-to-door across Canada looking for your wife. We both know
at. I, on the other hand, have a number of good connections that can get me a lot
information. I'm not going to bore you with every piece of trivia someone puts
t there. Canada—that's trivia. Toronto—not much better. Saskatoon, an
provement."

"I don't even know where that is."

"You don't have to. Here's what matters: your wife flew from JFK to Pearson
the 15th. Standby. Air Canada."

"And nobody saw her?"

"Everybody saw her, but nobody was looking for her. She have friends there"
"In Canada? No."
"I sort of knew that. From Toronto west to Saskatoon. Now if she doesn't ha
friends in Toronto, I'm going to assume she doesn't have them in Saskatchew
either. You don't have to confirm that—I checked. Now Saskatoon, that's a lit
smaller, maybe about the population of, oh I don't know, Jersey City. Still kind
big to go door-to-door. But she didn't stay there either. So now we're getting
the point where it would almost—almost—be worth telling you. She flew
Manitoba, scheduled airline."
"Where's that?"
"It's in...Jesus, it's in Manitoba. It's a province."
"What's the population?"
"Wrong question. It's about a zillion square miles. Random interviews are o
but she flew into a town called Churchill. It's more of a stopover than a destinatio
and an airport supervisor remembers an American landing there, a woman who f
Keira's description and who wanted to know what pilots flew out of there. I
trying to find out where she went next. Figure then we have something."
"Then just check the flights, the other airlines."
"Well, there's Canada and then there's way up in Canada. No one flies in
Toronto without being noticed or logged, but farther up in the wilderness there
lots of gypsy flyers, guys with WWII-vintage planes duct-taped together who
places you've never heard of. Hundreds of them, maybe thousands. There's
other way to get around."
"And we can't retrace her steps."
"We? No. Me? Give me a day or two."
"I can't."
"See, that's why I don't like chatty updates. Now you have a hard-on for flyi
to some place you don't even know."
"I could start with Churchill."
"Why don't you start at home? Check ATM withdrawals and credit charg
Unless she had about three grand in her underwear drawer, you're gonna find so
expenditures—tickets, luggage, clothing—it's chilly up there in the Arct
especially if you're dressed for Savannah."
"Then I'll know exactly where she is."
"Let the search begin. Don't be a stranger."
"Do you have a passport?"

cNally shakes his head. "Really? You want to search Canada together? Then
t, should we pitch it as a reality show?"
'm serious."
)on't be. Nunavut is huge, and it can be a little chilly this time of year."
unavut. He's heard the name before but can't imagine why.
/ou said Churchill. Where's Nunavut?"
3uy a globe and look near the top. And by the way, the airport information I
:, everybody has. If the cops are looking, and I don't know why they would be,
 might know she's in Canada too. Now she's not a fugitive and they aren't
ig to institute some all-out search or extradite her or anything cool like that."
This city cop, Hagan, he said to tell him if she was seen. Should I tell them?"
Jot much good comes from lying to the cops."
3ut then they'll stop looking."
3elieve me, a missing adult? They've already stopped."
Vell then I'm definitely not telling them."
cNally rolls his eyes.
Vhen the waiter comes back order some food. Hunger is making you stupid."

9

Nally is right, at least about the finances. Several hundred dollars has been
hdrawn from their checking account via two different ATMs, and their Visa is
ash with new purchases, some at the airport in Toronto, some farther west.
ira's underwear drawer is empty of everything except underwear.
If she had a rainy-day fund," McNally says later on the phone, "it's raining."
The crash and rescue continue to dominate the evening news, and survivor
eriences seem more and more elaborate. One woman feels "haunted" by
plendent dreams and a feeling of prescience and an older man claims to have
n his deceased parents as the plane touched the water. It's all so much bullshit
Wilkes. Simply seeing your life flash before you isn't good enough anymore, he
s. Now we require golden cities and hovering angels and mini-resurrections.
en you write your screenplay, Wilkes mutters to the television screen, tell me
y those angels couldn't divert the geese. The newscast ends with a poem
nposed by the five-year-old daughter of a survivor: he hears the first lines and
sses the mute button. Wilkes isn't much of a reader but he knows a poem when
hears one. This isn't one.
omeone from Long Island is publishing a book, a paperback detailing the thirty
so minutes between take-off and rescue. *The Hudson Effect* will be out Monday,
ere five days after the event. Such is the state of technology in 2009. Wilkes
l read it, of course, on the off chance that it elucidates something about a woman
h two children: he reminds himself that, to the world at large, Keira Wilkes is
rely one of 150. Same rescue. Same happily ever after.
le debates how much of the conversation with McNally to share with anyone.
tells the Easons only that the PI has been gathering preliminaries, but he shares
ttle more with his sons.
She may be in Canada," he says, "but we don't know for sure."
She helped me with my report about Canada," Brett says later. "We had to write
nething about one of the providences."
Provinces. Which one?"
At first I had Yukon because it sounded like the basketball team, but too many
s had the same one, so I took Nunavut because no one else wanted it."
Nunavut. So he has heard the word before.
When did you do the report?"

"After Thanksgiving. I showed it to you, remember?"

"Of course I do."

He does—vaguely. Something about the North Pole and Eskimos and the icec[ ] At the time he figured it was just one more incursion of the schools into polit[ ] some new indoctrination about global warming. "Did Mom help you?"

"She helped a lot," James says, perfectly willing to sell out his brother.

Brett glares at him, then adopts a penitent look, the innocent recipient of sto[ ] merchandise. "Wasn't she supposed to?"

"Of course she was. I was just wondering."

"She said things, but I had to copy stuff down and print out the pictures and pa[ ] everything."

"Did you get a good grade?"

Wilkes doesn't care in the slightest but thinks it might be an appropriate questi[ ] at which point Brett volunteers to retrieve the project.

"And listen," Wilkes says, "there's nothing wrong with Mom helping you w[ ] a report. It's what all the moms do."

He looks at James: the younger boy's mind is whirling.

"That's not why she left," Wilkes says quickly. "Helping out like that is[ ] wrong. Sometimes I help you with some words or when you had to collect differ[ ] kinds of leaves that time. Sometimes in work people help me. It's okay to do tha[ ]

James appears almost convinced as Wilkes examines the report. It's a hell o[ ] lot slicker than anything Wilkes ever did in the fourth grade, replete with grap[ ] and photos and just enough text to make it informational. On the cover is a pl[ ] called Repulse Bay that looks like a Vermont village without the mountains, [ ] snow plowed into large mounds on the sides of narrow streets. But the sky colo[ ] a deeper azure than Wilkes has ever seen in New England—hints at a cold [ ] murderous intensity. Another photo shows caribou hides drying on a buildi[ ] hung on either side of a basketball hoop.

"Nunavut," the caption reads. "A Remote Country."

"Do you know what remote means, Brett?"

"Mom helped."

"Did she say anything about it?"

"She said it must be hard to live there with all that cold."

"I'll bet it is."

He leafs through the project: a page for Repulse Bay, another for Gjoa Have[ ]

"Brett, how do you pronounce this?"

'Like joy with an a on the end. That's what Mom said."

'Joy-a," Wilkes repeats and flips the page. An Eskimo family is dancing in some
't of native garb—lots of fur and fringe and beads. There's the obligatory photo
a polar bear and the chartreuse and lemon glow of the northern lights. The last
ge is filled with a vaguely human shape seemingly balanced together by
ulders. The caption, printed in red, reads Inuksuit.

'Brett, what's this?"

'A stone man."

'That's what *Inuksuit* means? Stone man?"

'Mom told me it did. She said she knew about them. She's the one who found
 picture."

'On the Internet?"

'In a book, I think."

'Really? Like from the library?"

'I don't know. Maybe."

'She cut out a picture from a library book?"

'Did Mom do something wrong?" James again, looking for the rationale that
ould have put his mother on the lam.

Wilkes shakes his head. No explanation this time—it's Brett he wants to hear.

'What I mean," Wilkes says, hoping to sound more curious than angry. "Is—it's
t a weird thing to know."

'She said it was like totem poles in America."

'You're right," he says with a hint of a smile. His words hardly convince himself;
 doubts if they're convincing anybody else.

He closes the report. It's a decent effort, though Nunavut is not a country but a
rritory and that mistake alone should render everything after it somewhat
udulent. Still, on the cover sits a large A- scribbled in red by some enthusiastic
cher who has, it seems, not set his sights very high. If schools are raising the
r, this guy didn't get the memo. Or he's confusing slick with competent, an error
ilkes understands. Tolliver & Byrne's yearly reports, four-color pictures and
lashy graphics on photo-quality paper, rival anything on a newsstand except
ybe Architectural Digest, though it's commonly accepted that a simple PDF file
nt to stockholders would accomplish the same function.

'You did a good job, Brett," Wilkes says, then with the boys off by themselves,
ones their principal who has, in a past moment of expansive weakness, posted
r number on the school website.

"We haven't told many people," he says to her. "You know the papers. Th
jump on things like this."

It's a calculated comment: Barbara Woodard knows about the papers. Just befc
the holidays she came to the defense of one of her teachers accused of impro
touching. It turned out that the so-called victim had lied and the parents h
knowingly defended him, causing the school committee, which had demanded t
teacher's immediate resignation and arrest, to issue a public apology. M
Woodard spent most of her working hours between Thanksgiving and Christn
putting out a fire that didn't exist and charting the results in the media. Even if l
faith in that staff member had been corroborated, Wilkes doubted that either she
the accused considered the outcome a victory.

No, Wilkes won't have to concern himself with Mrs. Woodard's discretic
though she is quick to guarantee it. The school project was just a lucky break. I
wonders if more people have information they don't even know they have. Perha
if more people knew, if there were more conversations....

McNally does not agree.

"I don't think you want the story out there," the PI says, his tone clear enou
over crackling cell reception.

"Even if someone knows something?"

"We're both fairly sure she didn't run off with someone, but the undiscriminati
news hounds out there won't see it that way. There'll be those who attack yc
husbanding skills, an equal number who will claim she's in the equilibrium factc
getting her wheels balanced, if you get my meaning, and still others who w
hound you for details of the ransom note. The other ninety percent will know y
had her killed."

"Only ninety?"

"On the other hand—and if this is what you want, go for it—you'll become
instantly sympathetic figure for a few, especially when they know you have ki
There'll probably be a benefit concert arranged by next weekend. At least
pancake breakfast. Do you like pancakes?"

"Is this one of the consulting conversations I'm paying for?"

"You called me. I'm just saying, if you do go public, you'll leave yourself op
for a lot of quacks. See, I'm not entirely sure about the supernatural, but peo
don't disappear. They can go somewhere and seem to have disappeared, but unle
she's working with an illusionist, she still exists. So how much bullshit can y
tolerate? Can the kids tolerate? Her folks? You know your family better than I dc

f I do go public, how does that work? How do I do it?"

Vell, you can call a reporter. I'd call the police. In the end, it's the same."

Doesn't that get me in trouble? Wouldn't I have been withholding evidence?"

Vilkes, do you have any idea how many spouses disappear and how many of
partners hire people like me? It's a fucking epidemic. And the local cops
y have nothing to do with it—this is out of their jurisdiction. But if you want
ell them you're touching base—in case they hear of anything—something
g those lines. Tell them you don't suspect foul play but you can't rule it out."

sn't it the police who rule out foul play?"

And you help them. Prepare yourself, though. Once it gets out there—well, tell
boys what to expect. Maybe keep them home an extra day or two. Make sure
ybody knows you really do want her back—"

Of course I want her back. Jesus, why the hell would you?"

top. Just stop. That's exactly what I mean by how much can you tolerate?
en you talk to people, before you talk to people, practice. Practice not being
tified every time someone impugns your moral code or questions your deep
for your wife. But don't act mortified with me. You know that I know you're
ed at her."

'm angry."

And it's going to show. And people aren't going to differentiate between anger
the fact and anger that drove her away or convinced you to murder her and
e her in a ditch. You can be the anxious husband and the concerned father, but
d and vengeful lovers don't play well."

'or Christ's sake."

Now you're mortified again. Here's a little trick you can try. Every time you
t to be shocked at someone's slimy accusations, remember your little sexual
a in the garage. Or that Hendrickson woman next door, the one you keep
ng over. Maybe you are right now, though it's winter and she's probably
ting several layers of clothing. I'd bet the chances are good that you let slip to
end, maybe after a few of your Boodles, how you wouldn't mind an evening
de that towel of hers. Remember that towel? And Sandy Qualling discussing
al positions at work? How many of those little symposiums were you part of?
'll come up. Better thicken your skin a bit. And then stop reading the
spapers."

Vhat about a reputable paper?"

"Really? A reputable paper? For someone with no sense of humor, you do
off a good one on occasion. One more thing: what we already know is more
you're going to find out. I mean we have her narrowed down to a province
country, and maybe a city. That's a start. But the motive, that's still right here,
we won't know it until we ask her."

"Did I miss something?"

"I don't understand."

"Do you mean here, right here in this house? Did I not see this coming but she
have?"

"I don't think when your kid does a project on some distant place you sh
assume your wife is headed there, if that's what you're asking."

"There must have been other clues that I ignored."

"That's on you."

"That's why you're not going to Canada."

"That's why you shouldn't either. Reputable paper. I gotta remember that."

Afterward he gets the boys off to bed, Wilkes peruses the Nunavut project ag
Maybe it's better than he originally thought, or maybe he has ignored obv
clues. Or maybe he's overlooked everything where Keira is concerned. No
decides, it's the plane crash and the aftermath. It's cheating death and
reconciling oneself to that second chance. Some can handle it, some can't. It's
Hudson Effect: he should write a book.

He stares at the stone man for a few moments, then lays the project on the co
table and, at some point, falls asleep on the couch.

10

[Taggarik]

Repulse Bay, Auguste Demarais awakens to darkness and checks the clock by
bed. Three-thirty in the morning. The time hardly matters for his surroundings
l look no different an hour later, two hours, four. Even so, even in this place
ere the dark predominates and daylight is reduced to a few faint hours a day,
guste Demarais has always tried to maintain a semblance of normality in his
stence. By midnight he likes to be in bed; by 8:00 a.m. he likes to be drinking
 strong tea. The hours between pass in the brutal blackness of a planet tilted
ay from the sun by some millennia-old cataclysm that occurred before there was
)emarais, a Nunavut, a Canada. Before there was anything that walked or
athed or lay awake and stared into blackness. But whatever happened in that
historic nanosecond left behind this frozen and barren desert that stretches out
 a thousand miles in every direction. That event is the reason for the dark time,
zgarik. And all those twilight designations scientists were so concerned with,
il, nautical, astronomical, only the last one mattered: when the sun dipped so
 below the horizon that even the dimmest stars were visible, then it was dark.
d Auguste Demarais preferred to be asleep.

3arefoot on the uncarpeted floor, he creaks to the window to check the
rmometer; it was twenty-seven degrees below zero, Celsius. His mental
version. He grew up where temperatures carried an F after the digits, which
:sn't work well with negative numbers, but he knows that forty-below is forty-
ow, regardless. That mnemonic device simplifies the process a little; besides,
quibble over three or four degrees is a waste of thought, especially when that
ady breeze keeps the air moving, seeking out structural weaknesses and
:ealed cracks. He can feel it through the glass—fifty-nine, maybe sixty degrees
ow freezing.

\ streetlight shines outside the front door, illuminating a whitened earth. But the
ht is misleading. Years before, when Auguste Demarais left Nunavut for a time
l visited his birthplace in the states, he was constantly disabusing people of the
a that the Arctic comprised endless blizzards and a blinding amalgam of snow,
, and wind. Auguste preferred to call it the cold Sahara and explained to them
icepts like moisture sources and dew points and all sorts of meteorological

arcana. Sometimes he settled on "too cold to snow," the facile but comforta
explanation that seemed to satisfy everyone. In Repulse Bay itself, nobody ca
about any of this except Gordon at the government weather station, and he is p
to care. If anyone else lies awake at 3:30 a.m., it's probably Gordon, checking
barographs and anemometers and preparing a forecast the locals will proba
ignore. In the states, weather headlines the news twenty percent of the time, ye
Repulse Bay, where for six months of the year the temperature alone can kill a n
in minutes, it's never more than a passing thought.

One afternoon during the previous July, the temperature nudged twenty-o
degrees Celsius. A strict conversion would have yielded a Fahrenheit temperat
of sixty-nine and ninety-nine one-hundredths, but Gordon decided to forgo his us
exactitude and call it seventy. No one could remember a day that warm, and
unusual weather sparked all sorts of crackpot behavior among the normally st
citizens. There were shirtless people, men and women, basking on the shore n
the water aerodrome, and the co-op hawked small paper cups of vegetable oil
suntan lotion. Some murmured ominous warnings of climate change and an end
life as they knew it, but Gordon, cautious to a fault, urged them not to conf
weather with climate, assured them that anomalies were what made the averag
That same night the temperature dropped to the freezing point again, but the cl
did not allay the concerns of a coming Armageddon. Neither did an unpreceden
string of eighty-degree days in Baker Lake. Auguste Demarais found it worriso
too, had witnessed the subtle changes in the permafrost and the glaciers, and ev
though mornings like this made those fears seem ungrounded, he too could disc
the difference between weather and climate. Weather killed you in minut
climate took centuries but proved just as efficient.

In Colorado where he grew up, Gus, and he was Gus back then, that less forr
version of himself, often slipped outside in only his pajamas to pick the Post
of his mailbox. In the lower forty-eight, you did those things even on the cold
mornings. Maybe the weather was frigid, even dangerous, but it had lim
parameters. In the Arctic, though, words like frigid and dangerous beca
burlesques. A careless trip to the mailbox on a morning like this might me
death—a stumble, a fall, the least bit of debilitation that kept a person in
elements ten, maybe twenty seconds longer than he had anticipated, and that mi
signal the end, or the irreversible beginning of the end. He wouldn't be fishing
his cell phone to call the paramedics; he'd be dead before rescuers got their f
layer of thermal clothing off the hooks.

Auguste Demarais lives by the rules of this new normality. Rolling out of bed at first light enforces it; staring into blackness at 3:30 a.m. does not.

And there is no reason to be awake. There are no early morning people like in Colorado, the ones who bake the bread or brew the coffee or drop off the Denver Post in the letterbox by the street. Here the night presses against the buildings and keeps them shut up tight. He can explain it in English, but in the Inuit language, there are no words: the language doesn't work that way. A person can't just string together parts of speech until the combination of nouns and verbs produce some cogent expression. Here a "word" might be thirty letters long and contain within it a question with multitudinous parts. And the subtlety and inflection are maddening. He had once heard someone say thank-you; he was sure of it. But when he tried to repeat the phrase, a bystander erupted into paroxysms of laughter, explaining to him afterward that he had actually bragged about the mucus in his throat. Many times he longed for an English/Inuktitut dictionary, but the idea was laughable. The book would either be endless, or blank.

He wonders, at 3:35 a.m., if there is a concise Inuktitut word for insomnia, but how can there be? It probably takes the form of some oblique question like, are you one who sees the darkness while others have their eyes shut? or some such.

He stumbles to the bathroom to pee, then shuffles into the darkened kitchen where he opens the freezer, uncaps a bottle of vodka, and takes a swig—just one. Tales of people drinking liquor outdoors in the Arctic and freezing their throats keep him from gulping down more, though his own freezer is nowhere near as cold as the "freezer" that surrounds the bungalow where he lives. And his kitchen of course, as uncomfortable as he lets it get each night, is no match for the unrelenting chill beyond those poorly insulated walls. He pours a few more drops into a shot glass, warms it in his hands, and returns to bed with it.

The vodka relaxes him, but as it always does, unlooses the truth.

He has had the dream again, but nowadays—is he just getting old? forgetful? blasé?—he seldom remembers having it, just the feeling of having had it, of having seen the woman again. And this woman, she is not a beauty by any standards, either Anglo or Inuit. If she possessed classic features and a perfect figure, then yes, an obsession like this would be far less inexplicable. And if the dream involved sex, or it was one of those youthful fantasies in which, just on the verge of fulfillment, the person awakens, he'd understand that too. But even though she is always naked, he never reaches out to graze her cheek, her breast, her hand; he cannot remember even looking at anything but her eyes. The advancing years have not so

much robbed him of desire, but he has gone so long without making love to
woman that he is no longer sure how to proceed, how the dance progresses,
steps, the movement, the embrace. It has become easier not to try, to avo
rejection. He is sixty, too young to have abandoned the pleasure of a woma
touch but too old to start again.

Sometimes he awakens with his heart racing, his eyes desperately scanning
darkened room to find her, trying to retain the last vestiges of life before
unrelenting Arctic draws her in. But as with every episode, the ending is gradu
the figure fading almost imperceptibly through translucence, even as Augu
struggles to mold her back together. Unlike his wife, his former wife, he is a po
sculptor.

He warns the woman that she will die in the cold. He advises her about bo
temperature and hypothermia. He relates stories of survival and death in Repu
Bay. He has lived there, learned there, he is the observer she can never
disappearing as she does when the daylight arrives.

"You cannot be me," she says, then repeats it as the image continues to fa
becomes a bluish cloud, disappears altogether. He isn't sure what the words me
but the woman has said them once, or perhaps in every dream. He is never sure

Nor is he sure anymore where the dreams end, or if they end at all. This ea
morning that very woman lies in a derelict shack mere miles from him. She
cajoled him to take her there, then ordered him away. Now she will die. Or she w
be reborn. Or she is not there at all but merely another chimerical vision emerg
from the cold. Deserts have their mirages; arctic deserts are no different.

He finishes the vodka, the *angajaarnaqtuq*. He hears the wind rattle a loo
shutter, then go quiet, then rattle it again. Comforting repetition. He'll be asle
soon and the woman will not return—not tonight anyway. But next time, may
he will touch her, make a tentative approach to intimacy, and maybe she will ma
him feel something inside himself. Tonight there will be only darkness, many mo
hours of it before the pale sun slinks into view.

kes's benchmark for a reputable paper, the *Times*, buries the article amidst
onal news just above the story of a smoldering landfill that has some
geport neighborhood squawking about noxious odors. Wilkes shakes his head
wonders aloud why the complainers can't keep their windows closed, the kind
omment that Keira would criticize, but she isn't here to police him.

Miracle on Hudson Survivor Now Reported Missing

e *Times's* angle leans more toward irony than conspiracy, that someone who
ived a potential catastrophe winds up missing anyway, as if someone rescued
the *Titanic* had stepped onto the New York pier, tripped over a discarded
preserver, fallen into the river, and drowned. But it's the *Times*, and the
y is diluted in favor of objective presentation.
me of the other papers, perhaps targeting a different readership, tie together
geese that crippled the engine to wild goose chases in general, and another has
e inappropriate fun with "fowl" play. The approaches may not be the most
ful, but there are few hints of anything untoward, especially since the triumph
e rescue remains uppermost in people's minds.
e TV networks give this new angle short shrift, though one uses it in a longer
ure on the Hudson Effect, downplaying the single disappearance in favor of
erscoring similar kinds of psychological responses to near-tragedies—people
 have escaped from fires, abductions, prison camps. The Hudson Effect has
ady mutated into the Hudson Syndrome, a better movie title, Wilkes sneers.
even he feels that, all in all, the coverage has been remarkably subdued, even
reet.
ill, once the story is out there, Wilkes's private affliction becomes everyone's
ere concern. Casual acquaintances and long-standing clients, even relatives
 have ignored the family for years, find reasons to phone. His eighty-year-old
e in Savannah, he of the birthday party at which the family never quite arrived,
 for an update while insisting he is somehow to blame. Wilkes handles all the
-wishers with a modicum of grace, and most people seem to know what it
ns to keep a reasonable distance. It's the casual acquaintances that annoy him:
an't distinguish concern from ghoulishness, and eventually he stops trying.

In his spare moments he pores over the topographical map of Canada. And Nunavut.

On a flat map the territory is gigantic, all 1.2 million square miles of it, stretch from somewhat accessible and perfectly civilized Manitoba north and east to frozen Ellesmere, an island itself the size of New England, less than five hun miles from the North Pole and half that to magnetic north. There are forebo place names like Resolute and Repulse, unpronounceables like Taloyoak, literarily appealing Melville Peninsula and Cambridge Bay, and for su amusement, Igloolik. There are references to a past and tributes to the animals inhabit the region, but regardless of the nomenclature, the entire expanse, tho dotted by occasional settlements, defines desolation. The immensity is dauntin could contain the vastness of Alaska with room left over to pack in a midwestern states.

And it's been around, in its current form at least, since 1999. Wilkes won why someone hasn't mentioned it. Then he remembers a history professo college observing that, were it not for wars, Americans would never l geography. Nunavut seems a most inhospitable battle zone.

The boys are in weekend mode, still in their pajamas at 11:00 a.m., Wi phones Andy Campanella. Unmarried and living in a small walk-up in Que Andy is the kind of guy Wilkes can bother on a Saturday. But just to be sure waits until noon: if there's a woman with him, the pair has had more than enc time to reprise the previous night's sex.

"Nunavut," Andy says. The background is quiet—no TV or music. It sound if he's alone. "That new territory, broke off about ten years ago."

"Exactly ten years," Wilkes says. No sense letting this kid think he knows n than the boss.

"It's Inuit," Andy says.

"It's what?"

"Inuit, that's the native people, it's their homeland."

"Well, I have to get there. I may have a lead about Keira. Maybe," he says. " you do that?"

"The PI you hired. He found her?"

"It's a little complicated."

"But he's going with you, right?"

"No. Not...yet."

ndy is silent for a beat or two. Wilkes knows the request doesn't compute. Two
es against then: his investigator and his assistant. Fair enough, but neither one
narried to the woman, so neither really deserves a vote.

Mr. Wilkes, I can get you anywhere," Andy says seconds later. "It's just that
particular junket may involve some unscheduled airlines and smaller aircraft."
All the time he's talking, Wilkes can hear clicking in the background, tapping
's on a laptop. His assistant at work.

I know you like the big jets," Andy says, "but they don't fly there. I mean they
ght fly over the North Pole on their way to central Asia, but unless you jump
—"

Baker Lake is far from the pole."

Believe me, Mr. Wilkes, when you're anywhere in Nunavut, you're not that far
m the pole. I can email you some itineraries in minutes. Churchill, Baker Lake,
oulse Bay. Use those for starters. You can always add on."

Wilkes smiles at the speed with which Andy can accomplish such tasks. Ten
nutes. It would take Wilkes the better part of an afternoon just to get out of
Guardia, let alone reach some frozen village in northern Canada. He hangs up,
rs a coffee, awakens his laptop, finds a weather site, and types in Baker Lake.
almost noon in Connecticut, an hour earlier than most of Nunavut. Outside his
chen window the thermometer dial, shaded from the glaring sun, nudges thirty
grees and a stiff wind moves the leafless branches of a small redbud tree on the
nt lawn; but fifteen-hundred miles north and five hundred west, the thermometer
ds twenty-four degrees below zero and there are flurries in the air. He
nembers a few sub-zero mornings in recent years: the difficulty of starting his
, the delays on commuter trains when the cold froze the switches, the warnings
frostbite and worse. But twenty-four degrees below? Jesus! And in the daytime
less.

Of course he hasn't forgotten McNally's admonition about searching something
vast at Nunavut, so he phones Roche, the IT guy at work. Roche is McNally in
nirror universe. Slow, deliberate, measuring every word, he requires an hour to
ke a fifteen-minute technology presentation, not because he mumbles or stutters
lacks preparation, but because he keeps finding questions to ask himself while
speaks. And he ponders them, coming up with a solution to problems nobody
cares about. You're probably wondering—he says over and over: nobody ever
but that never stops him.

But if he's a geek he's also a Johnny Depp lookalike, and Wilkes often wond
what kinds of women this unusual combination nets him. Or men. Or maybe,
Roche's case, cyborgs.

"I need your magic," Wilkes says. "I need you to scan a computer for me."

"I read in the paper about what happened," Roche says. If anyone could ha
missed the story at work, it's him. "What exactly do you need, Mr. Wilkes?"

"I want to know what's on my computer."

"Then you should look."

This is probably a joke among IT-ers and Wilkes sloughs off the n
discourtesy.

"I need more. I need to know where my wife has been—you know—surfi
web sites, emails, everything. Is that what you call a history?"

"Is that what I call a history? I didn't make up the word. Actually differ
browsers tend to store their histories in different folders. Some continua
generate text files and—"

"I use Safari."

"It's a Mac, then," he says with a trace of disdain. Wall Street—most
business—is married to IBM and everything that IBM ever engendered. To Roc
the Mac is a nice little tool for the dilettante who takes pictures and listens to mu
nevertheless he's learned to deal with it. "When do you want to know this?"

"I can bring it in Monday."

"Don't you want the information before that? Don't you want it now?"

Roche lives on the other side of the Hudson, maybe ten minutes from the GV

"I can't leave the kids to drive to Jersey today. Monday will be fine."

Roche doesn't respond and Wilkes knows he has given the wrong answer:
just doesn't know the right one.

"Is there some other way then?"

Roche mumbles something, or grunts, some sound that says yes, there is.

"Mr. Wilkes, I'm going to send you an email with an attachment which you v
open, just what they warn you against, and this is why they do that. When you of
that attachment—it's not a virus and it won't erase your hard drive and it wo
access your credit card to buy me a new petabyte drive—when you open it, I v
be able to examine your computer, and for that matter, do whatever I want with
Is there anything on there you don't want me to see?"

"I want you to see everything."

"You're probably wondering why I asked."

"It's fine. I don't—"

"I'm not talking about porn here, but if I find indications of illegal activity, I'm
quired to report them."

Wilkes laughs.

"What do you think my wife was doing?"

"I thought that's what you wanted to know. People use computers to make drug
als, set up and maintain escort services, trade aberrant sexual photos, make
apons purchases, plan liaisons—"

"I get it."

"I can tell you how to clean it up first before I do any real excavating."

"Just...excavate."

"How about Mrs. Wilkes? Would she be concerned if she knew?"

"My wife the drug dealer?"

"I am not trying to be insulting, Mr. Wilkes, but you have to realize something:
licensed to use certain technology. If I don't turn over information on
galities to the authorities, I'm not licensed anymore. I make really good money
T&B and on the side—I'd like to continue. If we're agreed, then open the email
d the attachment and I'll get to work."

"How long will it take?"

"In a half hour I can send you the information or print it out and give it to you in
son Monday. Your choice. I'm going to hang up now—that way you won't have
get rid of me."

"Wait. Can we keep this semi-unofficial?"

"It's between you and me, within the parameters I already established. Let me
my license and read the wording so that you have a clearer idea."

"No," Wilkes says, almost too quickly. "Just semi-unofficial."

He doesn't fear Keira's involvement in organized crime or some terrorist cell.
t if he is going to spy on his wife, to become no better than a suspicious husband
ing to track an adulterous partner, he wants to do it unofficially.

"Print up the report. I'll get it in work Monday."

"Keep the laptop plugged in. I don't want the battery to crap out while I'm
ging."

Within seconds Roche's email arrives with an attachment named Snoopy. He
ens it and waits for the excitement, some sort of explosive burst of color and
phics. But instead a splash screen appears and on it, of course, a beagle,
illated and primitive, graphics from the eighties. Wilkes immediately wonders

if Roche, the stickler for legality and protocol, has used the image with permissi
As the cartoon dog dons a Sherlock Holmes hat, Wilkes can hear the whirr of
hard drive as the screen fills with jumbled and indecipherable text that indexes p
at a dizzying pace. Wilkes has heard applications referred to as "elegant." Snoc
is not one of them.

So this is a Saturday for someone like Roche. Then again maybe it's Roche a
not Campanella shacked up with someone from work. He can easily envision
techie sequestered in a small apartment crammed with keyboards and monitors a
hard drives and cables draped on clothes hangers or closet hooks, with encrus
coffee cup rings on the furniture and wrinkled clothing lying in scattered pil
And there, crawling among the peripherals, trying to find her clothes, is Sar
Qualling. After all, where else would Roche meet someone if not at work? Anc
she is screwing around as much as McNally says, then why not with Roche, a go
looking unattached guy with money? Across the river in Jersey. Safe from
husband's prying eyes and perpetual erection.

He shakes his head: he can't really imagine Roche with anybody. But
recognizes another disheartening fact too: he can't imagine himself with a wom
either. Keira has been gone only a few days, but it's longer than that since th
made love. He tries to remember the nights in reverse order: not Tuesday, that v
packing and preparation. On Monday, he watched basketball while she went
bed. James had had some stomach virus over the weekend and trying to fit in so
private time between his bouts of nausea seemed not worth the effort. Say a we
then, thereabouts, not that long, but already the idea of making love to Keira see
more fanciful than plausible. Then again, if making love requires intimacy, wh
was that while she was planning to leave her husband and children? What ot
intimacies has she kept from him? He fights off the temptation to phone Roche a
cancel his probe, but it's as much anger as curiosity by which he allows the so
to continue. McNally was right about that.

"I've got an IT guy scanning my laptop," he tells the PI. "I may have a bet
idea where she is."

"Oh."

McNally sounds aloof and bored. Saturday. Maybe he's slept in, just getting

"Did I catch you in the middle of something?"

"Nope. I'm good."

"You sound sort of...sure you aren't busy?"

"You...um...when you hired me, you didn't actually give me any restrictions.

Meaning what?"
already—you know...."
You hacked into my laptop? Who said you could do that?"
Well—actually—you did."
Bullshit, I never said that."
You didn't tell me not to."
I didn't tell you not to do a lot of things."
A lot of things don't matter. Your home computer does."
And how did you do it?"
I have friends in the business."
Why didn't you tell me? I'm paying the fucking IT guy from work to look at it
."
Roche. He's topnotch. I wanted him to do it but he said he'd need the owner's
mission and I didn't think he'd get it. Anyway, you got the best. My guy's a
or at Fordham, works part-time at some hamburger slop house. Roche will find
thing I may have missed."
ilkes is fuming. "I don't like this."
understand. Really. But that's what I do. I can't be asking you how you want
to go about it. If you knew, I'd be out of a job. Besides, you can always fire
,
don't want to fire you. At least tell me what this guy found."
The usual."
Was my wife having an affair?"
Doubt that, but in early January she zeroed out the unused space on your hard
e. Three passes, not the most secure but damn close."
That was me."
So maybe you're having an affair."
I have client information that needs to be securely erased. I burn it to a T&B
and they put it in secure storage off site. I do it every month."
There you are then."
ilkes's anger subsides, but if he's traveling north to follow what he considers
il, maybe he no longer needs someone poking around here.
Listen," he says. "I know you're good at what you do and all, but can you just
I me your bill through noon today and we'll just leave it at that."
guess I did say you could fire me, so, sure, no problem. It's after noon, though,
phone call doesn't count?"

"Count it."

"That kind of starts a new billing day. I can prorate—"

"Jesus Christ!"

"I'm just busting your chops, Wilkes. Getting fired is hurtful you know."

"I don't want you—anybody—working on this anymore. Bad enough s college kid accessed my computer. I'm not comfortable with any of it."

"People don't hire me when they're comfortable; they hire me when they to be comfortable and want to be that way again."

"Maybe the cure is worse than the illness."

"A lot of them are, but you'll have my bill Monday," he says. "Uh, th President's Day. You'll have it Tuesday. And let's say thirty days if you can care of it by then. And one more thing. I've done this long enough to know people who don't like my tactics wind up missing my results. I'm no unforgiving person. If you have a change of heart, call. You do a lot of searches?"

"What? No."

"My techie found some scraps of files, some map searches."

"That's because she's in Canada."

"I suppose. Like I said, I'll send you the bill. I could tell you what the col kid found, but you already have the best."

And that's it. Wilkes doesn't require a good luck or sorry it didn't work Another client is undoubtedly waiting to learn whom her husband has l sleeping with when he claims to have missed the commuter train home.

When Roche calls back, Wilkes feigns interest and gratitude: he owes colleague at least that much.

"Maybe you can email me the results after all?"

"They'll be encrypted but they'll open nicely with a password. Use your name, no caps."

"And the bill, send that here. This isn't a T&B project. Did you...um...find of map searches?"

"Fragments, mostly north of the border. Looks like some of it has l scrubbed."

"By me I'm afraid. Remember, the bill comes here."

Roche doesn't argue. Why should he? It's his job. And Wilkes wants no larg out of professional courtesy, not this time. The same holds true for Andy who

ne up with several scenarios to transport Wilkes wherever he thinks he wants to
 Wilkes is not ready to decide. Already he feels slightly lost without McNally.
arly in the afternoon his in-laws gather the boys to take them to eat at some
ily restaurant or other where pancakes pass for lunch and dinner. Wilkes sits
the dining room window with a an ice-filled juice glass of gin, justifying the
ess because he's not driving to New Jersey to pick up Roche's report. He
ices the Christmas wreath lying on a brush pile in the backyard. A few weeks
ore he and Keira had argued over it. She insisted that all decorations should be
noved the day after New Year's and Wilkes was procrastinating. The Saturday
ore the crash—Jesus that was only a week ago—he had found her outside in a
d rain, unstringing lights from the bushes.

you're not going to do it, she said, and he convinced her to come inside and
 off. For the next hour he ripped the lights off the branches and, though he had
nned to get another years' use out of them, crushed them into a black garbage
 and forced them into a trash can, snapping wires and popping bulbs in the
cess. Finally he tended to the wreath which he scaled across the yard like some
ural frisbee, watching it land near the birdbath. And so it lies, the first stages of
wn overspreading it, on a pile of dead leaves and broken twigs.

wasn't much of an argument, more like a dispute. It was not by any stretch the
mination of several little flareups that pushed her over the edge and sent her off
ome distant refuge. He knows his wife a little better than that for Christ's sake.
's known her forever, though, admittedly, she was not really his childhood
etheart. That status belonged to Leslie Jacobs who had dated Wilkes from the
dle of his junior year in high school right through graduation, had then gone
 to college and, within three weeks, informed him with a Peanuts Hallowe'en
d that she had found someone else. Assigning Charlie Brown the task of
aking off a relationship seemed a bit cavalier at the time, or maybe eminently
ropriate, but he never looked back. For two years he dated others, though dated
ame merely a euphemism for sidling up to some coed at a party and deciding
ose bed they were going to end up in.

Keira Eason had spent her early college career in similar experimental
miscuity, Wilkes never knew it, never asked. She hardly ever talked much about
 boyfriends, and Wilkes never mentioned his string of passing liaisons or the
ger one with Leslie, nor did he ever carry one of those "what-if" torches for any
hem. Those women were gone and might as well never have existed. That he
alled Leslie at all was more a result of the gin than the loneliness.

But maybe there had been someone important in Keira's life before him.
was twenty when they started up. There must have been some relationships in h
school, college, at work, on a summer vacation. Somewhere along the wa
twenty-year-old girl acquires some boyfriends, like maybe that guy at the airp
Maybe that was her first real sex. Wilkes was fourteen when he had his, on vacat
with his parents, at a cabin in which some girl's folks had been trusting enougl
leave her alone for an afternoon. Keira could very well have been doing the sa
thing somewhere else. He hasn't shared all his romantic activities with her; w
shouldn't she have adopted the same strategy?

Romantic activities. Jesus, talk about euphemisms. And childhood bullshit.

You always remember the first, they say. He sips his gin and tries to remem
the name or the face of that girl in the cabin. He can't remember either.

But maybe Keira remembers hers.

ien the doorbell rings, Wilkes gulps down the last of the gin and puts the glass
the sink, filling it with soapy water. He doesn't want to explain to his in-laws
y he needed a drink that early. Out the picture window a light blue Camry idles
the curb, its lights on, exhaust whitening the air behind it.

Saturdays are prime time for proselytizing Jehovah's Witnesses—usually
uples or small groups, usually black recently the split seems to be fifty-fifty
naling perhaps an uptick in religiosity among whites. It doesn't matter to
ilkes: he has become masterful at sending them away without insult or offense
accepting any of their barely-newsprint-quality pamphlets which he would
rely discard anyway.

But this time he opens the front door to a white woman. Alone. Her clothes more
sely resemble what he sees at work every day than they do someone selling
us—tailored gray pants and a Kelly green silk blouse that shows plainly under
r hip-length black leather. She has neither the ethnicity nor the uniform (nor for
t matter the pamphlets) of a door-to-door bible thumper, and though Wilkes has
ver seen her before and she wears no identifying markings, he knows she's a
p—he immediately dislikes her.

"I think your car's running," he says.

She turns around to give the vehicle a cursory glance, then shrugs.

"And I'm parked facing traffic. Wasn't sure you were home. April Staubley,
lton P.D.," she says, flashing the laminated card with her photo and town seal
it. Again she glances at her car but makes no move toward it. He asks her in but
e doesn't want to sit—she's too twitchy for that with body parts in constant
tion—her eyebrows arching as if in continual surprise, her fingers tapping her
imb in rapid succession over and over and over. She blurts out that she wants a
ir and for the next twenty minutes he watches her poke here and there, never
iching a thing without first asking can I pick this up? or can I just move this
er? or is there anything in this room I shouldn't see? It's his first experience
ing in a crime scene, and he tries to imagine the lamps and wall hangings
tooned with police tape.

Throughout, Staubley makes little grunts of…of what?…agreement? discovery?
ially she asks if the two of them (why does she need him?) can look around
tside. The yard is a mess: a recent thaw has left a sloppy amalgam of mud and

ice. Even so, they meander through it, leaving new footprints and retracing the
until almost no part of the yard retains any decent-sized untouched area.

"Snow," she says. "It covers everything, doesn't it? I may send some forens
people out here when this melts."

"It's melted already. Why not call them now?"

She shakes her head. "They'll want overtime on Saturday. Probably nothi
anyway."

"I wouldn't bury anybody here," he says. "Over near the woods there are so
brush piles…well, God knows what's buried under them."

"Not today," she says—there's just enough dismissiveness to be threateni
Near the car the stream of exhaust, diminished now, still rises behind the park
vehicle.

"No company car, huh?"

"I get mileage." she answers. "I never have to drive far and I don't usually
involved in high-speed chases. Might as well be comfortable. What does your w
drive?"

"It's in the garage," Wilkes says. "A Forester."

"Subaru—almost bought one. Been started lately?"

"No."

"You ought to crank it a few times, maybe drive it for a little while—no ser
letting it sit there and rot."

"It's only been three days. It would have been in the airport longer than t
without rotting."

Staubley ignores him. She puts her nose up against the garage window.

"You have keys right? I mean your wife didn't take off with the only set."

"Take off?"

"Yeah, I don't mean the plane—"

"So you think she took off rather than was abducted or…or harmed."

"There's no body, there has been no ransom demand—that's true isn't it?"

"What's true?"

"A ransom request?"

"How about the body? Don't you want to know that?"

Wilkes smiles when he asks the question—the gin hasn't quite worn off and
realizes why so many drunk drivers say so many stupid things when they're pul
over.

"Well that too," she says.

Jo body. No note."

Iow'd you get the car back from LaGuardia?"

Drove it."

And you've searched it?"

Jo, but…why? She never went back to it. It just sat there."

You gotta consider some sort of trauma, disorientation," Staubley says.

She took off—she may need some help getting back, but we can't get that to

until we actually locate her. I'll have someone go over the car anyway—you

er know."

've hired a private investigator and he's done things like that." He regrets the

mmediately, but Staubley seems unfazed.

Might I ask who?"

don't know if I'm required to tell you that, because my understanding of the

private—"

Not important. If you were coming home from work right now," she says,

mal day, and I told you your wife was visiting in a house nearby and you had

opportunity to knock on one door and find her, which door would it be?"

e scans the neighborhood. The Sandellis and the Hendricksons, the two

ilies that flank him, are not particularly friendly, their meetings usually

lting in little more than a casual acknowledgment. Across the street and three

ses down are the Teggs—that's a possibility. There's a girl there James's age,

a few times Keira has driven the children to school. That courtesy has not led

ny frequent socialization, but there has been the occasional visit and there was

east a possibility that Keira and Ginny Tegg might have gotten together

isionally for coffee.

ctually Keira likes Ginny more than Wilkes likes her husband Jonathan whom

onsiders pompous and overbearing and, for a bank executive, stupid—opinions

eels no need to share with Staubley.

he Teggs," he says, pointing to a dark green raised ranch. "Two g's…we're

of friends."

may stop there for a minute. Did they know your wife was missing, I mean

a the start?"

Before the papers got a hold of it? I don't think so."

Probably not worth a trip then. I doubt if she's holed up over there."

e looks at his shoes, at hers.

Did you want to come back in?"

"No," she says, and turns toward the car, peering up the street. Then she st
reaches inside her jacket, and pulls out a card.

"Call me if you hear anything," she says, then heads for the curb, backs
Camry down the street and into the Teggs' driveway.

He immediately regrets involving the neighbors, especially since, a half l
later when the boys arrive home, the Camry is still parked there. Now he'll l
to call the Teggs and apologize for involving them with this so-called detec
Keira's parents are also unhappy that the police have become involved, especi
when—as her mother says—sometimes a woman goes off to find herself. He f
the expression nonsensically clichéd, but refrains from commenting because:
off they're leaving and he'd like to have the house to himself, and second the
of an old boyfriend, a topic first broached by McNally, has begun to bother hi

"I was thinking before," Wilkes says, "and I know this is dumb, but did K
have any boyfriends before me?"

"Well like everyone else, she dated," Mrs. Eason says quickly, "and the
course she met you in college. That cop wanted to know that?"

"Yes," Wilkes says. It's not a complete lie—McNally is kind of a cop. "
know how the police are—they need to know everything."

"No they don't," she snaps. Her husband has already opened the front door,
returns and takes her hand. He's apologetic.

"She doesn't have any use for those people," he says.

"What people?"

She answers for him. "Investigators. Half the time they're just looking for d

"That's basically their job description," Wilkes says, a response that comes
a little too sardonic for his mother-in-law. He quickly switches gears.

"Anyway, thanks for taking the boys out like that," he says, then adds
whisper, "get their mind off it for a minute."

"Brett is angry," Mrs. Eason adds, contributing her own whisper. The thre
them resemble a clique of schoolchildren discussing a common enemy.

"James may not fully understand, but Brett does," she says. "He kn
abandonment. The sooner this all ends, the better off they'll be."

"You mean the sooner Keira comes back—."

But Mrs. Eason is already out of earshot, pacing toward the car with her husb
close behind. He overcomes the temptation to say it again—to lay the blame wh
it belongs, on their runaway daughter. Instead he notices Staubley's car and w

boys they will soon have a visitor. James is indifferent, but Brett—the one who
ially demanded police intervention—doesn't like it.

Why do we need cops?"

I thought you wanted the police to do something."

I don't want Mom to be arrested."

That's not going to happen. You know that, right? She didn't do anything
ong."

She ran away."

We don't know that."

Then where is she?"

With no suitable outlet for his anger, the boy kicks the bottom step of the
rcase. Wilkes disregards it.

If she ran away, that's not a crime," he says, "and if she ran away, then it was
a good reason. And she'll come back because she loves you." He holds up a
d to stop the denial, already forming in his son's brain. "And if we don't know
reason yet, then we will when she comes back and tells us. Now both of you,
brush your teeth."

They hardly reach the stairs when the doorbell rings.

I saw the car," Staubley says, glancing over his shoulder at Brett and James. "Is
a bad time?"

Not yet. Come in," he says. "Would you like some milk and cookies with the
s?"

Staubley smiles—she at least gets the gibe—but turns down the offer. She leaves
shoes—not a lot cleaner after her visit down the street—on the stoop.

Watching my weight," she says. "Driving around all day is not good exercise."

he's thin and angular, and if she has a weight problem, it may be keeping
ugh of it on to fill out her clothes. In the kitchen he barks some introductions.
ther boy is accustomed to a cop out of uniform, and so Staubley spends a few
utes defining her job, assuring the boys she is there to talk to their father. They
n't impressed, and James is disappointed—without the uniform or a visible
apon, she is just another lady, though with the kids her voice seems smoother
more controlled, almost soothing, maybe even motherly.

I saw your car at the Teggs'," Wilkes said. "Out of gas yet?"

I had to shut it off. Mrs. Tegg likes to talk, and she was shocked to learn about
s. Wilkes. I guess she had a number of conversations with your wife."

So did I," Wilkes says. "She used to live here."

Staubley studies him for a moment, seemingly unsure if the response is faceti
or rude. Wilkes intends it to be both.

"True," Staubley says. "I guess they talked about traveling, places to go. Did
know that Ginny Tegg was married before?"

"If I did, I'd forgotten."

"Her first husband was abusive. I guess she wound up in a shelter more tl
once."

"She told you that?"

"As I said—she likes to talk."

Wilkes glances at the boys—tries to ascertain their understanding of abu
Regardless, he doesn't think it's a fit topic for discussion, and though he co
simply say so—it's still his house—he decides to double down instead.

"Since they're both here, why don't you ask the boys if Mom and I hit each otl
They would know."

"I haven't asked any questions," she says, a trace of defensiveness in
response. "I simply said that one of your neighbors has been a victim of abuse.

"And it could be like what, a neighborhood virus? Tell you what—feel free
tromp around in the mud some more. But if there's nothing else right now….bc
say goodbye to Detective Staubley."

Her expression changes little—she has undoubtedly been in these situati
more frequently than the Wilkeses.

"Sorry to disturb your afternoon. I can show myself out. I may be in touch agai

"Don't forget your shoes. And next time why not call first, in case I want
attorney present."

"Why would you need an attorney?"

"Everybody has one. I'm sure you do."

"Whatever suits you," she says. her fingers are tapping again—her maternal r
has ended and she's a twitchy cop again. She offers a lethargic, almost spa
wave, constructs a weak smile for the boys, and she's gone.

"Sorry about that," he says to them seconds after the door closes. She can har
have reached her car when Brett offers his assessment.

"Witch with a capital B."

"Brett! We don't say things like that."

"You do sometimes."

"Adults sometimes say bad things, but they're still bad things. I don't want
using that word."

Witch?"

"Don't make me explain."

The boy nods, stands up, and saunters out of the room—he has made his point. nes looks bemused, but that's okay. Wilkes will let everything settle, then talk Brett again about inappropriate language. It will probably be a difficult task: ett has merely verbalized what Wilkes was thinking and, for that matter, saying nself with his tone.

Later that evening he goes through Keira's closet again. There are items missing, the meaning of their disappearance eludes him. Besides, if such a search were rthwhile, McNally would have done it himself. He closes the closet door and ens the top drawer of her dresser. He feels like a pervert searching through his fe's underwear, touching every item and trying not to remember what it felt like xt to her skin. But people often keep cash in their underwear drawers, and maybe ier secrets too. Maybe a trove of old love letters from the boyfriend her parents uldn't talk about, or possibly even a new one. Maybe one of them reads come me Keira—the Arctic is a lonely place without you. He smiles at the thought of nething that lame but riffles through everything. No hidden cash. No trove of :ers. No secrets of any kind. Not in that drawer or any other.

Another night alone, his third. He doesn't count the first one—the day of the .sh was chaotic and surreal. But this—this is the worst. It's a Saturday and he 1 Keira should be out with friends or seeing a movie or enjoying dinner newhere. But there's no they, just him. He gets the boys off to bed with a fatuous omise of better days ahead, then pours himself another gin, this time opting for raditional glass—smaller, more suitable. When he pours a second, though, he lizes that the size of the glass doesn't matter if he keeps refilling it.

Je calls McNally—it's been about twelve hours since he fired him. Wilkes dies himself for some late-evening sarcasm, but the PI is true to his word: he lds no grudges.

"Never a good day when a cop drops by," McNally says.

"I think she was accusing me of beating Keira, maybe killing her."

"I doubt if you did that."

"Thanks for the vote of confidence."

"Look, this Staubley has no clue, no idea. She wanted to annoy you because she sn't brought in on this. I'd say she was successful. I mean, I don't want to laugh, t the image of you and that cop tromping through the mud is funny."

"Not at the time. I've made preliminary arrangements to go to Canada."

"I hope it's to see a hockey game."

"I know you don't approve."

"What do you plan to do, call in the Mounties and say 'my wife is in your coun somewhere—can you help me find her?' Look at a map, Wilkes. Look at the s of that place."

"But you said Churchill. I checked the map."

"You checked the map? Was Keira's picture on it? What do you mean y checked the map?"

"I mean Churchill is a small town. It's like Wilton—sort of spread out but too many people."

"I'm sure people confuse the two all the time. Come on, seriously."

"Well I can't just sit here and wait."

"Are you rehiring me?"

"We're negotiating."

"You know my rates. What's left to negotiate?"

"Travel plans?"

"Don't have any. Your job is to sit there and my job is—was—to find your wif

Wilkes waits for the word paradigm to make an appearance but it doesn't. late. Mellow as he is from too much gin, he still can't face the prospect of anot night alone in that house.

"Maybe if…when I get back…."

"If you're so dead set on going, at least plan on success. Figure on coming ba together, then you won't need me. That is what you're planning, right? Becaus this is some junket you're taking because you don't know where to turn, why give it another day or two? Give me another day or two."

"I just want something to happen."

"That's because you've seen investigators on TV and they make the job lc cool. It's not cool. It's a grind. And missing persons—sometimes the why mal the what easier. Find out the motive and you figure out what happened. The w is somewhere around here and that's where I'm more comfortable, more effectiv

"So I should rehire you."

"You should go to Canada. You're gonna go anyway. But be careful. You'r man trying to find his wife, you're not a PI and you're not a cop. Don't come looking like one. Real cops don't like that."

"I can call Andy right now and he can get you a ticket."

have some feelers out and I haven't recalled them yet. Let's just say that your
is open but I'm actively pursuing a few others. It's pretty much true."
'm not going to have you working for free. I always pay my own way."
hen you'll be ecstatic when you finally get a bill. Let's say I'm on retainer.
p in touch."
Anything else I should know?"
Don't fill up on the in-flight snacks. All that salt'll kill you."
was serious"
hen lay off the booze. To me you sound a little buzzed. Maybe the gin makes
gs easier, but you don't want to look like some drunk any woman in her right
d would run from. Got it?"
'm not drunk."
ine, then, Ainngai. That's how you say hello where you're headed. It'll get
in the door. And Tavvaujusi will get you out. Everything between—good luck.
nngai, Wilkes repeats later. All well and good, but he doesn't have a clue what
I say after that.

13

7:00 the next morning Ginny Tegg is at his door, bundled up for her morning
. She looks cold, but more than that, she looks awful. If she has had any sleep
ly, it hasn't done her any good.
taubley.
he cop has upset her and now Wilkes has another fire to extinguish.
I know why you're here," he says, tying the cincture on his robe. He's half-
ssed and unshaven and, more than likely, looks as bad as she does. "That cop.
 sorry about that."
It's not her," she says, her words clipped, high-pitched. "We have to...I have to
, to you. Something—Jesus, I have to tell you something. It's about Keira. Can
me in?"
Of course."
I should have come last night. I should have come...damn it all…I should have
ie months ago."
It's okay," he says. It's not, and he doesn't know what's going on, but he
sn't want to contribute to the panic.
he won't move past the foyer, her shoes are caked with snow and she doesn't
it to soil the rug. Wilkes goes upstairs, throws on some clothes, returns. The
ire effort takes him no longer than a minute, but in that space he has figured out
y Ginny Tegg has interrupted her run. Of course it's about Keira—and
ieone. If Keira would confide an affair to anyone in the neighborhood, it would
Ginny. And if anyone would notice a man coming to the house while Wilkes
 away at work, that would be Ginny too. She isn't a busybody, but she is aware
ier surroundings, forever jotting down license plates of cars traveling too slowly
 thus, to her, suspiciously. Once she saved the life of a woman parked by the
 of the road, her car idling for what Ginny deemed too long. She called the
ice, they found an elderly driver having a coronary. EMTs saved her.
I don't care about the rug," Wilkes says. "Come in."
Let me just stand here. I'm fine."
Coffee?"
he shakes her head.
Let me just get this out. I got a letter about a month ago," she says. "Just after
inksgiving."

"From whom?"

"I don't know. It wasn't addressed to me. Well, it was. I mean, it had Keir name but my address. I just opened it with all the other mail. I didn't even look the name. It was Keira Eason. That's her maiden name, isn't it?"

"Yes, she still gets some college mailings addressed that way."

"This was not a college mailing, and this came to our address."

"And you opened it. What was in it?"

"A note card. It said, 'All these years—I can never forget you.' That's all it sa It was signed 'em.'"

"Initials?"

"No, I don't know, two lower case letters. I didn't know what to do. If I had opened it I could have just brought it over to her, but it was opened. She wo have known I read it. And if it was the worst...if...."

"You can say it, Ginny. I've thought it."

"Okay. Okay. If she was having an affair then—. She's my friend, but so you. Our kids play together, ride to school together, we've been at your hou Fuck it all, what was I supposed to do?"

He takes her hand, still mittened, and leads her inside.

"Sit down," he says. "Please."

It's like dragging a heavy sack across the floor, but finally he gets her int chair.

"Just relax," he says. "Sure about the coffee?"

"I'm sure."

"So you had this letter. Did you show it to your husband?"

"Not at first, but he knew something was wrong. In a way it was addressed him too."

"So what did you do?"

"Well, he thought no one would be so stupid as to send a letter to the house wh his lover lived with her husband. He thought it might have meant nothing, someone carrying a torch all these years. Harmless."

"But you didn't agree."

"No, someone that obsessed wouldn't have screwed up the address, wo probably have it memorized, probably driven by the house a few times. In the we still had the letter and it wasn't ours."

"So you gave it to Keira."

'John wanted to throw it away, but I thought what if she's in danger. What if this
n' is a stalker and this was her only warning? I gave it to her, told her the truth,
t I had opened it inadvertently and I was sorry."
'And she made you promise not to tell me."
'She didn't say anything. Said it had to be a mistake or a joke. We sat around
 a while, talked about the upcoming holidays. Just, you know, nothing. Then
en she went missing, I remembered the letter, and then that cop came by. I
aked. I should have come over last night. I should have told you last year."
'You told the person the letter was addressed to. What more could you do?"
'Martin, I feel awful about this."
'Don't. That was months ago. Maybe the two events are unrelated."
Wilkes doesn't believe it. Ginny doesn't either. But the theory does lower the
sion in the room a notch or two. He asks if she checked the postmark. It was
newhere in Queens according to the zip; the answer means nothing. Nor does
nny's suggestion that maybe Keira kept the letter. Maybe. Maybe she hid it in
in sight. But even if she did, then what?
'I'm sorry about that cop yesterday," he says.
'I didn't tell her about the letter."
'Good. She's a pain in the ass."
'She was okay with John and me, but—I thought maybe Keira told you about it.
'asn't going to be the one."
'No, I wouldn't expect you to."
She stands and moves toward the door.
'I have to finish my run. I hope I did the right thing, telling you."
He nods
'You did. And—I mean—there was never anything else, right? I mean anybody
e?"
'If there was, I never knew. Our conversations were always pretty dull: furniture
d clothes, kids and husbands."
He forces a smile.
'I gotta go finish, get the kids off to church. I'm sorry."
'Don't be. Enjoy your run."
He watches her jog down the sidewalk and accelerate into the road before
appearing around a corner. He'd love to turn the house upside down and find
t letter, but Keira has certainly destroyed it. He can give the information to
Nally, though he's sure the PI will come up with the same conclusion he did,

the one he didn't share with Ginny Tegg, the one that says Ginny was supposed
receive that letter and deliver it personally to Keira, thereby avoiding any chan
of Martin reading it. But Ginny wasn't supposed to read it first.

A good plan, 'em,' whoever you are, just not good enough. But whether or
Keira reciprocated, he doesn't know. And regardless, Ginny's admission does
alter Wilkes's plans.

The Easons will take the boys while their father is gone, and though they do
like his striking out on his own to some unknown region, Wilkes assures them t
he takes just as big a risk every time he drives into the City on I-95. And to sof
the departure a little more, he lies.

"I'm going with McNally," he says. "He thinks the two of us have the b
chance. We'll be back on the weekend."

"Just so you know," Keira's father says. "She was never serious about any
them."

"What?"

"Her boyfriends. Yesterday you asked us. She wasn't serious about them."

"Okay," Wilkes says. Dismissive. Nonchalant. They should have answer
yesterday. Now it's too late. Now he knows better—about one of them at least.

He gives Brett and James some last-minute guidelines: it's back to school
Tuesday. They groan, but he thinks they may welcome any reestablishment
routine.

"We'll take them to our place tonight," Keira's mother says. "It'll be a lit
vacation."

Wilkes is tempted to balk just to be ornery, but instead he packs them a duf
bag and kisses them goodbye. By late afternoon, with the house to himself,
vacuums the dining room, runs the dishwasher, then decides that the rest of
house can use a dusting and digs around for cleaning supplies he thinks Ke
might use. Mrs. Eason will do all these things while Wilkes is gone, but he wa
Keira's folks to realize what a genuinely fucking responsible husband he is, if
to impress them, at least to accept the fact that the blame for her disappearance
lie with him.

He celebrates his domestic achievements by cracking open a new fifth
Boodles, then stumbles to the back closet to dig out his carry-on, still packed fr
the trip he didn't take. The space is nearly empty. Of course it is: his wife and ki
luggage is at the bottom of the Hudson.

Oh yeah," he says aloud. "I guess I forgot about the plane crash. Who can ember shit like that?"

e smiles and repeats the observation, then practically doubles over with hter, holding onto a chair as his eyes begin to water. He castigates himself (it that funny, it's the gin, he says) then laughs some more. Finally he drags out arry-on, sits at the kitchen table, and tries to regain his composure. He knows drunk, he's ignored McNally's warnings, and he knows it's not the right time ll the airline. But those suitcases, they cost money.

website gives him all the information he needs, but the first call results in a u of choices, none of which appeals to him. He hangs up, calls again, pays er attention. Finally, jiggling the ice cubes on his second double, he gets a an being.

want to report a lost suitcase. It's brown and has tan trim. Tan trim."

e repeats the last two words because they don't sound right together. Or they d too right, like another word.

e voice on the other end is cordial. Carol or Karen. He was sounding out rum' while she was talking and he's not sure.

'm sorry to hear that. Let's see if we can locate it for you."

don't have that stub thing you know."

hat's fine. If you can just give me the flight number or the departure and ination and day of the week, we can start tracing it."

was 1549."

ere is silence on the line, but only for a moment.

ou said 1549?"

es...Carol." He takes a chance on the name. She doesn't correct him.

o this was before last Wednesday, am I correct?"

o, you are not."

e smiles. This is too funny, like some crank phone call you make to a friend. technically it's not a crank call. Suitcases that genuinely belong to him were ct on that plane and now he doesn't have them.

ir are you talking about last Wednesday's flight?"

es ma'am, that's the one. Where can I pick up my luggage?"

rol may be bemused but she isn't flustered. She launches into a report on tly how the airline is handling this, how they have contracted with some outfit exas to retrieve and salvage every item of luggage and its contents.

may be a while," she says. "It's a big job."

"Then they shouldn't have landed in the water."

"Yes sir. Did you receive a preliminary check from the airline?"

"I haven't opened much mail."

"Let me verify that it was sent. This is Martin Wilkes, Wilton, Connecticut?"

"I should have given you my name so that you could find my stuff."

"I can see it on the caller ID. My records indicate that you weren't on that fli I do have Keira E. Wilkes and a Brett—"

"The E is for Eason. That was her maiden name."

"Yes sir, and James."

"Those are our kids. My wife took two suitcases and I was supposed to mee in Charlotte."

"Did your wife and sons receive their checks? There should also have be ticket refund."

"I haven't been opening the mail. I'm the one whose wife is missing."

"My understanding is that nobody was missing."

"It happened after."

"I see. I'm not familiar with that particular situation. I can transfer you to—

"Well, maybe if you didn't live in India you would be familiar. Do you newspapers in Calcutta?"

"Excuse me?"

"Well it's obvious if you lived in the United States, you'd know what I talking about."

"Sir, I'm in Philadelphia."

"Well, even so—"

"We aren't fully staffed on Sundays, but I can let you talk to a supervisor. don't have to put in a formal claim on those suitcases. It's already being taken of."

"Do you know Jasmine at LaGuardia?"

"No, sir."

"Jasmine Pierce. She's pretty nice but she's in way over her head, you know

"I don't know who that is, but if—"

"Well someone should take a look at her, maybe a little job evaluation order."

"Are you registering a formal complaint? I can transfer you."

"Is there anything you can do without transferring?"

"I can answer questions about lost luggage."

doesn't matter. Already the joke is wearing thin.

Never mind," Wilkes says.

If you've received those checks, they can be used to tide you over until your
uables and belongings are returned."

But the stores are closed. It's Sunday night here in America."

Yes, sir. Is there anything else I can do right now?"

He has lost the thread of the conversation. He's thinking about the Easons and
ra's suddenly fucked-up childhood with boyfriends who never had names and
er meant anything to her.

Sir?"

Sorry...Carol is it?"

Karen Keelan—K-E-E—"

Got it."

I can give you my employee ID in case you—"

No, no, really. I guess you're a good sport," he says.

If you call this number tomorrow after 3:00 and ask for me, you can tell me if
have received those checks."

You mean when I'm sober."

I mean when you've had time to sort through the mail."

I thought it was Carol. I guess we had a bad connection. I could call you back,
ybe use your right name."

he sounds really pleasant, and she's only in Philly. Not in Calcutta or New
hi. He could have driven over, three hours, maybe four, and spoken to her
sonally. If she's at the airport they could sit and have a drink, regardless of how
inesslike she sounds. What the hell. He wouldn't want to go through the entire
rting rigamarole again, but it would be nice to be with someone who didn't find
repulsive.

You don't have to call me back," she says. "Did you say your wife is missing?"

My wife, yes."

His answer creates a silence: maybe the question was Karen's subtle way of
inding Wilkes that, if his wife is missing, maybe he shouldn't be flirting with
e woman on the telephone.

Mr. Wilkes, is there anything else I can do for you today?"

Yeah, could you not say 'thank you for calling U.S. Airways' or something
ally—what's the word?"

Polite?"

"Yeah, I guess that's it. Sorry."

"I have to say it, you know, or I will get sent to Calcutta. If you hang up first
course, you won't hear it."

So McNally was right. Drunk, he sounds exactly like a husband any won
would flee. Still, no reason to leave this Karen with a bad aftertaste.

"I think maybe, on second thought, I'd like to hear it."

And he does hear it, waiting silently for the spiel to end before hanging up.
still isn't completely convinced he wasn't speaking to someone in India, but
likes her anyway.

He stumbles into the living room and steps on the vacuum hose. His w
intentioned cleaning has left a trail of appliances and household products that
has no desire to put away. In the morning, he says, and drains the remainder of
glass.

e following morning he's sober and alert for his discussion with Andy, and four
cedrin have dulled some of the headache—temporarily.
Six hours from Saskatoon to Baker Lake," Andy says.
And this is where the Eskimos live?"
Inuits. Eskimo is considered a pejorative term."
Wilkes waves it off. It's hardly worth keeping up with what people want to be
led anymore. Andy brings up a map of Canada and it spreads out across
lkes's office monitor, the cursor lying just to the west of Hudson's Bay.
Right there—Baker Lake. You get there from the western territories. Now you
ald charter a plane in Montreal and fly directly over the bay, but planes with that
ad of range couldn't set down at the airfield there, and the planes that can land
re don't have that kind of range."
Airfield? You mean airport."
I like to distinguish the two, but either way it's a place to land. The airline and
airfield have a good safety record for a busy little air...field."
Sandy Qualling enters with a coffee and he flashes immediately to his earlier
ntasy of her and Roche, the one he couldn't maintain. Seeing her this morning in
bright red patterned peasant blouse and a tastefully snug grey skirt makes any
k to the usually disheveled Roche even more ludicrous, though McNally's
imation that she's slept around piques his curiosity. And the residue of the
vious night's binge, along with a nebulous memory of his failure to seduce
ne airline employee, makes him stare a little too long.
Thanks, Sandy," he says. He tries hard not to let his eyes drift downward and
ds off successfully until she turns to leave. He stops her when he remembers
letter, asks her how many of his clients live in Queens.
Several I would think," she says. "Would you like their names?"
Ie says he would, but even as he replies he realizes the futility of the task. Then
dy gives him worse news in several small doses: twenty-six hours of travel time;
overnight in Saskatoon, laughably expensive airfare; a Beechcraft 1900.
Do I have to stand outside and crank the propeller?"
It's a very good plane," Andy says.
The associate clicks the mouse and the image of an aircraft fills the screen.
Oh, Christ," Wilkes said. "It does have propellers. And what the hell is Pronto?"

"A small outfit. The plane is a turboprop. It's more of a jet than a piston—th
a propeller."

"Pronto. Sounds like they should be flying south of the border."

"You've flown on this type of plane before."

"Cramped. Noisy."

"And safe," Andy says. "Let me know what I should do next. T&B will proba
pay for it. Maybe we should talk about accommodations."

"An igloo will be fine. I'll rough it with the other Eskimos—or whatever they
called."

"They're called igloos," Andy says with a grin. "One more thing. Flights out
Baker Lake fill up sooner than flights in. We should book it as a round trip. Y
don't want to be stuck there."

Actually, Wilkes doesn't want to be there at all. He wants to return to his norr
New England life with his wife and kids and cars and vacations and meals
normal times and discussions with colleagues about salaries and cars and spc
and women—discussions that don't center on dicey landing strips and strar
liveries painted on small flying crates. He rubs his eyes and wonders how ma
over-the-counter painkillers a person can take in a day.

Andy clicks the mouse and the T&B logo fills the screen.

"I gave you six days. Tuesday to Sunday. That going to work?"

"It'll have to."

By noon Wilkes has emailed his itinerary to the Easons, and by 3:00 he's at J
with time to spare. But the flight to Toronto is a bear and Andy's "large jet" tu
out to be a small regional, packed and cramped, and Wilkes finds himself squee
in against a window halfway back, leaning away from a bearded man in his fift
with cufflinks and a tie tack and an unfulfilled need to talk. After initiating th
different conversations, however, and hearing Wilkes abruptly end them all,
man gives up. Sandy Qualling's list of Queens clients is in his pocket. He glanc
at it when she gave it to him, studied it a little more later, decided to hold on to
Now he checks it again. No Emilys. No Emiles. No Emerils like that TV chef.
last names that begin with *em*, and only Ellington begins with an *e*. He folds
list and puts it away, unsure of why he's bothering with it.

On the layover in Toronto Wilkes eschews a Starbucks for a bar and grille wh
he knocks back two gin and tonics and a bowl of salt interspersed with a nut
two, just the snacks McNally warned him about, and he's ready for a third dr
when he hears, incorrectly, that his flight is boarding. He leaves and races to

—forty-two minutes early. He decides to wait there and watch the area fill up
er than have that third drink: the liquor he's already consumed has put him in
ghtly better frame of mind.

e second plane is a slightly larger regional of the same type, and he finds
self, once again, in seat number 15-A. He feels certain he can carry on a
versation with whatever idiot occupies 15-C. When it turns out to be a well-
sed woman about his age, the prospect seems less dreary. But this flight is far
a full, and once the plane is airborne, the woman moves across the aisle to a
of unoccupied seats where she stretches out and, before the plane has even
hed cruising speed, sleeps.

e is nowhere near as pretty as Keira, probably nowhere near so young either,
gh her skin seems smooth; any wrinkles probably well hidden. And there is
ring on her left hand, for whatever that's worth. Keira has one of those too and
sn't stopped her from running off, and maybe even finding her own partner
whom to fly. Wilkes orders that third gin and tonic after all, this time from
flight attendant and, without being conscious of it, traces the outline of the
ping woman's leg under her brown wool pants and wonders what sort of
erwear a no-nonsense businesswoman in a suit wears these days for a trip
ss the Canadian plains. Or is she wearing any at all?

e third drink helps him visualize undressing her in a hotel in Saskatoon, until
emembers he has taken a room at the airport Travelodge, a more than likely
iceable establishment that a classy woman would never stoop to enter. He asks
light attendant for a hotel recommendation and she suggests the four-star Park
n near the river. He doesn't know what river, or that there even is a river, but
wes himself more than an evening in a utilitarian room listening to planes
ning above him, watching pay-per-view movies, and drinking out of plastic

hen he drowses back to his interrupted fantasy, the woman in the brown suit
evolved into Keira wearing those skimpy underwear she fills flawlessly with
lim, athletic body. Imagining his erstwhile seat mate wearing them, her thighs
ching the leg openings, he loses interest in what might lie between them. God,
besn't even fantasize well anymore; when did he lose that ability? He lies back
e dreary and unbroken snow fields of Ontario and Manitoba streak by beneath

e regional puts down in a thick drizzle, rendering the flight attendant's
rance of a "beautiful view of the park from your room" an empty promise. And

the hotel would never be confused with the Four Seasons, just a well-appoi
lodging in what seems to be a pleasant city. Maybe the star system in Cana
different; maybe it's metric and four stars is really two and a half. Later, chec
in and settled, he decides not to share his parochial observation with the barte
in the hotel lounge, opting instead for the safer weather observation.

"Rain," he says. "Not snow?"

"We get our share of both, these days," the bartender says. "Kind of warm
past few months."

He pours a double over miniature ice cubes in a heavy glass tinted a subtle gr
"If you just got in, I can get you food."

Wilkes declines. It's after 10:00 and he knows that eating at this time of n
means no sleep.

"Some snacks if you have them," he says, and the bartender places a small b
of heavily salted mixed nuts in front of him. Wilkes avoids them. McNa
prophecy seems to be dogging him. Four seats down a man who looks to be a
Wilkes's age fiddles with his cell phone while a beer goes flat in front of him
is texting, or playing a game, or participating in any one of the innumerable c
activities that make one forget he has just overpaid for a beer. A few seats bey
him a young couple leans toward each other, occasionally laughing out loud a
some shared secret, occasionally letting the bartender in on the joke. The lou
area with its cushioned chairs and marble tables is empty.

And the woman in the brown suit isn't there. Wilkes has decided that those th
would not be an issue after all and occasionally checks behind him for new arri
eschewing the very real possibility that she's already on her way to Tokyo or H
Kong, or maybe she's traipsing about naked in her room in the Travelodge, dr
from those plastic nips in the honor bar and looking for someone to fuck bec
the sound of planes whining overhead makes her horny. The nakedness woul
important; Wilkes is certain he's lost the skills needed to separate an unfam
woman from her clothes. He picks out an empty table and imagines the tw
them sitting there while he convinces her that an account with Tolliver & Byr
her best possible financial move and she unbuttons her jacket to give him a b
look at her chest.

"Is there someone you're waiting for?"

It's the bartender again, his white shirt and somewhat thin black tie suggesti
certain formality and legitimacy, both of which make his question even r
peculiar. He is younger than Wilkes and as thin as Wilkes was at that age.

Oh, no, not at all.

'Cause this is kind of a quiet place, most nights," he says, his words full of logy, "and this is one of those nights."

No problem."

he man wipes away some of the moisture near the now watery gin. "Couple rs down, if you're interested—I mean, if you want more excitement—there's Pelican. It's more of a night club, if you like dancing and all."

Vilkes is certain that "dancing" is a euphemism, or at the very least an inapt cription of what lonely men sucking down gin actually want, but he chooses to be coy with the bartender.

Too old for nightclubs," he says. "Just a drink before I turn in."

No problem," the man says. "Another Boodles?"

He doesn't want one but says yes, almost out of guilt.

Headed for B.C., huh?"

B.C.?"

British Columbia. Beautiful place."

Actually I'm headed north."

Man, you're already north."

Gonna go where it doesn't rain like this. Going up to Baker Lake."

Vilkes tosses out the name as if he's been there a thousand times. The bartender nts to Martin's glass and laughs. "Better get a few of these to go. One for the ht and one when you get there and see the place. After that you're on your n."

You've been there?"

Never had the pleasure. Talked to people who have. Tell you what, they claim summers are beautiful. There really is a lake. You wouldn't want to swim in it ise it never gets that warm, but the temps get up around eighteen degrees etimes. Not much different from a cool day down here. Of course this is uary."

Eighteen? What's that in English?"

Around sixty-five degrees. Not toasty, but not like it is tonight."

No lake, huh?"

Not a liquid one. What takes you up there?"

My wife's job."

he bartender nodded. "Thought you looked like an executive. Guess your wife o. What kind of mining?"

"What kind is there?"

"Used to be some gold; they come and go as people find a new seam. The talk of a big new outfit maybe 100 kilometers north of there. If it happens, Bake look a lot different in a few years. Is that what your wife's involved in?"

"More or less," Wilkes says. "Don't know much about the place. How do get around up there?"

"Same as here. You drive."

"But you can't get there by car."

"Dogsled maybe, snow machine. Of course you'd have to tote a few day's wc of food or fuel or both. No, you fly in or you don't go. Your wife have a pl there?"

"Company put her up."

The bartender nods. "Got some motels there I guess. Regular little city, jus the middle of nothing. How long has she been there?"

Wilkes is enjoying the fiction; his wife the mining executive. It transforms from an abandoned husband to a supportive spouse, one who does not requ companionship from some "escort" at the Pelican.

"Few weeks."

The bartender nods, takes another swipe at the moisture on the bar, then mo off toward another new arrival. By the time he drifts back, maybe fifteen minu later, Wilkes has acquired a new world view, the maudlin appreciation everything and everyone.

"You're staying here, right? I mean in the hotel?"

"Oh yeah," Wilkes says, and he slurs out a discursive narrative about cancel his room at the airport because he wanted to see this city, except when he tell he can't remember the name of the city.

"Because," the bartender said, "if I thought you were driving somewhere—"

"I can't drive in Canada," Wilkes says with a smile. "I don't have a me license."

He laughs more heartily than the joke deserves and the bartender chuckles to

"Still and all," the man says, his eyes studying his customer. "Maybe one m drink should do it, huh? At the most?"

"Not even that, gotta take off. Got that early flight and all."

"You have a safe trip. Stay warm. And hey, listen, I may have gone a little of bounds recommending the Pelican. I didn't see a ring so I thought...."

He looked at his left hand. No ring.

Wilkes is never without it, but he removes it in hotels. It's a quirk, and it's stupid, and aside from Keira, nobody knows about it. It's all about plumbing. He trusts his drains at home; knows which ones have mesh strainers and which ones don't. At worst he's a pipe wrench away from retrieving anything that slips into a home drain. But in a hotel, who knows? His ring is on a desk upstairs, safely away from drains.

"Don't wear one," he says. "If you need a reminder, you're not really married." Wilkes signs the room tab and leaves a five on the bar. American money; he hasn't converted any currency yet. Waiting for the elevator he considers again the bartender's suggestion—the Penguin, or the Pelican—whatever nightclub the guy suggested when he thought Wilkes was interested in a night of whoring. Maybe that woman in brown is there, but the prospect of braving the rain only to vie for her affection with other suitors stops him.

Inside the room he finds the ring, slides it back on, and smiles. His wife, the mining executive. And not just any mine: gold! At least if he has to make small talk on the next leg of this dismal journey, he has a topic. And although he doesn't care to see Keira at the moment, this woman who has left him to a wretched world of unfulfilled fantasy, finding her seems even more appealing, like looking for a new, exotic, mysterious stranger. Maybe when the gin wears off he'll reconsider, but at the moment he can't help wondering what a mining executive is like in bed.

as the hotel bartender said: in Baker Lake people travel by car. In Wilkes's
, it's a green, mostly rusted out Mercury Grand Marquis of uncertain vintage
he shares with two other men in matching orange parkas and a woman with a
ll child on her lap. Nobody speaks on the ten-minute ride from the airfield to
center of town, so Wilkes doesn't have to share his new identity as the mining
cutive's husband. It's just as well since, for all he knows, the men in the parkas
ally are mining executive's husbands.

he flight, more tedious than disconcerting, was comfortable enough, and the
-jet proved to be less a thrill ride than just another dreary conveyance between
 points. He leafed through some magazines, imitated Keira by trying (and
ting on) a crossword puzzle, and used his laptop to check some client
folios. As flights go, it was comfortable and nondescript.

ot so the Grand Marquis, the ungainly throwback whose springs or shocks or
tever once steadied the ride had failed many potholes before. It lumbers over
snow-packed road at a cautious pace, constantly and noisily overtaken by
ter snow machines, before finally depositing its passengers at the Baker Lake
l. If there is an antithesis of the Park Town, it's these two adjacent Quonset
 with a small connecting structure between. On the lintel above the entry is a
 with some odd looking letters on it. Wilkes assumes it is the Eskimo
slation of welcome, but he doesn't contemplate it much, nor does he worry that
ight mean no vacancy: he has been assured that the hotel is never filled in the
er and that finding accommodations will present no problem.

he cold has already stunned him once at his first step off the plane. He is dressed
winter, New England winter, but has made no special provisions beyond that.
ore leaving, Andy had offered him temperature profiles and McNally had joked
it the climate, but Wilkes didn't plan to be outside at all. His vision of a search
lved Q and A in warm buildings protected from the elements en route to a
dy resolution. But even the short walk from the plane to the cab and now this
to the hotel entrance take his breath away. It's as if the air itself has solidified.
s obscure his vision and he's fearful that even a few extra seconds of exposure
going to cost him an earlobe or two. He always thought the term bone-chilling
a childish hyperbole, but now it seems insufficient.

"Not much wind today either," the hotel clerk says when Wilkes mentions chill. "When it picks up and blows the snow around, that fleece of yours won' nearly enough. You head on over across the street. The lady will fix you up."

She points toward a storefront with a faded, formerly red sign. Karoline's.

"Fix me up?"

"'Round here if you don't have clothes to live in, you die in 'em."

Eskimo humor, or cliché, he says to himself, though the receptionist does have native features and the home-spun wisdom may have been acqu secondhand. But her sleeveless down vest and layers beneath it, at least t neckbands Wilkes can count, speak to her appreciation of the elements.

She points him down a dimly lit hall. "Number eight on your right," she s "You may have to work the key a little."

He doesn't, but he nudges the door open with some trepidation only to fi space not dissimilar to most of the other business rooms he's occupied in Det Cincinnati, St. Louis. And it's warm: too warm. Near the thermostat, thoug warning is posted: lowering the temperature at night can risk pipes freezing slides the dial back a few ticks only.

He carries one small suitcase, carry-on size, and since he never has been on those travelers who unpack, he tosses it on to the only extra chair and turns to l again, but not before he unpacks some thermal shirts and slips one of them on. desk clerk's warning has disconcerted him and he recognizes the risk in me crossing the street. It's twenty below, maybe more. He knows the math, he doesn't know the science.

Karoline's store sign isn't much bigger than the sign on his own house, the he and Keira argued over. She wanted an apostrophe after the s but he insisted were the Wilkeses, just like the Smiths and the Sturgeons and the Maglic Logically and grammatically his argument was impeccable, but when he ord the sign from a local artisan, the man asked him if he was sure he wa "Wilkeses" because it sounded awkward. Tired of arguing and debating devising cogent rationale, he told the man to paint "Wilkes." No apostro nothing. Let passers-by figure it out.

With Karoline there's no argument: an apostrophe and an s and the word c after it. Wilkes never really understood how a co-op works, but he figures once inside, he'll be in a quasi-Salvation Army store, one that carries everyth yet, in its own hapless way, nothing. But he's made it there, escaping the

mentarily, and the first items he sees inside are rows of anoraks. As the desk
·k said, Karoline's will fix him up.

. woman's voice interrupts his little moment of gratification.

Bonjour!"

ehind the counter stands a decidedly un-French woman, more a girl, maybe
nty, twenty-one? Her features are that of a Native American, but since he has
his native America a thousand miles behind him, that nomenclature probably
longer holds. So this is an Eskimo, or would have been before Wilkes learned
the expression had fallen out of favor.

Français?" she asks.

Anglais," he says, quickly depleting most of his French vocabulary.

I speak both, and some Inuit. Let me know if you need any help."

uit, Wilkes says to himself, that's the word.

Inuit is the native language?"

Inuktitut is the real word," she says. "To say I speak Inuit is like saying you
ak England, but it's easier. What can I help you with?"

Ie repeats the word to himself. Inuktitut—like Connecticut. Maybe he'll be able
emember.

Are you Karoline?"

Oh, no," she says and smiles. "Even in this climate I would not be that well
served. My aunt died in 2005. I'm Jacqueline, Jackie."

That doesn't sound like an Inuit name."

Manitok is my Inuit name, but it's more of a nickname. Not official. I'm going
ry it out a few more years. When I'm thirty I'll decide."

That's a long time to try something out."

I'm not as young as I look. And you are—?"

Older than I look," he says, then laughs. "Martin Wilkes. That's my name for
"

Maybe you'll find one here you like better. Are you with Autumn?"

Autumn?"

Then I guess you're not. Autumn is the mining company," she says, her voice
ged just slightly with disdain.

Oh, no, not at all. I'm just here on...I'm looking for somebody."

Mon dieu," she says, stifling a laugh. "Have you come to the wrong place!
fee?"

Behind her a carafe is steaming and next to it lie some sugar packets and eve
plate of cookies not quite dark enough to be chocolate. Molasses maybe, the sa
hue as Manitok's apparently ageless face. Can she really be close to thirty and
look like a high school student? Maybe all those warnings about the sun's ag
qualities are true, though the cold (and he's had but a few moments of it) m
inflict its own ravages.

He turns down the coffee.

"This counter is just a formality," she says. "You can come back and get your
a cup when you want."

"I just had some at the hotel, thanks. What'd you mean I came to the wr
place?"

"Well, people come here for a lot of reasons. We have trout fishing in
summer. It's beautiful country when it's green and...thawed. But now, not e
February yet. When people come here they're working for the mines or visitin
relative. Of course you might have come here to icefish, but you don't seem
type. Who are you looking for?"

"A friend."

"And he came here?"

"It's a she."

"Uh huh. And you know she's here? Why?"

"Why do I know?"

"Yes, that too, but why did she come here?"

"I'll have to ask her when I see her."

Manitok looks wary: Wilkes isn't surprised. There's something sinister abo
man searching the hinterlands for a woman—something threatening and off-ki
If the cops are asking the questions, well, that's what cops do. If some underdres
visitor is doing it, there's something untoward involved: abandonment, a custe
dispute, divorce, revenge, abuse. Is he there to retrieve this woman or kill her?
tries to set the clerk's mind at ease by showing a small photo of Keira—smili
seemingly happy.

"That's her," he says. "Have you seen her?"

"Are you some sort of detective for the mines?"

He laughs.

"They have their own detectives?"

"Are you?"

No. I'm a financial advisor for Tolliver & Byrne in New York. You probably ven't heard of them because they haven't been shut down yet and no one has :n arrested."

Ie hands her a business card. She glances at it.

'This is Canada," she says, and returns it.

The reply is not so impolite as it is dismissive. Whatever financial mischief is)pening on Wall Street doesn't concern her.

Manitok holds the photo up to the light. "What's her name?"

'Keira Eason."

She examines it for a few more seconds before returning it.

And if I called the number on your business card and asked for you, they'd)w who I was talking about?"

Ie takes out his cell.

'If you'd like, go ahead."

She shakes her head.

'Cell service is spotty around here. If you leave the picture I can ask around. erybody comes in here."

Ie hands it to her—he has five more—and she tapes it next to the cash register.

'Thanks," he says, though he's certain no one will even notice it. "What I really d is for someone to help me pick out some clothes. The lady at the hotel doesn't nk much of my winter wardrobe."

She's right. I'm surprised you made it across the street."

She leads him to the anoraks alongside tables filled with mittens the size of ving platters.

And that baseball hat and earmuffs you're wearing? Mr. Wilkes, you're begging trouble."

She lifts a thick wool toque from the table and hands it to him.

Someone knitted this?"

Someone did."

Ie examines the label. China.

Sheep don't like it up here," she says, "and it's hard to make a good wool cap of sealskin. Try it on."

Ie hates wearing caps: something about the look has always reminded him of a allus with a condom at the tip. But given few options, he slips it on.

I never liked these," he says. "The look is—well..."

"Like a penis, yes, but the first time the temps reach forty below, you won't c
what you look like."

"It gets that cold?"

"This year has been bad, dangerous. Warmer than I can remember but with th
horrible cold spells."

She points outside and he follows her lead as someone walks past the windc
Wilkes can't tell if it's a man or a woman or a polar bear walking upright,
clothing is so enveloping.

"You want what they're wearing," Manitok says, and assembles a survi
wardrobe as Wilkes watches. If this woman hasn't seen Keira, it's unlikely anyc
else has either; and if he's going to have to root around this open-air icebox,
can't quibble over money or appearance. Two-hundred American dollars later h
back in his room with his former outerwear in a plastic bag by the waste bask
It's a bargain; he's paid that much for a Brooks Bros. shirt in his former life. 1
thermal socks make his feet feel like mallets, but he steps outside the hotel a
trudges to the street and back without toppling over. The cold is just
overwhelming, but he's fairly confident it won't kill him.

Back inside he shows his wife's photo to the hotel clerk, Hannah, he fina
notices the nameplate on her vest, but she shakes her head. She hasn't seen h
nor has anyone in the next three businesses he approaches: a bank, a print shop
convenience store/deli. Wilkes never thought McNally possessed any particu
skills, but he may have underestimated him: a practiced PI would not be stuck i
town where nobody would speak to him.

More small businesses line the main strip, but the farther he gets from both
hotel and the co-op, the less he trusts his ability to withstand the cold. He convine
himself to try one more place that looks like an artisan's gallery, when he hears
name shouted. It's Manitok.

"Come back to the store," she says.

"I'm fine. This clothing—"

"She was here. That woman in the picture."

u lied to me," Manitok says. "You're not looking for a friend. You're looking
our wife. And her last name—"
ason was her maiden name. I thought she might be using it. Why should that
er?"
t matters because you didn't tell me the truth."
said I was looking for a friend. That's the truth. It's just—"
on't tell me it's semantics. I'm not an idiot."
ilkes stops mid-sentence, the *s* on his tongue. Manitok leans back and folds
arms.
r. Wilkes, we're not innocents up here. I'm glad your wife is your friend, but
t expect me not to know the difference. I have a lot of friends. I don't have
lren with them."
Who said anything about children?"
e glares at him, a withering and icy look more than commensurate with the
ther outside. This Manitok is as outspoken and forthright and incisive as any
s investors—like Robert K. Blackmoor minus fifty years—and Wilkes knows
e spent an hour with Blackmoor quibbling over language, Tolliver & Byrne
ld fire his ass before the next pay cycle.
, we, have two children."
e nods but remains silent.
should have been more forthright."
s that really the word you want to use? Forthright?"
ruthful?"
was hoping for honest. So I'll be honest. I'm sorry I sent you out into the cold
profited from it. Now tell me you don't mean that woman any harm. The fact
you're looking this hard for her—"
he ran off," he says, and distills the previous week's chronology into a one-
ute capsule. Manitok listens without any visible reaction and says nothing
n he's finished.
t's true, all of it."
es, this time," she says, her eyes narrowed slightly. "Maybe it was pride that
e you lie before. I guess I can understand that. Now I'll tell you the truth: your
was here. Saturday."

"Here? In this store?"

"I remember her eyes. They're almost amber."

"She always claimed they're hazel. Was she alone?"

"I didn't see her with anyone. She came in, like you, and needed clothes, b[c] I know that because we had only one pair that fit her—"

"She has big feet."

"—The boots were very expensive."

"But she bought them anyway? That's a concession she wouldn't mak[e] home."

"She paid cash."

"She took a lot of it with her. Do you know where she went?"

"I work odd hours, Mr. Wilkes. Eight hours today, tomorrow twelve, then off, maybe, unless I get a phone call. I can go a long time without crossing p[aths] with folks. I did have the feeling she wasn't planning to stay here."

He finally slips off the mitts and removes his toque while Manitok pours cups of coffee. She nods toward the cream and sugar. This time he accepts it. [This] time he can't seem to warm up.

"You think my wife left here and went back home?"

"I thought she was on her way to somewhere else. With those clothes, I dou[bt] it was home."

"Where does a person go from here, if not home?"

"Your wife, and I don't mean to be... indiscreet...."

"You mean nosy?"

"I guess I should learn more English. Is she running from something? Lik[e] law?"

"I'm really not a cop."

"You could be a private detective."

"I already have one of those. Or I did until I fired him. Do you even have [one] here?"

"Somebody has to arrest the petty thieves and dry out the drunks. We ha[ve a] police force, EMTs, a fire department. I don't think we have a missing per[son] bureau, though. So she is running from something?"

"I have no idea," he says, then forces himself not to include her abandonme[nt of] the children on a bus. The thought of it infuriates him, but Manitok might dis[cern] the anger and pull back. "What's after—here?"

Manitok shakes her head. "I don't understand."

I mean she flew into Churchill because that's a stopping off point to Baker Lake. Is this a stopping off point too?"

Manitok shrugs. "I'm not sure if there's a real answer to that, but I'll show you something."

On the wall near the outdoor clothing section is a detailed map of Nunavut the size of a museum poster.

"We're here," she says, pointing to a dot at the end of a long river. "Baker's different. Every other town up here, every settlement is on the bay, Hudson Bay, the Passage. We're pretty far inland."

She slides her finger north and east.

"Now this up here, this is Repulse Bay. Over here to the east, maybe six-hundred miles, you got Iqaluit, the capital. Thirty-thousand people. If you want to hide, I guess that's the place."

"I don't want to hide."

"You'd need warmer clothes anyway. Over here is Qausuittuq."

Wilkes searches the map. The letters and the sound don't match.

"I don't see it."

"That's the Inuit word for it: the place with no dawn. Resolute."

"How many miles north is that?"

"Six, seven hundred."

"Jesus! And you can fly from here?"

"No other way in. If I wanted to get lost—"

"And it's a city?"

"Not quite as cosmopolitan as this one," she says, and winks. "It's a research center. Mostly scientists. A civilian would have no purpose there. Lot of climate studies."

"Global warming. Today I wish it were true."

"You don't go along with that, huh?"

"The climate is always changing."

Manitok leans back. "I guess I should admire your forthrightness, Mr. Wilkes. You know that we're probably sensitive to environmental issues but you just say what you think. So let me be forthright too. Exxon may be an investment to you, but not to us."

She says it with a smile, but Wilkes catches the drift immediately. Exxon, the Exxon Valdez, the environmental disaster a generation before, Alaska, Eskimos, Inuits, Manitok. His standard retort, you can't blame a corporation for some drunk

at the helm of a ship, seems inappropriate, maybe even callous under
circumstances.

"I do buy and sell oil stock."

"Just business," Manitok, her tone slightly cooler.

"Business. Like you selling me that knit condom to wear on my head."

She suppresses a smile, but traces of it seep through. "Like that, yes. But if
condom breaks, you don't destroy an ecosystem."

He nods. The photos of wildlife coated with viscous crude are ingrained
everyone's minds. Birds, fish, mammals, all terrified, agonizing, dying, or dea

"It was not your fault," she says, her tone losing its chill. "I won't hold
responsible if you won't ask me to forget about it and ignore what's coming."

"What you think is coming."

"Fair enough."

A young woman approaches the counter with a child gnawing on a piece of to
They both regard Wilkes warily, pay, then leave.

"Strangers," Manitok says with some regret. "Since the mines they're no
welcome as before. We're suspicious now. We think everyone wants someth
from us."

"Were they suspicious of Keira?"

"I don't know how many people she actually met."

"If she were still here, would I be likely to find her?"

"In August, maybe, when everyone's out and about. But now, we tend to s
indoors."

He looks at the posted picture of his wife, taken two years earlier at Jam
fourth birthday party. Her mouth is slightly contorted from having helped her
blow out the candles rather than spit them out (something at which he was ad
and her eyes reveal the beginning or ending of a smile, Wilkes cannot remem
which or, for that matter, why he even snapped the picture.

"I'm going out to look around," he says. "Can you just, you know, ask peo
maybe show the picture?"

"Sure."

"And put in a good word for me so that people don't think I'm from the mine

"I'll say you're from Exxon."

"Thanks, You'll find me in a ditch somewhere."

"Mr. Wilkes, listen. The mines, the oil, the visitors spooking the wildlife.
need the money but we hate to give up our heritage. We're no different fr

one else and sometimes we don't like ourselves for it. Do you ever feel that y? I mean you deal with the wealthiest people while millions of others live hand-mouth. Does it bother you?"

Sometimes probably." It's the answer she wants to hear, but that kind of lection constitutes very little of Martin Wilkes's persona.

I may live another fifty years," she says, "even more if I'm lucky. I'm going to changes. We all will. But my grandchildren and their grandchildren won't live a place like this. It may still be called Baker Lake, but there may not even be a e. Or maybe there'll be only a lake. You can't blame people for wanting to hold "

I don't."

By the time the locals realize your intentions are good, you'll be gone anyway. tread lightly. If you can, with those boots."

he looks at the clock, scans the store. A few people are picking at merchandise most of her customers are eating.

Around three," she says, "things slow down in here. I can go with you. It might safer."

That's two hours. It wouldn't give me much daylight."

Less aimless wandering though. And up here, traveling alone is never wise."

But I'll be close by."

Forget the numbers below zero," she says. "That's just math. Use your agination when you go outside. Imagine what cold really is."

Ie considers her offer to wait, but he doesn't have that kind of time to fritter ay. He slips the goofy-looking toque over his head, gives Manitok a smile of ignation, and heads back to the hotel where he makes several futile attempts to ch McNally on an outside phone line that keeps shutting down. After a half zen attempts, he gets the answering machine.

It's Martin Wilkes," he says. "I'm in Baker Lake and it's, well it's light today I I'm going to look around. Just wondering if you had any advice, so, you know ou can, give me a call and...."

Ie continues to flubber through the end of the message when he hears a click.

I'm here," McNally said. "I would have picked up earlier but I was laughing hard. It's light today? Now there's a testimonial."

It's not a bad little place. Looks like some small towns in Connecticut."

"Well, I'm looking at this website and all I see is quonset huts and shacks. (wait, let me zoom in. I think I see an eight-room colonial with a pool and a tennis Never mind, it's a quonset hut."

"I didn't mean the architecture was the same. It's just a small town."

"Nice beach though. I got a feeling the picture I'm looking at wasn't taken February."

"Are you finished?"

"Nowhere near," McNally says, "but I'll give it a rest. Are you calling to reh me?"

"You want directions on how to get here?"

"Let me rephrase. What can I do for you in an advisory capacity, 'cause I s' as shit ain't going there, despite my wife. She's busting my chops for accompanying you. Says I'm shirking. Do you think it's true? Am I shirking?"

"So now what, no privileges for a week?"

"I hope you mean TV, because everything else here is just fine thank you. I fault for bringing my work home."

"If worse comes to worse and she throws you out, let me know. I can find yo nice Inuit name and get you all settled in."

"I worked too many years for that Mercedes to settle for a dogsled. Anyway, my advisory capacity—"

"I get it, you're charging me."

"I'm not. I told Lynne I'd advise you for free until you got back."

"And Lynne is—?"

"My wife. No wonder you need a PI. Talk as long as you want. Do you ha enough pips for the pay phone? Can you turn the crank or is it frozen?"

"I thought you were giving it a rest."

"Officially resting. What have you found?"

"A store clerk claims she saw Keira."

McNally's tone changes.

"No shit. What did Terry say?"

"That's not her name."

"I didn't ask that. I'm looking at the map here and I'm gonna guess you did walk from the airport. I'm basing that on the fact that you haven't been eaten wolves or frozen into a lump. There's a 50-50 chance Terry from Terry's T drove you. Maybe he drove your wife too. Check the rest of the cabbies too. T store clerk, was she hesitant at all? I mean was she willing to provide informatio

Not at first."

"She didn't trust you, but she was young, right, and wanted to be helpful?"

"Fairly young."

"Gathering information as an outsider may be difficult. She's sure about your ?"

"Said she was in Saturday."

"Not since?"

"Apparently not. She thought Keira might have been passing through."

"Then you better hurry up and line up those cabbies, because if that clerk is right, of them saw her twice at least, coming and going. After the cabs, try the stores. ck the mall. Women love to shop. My wife prefers Nordstrom. Got one of e?"

"You can't help yourself, can you?"

"It's hard. Try the co-op first."

"That's the clerk I mentioned."

"What's his name?"

"Her. Manitok, but she goes by Jackie."

"If she's Inuit, you call her Manitok. Show her a picture of your kids."

"Don't have one."

"Listen, Wilkes, don't take this personally, but what kind of loser doesn't have ture of his kids? Can you buy a wallet in that co-op?"

"suppose."

"Sometimes they come with sample photos. See if you can find one with some in it."

"This woman isn't stupid, you know."

"Then tell her you just had portraits taken but they haven't come back yet. And ess concern about Keira."

"am concerned."

"know you a little bit, Wilkes. Not much, a little bit. I'll bet you never told this itok that you feared for your wife's safety, or how much you missed her."

"don't remember."

"Then you probably didn't. If she thinks you want her back but doesn't know , she won't be quite so helpful. Maybe she'll start thinking your wife doesn't t to come back."

"Is that what you think?"

"Please, don't make like I'm hurting your feelings. She left on her own. I
about a newspaper? Do they have one?"

"I'll find out."

"I already did. The Messenger. Fellow named Tad Burton runs it. I don't t
that's his Inuit name. Maybe he's got some information. You don't have a
recorder, do you?"

"No. Why didn't you tell me these things before I left?"

"Because I told you leaving was a bad idea."

"But I found her."

"No, I found her. You're just standing at the end of the earth talking on
phone. Though—I am surprised you got that close to her that fast. Just remem
half the people are going to lie outright and half the remainder aren't going to
you with the whole truth. And the other half won't give a shit."

"I'd love to see that pie chart. Anything else?"

"You got Mounties there on the main drag. I don't know how many, but the
some kind of headquarters on that street along the lake. Be careful, cops espec
don't like an outside investigator coming in and doing their job, especially w
the outside investigator ain't one and there is no job."

"I'll get back to you if I hear anything."

"If you'd like."

"Aren't you interested?"

"Sort of. Tell you what I will do, since this whole journey demonstrate
unprecedented lack of good sense on your part. I can go to your house and gr
photo of your kids and maybe email it to you. A picture on the phone equa
picture in your wallet."

"I don't need it."

"Whatever you say. I just checked tonight's forecast for Baker Lake. Thirty-e
below zero and clear. Fahrenheit. That's when you stay inside and do al
paperwork, the flowcharts, prepare for the next day."

"I think you're worried about me."

"Would you be worried if I were handling your portfolio?"

"I'd be terrified."

"There you are."

McNally clicks off, or the line goes dead. Wilkes isn't sure which. He still h
told the PI about the letter. There aren't too many stupider approaches
withholding information from your own investigator, but he just doesn't

Nally to know this. Besides, the day has not been a waste: he has made some gress on his own (even McNally seemed a bit impressed) and has no reason to k it won't continue. He's been a salesman all his life. He simply needs to keep licizing the prospectus until he finds the right investor.

e Mountie office has been abandoned for a small storefront where two former
ice officers of indeterminate age alternate weeks on duty, a retirement gig for
h of them. Someone named Stevens is on this week. He's from Cleveland and
er to help, but just as eager, it appears, for company, a break from the towering
'D pile of early TV sitcoms that apparently fills up his days. He pauses an
sode of M*A*S*H to take down all the pertinent information, then hints at
nething McNally implied an hour before. It isn't the law's job to find people who
't want to be found. Rather than debate with him, Wilkes leaves the retiree to
 history of television.
Jeither taxi driver volunteers anything about some woman from the states;
rse, each acts like a priest forbidden to repeat what he's heard in the
ıfessional. The dead ends leave him exhausted and frustrated.
It's the cold," Manitok says. "It takes so much energy to keep warm, there's
hing left for anything else."
Is there anything else? Anywhere else?"
We have a few taverns," she says, "and a real restaurant off the motel. Oh, and
exercise place over on Arluq on the way to the airfield. Mostly college kids use
ecause the school itself is pretty limited.
College kids? Seriously?"
College of the Arctic."
So it's like a branch of something?"
Tell you the truth, I don't know. Never went."
Manitok leans across the counter. "Can I just ask you something, and I don't want
ı to feel insulted."
An insult usually follows that question, but go ahead."
When you came here, how much preparation did you do?"
I packed."
And not very well. What do you know about this place? About Nunavut?"
I was rushed. I had to make arrangements for the kids, I had to—"
You have pictures of your kids?"
No. We keep meaning to have a family portrait done, but you know, we kept
ting it off."
You don't have a camera to take your own picture? How old are they?"

"Brett is nine; James is six."

"Two boys. You didn't tell me that before."

"I'm not looking for them."

"I suppose not. That college you didn't know existed. They have a library. May
an hour there would fill in a lot of holes in your learning. I can take you."

"What about the store?"

"Everything here is self-serve, and I have an honor box. I don't sell liquor or gu
so I'm not endangering anybody. Someone needs something they'll take it a
leave me the money or a note. Come on."

He doesn't want to waste a single minute in a college library. He hardly ever
that in college, for Christ's sake. But he can see the upside: being seen with one
the town's citizens might afford him some credibility, respectability, and may
others would be less reticent about sharing information. Besides, Manitok i
pleasant enough girl with a quick mind and an understated sense of humor, a
who works cheap, especially compared to McNally.

"Those pictures," Wilkes says, pointing to two cheaply framed photos on
wall near the cigarettes. "Those were taken here?"

"Don't sound so surprised. I'll be ready in a minute."

While she involves herself in an animated conversation with the remain
customers, he examines the photographs. One of the photos looks like what he l
already seen: a barren expanse of white with the occasional pile of plowed sn
to interrupt the monotony. Two cars and a snow machine share the road, or m
correctly the snow that covers the road. He can walk outside with his cell pho
and replicate the image, except for the single polar bear menacing
photographer. He hasn't seen one of those and isn't sure he wants to.

But the other photo defies everything he has seen in Baker Lake. It might as w
be Wellfleet on the Cape, or Nantucket, or Montauk. Maybe a Maine seaco
village on Booth Bay. That the photo could have been taken in this snow-bl
wilderness stretches all credulity, and yet the landscape is unmistakable: barr
treeless acreage sloping gently toward a lake which, though currently locked do
by months of ice, shines clear and placid in what appears to be morning sunshi
It's almost disconcerting in its beauty.

"It reminds me of places in New England," he tells Manitok when she retur
"You've never been to America, have you?"

"Never on the east coast. Is that what it looks like?"

More trees, but yes, this is exactly what it looks like. There's a word scribbled
ne picture."

uraq. Summer. The solstice. It never gets really dark that day, just twilight.
s far from the dark time as you can get."

"he dark time?"

Jow. Today, even though we're a month past the winter solstice. We have the
but it's like having a light bulb in your lamp but there's never quite enough
age for it to work. That photo from *Auraq*, that's 3:00 a.m., even before the
rmen were out. Of course they're too drunk to go out on the morning after.
's why the lake is empty."

nd that shack," he says, pointing to what amounts to a whitewashed carton on
ks with one visible window, the door apparently on the other side facing the
. "A fisherman lives there?"

ort of. It's just there for people who need it."

Vho owns it?"

"I tell you that *Anirniq* owns it just as he owns everything, you would either
npressed by my wonderful simplicity or amused by my naiveté, right?"

nirniq? He's what, like God or something?"

guess. But we don't really have a God. We're all responsible."

ut isn't one more responsible than the others?"

e laughs. "We don't have just one prime mover. That's what makes us so
nt. I said I was in your country—even took a theology course. I know that
f of God."

o no prime mover? How about a more major mover?"

orry," she says, fending off the gibe. "All our movers are prime, even the
als. That's why we pay a price when we kill them."

o that shack...you have to keep it presentable for that...entity?"

hink of it as a soul. I'll concede you that much. It's a nice European concept
can wrap your Christian head around and one that I can almost accept. A soul
in that cabin, but only when it wants to. Sometimes it probably wants heat
running water and comes into town."

ilkes studies the photo again and tries to imagine how Baker Lake in January
become this tranquil and almost enticing little postcard village in June. He
, and that cabin—it's still a shack. For that matter, he learns a few minutes
after a short and frigid walk, the college isn't exactly a college, but part of a

building that also houses, appropriately enough, a high school. And the libra
essentially four desktop computers lined up in carrels against a wall.

"We don't have much space," Manitok says as she squeezes between a table
a filing cabinet. "We do have a book room, but it's mostly for texts. In here it'
computers and some local histories."

She leans over to log in, then drags over a chair.

"It's all yours," she says. "Can you find your way back after?"

"I left a trail of bread crumbs," he says, and winks.

"A bear has eaten them by now."

"I saw one in that picture. What's the word for polar bear in your language.'

"Too many to list. I like the ones the poets use, *Pihoqahiak*, the ever-wande
one. All the other words make them out to be big oafish brutes."

"And they aren't?"

"Do any of us want to be called what we really are. I mean human so
harmless enough, maybe complimentary given all those years of hearing it
that way. But it doesn't encompass all our evils. Anyway, don't let a *Pihoqa*
get you on the way back."

"I thought he was my soulmate?"

"Not when he's in a bad mood, or hungry. Come back to the co-op when yo
done. Half hour, then we'll look around a little."

She leaves him in a room with several students, though only he is staring
blank screen. He pokes at a few keys and makes it look as if he's involved. He
Two weeks ago he was a comfortable Fairfield County commuter, riding Am
to the city and taking his six-figure salary back to Connecticut. He was helpin
kids with homework and taking his wife to the movies; having regular meals
regular sex; following the news and watching the markets and lamenting
inauguration of a Democrat and, in short, leading the life his career had bro
him to. He had complaints like everyone else: a wife who was losing some pas
for him, maybe passion altogether, and kids who sometimes lacked respect.
these were the fodder of jokes and benign laments, not of resentment. These
complaints uttered over a beer with the guys after work, uttered before you
home and hugged your kids and made adequate love to your wife. That
normality. But this, this was—he should have asked what the Inuit term for fu
up was. In a place where it never gets light and then never gets dark, there ha
be several of them.

the nominal College of the Arctic he learns that Baker Lake is 90 percent Inuit.
e didn't feel like an interloper before, he does now. He knows that Mexicans
r to Americans as gringos, and Hawaiians, still leery perhaps of the
onization (and some even resentful of statehood), call them *Haoles*. Neither
n is particularly insulting, can even be endearing. Neither can match the the
cor of mainstream American words that isolate blacks, Hispanics, Jews,
ians, and in the new century, anyone from the Middle East. But what is he to
Inuit, these people who struggled for decades to have a territory of their own—
possess this Nunavut? What do they think of some Anglo from the states
ndering about with no fixed purpose, neither a tourist nor a visitor, just a guy
oking for someone"?
e logs off when he notices a young lady waiting for a workstation.
I was just leaving," he says and glances at his watch, still on Eastern time. He'll
e to remember the zone difference, merely an hour, when he calls the boys
ight.
nd what will he say to them? He has told them so little to begin with that being
ue now will be easy. But he can't regale them with stories of bizarre wildlife
en all he's seen so far is a couple of dogs, one of them a golden retriever that
ked for all the world like any other walking companion on some lane in Wilton.
midnight sun, no Aurora, no reindeer. He isn't even sure he should mention
nitok's having seen their mother, not until he has seen her himself and started
home.
e shuffles past some storefronts: a barber, a hardware store, a gallery, a real
ate office with pictures in the window of houses of varying styles. He tries the
r; it's unlocked, but the office is empty. On a small table are brochures on home
ership and a looseleaf notebook filled with architectural drawings. McNally
y have joked about a colonial, but there's a listing for a cape and several ranches.
ybe the mines far to the north presage a new way: more money, more work,
red lives. He doesn't need to be Inuit to know that. They're sixty miles away,
se mines. How weird, he thinks, the distance from Wilton to New York City is
about the same and he does it almost every day either on rails or paved roads.
Not around here," Manitok says when he gets back. "Sixty miles on a snow
chine isn't that big a trip, but not every day. Men will probably come home on
ekends."
So the adjustment will be minor?"

"Open-pit mining will scar that area forever, but it's safer than sending our peo
into a hole. We argue that subject just as you argue in your country. You h
fracking to find natural gas, I read about it, poisoning billions of gallons of wa
Something that awful would be a hard sell around here. But in America—"

"It's been unjustly criticized, the dangers exaggerated."

His sudden defensiveness silences her, though the response itself is essenti
robotic, emanating from his unshakable trust in that ancient Calvin Cooli
bromide about the business of America being business. And in Wilkes's partic
business, energy company holdings pad a good many portfolios and provid
multitude of investors with a blithe security. He has always assured his clients,
few who bothered to inquire, that the processes used to access these fuels were
the ecological disasters some watchdog groups were claiming. He has the dat
refute the accusations and justify the process, and not only that, he can sleep pr
well at night.

Despite all that, Manitok's slightly doubtful look stings like a reprimand.

"What I meant," he says, trying to remove the new chill he himself has effec
"is that it's not always as bad as people make it out to be. There are alw
sacrifices. The animals you kill—"

"And we have protests here, old-timers and young people who would like to
the mines disappear or never come to fruition, but they have to eat too. We all

"How often do people go up to the mines?"

"By the spring maybe we'll start to see a real exodus. Workers will live there
a month or two, then get some time off. I guess there'll be some sort of rota
schedule. Ten years."

"Ten years!"

"That's the presumed productive life-expectancy. Then when it runs
everyone goes home."

"And leaves an open pit."

"A million years from now someone will wander through there and thin
meteor hit and left a crater and that's how this beautiful lake came to be. Or a
legend will grow up."

"Do you think you'll still be around a million years from now? I mean the Inu

"Will there be any cultural group? Any mythology? I know there won't be
Americans. Or Europeans. or Asians."

"Or humans?"

I can't believe there will be, but I try to be optimistic, just in case it turns out
 still here in some form—wandering the outskirts of Baker Lake foraging for
d with my cubs. Anyway, only egotists worry about such matters. You and I,
're here for the short term, then someone else takes over."

But you just said—"

If I am still here, I'm not going to know it anyway. Did you enjoy our college?
you stop in the gallery on your way back?"

I didn't see it."

Too bad. It's two doors down. Some nice things that the locals do. Native art,
k art, what some call primitive art. We don't have the pastels and oils you're
d to."

Just like New England," he says. "Fishing villages and artists colonies."

Your wife," Manitok says, checking off packaged items in a large carton. "Is
an artist?"

She would say a failed artist, I'd say unrealized. I guess she was pretty good in
h school. One of her teachers suggested she continue in college."

But she didn't?"

No. Maybe we can stop over at the gallery."

Go now. I have to register these jackets."

But you were going to come with me."

he points to the open carton and Wilkes sees a half-dozen more.

I can't leave these here."

I have a limited amount of time," Wilkes says, the frustration more apparent. "I
uld be looking for Keira, not wasting my time in some gallery."

Fifteen minutes. Promise. You can wait here if you'd like."

I can only drink so much coffee," he says. "Fifteen minutes."

's as close to an ultimatum as he can issue, but if the tone is peremptory,
nitok ignores it.

The sign says Takuminartok," she says. You can't miss it. And it's more like a
rkshop. This time of year with so few tourists around, artists are more likely to
g out together, work together, chip in on fuel money together—heat one place
ead of twenty. *Takuminartok*."

Don't bother spelling it," he says. Why waste another fifteen minutes cobbling
ether random letters to spell something he doesn't care about? "Maybe they
n't let me in. You know, being an alien."

She laughs. "We're not so primitive that we don't recognize a potential custom when we see one. Buy yourself something to take home. Come back in fift minutes. I'll take you around."

Wilkes arranges his outerwear so that virtually no patch of skin is showing, th repeats the name of the place, butchering almost every syllable. Manitok smile

"It means nice to look at. Have fun looking."

He glances at the summer photo again. The lake, the shack.

"Those places on the beach, are they heated?"

"Most of them are lucky to have doors."

"But are any of them livable?"

"This time of year, there may be one or two with a pellet stove, kerosene. I d know about livable."

"We'll check them out?"

She nods.

"Fifteen minutes," she says once more, then rips a utility knife through the box

He could have told Manitok more about Keira the artist. At a high school show where some of her paintings hung, a young English teacher told her tha Sylvia Plath had been an artist, these were the pieces she would have painted. Ke didn't know Plath, but found out easily enough that she had been an extraordin poet who one day, at thirty years of age, already a successful poet, a wife, a moth filled her apartment with gas and killed herself. With her death she became poster child for a generation of youth leading tortured existences, real or imagin Keira would not have minded being an inspiration, she told Wilkes once, but hoped to live past thirty, not be known for her darkness, and not fulfill so English teacher's offhand prophecy.

And as for Keira's skills, Wilkes is probably not the one to ask. On a trip to Metropolitan once he referred to a number of small pieces as tchotchkes and pr much infuriated her. Since then he has tried to keep his artistic judgments himself.

re may not be any bears on the streets of Baker Lake, but the workshop is filled
them—sculptures, paintings, drawings. And other animals too: a walrus, a
ou, and some creature that might be a teddy bear were it not for its sheep's
. Takuminartok looks more like a high school art class than a gallery, with
rent workers engaged in diverse projects in various stages of completion. One
who looks to be Wilkes's age is squeezing a tube of reddish pigment unto a
tte, fitting Wilkes's description of a real artist, but the others are carving and
pting to the clink of stone hammers and the whirr of a wheel. An older man
ks with a soldering iron and some bluish gemstones; another with a number of
l chisels, a simple jackknife, and a block of pine, a medium that certainly didn't
lop in this treeless northern desert. Everyone seem oblivious to everyone else
to Wilkes, but one person does appear to be in charge: a stubbled man in string
nd jeans. He lacks any obvious ethnicity, but his blue work shirt might easily
come from Wilkes's closet back in Connecticut—by way of L.L. Bean. He
les with the tie and makes eye contact with Wilkes, but there is little of either
ome or exclusion in the man's glance.
eel free to look around," he calls from across the room, nodding toward the
hed products on a long wood table near the back door, then continues flitting
station to station and conversing with, maybe mentoring, the workers. No one
s unhappy to speak with him, and if his brief visitations are interrupting their
in any way, they certainly don't show any displeasure or annoyance.
nally his his meanderings bring him to the display table.
an I help you with anything today?"
Martin Wilkes. Manitok at the store sent me over."
call her Jackie. I butcher the Inuit names pretty good."
ut this place—"
on't remind me of the name. I'm Leo. You came in on the plane yesterday,
?"
ow do you know?"
eceptionist at your hotel, cab driver, few others. Come in from Saskatoon?"
y way of everywhere."

"That's the way travel is around here. That's why when we get somewhere stay. I came here from Halifax. Going home now seems like too much troubl now I'm the curator here, in a very general sense. What brings you to Baker La

Business. The word is almost out when he changes his mind. Evasiveness d work with Manitok, maybe honesty might.

"I'm looking for somebody. Woman named Keira."

"Fugitive?"

"No, of course not. I'm just looking for her."

"You a cop? Mountie?"

"Manitok—Jackie—asked me that too. Neither. Just looking for her."

"Well," Leo says, his tone noticeably cooler, "that sounds a little ominous."

Wilkes pulls out the photo. Partial truths play as poorly as lies in this place.

"This woman," he says. "Have you seen her?"

"She's pretty. No wonder you married her."

Wilkes thinks better of denying it.

"Twenty years," he says. "It's a long story."

Leo smiles.

"I don't want to sound like some wilderness wise man, but every marriage long story, even when it ends. The problem is, the story seldom ends with marriage. So, why is she here?"

"Something happened. I don't know what. Maybe she just wanted to be awa hide. I honestly don't know."

"Not many come to Baker to hide. It's too small. Everyone knows everyone and no one can come into town without being noticed. You need a big city to lost in. What made you think I might know her?"

"She used to paint a little when she was younger. I thought she might grav to an art gallery."

"And when you find her, if you do, then what?"

The impertinent question catches Wilkes off guard, but even more distres he has no ready answer. He has considered Keira's departure the workings over-stressed consciousness, felt that maybe a calm and gentle conversation w put her on the right track again. And of course there are the kids: reminding h familial responsibilities is bound to right the ship, no matter how close it may come to foundering. He doesn't anticipate having to do anything other than sir appear.

"One step at a time," Wilkes says. Evasive, but it's an answer.

You're welcome to browse," Leo says. "Any items for sale are marked with a
e tag. Canadian currency I'm afraid, but similar to your dollar. Maybe add five
 cent. Everything is negotiable."
Wait a minute," Wilkes says. "You didn't answer me. Have you seen her?"
I told you this town is too small to hide in. A few days ago someone looking
 that came in, but not since. I thought maybe she went home."
You're sure it was her."
Except for the name. She said it was Sylvy."
Sylvy? Like Sylvia?"
I guess. She came in here twice, asked about the place, what we did, how we
 our raw materials, things like that. Her training is a little more formal, I think.
 didn't seem comfortable with our work."
She used to paint."
That's what she said." Leo points to a gray-haired woman in black jeans and a
or-spattered green smock "She watched Barbara over there for a while but they
n't speak at all. I think if we were set up for traditional Western art, she'd have
n better."
And what, worked here?"
I don't hire people. Artists need space and I rent them some. If she'd wanted to
that, I always have room."
And she called herself Sylvy?"
Yep."
And you haven't seen her since."
This town is pretty much shut up during the winter. We see people at the co-op
he new warehouse market up on the hill, and maybe on Saturday night for
cing or a movie. Otherwise, the weather being what it is, we don't bump into
ple."
But if she were still here, wouldn't she be in a motel or an inn?"
Not necessarily. In the summer we get a lot of fisherman up here with the
ists and there's never enough motel space for everyone. Families take in
tors all the time."
Their houses are that big?"
eo doesn't answer. Instead he nods toward an older man who has removed his
ses and is glaring at the two of them.
Sorry for the interruption," Leo says to him, then points Wilkes toward an open
r. "That office," he says. "We can talk in there without disturbing anyone."

The so-called office is barely the size of Wilkes's motel bathroom. Two cha
a somewhat antiquated desktop computer and tower, an unplugged fax mach
layered with dust, and a metal filing cabinet. That's it. There is no desk other t
the table on which the keyboard and monitor sit.

"Not much," Leo says, "but we need some place to keep records. Sorry ab
Wilcox out there. He thinks this should have the ambience of a library. He thi
the quiet..."

"...I understand. You were saying people here take on boarders."

"In the winter we store all our boats, tackle, gear—we pile them into all th
shacks along the lake. It opens up living space in some of the houses and peo
can make a buck or two as makeshift B & B's, usually without the second B. Y
probably saw the shacks."

"In a photo, and I haven't actually seen the lake."

"Easier to spot in the summer. Anyway, we use those shacks for storage, pa
them bright colors. Tourists think they're rustic reminders of older and simp
days. Like your diners."

"What do you mean?"

"Well, you have picture books of diners. I've seen them. Why?"

"Nostalgia, I guess."

"They're ugly. And all those paintings of lighthouses: you see them as par
some cherished American aesthetic. Your great painter, Edward Hopper, it's
fault, you know. He started painting them and suddenly people thought they w
somehow beautiful. Phallic symbolism aside, they're architecturally insignific
and common. Hopper painted them beautifully, but he knew all that. It was
little joke."

"It's not the architecture: it's the—"

"Nostalgia. In Nova Scotia where I come from, we have some beauties. Hop
missed out by not hopping the ferry. But listen, I never argue with people over
they might be customers who want a painting of a shack.

"No one lives in these shacks during the winter, right?"

"No one is supposed to. We have some homeless who use them as shelter."

"Manitok said some are heated."

"A couple of them have cookstoves. Of course one of them burned down a
winters back so we're better off leaving them unwinterized. Less of a temptatic

"And these homeless?"

A small stove can keep someone alive, and at the very least it's shelter from the
 id. One of our mounties patrols the shore. If he finds anybody trying to live in
 m he generally gets them up to the med center or, if the person seems all right,
 lock-up. Last winter we didn't lose anybody. That was rare."
You mean no one died?"
Yes. Usually somebody'll crawl in there either drunk or with the means for
ting drunk. It's odd. They say you can't freeze to death in your sleep, that your
ly will shake you awake. But when you're drunk, it doesn't work that way. That's
y we need the Mounties to check."
The two American cops."
We like mounties and they don't seem to mind the name. I doubt if your wife
uld be living in one, not with all the spare rooms in the off season, but if you
re to see smoke coming out of some shack, it might be worth a look."
When you saw her, this Sylvy, how did she seem?"
Not like a tourist. You know when you're in a strange place you always seem a
 le lost, not knowing where things are or how to get things done. She never struck
 that way. She seemed to be at home, comfortable."
Was she depressed?"
Am I? Are you? It's not like on TV where there's sad music playing in the
 kground so you know. She didn't seem it, for what it's worth. Pensive, maybe.
 rious."
And you said she was alone?"
I don't think I said that, but she was."
Vilkes isn't entirely sure why he asked that last question, but Leo's claim that
 didn't look like a tourist bothers him. What if she really were traipsing about
h some secretly acquired lover? What if the plane crash had interrupted more
 n a flight to Savannah? Maybe the original plan was to get the kids to Charlotte
 complete the first leg of the journey, then blend into the crowd a bit and escape,
 ving her sons to wait for their father who would be arriving soon anyway. But
 river landing and the rescue: nobody could have anticipated that little glitch. In
 anic she took the first flight anywhere. Toronto? Sure. Why not? Passport?
 ht here. I was going to use it to fly to Spain with my lover but...
 he scenario disintegrates around him: Keira wouldn't do that. Then again, the
 ira he knew wouldn't become someone named Sylvy, and he doesn't know what
 vy might be capable of. One thing he would bet on: Keira Wilkes, in whatever
 sformation, would be unable to trade all her accustomed creature comforts for

some utility shed, let alone a hovel open to the weather. And to be shacked up v
someone in an actual shack, well aside from the nice irony of the term, that i
her. Still, if the thought of surveying those shacks had been a mere vagary bef
it has now assumed greater significance.

He thanks Leo for his time and reenters the gallery. Near the front door, c
white pedestal sit a number of small pieces. Several of them resemble the st
man in Brett's project.

"I know what this is," he says, "but I forgot the name."

"*Inuksuit*," Leo says. "Man of stone. *Inukshuk* is the more pop
pronunciation."

"Stone man," Wilkes says. He looks at the tag. $50.

"Canadian?"

"If it's cash, we don't much care."

"My older boy might like this. I'll come back," he says.

And he intends to until he steps outside into a stunning rush of cold that insta
propels his mind into survival mode, and though Manitok's store is merely
doors away, all thoughts of tiny sculptures and mementos and wilderness wise r
vanish. He takes a few more breaths—they come more easily—and decides h
dressed properly, that a healthy adult can survive the rigors of what is in fact
more than a little village. He leaves Manitok to her cartons and invoices and
off to explore on his own.

lake itself is just another snowfield, albeit smoother, and the shacks are in no
 quaint or picturesque. The first one he sees is missing a door; the next
esses one but the knob is apparently elsewhere, replaced by a simple gravity
 one might find on a picket fence gate, a latch so misaligned and rusted that it
onger serves any function whatsoever. On a metal eyelet above it hangs a
ock, already snapped shut, protecting nothing but itself from theft. In the dim
ior a boat maybe ten feet long with a squared off prow has been squeezed in
 mere inches to spare. He can't imagine what kind of calisthenics it took to
euver that thing through the door, but now that it's in, it doubles as the storage
: rod and reel combinations, several metal boxes undoubtedly filled with lures
hooks, a small wooden table with the point of a serrated knife stuck into it like
nveiled threat, some paddles leaning in a corner, a few life vests and seat
ions, a pamphlet on fishing in Nunavut. This is all proof that notwithstanding
January climate, the lake can exist in a liquid state, fish can swim in it, and
ists can go out on it.
cked to the wall near the door is a 2008 calendar (a promotional gift from a
ware store somewhere in Quebec), a generic exposition of photos that bear
 resemblance to Baker Lake. Beneath it a pair of boots is laid neatly next to an
sized mahogany cabinet that runs the remainder of the length of the shorter
. He slides open the top drawer—empty. The one beneath it contains an
lded red corduroy shirt and a pair of thick gray socks, a toothbrush in a plastic
, two ballpoint pens, and a tack hammer. In the other drawers he finds some
logues and fishing magazines—outdated, ratty, and forgotten. He feels like an
loper.
the next shack—all windows and door intact—there's a bunk bed without
resses, a set of horseshoes, some utensils in a clear plastic bag, and a team
er of the Montreal Alouettes from 2002. They appear to be a football team;
es has never heard of them.
d there's a stove, a black box the size of a small freezer, its pipe vented roughly
ugh the wall. Some ash lies about the metal base, but when Wilkes looks for a
d pile, he finds none. No surprise: he hasn't seen a tree since he left Saskatoon.
, he thinks, or kerosene, or pellets maybe. He makes a cursory search, but he
 staying—as cold as he is, he doesn't need a fire.

Outside again he scans the lake and sees, here and there, outlines of hu
figures, stationary and small. Manitok mentioned ice fishing: it's possible tha
figures in the distance are doing just that, that one or more of them could be u
one of these hovels as a home base, as their own home base. He'll have to be ca
not to look like a thief in case one of them has a rifle and shoots him as a trespa

The footing is slow, a mixture of loose sand and talc-dry snow, and fatig
overtaking him. There's a limit to how much of this he can do, but he doesn't k
what that limit is and how the cold affects it. The next three shacks contain no
no stove, no burner, no heat source of any kind, just unclassifiable implem
devices, junk, the stuff of spring-cleaning refuse collections. One of them cont
only a card table upon which sits a crucifix on a stand, alongside a photo of a yo
Inuit—he couldn't be more than twenty—and some artificial flowers. The dis
reminds Wilkes of those roadside memorials that seem to arise spontaneous
accident sites. It's possible that some local fisherman took to the waters
morning and, as sometimes happened in the seas off New England, never retur
Perhaps the family came by and hauled away the belongings, and other resid
left these objects out of respect, or superstition. Perhaps the soul (Manitok ag
to the use of the word) of that dead fisherman pervades the building, shur
others away. Wilkes isn't ready to accede to any of that hocus-pocus, but he do
stay inside very long either. He remembers Leo's comments about dead bc
having been found in these places, and he doesn't want to become one or disc
one.

"A few more," he says aloud, surprised at how difficult it is to form word
how the cold prevents his mouth from working that well. He approaches ano
sloppily painted a dazzling turquoise one might associate with the tropics.
much taste, he says, but at least a sense of humor. He's about to turn away v
he sees smoke rising from a metal pipe above the roofline, and there's an ac
doorknob on an actual door that seems shut up tight. He turns toward the
again. Can the ice fishermen see him? Is this their shelter? Do they have rifles
telescopic sights trained on him?

He hears a voice inside—then another—neither of them recognizable. B
there are two persons inside, there could be three. Or more. Maybe a recogniz
one that hasn't yet spoken. In an instant the fear of never finding his wife becc
the fear of finding her after all—of finding her here with somebody—or of fin
her dead. He considers returning to the hamlet and rousting that American cc
things were to go sideways here, a man with a gun might be a resource.

he smoke continues to belch sporadically from the stack on the leeward side,
stly gray, sometimes black, dry and wet fuel mixed together. He rests his
tened hand on the doorknob. He has enough mobility to turn it, but he backs
 In the real world he would knock, but he has left the real world somewhere in
katoon, or maybe long before that.
e cups his hands around his mouth and shouts hello, but the thick mittens seem
bsorb the words and they come out muffled. He hears movement, something
tering. He remembers the knife stuck in the table of that first building and
gines someone bursting through this door and dragging a serrated edge across
throat, leaving a blotch of red snow for the so-called mounties to find. He backs
y and considers ways to retract his greeting, but the door opens and a young
 in a thick tan sweater and jeans faces him, a green knit cap pulled down to his
k eyebrows. Behind him a haze softens the interior.
You looking for Deidre?"
'm—no—I'm looking for a woman named Keira Wilkes."
Who the fuck is that?"
Sylvy?"
Make up your mind. Who you looking for?"
he young man pulls the hood of his sweater up over his cap as the out of doors
vs in. He uses both hands to do so: he is not holding a weapon. But even so,
 big and muscular and easily capable of kicking Wilkes's ass back to town. A
fe with a serrated edge would be mere window dressing.
Her real name is Keira Wilkes but sometimes she uses Sylvy."
Why?"
Nickname. Someone said she might be hiding in one of these...cabins."
he youth stares at him, shakes his head, blocks the doorway with his bulk.
You know," he drawls, "if you're looking for Deidre, if her old man sent you,
 say so. Ain't no fucking deal."
Wilkes tries to look past him and a whiff of something catches his senses. Pot.
 don't know anyone named Deidre," Wilkes says. "Can I show you a picture of
woman I'm looking for?"
he young man shrugs, glances at the sky. The daylight is fading and he and the
g inside probably want to finish their weed and get out.
f I could just come in out of the cold for a second, dig out that picture?"

The young man doesn't move and Wilkes struggles through layers of clothing
produce it, aware that even a few seconds of exposure could cost him a finger
two.

"Put your mittens on," the young man says, dismissing the photo with a qu
glance. "Ain't seen her."

Wilkes examines him more closely. He has no beard, no stubble. He looks bar
old enough to shave. He isn't a young man: he's a boy.

"You're sure? I mean the light here—"

"I can see clear enough. I ain't seen her."

"What about—anyone else in there?"

"Who says there's anyone else in here?"

"I'm not trying to make trouble. I don't care about the pot. I just want to know
"

"What pot?"

"The weed, whatever you want to call it. It doesn't matter."

"I told you, we ain't seen her."

"You said *you* didn't see her. What about your—company?" Wilkes is push
more, emboldened by the youthfulness of his adversary, hoping for so
hesitancy. He doesn't get it.

"Look, if Deidre's father wants—"

A girl's voice interrupts him. "Henry, let him come in."

The boy steps aside immediately and Wilkes sees a girl's face, pretty v
features and coloring like Manitok's but with shoulder-length hair dyed the ora
side of red and razor-lined bangs that cover most of her forehead. Without the d
job she might be a starlet from the fifties or sixties. She's Inuit. Until then he di
realize that the boy is not, that he's white, or Anglo, or whatever designation
minority carries. Wilkes doesn't know if a mixed couple like this is an affron
the community—it still happens in the United States—or if adults here are
adults everywhere: they just didn't want their kids sneaking off to have sex. A
this pretty young girl, wrapped in a patchwork blanket and more than lik
wearing nothing under it, if she were Wilkes's daughter he'd probably want to w
that serrated knife across this guy's throat or just cut his balls off. But she's
and though Wilkes may be a father, he's not her father.

"I'm Deidre," the girl says. "Henry here didn't introduce himself."

he pokes her boyfriend, he can't possibly feel it through the layers, and almost racts a smile from him. He shrugs while she glances at the photo, then returns Wilkes, holds up the joint.

Want some?"

No, thanks."

We won't tell."

What if I'm a cop?"

I saw you in the co-op before bullshitting with Manitok. If she trusts you, I trust . Hit?"

Wilkes laughs.

No. Tell me about Keira—or Sylvy."

Show me the picture again."

Ie does. Deidre laughs.

So different. Her hair is shorter now and she was wearing glasses."

You saw her?"

I talked to her."

When?"

Couple days ago, down here by the lake."

Deidre waves Henry over to sit by her, to share the joint. She's affable and rming, and she deserves better than Henry. Wilkes is pretty sure she'll figure t out eventually.

Was she living in one of these places?"

I don't know—I didn't ask. I thought maybe she was, but nobody pays attention hat kind of thing around here."

What kind of thing?"

People hanging out, getting away. I thought maybe she was a criminal or aped from prison. Is that why you're looking for her? Are you a cop?"

I might as well be. That's what everyone thinks. I'm her husband."

Whoa," Henry says, his voice gravelly from an afternoon, or many afternoons, smoking. "How bad did you beat her to make her come up here?"

Deidre pokes him again, this time it's more of a jab.

Don't be an asshole, Henry."

It's a fair question," Wilkes says. "But I never hit her. I don't know why she's e."

He condenses the story of the flight, the rescue, the abandonment. Even up h
everyone has heard of the crash on the river—the miracle—but Henry i
convinced that this stranger was part of it.

"It's famous news," the boy says. "Maybe you just added yourself to it. Mayb
was in the twin towers when they were attacked and I escaped. How are you go
to prove I wasn't?"

"You aren't old enough."

"Maybe I went to work with my father that day, just like you had to work at
last minute. See, anyone can make up a story."

"We have two children."

"So?"

"So explain to me why she would leave them with a dangerous man like
Why wouldn't she take them along?"

"Because she had to save herself first. Then, maybe in time, she'd be able
send—"

"Stop, Henry." Deidre's tone is gentle, cajoling. "This man's not lying. He di
hit her and she was on that plane, she and her kids. I told you that's not why
left."

Henry backs off. They have all wound up, by very gradual steps, nearer the h
from the cast-iron stove. Deidre pulls the blanket tighter.

"Does it bother you that we're smoking?"

"Pot's not illegal up here," Henry says quickly, though he makes no move tow
lighting another joint. "I ain't selling, or growing."

Wilkes barely hears him. "She told you why she left?"

"We talked," the girl says. "She said it was like having a daughter—or a sist

"She has a sister."

"But they don't get along and she lives far away."

"That's true," Wilkes says with some surprise. It was Keira then unburden
herself to this—kid. "You said she told you why she left?"

"She said she wanted to—she wanted peace."

"You mean, like world peace?"

Henry, surly but honest, corrects him.

"She wanted to die in peace," he says.

Deidre glares at him. "Damn it, Henry!"

That's what you told me," the boy says. He doesn't like being doubted and sh
away a little, opens the stove door, pokes around inside with what looks like a l

wdriver before slamming it shut. The afternoon has not gone well for him, and
ex that was probably scheduled for just about now? That wasn't happening.

Henry," Wilkes says. "Did Keira say that?"

he boy stares down at the floor. "I ain't saying nothin' more. Deidre's the one
talked to her."

nry's decision to remain silent doesn't matter, but he can't afford to have
Ire do the same.

ou two have plans for today, right? Well I do too. And one of them is to find
what my wife told you so that maybe I can find her and bring her home. Now
y plans interfere with yours, then we'll just sit out here until it gets dark and
kids have to go home. No rush. I don't have a schedule. But if you just tell me
ything that happened with my wife, I'll leave you alone."

nry remains shut down; Deidre doesn't.

eople say all kinds of stupid things," she says, "especially up here in the winter.
darkness gets to you after a while."

's not dark yet. Did she really say she wanted to die in peace?"

es. I'm only telling you what she said. I just figured she had some kind of
y bad cancer and didn't want to face all the chemo. I had an aunt—"

he doesn't have cancer."

o maybe not cancer? Some other disease?"

o other disease either." His voice crackles as if frozen itself, the tone
tening. Even the hulking Henry seems less formidable. "I'm sorry," he adds
kly, afraid he might lose Deidre too. "I don't mean to yell. It's just that I know
vas fine. What else did she say?"

alked about her kids," Deidre says. "About her home, about you."

Vhat about me?"

aid it wasn't your fault, wasn't anybody's fault. She just wanted, you know....

d her that she was too young for that kind of talk—she's like the same age as
nother—but what could I do?"

nry drapes a bulky arm over Deidre's shoulders and breaks his silence.

ike in that song, I guess, everyone dies alone."

don't know what song you're talking about, but you're born alone, too." Wilkes
, angry at bullshit passing for profundity. "It's the time between you're
osed to share with others."

idre lowers her eyes. She gets it if her boyfriend doesn't.

"He just meant—you know—we don't want to argue with you," she say
just—if she wasn't sick then, geez, I don't know."

"And she told you here? In this—hut?"

"Another one up the beach."

"And she's not there anymore?"

"I checked before. I was afraid—you know—around here—anyway, th
nobody there."

"Did she seem depressed? Suicidal?"

"She was funny. I mean, sort of joking about the cold, the town itself, even a
dying."

"Did she joke about me? Her kids?"

"She didn't want to leave the kids, but it was the only thing she could do to
them."

"Save them from what?"

"From her."

Wilkes's mind is racing. With daylight fading he can't check every structure
contact every family with room to take on a boarder. But if Keira is here
threatening suicide, he can't be wasting his breath talking to these two.

"I can pay you," he says. "Both of you. Will you help me find her? If we
up—"

"Almost dark," Henry interrupts, "and me and Deidre, you know, we got s
things to take care of."

"If you help me," Wilkes says, "you can have my motel room to take ca
those things. It's gotta be better than freezing your asses off in here."

Henry shakes his head. "We'd never get past the front desk. Besides, this is
of our place."

"Where anybody can just walk in on you?"

"No one ever did until today."

The surliness returns. Of course it does. Henry has to reestablish his lost vi
if he hopes to have sex with Deidre. And though she looks embarrassed by it
reaches up and touches the boy's elbow—a show of unity perhaps, or mayb
indication that she is through arguing her own side and has come around to his
Wall Street or in the Arctic, Wilkes knows when a conversation is over.

"What shack was it, where my wife was?"

"Down the beach. It has an olive green door. But I told you, I checked."

"I'll have to take a look."

Vait," she says, and it appears she has something important to add but checks elf. "You're new here. When the sun goes down the temperature can drop fast. need to be out of the cold."

'hat's it?"

e nods.

'hanks," he says, his lip curling just enough to let it show, "for the information." ie door bounces shut behind him in the freshening late-afternoon breeze and a moment he stops and faces the frozen expanse of the lake. The flurries have ped and he can discern mountains on the other side of some range he has never d of, bearing some polysyllabic Inuit name he will never learn nor, if he does i it, will never remember. Closer by a single-engine plane lifts its passengers the tundra, headed off for what has suddenly become tropical locales— catoon, Winnipeg. If he wanted to, right then and there, he could traverse the and wind up, two miles later, at that airfield, waiting in the one-room terminal he next flight out. There is nothing valuable in his hotel room, and they have credit card imprint. They can keep his clothes, give them to charity, maybe them in one of those shacks so nice young people like Henry and Deidre can hem on when they aren't fucking or getting high.

two-mile walk to the airfield as night falls: that would make him the cautionary of Baker Lake for the next decade at least. Besides, he can see the shack with olive green door, inasmuch as the twilight allows for color. He has no hope of ing anyone or anything: Deidre says it's empty and she, unlike her boyfriend, ns to have no ulterior motives. He approaches the place anyway and finds the is ajar, wedged open with an irregularly shaped brown rock. A cold stove sits ie corner, next to a cot and across from a few stools and a small table. The s are graffiti-covered with gingerbread men or teddy bears, as if a child has left unattended with a box of sidewalk chalk and told to draw *Inuksuit* ywhere. Keira has drawn them, he's sure of it, but done it without a scintilla of sm. No initials, no name, nothing to prove that these makeshift murals nged to a runaway from the United States, from Connecticut, from his house, i his marriage. Her escape is not some cry for help. It's a cry to be left alone. n the return to town, he passes the turquoise shack again, deliberately aining far enough away so as not to eavesdrop on its inhabitants. They too want e left alone. He has no reason to disturb them.

lat girl, Deidre, talk to her alone."

McNally doesn't have much long-distance advice beyond that, and he's not ticularly surprised at the name change, despite Wilkes's contention that it makes seem like a criminal. Irrelevant, McNally claims. Just appearances.

Incidentally," the PI says, "I had some time to kill so I spoke with your in-laws."

Why? I really don't want them involved."

This is where I'd put a smiley face if I were emailing you. She's their daughter. ey're watching your kids. They're involved."

I mean I don't want them bothered."

By a crude detective, I got that. I was polite and I didn't ask them half the things ranted to, but eventually, when you rehire me, I will. Is that going to be a blem?"

I don't know what you mean. Did they do something wrong?"

Illegal? I doubt it. You know they haven't lived in this area all their lives."

Keira said she grew up in Haddam or Hamden. I don't know, she doesn't talk ut it much. I always had the feeling she—they—struggled."

Struggle isn't in the Easons' dictionary. Neither is communicative. But there's nething there, I know it."

What did you say to them?"

That I was interested in her childhood, that sometimes adults get overwhelmed try to return to a simpler time. Just psychobabble of course, saw it on TV, but ought I'd give it a shot."

Why is that psychobabble? Do you believe anything you can't actually see?"

I am a Catholic, thank you very much, but to answer your question: no. Tell you at I do believe, though, they're hiding something."

Something relevant?"

Wish I knew. Permission to speak to them more, sir?"

I'd prefer you didn't."

I'll take that under advisement. Officer Staubley called me too."

Since when do cops call you?"

I guess when they don't want to drive an hour into the neighboring state. She ed if I was working the case."

Can she do that?"

"She can ask whatever she wants. I don't have to answer except in court, an
don't think she had a subpoena in mind. Sometimes cops ask you things you do
have to answer just so you know they're wondering about you."

"Why?"

"She did remind me that if I were deliberately breaking the law in order to serv
my client, I was liable to arrest and prosecution. I laughed."

"That's funny?"

"It's stupid. Of course I know that. Statements like that don't bother me so mu
as piss me off. I'm not withholding evidence. They know as much as I do. Anyw
I'm keeping busy. So is that going to be all right with you, you know, if I alien
everyone you've ever known?"

"I hope that's an exaggeration."

"Your kids are off limits. Everyone else, though—"

"Do what you have to do."

"So I'm working again?"

"For me? Yes."

"I'll start billing at midnight, that makes the paperwork easier. Once you s
breaking the day into twenty-four units—"

"Central Time."

McNally laughs. "Touché."

"One more thing," Wilkes says. "In your discoveries, have you found any
named Emily, Emile, anything beginning with EM?"

"My wife has an Uncle Emil. Do you think he has something to do with this
there something you're not telling me? Another garage girlfriend?"

"Just—no, nothing. If you do come across a name like that, could you let
know?"

"Sure, but any other two-letter combos are going to cost you extra, unless
tell me why."

"It's nothing, really."

"I doubt that," McNally says, "but it's your call."

Wilkes hangs up, gives himself a moment to settle, then calls home and
again. Nothing to report, he says, no trace. No hint. He'll stay on it. The boys so
like the boys. If they're living in constant anxiety, their voices don't reveal
They've had dinner, subs from some deli in White Plains, and now they're ho
again with school looming.

miss you both," he says, then fearful that they won't respond in kind, launches
a fuller description of Baker Lake. But the narration lacks the excitement of a
paging polar bear or a marauding wolf pack, and he's too tired to concoct such
ons. In truth he could have frozen to death that very afternoon, but even the
t extreme cold lacks the cachet of marauding wild animals. He promises them
 be home by the weekend.
; for his in-laws, he has always chalked up that seeming reticence to their liking
a more than him. He can hardly hold that against them. But if McNally is on
omething, let him have at it.
 falls asleep trying to map out the following day, and continually awakens to
 the schedule. In the utter blackness of early morning, feeling unrefreshed and
gy, he skips the complimentary quonset breakfast, opting instead for coffee at
general store where Manitok is already busy with the morning crowd. He grabs
p and fills it like a regular, then glances at a copy of a Nunavut News that
ably arrived on the plane with him.
hate to bother you so early," he says when he catches Manitok taking a breath,
 when you get a minute."
lways have a minute. Sorry about yesterday. I'm supposed to log in
chandise when it arrives, get it on the shelves. Then you didn't come back—."
veryone has to sell," he says, seizing on the tenuous connection between their
 "I just explored a little. Do you know a girl named Deidre?"
know Deidre Laird," she says. "Don't know any others."
oung girl, maybe seventeen, eighteen, freaky hair, has a boyfriend?"
he Deidre I know has a lot of boyfriends," she says. "Good kid, could be a
 more choosy. What about her?"
found her yesterday not being choosy with some Henry character."
nson. Big white kid. They're a couple sometimes, I think mainly when he gets
 dope. Were they naked when you found them?"
m afraid I may have interrupted the clothing removal process."
ood. Either you prevented a death by exposure or an unwanted pregnancy. I'm
ure they use protection."
hope they did, 'cause I'm sure they got down to business after I left. Do you
v where I can find her? I think she would have told me more about Keira if
vere alone."
old you? She met your wife?"
o she says. Can I trust her?"

"Deidre has a lot to learn but she's pretty honest. There's school today," Man
says, glancing at the clock, "or will be in an hour or so. I can call over there. I k
the secretary."

"And maybe get her out of class for a few minutes? She claims she h
conversation with my wife, a long philosophical discussion of life and dea
don't get it, but I don't think she made it up."

"She does get around. I don't want to call the school until eight. Have s
breakfast," she says.

Wilkes, suddenly hungry, takes a sugared doughnut from the case. Since he
already finished the newspaper, he peruses a bulletin board by the entra
surprised by how much the notifications and announcements resemble thos
home: garage sale, reading group, free lecture on finances. The trappings of a s
community are the same everywhere.

He returns to his hotel room and passes the thermometer flashing negative th
five degrees Celsius; he doesn't wait for the Fahrenheit conversion. Does it ma
In his room he showers and shaves and prepares as he would for a day at Tol
& Byrne. Except he's not at Tolliver & Byrne, and he's traded his tailored gray
for thermal gear big enough to fit another inside with him. It would
disingenuous to complain. All those dual layers of wool and polyester are kee
his internal organs from shutting down.

"Ten minutes," Manitok yells when Wilkes returns. "Deidre will be in the
office."

He nods and tosses five American dollars into the plate for two coffees a
doughnut. It's probably too much but he doesn't want to dicker with conver
rates. Manitok points him in the right direction and he winds up back at the co
where, this time, he follows the signs for Baker Lake Secondary School and
Deidre sitting on a long bench seemingly designated for miscreants.
recognizes him.

"I suppose I'm in trouble for yesterday?"

"Why would you be?"

"I mean for the dope."

"If he was a dope, you shouldn't have been with him."

Deidre nods. "If Henry isn't here to defend himself, it's not fair for you to
about him."

"Sorry about that. Look, I'm not trying to get anyone in trouble. I just tho
that, maybe yesterday with your boyfriend around—"

"He's not my boyfriend."

"Then with Henry around, I thought you were less than forthcoming."

"What does that mean?"

"It means you could have told me more—about my wife."

The girl looks down at her lap and unnecessarily smoothes her suffocatingly tight jeans.

"So is there?" he asks. "Is there more?"

"I think she might have been drinking."

"Are you sure?"

"No, but she seemed unsteady, spacey. Drunk or on meds."

"So it makes sense you thought she had cancer. And she was living in one of these shacks?"

"She was in one. I don't think she was living there. When I saw her the first time—"

"You saw her more than once?"

"Henry and I, we use those places a lot. All the kids do. Not just for dope. We, you know, use them."

"I get it. We used to use our cars. Nobody complains?"

"We clean up after ourselves. The cops leave us alone and we don't get hurt or mess around with any hard drugs. I don't even drink."

"Just recreational drugs then, and the sex?"

Deidre pulls back. "Did you come here to lecture me or to talk about your wife, because I got a lecture going on right down the hall that I'm missing."

"I'm not lecturing. I have kids, too."

"So? Lots of adults have kids. It doesn't stop them from fucking up."

He nods. She's right. He's lecturing.

"I'm not here to criticize. God knows in my situation—"

"What exactly do you want to know, Mr. Wilkes?"

"Whatever you can tell me."

"I told you, I think she'd been drinking. She was really talkative, said she liked here, told me she was from America but had no more ties there and wanted to start over while she still had time left."

"Start over? Yesterday you said she came here to die."

"I told you, she didn't always make sense. She was all wrapped up in some oversized coat that she must have picked up at the second-hand store."

The thought of Keira wearing hand-me-downs is ludicrous, almost as ludicr
as talking about still having some time left.

"That doesn't sound like my wife."

"The picture matches. She made up some story about her luggage getting l
but I knew she was, you know, making it up."

"Lying."

"Yeah."

Even though Deidre makes almost no eye contact, Wilkes believes her. S
embarrassed more than deceitful, sitting here as she is, informing a husband
his wife has traded a hospitable existence for a life of discomfort and want.

"What else did she say?"

"About what?"

"Anything. Why she was here and not somewhere else?"

"I told you. She wanted a fresh start. She wanted to die in peace. Nothing m
any sense."

"But having no ties. Did she explain that?"

Deidre presses down harder on the tops of her thighs, as if those stubb
invisible wrinkles just won't stop reappearing. Beyond a small partition Wi
hears voices, some discussion about a delivery that has or has not been made,
then a woman peeks around the corner.

"Everything all right, Deidre?" she asks, then glances at Wilkes. He feels li
child molester and moves away slightly.

"We're just talking," he says, as if that were some sort of defense. "Jacquel
Manitok at the store, I promised her I'd just be a few minutes."

The woman nods, if not with approval at least with less suspicion. Man
carries some credibility, a counterbalance for Wilkes's lack of same.

"Don't keep her out of class too long," the woman says. "Deidre needs all
learning she can get."

She winks at the young girl—it's all part of their threadbare but harmless l
act—and walks away.

"I'm a good student," Deidre says. "Mrs. Cole likes to give everyone shit."

"I think she was looking out for you."

"No need. You asked about her having no ties, right. Remember what I sa
think she was, you know—"

"Drunk, yeah."

She said her family had been killed in a plane crash and—um—she had to go
neplace where she wouldn't be reminded of it. She said you can't run from
gedy, it always comes back."
But the plane—"
I guess that part wasn't true, I mean what you said yesterday. There was a plane
sh and all, but no one died. I thought maybe a few—"
Everyone survived, including her kids."
Deidre looks hurt.
So she lied to me. I guess I should have been more, what's that word,
thcoming?"
No, she should have been more forthcoming. You should have been, you were
e. You can't automatically believe someone is going to lie to you. Just one more
ng. Did she mention a man named Emile or Emil or anything like that?"
Not that I remember."
's obvious Deidre feels bad about Keira's lie. It's funny, Wilkes thinks, the girl
vise enough to know that someone like Henry would bullshit her, probably tell
' he loved her to get inside those jeans; and maybe she'd lie in return, telling him
v much she enjoyed sex with some asshole because getting high was worth it.
t she probably isn't inured to lying in the adult world, to the insidious and
vasive quality of it. Politicians lie to their constituents; patients lie to their
tors; defendants lie to their attorneys; hell, diners lie to their waiters...
verything all right sir?
Oh, excellent....
nd yes, financial advisors lie to their clients, sugarcoat things anyway. So
est and honorable Keira Wilkes has offered Deidre a vision of that adult world,
ere lies no longer revolve around who smoked what and where, or who flirted
h someone else's boyfriend. Now the lies transcend the mundane and evolve
faithlessness and betrayal, life and death. They disrupt worlds, unalterably
nge them, create new ones that bear no relation to reality except in the mind of
creator. Deidre may feel hurt, but she owes Wilkes no apology.
You couldn't have known," he says. "Is there anything else?"
The second time I talked to her she said this wasn't the right place. She wanted
now what other towns were around here. I think she knew there weren't any.
s is it. There are no suburbs of Baker Lake. No neighboring communities."
Did she mention any other place, even in passing?"
No, but I got the impression she wanted to be farther away."

"From where?"
"From, you know, whatever it was that—"
"From me."
"I didn't know there even was a you."
"I know. Do you know anything about Repulse Bay?"
"I was there last summer," she said. "Went with my folks. It's beautiful August."
Wilkes smiles. "Everything around here is beautiful in August. Is anyth beautiful in February?"
She returns the smile. Tentative, still hesitant to open up. "What do you think
"Could she have gone there?"
"Of course," Deidre says, still looking down. "If that's what she calls 'the n town over,' then maybe that's where she is. But then what?"
"You mean if she's left there too?"
"No," she said, looking at him closely. "I mean what if she is there? What you do?"
It's Leo's question again. This time he's almost prepared.
"I guess we'll have to talk about it."
Deidre nods. The answer satisfies nobody. "I should go back to class. Okay?
"Sure," he says, trying to sound a little more positive, grateful. He still thi there's more, but whatever it is, Deidre has chosen not to share it. "I appreci your help."
"Wasn't much help."
"Your insights then."
She turns to walk away, then stops.
"You seem like a decent guy, and I really don't know what's going on with two of you. If I thought you were beating her—"
"I never would."
"You could be just saying that, how would I know? But you seem like a dec guy."
He waits. There's more.
"Your wife, the second time, when she talked about leaving. She was someone."
"With? Like you were with Henry?"
"I don't know, but she wasn't alone."
"Who was it?"

e shakes her head.

n old man, older than you. I didn't know him."

thought everyone knew everyone."

didn't know this guy. I've seen him around here but he isn't from Baker."

ey stand facing each other, five, maybe six feet apart. Neither says anything
the silence is interrupted by a phone in the nearby office and a secretary's
e screeching from behind a partition, "Deidre, you're supposed to be back in
."

e girl shrugs, her final apology, then shuffles back down the corridor, turning
.

he old guy, he might be from up in Repulse," she says, then turns the corner
disappears.

long as Wilkes continues to be gainfully employed by Tolliver & Byrne, and
long as Byrne himself retains a modicum of guilt for keeping the Wilkeses
arated that day, money is not an issue. But when Wilkes gives Byrne himself a
rtesy call to advise just how much it will cost to "hitch a ride" to Repulse Bay,
conversation becomes decidedly less informal. For the first time words like
eipt and *authenticate* enter the discussion. Byrne won't deny Wilkes anything—
lt is a wonderful motivator—but Wall Street continues to endure angry public
itiny, and this is not the time for sloppy accounting practices. Dubious travel
enses in some miscellaneous account to sanction a semi-clandestine search for
issing woman would be a PR disaster for a company that has so far been above
fray. He'll handle it, Byrne says, but he needs documentation.

/ilkes agrees without protest. He himself knows that, to an outsider, this search
ears to be little more than a perverse scavenger hunt with little hope of success,
the conversations with Deidre Laird, conversations whose particulars he
oses not to share with the New York office, have given him hope and
anized his resolve. He leaves Byrne with a raft of numbers and dates, a
ulous promise to keep costs down, and an offer to pay his own way if T&B no
ger feels able to meet his needs. Wilkes is gambling on Byrne's reluctance to
a top performer, but both men have been around long enough to understand
no one on Wall Street, or any other street, is irreplaceable.

xcept maybe Manitok in Baker Lake.

/hen Wilkes tells her he needs to get to Repulse Bay, she rummages through a
ver behind a counter and pulls out a business card. Imprinted on it is a neatly
led paper airplane with a name above its pointy fuselage: Curt Brantley.
lerneath it, in a gaudy fuchsia, are the words "Traversing Nunavut since before
e was one."

le could use a better slogan," Wilkes says. "Do you know him?"

le comes in once in a while. He's a little quirky, but as long as you do what he
you, no problem."

ne can't give away the card, she has only the one, so Wilkes takes down the
rmation while she tells him to wait. She'll make a call.

You're in luck," she says a moment later. "He's at the Polaris. He'll be the only
there wearing a tie. You'll pick him out."

The Polaris. That's a bar?"

"They have food, too."

"It's a little early to be drinking."

"Pointing that out to Curt isn't going to get you to Repulse Bay, at least not v
him."

"Do I want to fly with a drunk pilot?"

"He keeps flying and landing. Go meet him. Then decide."

Manitok is right. Curt Brantley is the only man with a tie, a regimental stripe
contrasts nicely with a pale yellow shirt and doesn't look terribly out of place v
his jeans. Manitok said quirky. She could have said preppy, but she also could h
mentioned that he was black, a fact that might have made the identification proc
that much easier. Brantley sits at a large round table with two other men an
woman, all white, all less formally dressed than he. They do not appear to b
foursome of rugged adventurers sharing raucous stories; instead they look like f
investment analysts discussing margins and futures on casual Friday in sc
weirdly rustic lower Manhattan boardroom.

"Excuse me," Wilkes says, approaching the table, "Mr. Brantley? The pilot?

"Not right now he ain't," a woman says, her eyes watery, her face flushed v
the tinge of too much alcohol too early in the day. The others laugh, but
Brantley.

"I could still fly through a barn and not scrape a wing," he says. "Who want
try me?"

"By the time we got the barn built, we'd all be sober," the woman says, t
smiles at Wilkes. "That's him all right, Brantley the pilot."

"I was over at the store talking to Manitok—" Wilkes begins, and waits.

Nobody seems impressed by the name drop.

"Anyway," he continues, "she said you might be able to fly me to Repulse B
Again no one responds, as if they're all in on some joke.

A few seconds pass, the only sound a muffled radio playing in the kitchen.

"Look," Wilkes says, "when you're free. I don't want to interrupt you. I'll b
the bar."

Brantley stops him. "Too early to drink alone. Who the hell are you?"

"Martin Wilkes. I'm from the states."

"Well, Martin Wilkes," Brantley says with a grin. "I think we all knew wh
you were from, eh? Whyn't you join us, Martin Wilkes from the states? We w
hold your heritage against you."

You sure you want him to join us?" the woman says to Brantley. "He won't
nt to fly with you after he hears all your crazy-ass stories."
Wilkes grasps the dynamic of the group immediately and knows that, even
ugh he's the outsider, he's better off near them than watching from a distance.
 drags an empty chair to the table.
Annie here tends to exaggerate 'cause she's too chicken-shit to fly and too smart
fly with anyone else, ain't that right sweetie?"
Maybe the chicken-shit part."
he raises a glass to her own cowardice.
Repulsive Bay," Brantley says. "Jesus, mind telling me why you want to go to
t place?"
Actually, I'm not sure."
It's a woman," another man says, the oldest of the group though he can't be
ch past fifty. "Take my advice, stay down south here. The surroundings are
ttier. The ladies too." He smiles and nods toward the woman, who feigns
barrassment.
Yeah, stay where it's warm" the youngest man says, tipping back the brim of a
e and orange baseball cap bearing some NHL logo Wilkes doesn't recognize.
That true?" Brantley repeats. "You chasing a woman?"
I don't want to seem unfriendly, but it's kind of a private matter."
Brantley scans the table, then stands and leans on his hands.
You folks give me a minute while I see what's troubling this Yank who's buying
 next round," Brantley says.
here's a forced cheer from the table.
Don't worry, Martin Wilkes from the states," the pilot says, shambling toward
 bar with Wilkes in tow. "They accept credit cards here. Now come on, what
ms to be the private matter?"
It might take more than a minute."
Give me the short version," Brantley says, "'cause here's the thing. I'm flying
se three science types up to Resolute tomorrow where they'll be until the
stice. Repulse ain't exactly on the way, but I can drop you, pick you up in a few
's."
I was hoping to go tonight."
Tonight? Then your condensed story'd better be especially good and especially
densed."

Wilkes begins with the Hudson landing; once he mentions that, Brantley the pi
is a captive audience, one whose awareness of the event encompasses the minut
detail.

"Not a flyer in the world not tipping his hat to that Sullenberger," Brantley sa
"You can't imagine what it took to get that plane down."

"Miracle on the Hudson."

"Fuck miracle. Weren't no angels doing that. Give the guy some credit. Whe
die up here I don't want someone saying shit like that, don't want 'it was his ti
or 'God was calling him home.' I got no kick with religion, but I hate bullshit. A
your family was on that plane? Man! You gotta tell the others."

"You can tell 'em later, after I've gone. Now what about Repulse?"

"You know how it got its name, don't you? Some explorer was looking for
Northwest Passage, got turned back there. Repulsed. How do you know that wo
happen to you?"

"I don't."

"And what if she isn't there?"

"Then you take me back here and I take a scheduled flight home."

"You give up easy, Martin Wilkes."

"I'd come back when I could, maybe find another way. But I have kids. I ca
just—"

"Yeah, I heard the kids part of the story. Look, I'll help you, but I have to
straight with the others too. I gotta throw them a bone or I gotta say no to you.

Brantley gets the bartender's attention and orders another round, yanks a thu
toward Wilkes to indicate who's buying, then leads him back to the table and
him down.

"Our American friend here," he says, "he's looking for his wife, and he's
answering questions about it so don't ask. It'll give us something to talk about w
you're going stir crazy up north. Anyway, I'm rescheduling. You know what a so
I am for romance."

The young man in the hat shakes his head. "Your wives might not agree."

"Former wives," Brantley says, smiling. "I'm not a bigamist. Anyway, I'm tak
this guy, who you remember has generously agreed to buy this round, to the m
repulsive of bays, and coming right back. And I'm changing your flight," he st
to point at his three passengers," to 3:00 a.m. tomorrow. Now since you're
sleeping in the same bed anyway—"

ley," the woman yells, feigning indignation. "Don't give this guy the wrong about me. I have better taste than that."

hree a.m. Set your alarm for 2:30. I'll get you to Resolute then come back and t up with Marco Polo here."

ilkes stops him. "I might not be ready to come back."

hat's a given," Brantley says. "But maybe I can help you get around in that e."

e older man has been quiet, probably because he was working some figures in ead.

hat means you'll have to refuel at the Haven. In the dark."

ou forget," Brantley says with a wink. "The vending machines illuminate e of the runway. Lighten up, Carlie, I have my landing lights and a flashlight. when have I ever let you down by crashing a plane with you in it?"

doesn't wait for an answer but turns back to his newest customer.

ull disclosure, Wilkes. I fly a 1973 Beech Bonanza. I'm guessing it's about as as you are but probably in better shape. Ain't no pressurized cabin. No nding and contracting skin gonna blow off the frame after a couple thousand ions. You baby up the engine and lube the cables, and it's good for another y-five years. Now Carlie here, he gets a little skittish."

nly when you're flying blind."

lso," Brantley goes on, ignoring the interruption, "and my frequent flyers v this, there was a complete refurbishment in 1999. New leather seats, new eting, new wall panels, new headliner, and new seat belts."

n't that all, you know cosmetic?"

o, I mentioned seat belts. Let's go, Martin Wilkes."

hat do you mean, right now?"

s soon as we find an ATM that gives you air fare. You packed?"

ive me a half hour."

e'll need that for the round you're buying. A twenty ought to do it if your t's maxed out. It isn't, is it?"

ilkes leaves a twenty on the table and mumbles a perfunctory goodbye before ng up with the hotel, straightening his already packed suitcase, and getting to eserted airfield, deserted but not silent. One cold, sputtering engine smooths ot fifty yards from the only counter, itself deserted. Once Wilkes climbs inside -tailed Beechcraft, Brantley's assessment seems true. It looks clean and new, gh the ambience is decidedly 1970s and the only digital readout is a small

clock recessed into the pilot's-side yoke. Everything else is gauges, dials, to
switches. The 70s, by way of the 40s.

And it's freezing, like a car that's been left out on a January night. Wilkes
smell heat, but displacing the cold may take a while. He wants to ask if
temperature might rise during flight, but he remembers something about
increase in altitude bringing a decrease in temperature, a depressing realizatic

"You sit up here with me," he says. "Smoother ride. And if I have a heart att
land anywhere flat. Probably want to pull up the gear first, belly-land, skid
stop. It's mostly flat up to Ukkusiksalik, then, well, it's flat after that too. Just
the nose up and glide her in. They practically land themselves."

"You're joking right?"

"I'm getting' up there in years, got a little hypertension, you never know wit
African-American types. One of those cultural things. Just to put your mind at
had a physical in the fall and I'm feeling pretty good. Of course that could be
whiskey talking."

After the brief tutorial on how to land a plane on the Nunavut tundra (after w
event, of course, Wilkes would freeze to death within the hour) Bran
loquacious as he was in the bar, says little more for the next ninety minutes u
it's to point out some visual reference point that engenders a course correction.
Beech has GPS, but it's turned off.

"Satellites and computers," he says. "They crash all the time. I don't."

After another prolonged silence he starts dropping altitude and Wilkes cat
his first glimpse of civilization: some small structures dotting an otherwise b
landscape, then a few more, and then finally what appears to be a town.

"Tough to get building supplies up here," Brantley says. "People gather so
of lumber and throw up sheds, but the town won't allow that kind of structu
these people live five, ten kilometers out in the wild. Hard to believe there'd
slum here, but there is."

"Like the fishing sheds at Baker."

"'Cept people don't try to live in those. Up here they do. And in Baker, th
right there a few steps from town. Up here, out of sight, out of mind."

He points off to his right where a spotlight seems to aim at nothing in the ar
sun of early afternoon.

"Airfield. Buckle up."

ilkes cinches the strap tighter, but the landing turns out to be uneventfully
ooth and the plane rolls past a few small buildings, one of which appears to be
aintenance hangar, before coming to a gentle stop.

You won't need a cab," the pilot says. "Not too many airfields right in town
more, but this one is. You have my cell."

What good will that do?"

There's a little service here. See you tomorrow. Around noon, I hope. I'll find
."

Be careful."

How do you think I survived this long? Get a room, look around. Tomorrow if
don't have any luck, we'll get cracking. If you do find what you're looking for
hange your mind, call. Just so you know, missing a flight could mean a long
t for another."

Wait," Wilkes says. "Where do I start? In Baker Lake—"

Repulsive ain't Baker, tell you that. Baker is laid back. It's a goddamn fishing
age. It's not even in the Arctic circle."

Does that matter?"

Hereabouts they make fun of Baker and their College of the Arctic—which ain't
n in the Arctic. Repulse is."

Baker isn't exactly tropical."

t's a question of perception. You live in the Arctic circle, you treat the world
a hostile place, darker, grimmer, more dangerous. You know there's more
ism here than there is in Baker? Lots more. People travel to Repulse from all
r hell, from Winnipeg to places you've never heard of just to wind up here. By
y when the bay opens up and the cargo ships and tankers make it through, you
get here by boat, come up from Moosonee. Things get a little friendlier then,
not in the winter."

So there's no one to see?"

f you were Inuit, I'd say talk to anybody. But you ain't, so you talk to me."

The natives, they're suspicious of, you know, us?"

You mean us white people, 'cause in case you haven't noticed—"

meant strangers."

Strangers asking questions? Yes."

What about tourists?"

"Tourists ask questions like where's the best place to see polar bears or what
get attacked by a caribou or what time is the Aurora scheduled for. But have
seen this woman? That's different."

Wilkes takes out his photo of Keira.

"I'm looking for her. Did you fly her in here?"

"If you had a picture, why didn't you show me before? Not that it'd mat
Haven't seen her."

"You'd remember, right?"

"It'd be on my log unless I want to lose my license. I'd remember. Plus she
good-looking woman. I doubt if I'd forget that face. She the one you're lookin' fc

"She would have been with somebody, a man."

"I figured it was something like that." Brantley turns the picture over in his ha
a few times, shakes his head, then returns it. "You be careful up here. An an
stranger asking questions ain't gonna cut it, especially one looking for revenge

"I'm not angry."

Brantley stares at him. "What are you then?"

"I just, you know, want to find her."

"Is this hide and seek? It isn't, is it? I mean I've read about things like t
Executives playing tag and flying thousands of miles to say 'you're it.' This i
about something asinine, is it?"

"No. What I told you before is true."

"And you're not angry? God bless you. Okay listen, find the *Naujat*, it
restaurant, get something to eat. A few doors down there's a gallery. I know
woman who runs it."

"I was at a gallery in Baker Lake."

"Leo's place, I know it. This one is different. I just figure before you go barre
through the town waving a picture of your wife at everyone, you might start v
a friendly face. Someone who knows me. I would be a...a reference, you know,
way you threw around Manitok's name back in Baker."

"It's that obvious?"

"It's that obvious."

"Do I really need a reference?"

"The women up here, they're equals."

"They're equals in America."

"Really? Is your boss a woman?"

"No, but there are women doing my job and getting the same pay."

Name all the people you know doing your job and tell me how many are men. Hell, you freed us before you freed women. Your Constitution is 250 years l; ours is twenty-five."

New isn't better."

Men wrote yours, and they wrote it for men. They even ignored their roots. rope had had female rulers for hundreds of years. How many women presidents /e you had?"

We have a black president."

Did you vote for him?"

I don't talk about politics."

That's exactly what we're talking about. All I'm saying is this, Mr. Wilkes. Once got our own territory, we modernized fast. The old rules about being in charge 1't necessarily apply anymore. Some of the men aren't handling it well, but y'll come around. If you want information here, you have to be one of those n who handle it well. If you sound paternalistic, no one's gonna help you."

Paternalistic?"

I did attend school at one time. Look, Martin Wilkes, I know you deal with ple's finances. What you do beyond that—if you're a nice guy, if you steer ple right—all those things are secondary. People come to you because they e money and want to make more. Jane doesn't want your money and she won't impressed by your man-job. She'll sell you something, but only if you like it she likes you."

Jane, that's her name?"

Yes. There'll probably be a few other women in there, too. She'll be less white."

Is she gay?"

rantley shakes his head. "Why don't you ask her? That's always a good ice-aker. Then if that fails, ask her how she got to be black, you know, just to keep conversation moving. You sure you're going to be okay here?"

'll be fine. You two are related?"

She's my sister, but some days she'd rather not cop to that. Look, I owe those er three in Baker; otherwise I'd hang around."

'll be okay. I'll just remember: Jane, black, not gay."

You're not an intuitive learner, but you're quick. Keep in touch, eh?"

rantley's Beech is airborne before Wilkes reaches the *Naujat* where he finds 1ewhat traditional entrees and settles for grilled cheese and a beer, then another r before finding the hotel and taking a room. It's late in the afternoon when he

locates Jane, then follows Brantley's advice to the letter, mentioning the pi
admitting a lack of artistic expertise, and asking a few innocuous questions. H
in and out of her gallery in five minutes, short enough to be unobtrusive, lc
enough so that when he returns the following day, and he knows he will, he'll b
familiar face. And he's honest with her—almost: he's less than candid only wl
she asks why he's in Repulse Bay.

"Business," he says. "Just business."

tin Wilkes is 2500 kilometers northwest of Montreal and a slightly greater
nce from the North Pole itself. His world of sedans and SUV's has given way
ne of snow machines and ATV's, along with decades-old, battered, and
ized pickups and station wagons. Pedestrians are rare, and they know better
to venture out very far. Besides, even with the proper apparel, there is nowhere
).

the evening he's back at the *Naujat*, drinking coffee and talking to his sons on
d line. He sloughs off specific questions in favor of a few general comments:
asn't found Mommy but he thinks people might have seen her. And he avoids
ls like abduction and danger, though to him they are more palatable than their
e likely alternative: escape. His in-laws request few specifics. They know
er: if Wilkes found their daughter, they wouldn't have to pry an answer from
 And after McNally's discoveries, he feels uneasy telling them much of
hing.

few gins and the image of Brantley flying blind in that crappy old plane keeps
from sleeping. He lies in the adequately serviceable bed and imagines the pilot,
ing and circling a darkened airport before finally saying, "fuck it, let's give it
ot" and descending through the swirling snow nose-first somewhere near the
ay. It's not so much a nightmare as it is a vision. He looks outside and notices
ura around one of the street lights. It is, in fact, snowing.

 dozes fitfully after that until, in the darkness that never seems to relent, he
ly gives up and makes his way to the lobby. Brantley is already there.

parachuted in," he says. "I have no idea where the plane ended up, but like I
 they practically land themselves"

ilkes, almost ecstatic to see him alive, decides not to share his recent
mares.

o you made it through the snow. Everything go okay?"

 doesn't just happen. You have to make it go okay. You saw Jane?"

e talked."

ood. Let's get some food and talk some more."

e *Naujat* does a better breakfast than a dinner, and while they devour some
 of dark-grained and gritty pancakes, Brantley ruins Wilkes's digestion with
es of famous Arctic air crashes.

"It's a hostile place, but you know, so are Hawaii and the Caribbean and all t'
other warm places with hurricanes and tsunamis and sharks. We just think i
weather's warm, we're okay. We're not. Actually up here there are fe
surprises—except for the temperature, one day is pretty much like the next. H
your room?"

"It's a room. Can't expect too much."

"Lonely, huh? You get used to having someone in bed with you, then you d
It's not pleasant."

This is not the type of conversation Wilkes cares to have with his pilot, any i
than he would with Roche or Campanella back in the city, but he can't ap
unfriendly to his only link to the rest of the world, so he nods politely.

"Married?"

"Timmy back in Baker mentioned my wives. Let's say I've been there," Bra
says. "Eventually you get used to sleeping alone. Let's go see Jane."

"This early?"

"I know her pretty well. She's in the gallery by 7:00."

"I guess this far north there's nothing else to do."

"I know you think Repulse is the northern end of the earth. It isn't, not to an
You take Cape Dorset: now that's more like it."

"And you fly there?"

"What's another 400 miles when you're this far into oblivion? But don't get a
of yourself."

He tries not to, but he can't continue to play this massive board game w
planes hop from square to square as the playing surface continues to ex
northward and only Keira comprehends the rules. All these places he has n
heard of, all these Nunavut hamlets, in the course of a few days not only have
become part of the vernacular; they've begun to comprise his world. This mor
it centers on Repulse Bay. Tomorrow morning? Who knows?

Brantley bangs on the door of the gallery storefront. The place reminds W
of the unpronounceable "nice to look at" gallery in Baker Lake. No response
bangs harder. A child, he might be about Brett's age, comes to the window
mouths the word "closed" until he beams a gigantic smile and flings open the o

"Uncle Curt!" he screams, and throws his arms around his waist. "Mom
back."

he boy, neither black nor Inuit, hitches up his pajamas and disappears behind a
ded curtain to deliver the news. Seconds later Jane appears, wiping clay onto
apron. The hug he received from his nephew is not repeated.
You're out and about early. Couldn't sleep it off?"
Flew in overnight. Had to prove to my friend here that I could land a plane in
dark."
he looks at Wilkes, offers a noncommittal nod.
We met yesterday," she says, her voice as flat as a jury foreman, then turns back
Brantley. "Can you occupy yourself for a while? I'm really busy this morning. I
e the kiln later," she said. "Gotta get things ready."
My friend here," Brantley says. "He saw some pieces he thought he might like."
s that true," she asks, "Mr., is it Wicks?"
Wilkes, yes. I'm not sure if I want to haul home anything big, but maybe you
ld send something. I'd pay for the shipping of course."
he woman laughs. "Why wouldn't you?"
 just mean—"
ook around," she says. "Take your time. I'll just be in back."
he again wipes her hands on her apron and shifts aside the curtain that separates
rooms, disappearing behind it.
Wilkes shakes his head. "She looked at me weird."
So did I," Brantley says, "when you offered to pay for shipping."
t wasn't that. She knows something."
Yes, she knows you because you introduced yourself yesterday. She's not a
italist or a tarot card reader, though there is one a few doors down. The place
ht be open if—"
'm telling you—"
What you're doing isn't criminal. You're looking for your wife."
 didn't tell her that part."
That part? You want to find her or not?"
rantley doesn't wait for the answer, but pushes aside the curtain.
Sis, before you start to throw again, can you come out here? Five minutes.
nise."
Your friend found something he liked?"
Sort of," Brantley says. As soon as she reenters the room, he adds, "My friend
 forgot to tell you that he's trying to find his wife. His memory isn't what it

used to be, or maybe the latitude confused him. Anyway he has a picture to sh
you."

Jane looks at Wilkes. "Is my brother right?"

Wilkes slides the picture out of the plastic sleeve.

"This is her," he says. "Keira. I'm trying to find her."

"Here? In Repulse?"

"I don't really know, but I was told she might have flown here."

"How did you misplace her?"

"I don't know that either."

"And if you find her, then what?"

He'd love to tell Jane just how tired of that question he has grown, but suc
response would accomplish nothing.

"We have children. I want to know what her plans are for them."

"And for you?"

"That too."

She looks at Brantley and frowns.

"You know you shouldn't bring people in here like this."

"Sis, it's his wife."

She shakes her head. "I don't want my life tied up with Auguste and his cry
ball or Ouija board or whatever he's using for premonitions these days. I think
know that."

Wilkes doesn't have a clue who Auguste is, but he doesn't miss the gist of
sentence.

"Premonitions?"

"See?" Jane says with disgust. "This is how days go to waste." She removes
apron and tosses it on a low table, exposing grey jeans dotted with various pow
and colors. Only a darker grey t-shirt with some decorative totem emblazone
green looks unscathed.

"Now I'm not working, and that fresh batch of clay—"

"Five minutes," Brantley says. "Less. It won't dry up."

Wilkes doesn't care about any clay.

"You have premonitions? Are you a psychic?"

"No."

"Then—" he looks from the artist back to Brantley. "What did you mean?
mentioned premonitions."

Wilkes holds up the picture again.

I saw it already," she says and stares at the floor. Her clunky black boots show residue of endless hours of clay, paint, tints of whatever media she chose to fill eclectic schedule, the one Wilkes and her brother have screwed up.

Put it away," Brantley tells Wilkes. "Jane, why don't we run out and grab a fee, maybe relax for a minute."

What world do you live in Curt? I have a child to get off to school and a day's rk ahead. I can't just run out for a coffee. You get that, right?"

Just to the *Naujat*."

No. And the woman in the picture, I haven't seen her."

he denial is weak, hesitant, but when Wilkes calls her on it, she digs in.

Curt," she says to her brother. "I answered his question."

Okay," Brantley says, and turns to Wilkes. "I told you, my sister here is not a chic. She's just unfortunate enough to have been married to one. Of course if had had the good sense to leave here—"

He's the one who should have left," she snaps. "I live here too, and work here. supposed to take my son and just up and leave? And go where?" She turns ard the beaded doorway and yells. "Are you dressed yet?"

feeble "almost" barely makes the passage from one room to another.

In case you don't know, Mr. Wilkes, Ben and I live here, out back, in rooms oved from the gallery. Right now I'm not in the artist mode."

he turns again and yells to her son.

Hurry if you want to say goodbye to Uncle Curt!"

My wife," Wilkes says again. "Even if you haven't seen her, have you heard thing?"

ane glances at the clock.

I told you—"

You haven't seen her. But sometimes people hear things."

he shakes her head, then turns away from them.

Ben, hurry up."

he three of them stare at the door as if, behind it lies the meaning of all life. As onds go by and nothing happens, the scenario becomes ludicrous. Wilkes can't ak the silence, but Brantley can.

Tell us where Gus is and we'll leave you alone."

You know where he lives."

Tried there already."

Well, then, he's off somewhere. Check the neighboring planets."

"Wilkes here doesn't have time for that. Come on Janey, help us out. Please."
"Oh, please? Your vocabulary is expanding."
The two men wait.
"Okay," she says, still reluctant. "A couple days ago Auguste flew to Baker La
It's not that unusual. He has friends there. He came back with a young woman.
"He told you?"
"I heard. Not that it matters, Mr. Wilkes, but Auguste is older than me, ninet
years. He's sixty. The woman he brought back is twenty years younger, may
more. My ex is not a womanizer, but this one could have been your wife."
"Is she here?"
"I don't know that. I don't follow his activities. I'm not being cryptic, Mr. Wilk
or evasive, or mysterious. She could be next door, across the street, kilometers
of town. Or she could have left and the rumor mill hasn't picked up on
Although—I think I'd have heard. I hear about everything he does. I might as v
still be married to him."
"Do you think my wife might be, you know, with him?"
"I stopped keeping tabs on Auguste's sleeping arrangements a long time ago.
The image startles Wilkes and his expression changes. Brantley sees it ri
away.
"Jane," he says in some chastening older brother tone he probably has
opportunities to use. This time she doesn't hit back.
"Sorry, that was insensitive. A woman did come in a few days ago, look
around. I was in back, didn't pay much attention. I usually don't. When she le
poked my head out; it might have been her."
"What did she look like?"
"Like an anorak walking away, like everyone else in Repulse in January."
"Did you see which way she went?"
Jane smiles at Wilkes. "Would it really matter if she went right or left?"
She lifts the apron off the chair and slips it on.
"I don't want to be rude," she says. "But I have things to do."
"Just one minute," Wilkes says. "What did you mean before about reading mi
and sharing premonitions? Your husband does that?"
"I'm not married."
"Your ex then."
"So he says. You can ask him."

le isn't at home," Brantley repeats. "Look, I know you have things to do, but guy here, I mean, he's come a long way. We can't just blow him off. Just tell what you know and we'll leave."

le said he was here on business."

Maybe he was a little reticent."

hey used to call that lying."

aney—"

get it. If she ran off, it's embarrassing. I was married to a loser who divorced I get that humiliation stuff, but"—and she stares directly at Wilkes—"you can't people who might help you. Still here on business?"

shouldn't have said that."

ne ties the apron. "I'm sorry would have been better."

is."

esus, Curt, I've got clay drying up back there."

eems to me," her brother says. "You told me once as long as the clay hasn't fired you can still use it. Just add a little water. I could go back there and spit for you if you'd like."

ll use my own spit," she says. "Your wife, Mr. Wilkes, I knew she was coming. uste has talked about this for years. Not Keira, though, that's not her name."

's Sylvy," Wilkes says, his stomach beginning to churn.

es."

nd she's only been gone a week. How could you have have known for years?"

Maybe my former partner can answer that. This woman he envisioned, that's an ongoing staple in his repertoire of craziness." She looks at her brother, softens her tone. "I don't blame you for trying to help this man, but Auguste arais isn't the way to go—not for anybody."

Maybe this time he is," Brantley says, and backs away. "We'll leave you alone "

n not anti-social," she says, "I'm really not. I'm just tired of dragging his hit around, Mr. Wilkes. That's what divorce is for."

an you just tell me how he talked about her? I mean like a lover?"

e said he had to help her find something."

id he say what?"

ou don't ask Gus those questions unless you want him to become sophical. He'd probably ask you why you want to find her."

ecause I'm worried about her. I want her to come home."

"And that's it?"

"That's not enough?"

She frowns a little, then turns to her brother.

"And you be careful," she says. "You think I didn't hear that crate of yours c
hurtling in this morning—in the dark! I kept waiting for the explosion."

"I don't carry that much fuel. It would have been a small explosion."

"Ben wouldn't think so. He likes you, God help him."

Brantley exhales. "You know me, sis. No one more careful than I am."

She nods and backs away. This time she doesn't come back but sends Ben o
hug his uncle before racing back to finish his breakfast.

"Cute kid," Wilkes says.

"My sister is a good mother. A little harried this morning. That's mostly
fault."

"I'm assuming Auguste is white?"

"Because the kid is? Yes, her ex is white, but my sister took Benny in whei
own parents died. They'd flown to Winnipeg for a second honeymoon, got ii
car accident, that was it."

"Jesus. When?"

"Three years last fall. My sister knew the family, it was cut and dried. She al
said she didn't want kids, but my feeling is it was Gus who didn't want them.
imagine what those conversations were like."

"She's a beautiful woman."

"Maybe you can pay to have her shipped back to the states. Come on, let's

"Where?"

"Check around town, maybe find Gus."

"Those shacks we saw when we flew in. We should check them out. They
them in Baker Lake too. Found a fornicating couple in one of them."

"They're good for that, in season."

"My wife used one for shelter, apparently."

"Maybe," Brantley says, "but in Baker they're practically in town. Up here y
die before you reached them on foot."

"So we get a snow machine. You have connections."

"Most outfitters rent only to groups, and you get a guide. You can't let peop
off on their own up here. They tend to come back dead. It's not a good idea."

"I'm out of good ideas," Wilkes say. "I ran out a couple thousand miles
Come on, you fly a fifty-year-old plane from outpost to outpost and you land

way illuminated by a soda machine. Now you're afraid to take a snowmobile a
 miles out of town?"

Not afraid. Aware. You live in the wilds of Connecticut, right? I don't know
at kind of animals you encounter. I'm guessing squirrels, mostly, a chipmunk or
. Maybe the occasional raccoon tips over a garbage can and you have to pick
some jars and bottles, or a rabbit eats your lettuce. It's different here. Those cute
 cuddly polar bears can collapse your skull with one swipe, and those majestic
ves you see through binoculars aren't quite so majestic when they're divvying
your body parts. Up at 10,000 feet where I live they don't bother me much;
n here, they do."

So can't we get a rifle at one of these outfitters?"

Have you ever fired a weapon?"

Yes."

Not counting amusement parks?"

My father used to take me duck hunting."

So maybe you can handle a firearm. Thing is, if you miss the duck, he's unlikely
urn around and charge you, or gather the other ducks into a pack and drag your
eding corpse back to his den. You don't want to be shooting wildlife from a
wmobile, not if I'm anywhere around. Not to mention, it's illegal."

Ducks don't have a den."

Now we know how you survived your childhood."

Then find me a snowmobile and I'll go myself."

That would make me complicit in your death. I'll fly you over, take a look-see.
 there out of town I can get down to a couple hundred feet and not bother
body. You'd be able to tell if there's activity around any of the places."

How slow can you fly?"

Fifty maybe. That's about stall speed. Are you familiar with that term?"

Familiar enough. I almost got into a fight about it. What are you gonna see from
uple hundred feet in the air at 50 mph?"

Fifty knots."

Even faster. We have to be on the ground. Come on Brantley, you must know
eone who will help."

There's something else about those shacks. Gus considers himself their
ector, likes to make sure they're okay. To him they represent the old ways."

Manitok said that's where souls live."

"In rotten lumber and scrap? I'd hope they can afford better. But they're close
the antiquities, some remains of earlier civilizations. My ex-brother-in-law thi
they need to be guarded."

"Like with weapons?"

"He isn't a radical, and he might even see the futility of what he's doing, but
hard to come between an old man and his beliefs."

"So we'll be careful. This is my wife we're talking about here, not so
sightseeing tour. Just tell me if I'm on my own here."

Brantley tells him again he refuses to be responsible for a death, and mome
later they're bargaining with a former pilot whose Inuit name sounds like Tu
He owns four snowmobiles, two of which he is willing to rent out, along with so
sort of thermal jumpsuit and fur-lined boots he claims will keep them both fr
solidifying. Wilkes gives him $300 and Tunic promises to return half when
vehicles are returned safely.

"I don't want to know where you're going," the man says, pocketing the b
"but you don't shoot anything, understand?"

"We're looking for someone," Brantley said. "We have no weapons."

"Who are you looking for?"

"I thought you didn't want to know?"

"I don't care where. I want to know what."

"Auguste Demarais."

"That might be difficult. You know that."

"We're limiting our search to this planet."

The man smiles, then jerks his thumb backwards like a hitchhiker.

"Out back," he says. "Come on. You know the drill."

Behind the house the machines are linked together by heavy-duty chain
unevenly spaced padlocks. The Inuit releases a few, then moves in close
Wilkes.

"You're American."

"Yes."

"New York?"

"Near there."

"I read about that pilot. He landed the plane in the water. Did you see it?"

"I was a few miles away. I saw it on TV."

"Sullenberger," the man says, then repeats it like a mantra. With all the I
names Wilkes has heard recently, a name like Sullenberger sounds absurd, ma

, a spoof. But the guide accents the final syllable and pronounces it sullenber-
ly, making him sound like a Montrealer. The man winks at Brantley. "Can you
that? Land on the water?"
I can walk on the water," Brantley says. "You know that. Are these things
sed up?"
You'll freeze to death before you run out of fuel. And remember, around here a
shot from five miles away sounds like it's next door."
We're not armed," Brantley says again.
he Inuit smiles. "I am. You shoot anything, I shoot you."

bled together from shipping crates, cardboard, and charred wood, the
eshift hovels strewn along the frozen ridge outside Repulse Bay make their
er Lake counterparts seem like a gated community. Most are windowless, and
e that aren't display openings filled with cold-shattered plastic flapping like
en moths in the breeze. Doors are ajar, when there are doors at all, and the first
e Wilkes and Brantley approach has merely half a roof, the remainder having
apsed under either the weight of the snow or, more likely in this dry and snow-
ed Arctic desert, its own weight.
e doors, like the windows, always face south, as if some wag of a home builder
sited a grotesque subdivision in a place nobody would live, then provided an
le, year-round view of the purposeless sun. Some structures are whitewashed;
rs "fixed up" with four-by-eight sheets of rough plywood. Occasionally a roof
ts actual shingles, though even then they've been hammered in at amusing
es, seldom matching each other in color, shape, or composition.
ough Martin Wilkes may be a visitor, or an interloper, or whatever the native
lation would choose to call him, he is not so innocent or sanguine as to believe
survival is possible in these shacks, not under these conditions. But he has
e too far to ignore them, and if Deidre's words were true, if Keira has come
 to die, for the first time Wilkes believes that in a place like this it can happen.
 though it would have been foolhardy to explore this unforgiving wilderness
e, he wishes, at least at the moment, that whatever discovery he is about to
e didn't need to be shared with some bush pilot whose only talents lie in a
pit at 10,000 feet.
aneuvering the snowmobile requires a minimal skill set, but Brantley leads,
ing the least treacherous routes, the ones with fewer opportunities for a
ap, such as flipping and subsequently dying under the weight of a half-ton of
led plastic and the machinery encased within. Brantley has made it clear that
 is no rescue inside the Arctic circle, not when the thermometer reads forty
w.
entigrade or Fahrenheit?" Wilkes says.
antley shrugs. "Whatever looks better on your death certificate."
ey enter the first shack. Unheated. Windowless. Dark. Covering everything is
 layer of what appears to be dust but what is actually a fine snow that has

pinched through the poorly fit lumber and settled on exposed surfaces.
impossibly big kitchen table made of off-white formica with molded chrome
an escapee from the 1950's, takes up almost the entire area. Wilkes can ha
imagine what kind of journey brought it here.

"How?" he says to Brantley.

The pilot shakes his head. "I don't even ask anymore," he says. "I don't k
where anything comes from."

They poke around among some small wooden crates that may have been us
send sculpture or carvings or anything that could be damaged in transit. Ther
unmatched chairs and a cabinet from a console TV people bought genera
before, when a television was still a piece of furniture and not a wafer thin sl
pixels. Inside its hinged doors are magazines and books and even food: a bo
corn flakes, some canned corn undoubtedly frozen solid, a bottle of ketchup
remainder of a loaf of bread with even the mold solidified.

Brantley tosses a slice to Wilkes. It falls to the floor and breaks. These p
have a different feel from those in Baker Lake where the eccentric colors offse
gloom of the construction, and where the lake, although it was no more tha
expanse of ice, made everything less inhospitable. Up here, so far from the t
there's nothing to relieve the despair.

They move on to a building piled high with dozens of Nike boxes. Wilkes
at one with his mittens and it opens to reveal a broken light bulb. He leaves the
alone and turns to Brantley, accusatory, critical.

"I can't believe they let people live like this."

"They?"

"This—territory—whatever it is."

"America has its slums."

"But we have social services."

"We do too," Brantley says. "There are people in Repulse who do what
doing today, except they come out with food and supplies on the off ch
someone will be here. Sometimes they bring kerosene too, just in case. In
ways, they do more than you and I are doing. Even Gus, unhinged as he ma
sometimes carries supplies on his little missions."

"I wasn't criticizing—you—it's just that something should be done. At leas
these down and build something close to town."

"Affordable housing?"

"Yes. If that's what it takes."

Like in America? I know what you do for a living, Wilkes. Do you encounter a
of clients living in affordable housing?"

That's not the point."

Then tell me the point."

Well, social services—"

I just told you. Everyone in town mucks in together. What more would you
it? You don't strike me as a reformer."

I can still have empathy."

What you have isn't empathy," Brantley says, his voice matching the chill
und him. "Empathy requires vision: being able to imagine what it's like to live
this without ever having done it or seen it. You're standing right here. You
't have to imagine the squalor or the misery. You're in it."

Then I sympathize."

Or pity."

Semantics," Wilkes says. It's an easy way out of losing arguments, but not with
ntley.

Not semantics," the pilot says. "Definitions. But I'll give you an escape, a little
that makes wealthy people like you feel better. Many of the native poor don't
it help, refuse to take it. And some people want to die."

Nobody wants to die," Wilkes says. "They may want their suffering to end, but
don't want to die. It's immoral."

Or brave. Facing the unknown like that, not certain of what comes next. If
thing. Survival may be the coward's way out when you know the next day will
ust as miserable as this one, and the previous one."

No one knows what the next day will bring."

Most people do."

But you, could you let yourself die?"

'm not miserable and impoverished and cold and hungry, but I'm ready. I'd have
e to do what I do. Hell, I've flown this area for thirty years. If that little Beecher
is out, I'm good enough to land it anywhere. Maybe even survive a week or two
he summer. But the chances of being rescued, they're not good. And if it's
ter, and the landing is rough and I'm injured at all, that hour when I can't take
of myself and do the things I need to do to survive, I'd just be another frozen
ropping in the Arctic tundra. Like I said, I'm prepared. And freezing to death
so bad."

"But getting there is," Wilkes said. He can remember a story he read in colle
some gambler marooned in a blizzard who chose to shoot himself instead.

"Unfortunately, yes. But when you get past the panic and the discomfort and
uncontrollable shivering, you arrive at a tranquil warmth, almost like a morph
high. You just drift and drift and then you stop. It's not unpleasant. And if you
speed up the process through loss of blood—"

"So if you crash and the odds are stacked against you—"

"I have a hunting knife."

"And you'd stab yourself?"

"Stabbing yourself, that's what crazy people do. I'm pretty sure I'd make a cu
the femoral artery, bleed out pretty quick, right about here." He points to an a
just below his groin.

"And what if right after you do that a helicopter happens by and sees you
finds that you've lost too much blood? Then you've killed yourself for nothing

Even with the hood covering most of the pilot's face, Wilkes discerns a smil

"You've been in the Arctic for a few days. I've lived most of my life up h
Maybe you're used to looking up from your yard work or your gas grill or y
golf outing and seeing an aircraft happen by. Up here nothing happens by. No
the ground and not in the air. Everything happens by design. No Sunday p
taking his family out for a ride is going to happen by a crash site and radio for h
We don't have your miracles."

"Then what are you doing here today? What master plan brought us here?"

"Well, I'm just trying to keep you from killing yourself, since you don't s
ready to die. But if we don't keep moving, we'll die anyway."

"Wait. If you kill yourself—"

"I'll go to hell. So you're a Catholic too. Lapsed, I'll bet, like the rest of us.
somewhere along the line you've held on to a few precepts that you'll carry v
you all your life, and one of them is that suicide is very very bad. No buria
consecrated ground. And then of course, no heaven. Not even purgatory. I stud
catechism too."

"You don't accept it?"

"The people up here don't put much stock in that paradise in the sky routine

"You're not Inuit."

"I'm not Jewish either, but I got no problem with the Old Testament. For
Inuits heaven is just a place where you don't worry. Look around this shack.

u seriously believe that a life led in a place like this is better than the
ernative?"

All life is better than the alternative."

Absolutes never make sense, except the one I just said. Come on, it's not good
stand in one place too long. Your boots will freeze to the ground and you'll die
nding up."

Bullshit."

Inuit humor. You'll develop a taste for it. Let's go."

he next stops are similar to the first two: no people alive or dead, and no signs
any recent habitation. No tracks either, animal or human or machine, just wind-
ven snow as fine as ash, filtering through the cracked seams and open windows
l half-missing roofs of one sad building after the next.

t's barely past noon but they're losing daylight. Even Wilkes, neophyte though
may be, understands that the bitterness of an eighteen-hour night is not
nething to scoff at. More shacks are in their sight lines, all as foreboding and
olate as the others. With Wilkes in the lead, a concession Brantley has made to
ow his partner some respite from the two-cycle engine fumes, they stop at none
hem. Brantley pulls up next to him and waves him over.

Giving up? If you are, you're still heading away from town."

A few more," he yells over the engine sound and points. "Those two over there."

Lead on, oh wise one, and slow that thing down or you'll be resting in your
holic cemetery faster than you expect."

ight, almost invisible flurries of snow begin, end, then begin again, though the
y real clouds remain gathered on the southern horizon, their shading a subdued
let. Keira is partial to that color. He'd given her a wool scarf just that shade the
vious Christmas. He tries to remember if it was among the items left behind,
can't. Perhaps she's wearing it now, maybe traipsing through Repulse Bay,
iting the galleries, or maybe at the *Naujat* having a spiked coffee and making
ll talk with the locals. She's probably had enough of this respite from being a
e and mother and is ready to return. Maybe that wool scarf has provided the
mth to keep her alive and later, in a satisfying turn, the impetus to return home.

e hears Brantley yelling. "What are you doing?"

What do you mean?"

I mean, what are you doing? We should be moving."

I'll bet Keira is in your sister's gallery right now."

My brother-in-law is the psychic. That's why we're looking for him."

"I think she's there."

"I think she isn't. My sister would have the authorities out on a rescue miss
for us."

"We need rescuing?"

"We will if you keep daydreaming. Let's move. Or you can gawk at the horiz
then I'll stop by and retrieve your body later."

On the next door someone has spray-painted 2009 in fluorescent orange abov
scattering of liquor bottles. The residue of an unsupervised New Year's pa
Brantley says, but then stops the snowmobile and holds up a hand.

It's only then that Wilkes notices some disturbed snow near the door, a t
column of smoke rising from a makeshift stack, and a ludicrous veranda on th
sides, apparently designed to hold a beach chair or two so that people can sit
watch the sunset, and die of exposure. The door is closed tight.

"Shut that off," Brantley says. "And wait. Let me do this."

"Do what?"

"Let me check this out. Stay back."

The command, unusually peremptory for Brantley, sets Wilkes's stom
churning. Moments before he was ready to give up the search, to believe again
Keira was just another visitor in Repulse Bay, that he could speed back to to
and bring her home, pick up their lives where they left off. The possibility
she's merely yards away makes the prospect of a joyful solution, even a beara
one, that much less likely. No one can be okay in a place like this.

Brantley makes a circuit of the building on the snowmobile, then again on fc

"I don't want to surprise anyone," he says when he comes back. "Come on."

"We're going in?"

"Not until we knock."

"Why?"

"Because inside there could be someone with a gun. He certainly heard us cc
up and he has the right to protect his place. And if he shoots you, I'm not dragg
your corpse back to town. I'll bury you in the snow and let the wolves have you
a few should happen by."

"Whoever's in here must have heard us. I'm not an idiot."

"That's why we knock. And say something, maybe an American greeting
hello would be appropriate."

Wilkes waits a beat or two, then takes a deep breath and, surprised again at
the cold hurts his lungs, knocks.

lello."

ey wait. Nothing. He can sense Brantley close behind him.

lello," Wilkes repeats, then knocks again, harder. The door gives way and
ks open an inch. It isn't locked.

lamar," Brantley yells, then waits. "Friend."

e response from inside is immediate.

urtiss. You should leave."

's Gus," Brantley whispers. "This isn't good."

ut we found him," Wilkes says. "Isn't that why we're here?"

his isn't good," Brantley says again, then nudges him aside. For a moment
es expects a gunshot to explode from inside and kill them both.

us," Brantley says, his voice calm and placid. "Are you okay?"

ou should leave."

re you armed?"

o you think I would shoot you, Curtiss?"

hen can we open the door?"

isn't locked, but I asked you to leave."

us, listen to me, are you alone?"

m with a friend. We don't want to be disturbed."

it a woman?"

lan or woman, what does it matter?"

hat's enough," Wilkes says, his apprehension smothered by impatience and
r. "How long do we play this game?"

hen let me go in first," the pilot says. "Gus can be a little weird."

o, not after all this," Wilkes says. "I don't even know the guy and I'm tired of
ullshit. And yours."

steps around Brantley and roughly pulls the door open. With nothing to slow
ogress it swings around and smacks the outer wall. The sound pierces the cold
silent desert, seems to reverberate off the other buildings before returning. In
mal world, a person might apologize for something so rude and careless, but
es has lost track of anything resembling a normal world.

he Wilkes home, small framed photos dot end tables and bureaus, marking the
sage of time as well as or maybe better than any atomic clock or quartz
epiece or perpetual calendar. Through these photos Martin Wilkes has watched
self age and, to a lesser degree, watched Keira do the same: the creases near
r eyes, the slight dullness in their skin, the subtle drooping under their jaws.
had begun to joke about gray hairs, about her too-small-to-sag breasts
inning to tilt earthward. He would counter with an admission that he'd gained
und or two (or five), become fatigued a little easier, been less than spectacular
ed a few times. Maybe, he said one evening, all those Viagra commercials were
ed at him. But the decline, if that's what it was, had been imperceptibly slow.
ow it's as if someone has fast-forwarded the scene, has taken Keira and, as
ice artists sometimes do with missing children, drawn a projected likeness five,
even twenty years away. This is Keira a decade from now, maybe more, lying
k still in that rude shelter, more a part of the polar landscape than some
stration of human life. Only her eyes, barely open, give some sign that this is a
ug form, not the remains viewed at a wake.
ilkes can do nothing but lean against the door frame, to seek some momentary
nce before taking a few steps toward her. He says her name, expecting no
onse and receiving none. He steps closer, says her name again, louder this time.
ra. Her real name. Not some made-up fantasy that brought her here. Closer, he
ts to touch her but her face, pale and expressionless, seems too frangible to
h or even approach, and Wilkes has the sickening sensation that she will
ter like the brittle plastic on those makeshift windows. Just as unnerving is her
r: that light azure that pervades every aspect of the region surrounds her like a
abre aura and tinges every aspect of the room: the faded red blanket wrapped
nd her, her bare ankles extending out from beneath it, her feet blue and almost
inous. Necrosis, he knows the word, has read it in warning pamphlets in the
hern hotels and stores and cafes. First the flesh dies from the outside in, then
person does the same.
ut nothing in Wilkes's life has prepared him for the moment when immediate
on was needed. Even his job, no matter how tense and pressured he may feel
mes, relies more on thoughtful consideration than precipitous action. He is not
of those who stalk the floor of the exchange making rapid life-altering

decisions, who waves a hand and sends a billion dollars on its way. If he were would not be transfixed, trying to reason out his next step, or at the very l finding something to say. And something should be said. Because even i situation that one can never prepare for, anticipate, even imagine, someth should be said. He tries again.

"Keira."

He says it clearly and almost casually as if they were conversing at dinner. moves into her sightline, kneeling so that she cannot miss him. In her eyes the a suggestion of movement, like a baby following light. Maybe it's mere reflex it's something. Maybe she's been drugged, or hypnotized, or brainwashed. It's c at that moment that he remembers that he and Keira are not alone in the room. I he been there seconds? Minutes? He has no inkling until Brantley's voice le some perspective.

"Gus, what's happening here?"

Gus. Auguste Demarais. Wilkes turns and sees an old man. If he is, in fact, c sixty, he does not wear his years very well. Bundled against the elements he se frail and slightly stooped, and the long overcoat seems to weigh him down e farther. He draws deeply on a stub of a cigarette, exhaling downward through lips. The cloud hangs in the air for a moment, then strays across the space betw them toward Keira, caught on a drift of air that has broken through the unse walls. She doesn't respond as the haze slips past.

Brantley mumbles something else Wilkes can't quite decipher, but the so breaks the spell and Wilkes moves closer to his wife, says her name again. waits. There is neither acceptance nor rejection in her body language. There i body language, no language of any kind. He turns back toward the smoker waves the next volley away from her face.

"She doesn't like cigarette smoke," he says, as if somehow the entire prob can be distilled down into a simple disregard for personal preferences, as if c this smoke is gone, the whole scene will be expunged from what is no more th poorly conceived play. Once the room is cleared of smoke and the curtain falls, wife will be able to return to Connecticut, to her children, to those small fra photos.

"She didn't tell me," the old man says and grinds out the cigarette on the plyw floor. His voice is strong and forceful without a hint of shame or embarrassn or apology. Wilkes turns away from him back toward Keira.

"Are you warm enough?"

More silence at first, then a narrowing of the eyes, slight but perceptible.

"I have this blanket," she says, her words scratched out painfully through vocal cords that seem as brittle as her skin. It's not the voice he remembers, but it's a voice nonetheless. A living voice.

Brantley says something but Wilkes pays no attention. He spies the stove near and next to it a bag of fuel pellets: someone has outfitted the place for the winter, but undone his own preparation by never sealing the cracks or repairing the broken windows. There's no thermometer visible, but Wilkes guesses the temperature inside. Twenty above, maybe, a little higher. Cold enough to die of hypothermia eventually, but not enough to freeze someone in his tracks, not like walking through Repulse Bay in the early morning. And Keira in that heavy wool blanket: if she is shivering at all, it doesn't show. Maybe he can get some pellets to that stove, get the temperature up.

"We have to get her out of here."

Brantley again, somewhere uttering pronouncements. But Wilkes knows his fate. If only he can warm the room, he thinks. But then he sees, on a crate next to her, clothing is strewn, the heaviest and thickest items near the bottom. On top is a red silk blouse he recognizes, her underwear, a bra dangling touching the floor. She's naked under the blanket.

The old man follows Wilkes's eyes and appears to guess his thoughts. "I found her that way," he says.

"Under the blanket?"

"I got her the blanket, and I lit the fire."

"And you took her clothes off?"

"I told you. I found her that way."

"Naked. She was lying in this—this fucking dump naked?"

The words are charged now, even in these surroundings. His wife naked with another man. Deidre and Henry naked in that disgusting shack on Baker Lake. Everyone knows what it means.

"You just happened to find her that way?" Wilkes says. "Who the hell are you?"

Brantley steps between them, facing Wilkes, but the answer comes anyway.

"Auguste Demarais," the old man says, then steps around Brantley and extends a hand. Wilkes stares at it for a moment, then shoves it aside.

"Are you out of your mind?"

Brantley is about to move Wilkes back physically when they hear Keira, barely audible, barely words. "I don't want to wear those things anymore."

"But it's cold, you have to." Wilkes, kneeling now, sounds like a parent argu with a refractory child, a child with no say in the matter but who will not give He turns and glares at Demarais, then pulls the blanket tighter around his wi neck. She offers neither resistance nor gratitude.

"I'm warm," she says, the words clear but chopped, as if different sentences been spliced together by some devious sound engineer.

"Wilkes," Brantley says, and motions toward the woman. "We have to get he

"She's okay," Wilkes says, convinced for the moment that under that blanket wife is, as she claims to be, warm and safe, that when he clears the shack of th two men, he can get her dressed and back to town and back again through all steps that brought her here.

"She's not okay," Brantley says. "I can take Gus here and go back for help."

"Gus? Is that his name? I thought it was Auguste something."

"Not now," Brantley says. "We need medical help."

"I told you, she's okay."

"And I'm telling you she's not. Look at her."

Wilkes is barely listening. He has moved his eyes away from his wife and fi them on Demarais, who has lowered his hand and taken out another cigare Wilkes reaches out and slaps it out of his hand: it flies across the room, land near the door.

"Didn't you hear me? Keira doesn't like smoke."

Brantley misses the exchange. He drags his cell through the air, then shove back into some inside pocket of his anorak.

"We have to go back to Repulse. I can't get a signal here."

Wilkes barely acknowledges him. He is still fixated on the old man who sta bewildered, at the perfectly good cigarette on the ground. He may be surprise Wilkes's sudden violence, but he doesn't appear angry.

"Gus," Brantley says. "Don't smoke."

Demarais lifts his head as if he's just awakened from a nap.

"I don't know anyone named Keira. There was no Keira in my dream."

"Goddamn it, Gus!"

In the close confines, the pilot's voice expands, straining against the sho structure. Wilkes has never heard the man yell, and apparently neither Demarais. The old man's expression changes, and though his eyes still display fear, he seems more willing to be a participant and not just a witness.

Wilkes makes eye contact, tries not to glare.

Vhat dream?"

. woman on a plane, a big plane. There were children everywhere. Some of
. belonged to her. Boys. You have two sons?"

'our ex-wife back in town knows that much," Wilkes says. "I wouldn't have to
 psychic to ask her."

antley grabs Wilkes's arm.

ater. You stay here. I'll take Gus and get help."

.eira is fine," Wilkes says again, and glances at her perfunctorily. "I just want
 1ow how this so-called psychic—"

Ve're wasting time, Wilkes."

ioddamn it Brantley, it's my time."

Io it isn't. Look at her, for Christ's sake."

.nd what happens to Kreskin here? He disappears into the Arctic night while
 vait for the EMT's?"

antley shakes his head, struggles to lower his own volume.

ius isn't running anywhere."

ilkes ignores him.

ell me more about the dream of yours."

o you have a daughter, Mr. Wilkes?"

'ou tell me. You're the psychic."

Vhat I saw in my dream. There was a young girl. She was lying in the dark.
 was hurt."

n the big plane?" Wilkes scoffs. "Better get your research straight. Nobody
 urt on that big plane."

marais nods. "She was already dead."

ow you know the dream," Brantley says, inches from Wilkes's ears. "I'm
 g Gus back to town and sending help. You keep your wife warm, keep that
 ;oing."

t now Demarais ignores Brantley too, stares at Wilkes.

our wife, does she dream?"

Ihat my wife does is not your business."

 glances over to her again: she may be aware of the conversation but she is
 1gaged from its significance. It's a familiar look for her, one Wilkes has seen
 re at boring, compulsory gatherings (usually work-related): the appearance of
 ing on someone's words while immersed in other thoughts entirely. She's good

at it, maybe that's what she's doing now, except this isn't some penthouse party
dragged her to against both their wills. This counts. This is important. This mat

"People share dreams," Demarais says, snapping Wilkes back to the presen
she didn't share them with you, maybe she didn't dream. Or maybe she kept t
a secret."

Wilkes flinches at the implication. Keira dreamed all the time, must
mentioned hundreds of them to Wilkes. He remembers the conversations, bu
the dreams themselves. Was he supposed to? Was he being counted on to char
activity of his wife's subconscious? What does that have to do with intimacy?
besides, he isn't the one guilty of abandonment, even if Demarais is right. So v

He backs away and kneels by his wife again. Her eyes move slightly toward
There is some...he doesn't know what...recognition? Acceptance? Gratitude?
is either glad he came for her or anxious for him to leave. He has no idea w
and, at that moment anyway, has no idea who she has become. He touches
shoulder, still fearful she will break.

"Keira," he whispers. No response. He looks up at Demarais. "It was Sy
right? The girl in your dream?"

Demarais nods.

"And you, are you Em?"

"Em?"

"Yeah, like Emile. Keira had a different name. Was that yours?"

"I have no different name."

"Everybody here has a different name. What's yours?"

Demarais looks bewildered. So does Brantley.

"He knows what I mean," Wilkes says. "He knows about the letter. He had i
from New York but he wrote it."

Brantley faces him and takes him by the shoulder.

"New York? And Gus here did that? Gus?"

"Well, listen," Wilkes announces, pulling back from the grip. "I don't know
Sylvy. We never had a daughter and we don't have any dark secrets in our liv
least we didn't until she came here and started dealing with this guy. Tell him K
he says, "tell him that wherever his ideas are coming from, he's wrong."

Even Brantley has gone quiet now, sucked in like gullible moviegoers at a p
contrived melodrama: they've bought their tickets and they deserve to see
schlock ends, they want to hear Keira's answer.

But her silence seems only to corroborate Wilkes's accusations.

So your dream was wrong, old man," he says.

Forget about his dream," Brantley says.

We will," Wilkes whispers to her. "And then we can go back and see the kids, back to normal."

His pronouncement rings with such authority that neither Brantley nor Demarais reply. But Keira does.

This is my place now."

It isn't," Wilkes says. "Your place is with me, with Brett and James. They—"

Auguste says it belongs to everyone," she says.

Well, Auguste is wrong. And he's been wrong all the time. All his mystical shit. You should know better. You don't even go to church."

He intends to be logical but it sounds like an accusation, angry and impatient.

What will you do if you find her?

Deidre in Baker Lake had asked that. And then Brantley too. The answer seemed obvious: he never once considered her refusal to come back with him. Now she sending him away, and he can do nothing but repeat what he has already said, time softening his tone, forcing himself to be civil, calm: she's a client and putting together a portfolio for her. No anger, No urgency. Just the calm of a figure executive selling an idea.

Now when these two leave I'll get you dressed and—"

The woman is right," Demarais says passively, interrupting. "You shouldn't take her leave this place. It doesn't belong to you."

Or you," Brantley interrupts, breaking his own silence. "This is not the time, s. We can't just let her die here. We're going for help, you and me."

Brantley has strength and age on his side, but Demarais seems suddenly implacable, like the stone man from the flag and the gallery and Brett's school ject.

Fine," Wilkes says to Brantley when he notes Demarais's resistance. "You go help and let the pervert sit here while I get Keira dressed. He's already seen her ed, it hardly matters, does it?"

Wilkes removes his mitts and starts assembling her clothes, but the cold inhibits

No," Demarais says, horrified. "If you take her away, who will watch her?"

Wilkes bolts up, lunges forward, and swings his bare right hand catching Demarais in the chest. The old man tilts backwards until he crumples against the l before pitching forward to the floor and landing on his knees. A sharp pain races up to Wilkes's elbow, past it, through his shoulder, to his neck. He grimac[es] and grabs his right shoulder.

"Jesus Christ," Brantley says, grabbing Wilkes. "What the hell is wrong w[ith] you?"

"He has no right to say—"

Brantley hangs on to the front of Wilkes's jumpsuit.

"Take care of your wife," he says. "Don't fucking mess with me. I'll knock [you] on your ass right here and let them find your body."

"Let me go."

"Do I appear to be joking? I'll let you go when you get your head straight."

"I'm okay now," Wilkes says. He isn't frightened, but he knows that Bran[tley] does not make idle threats.

Brantley releases him and tends to Demarais, now seated on the floor, conscio[us] rubbing at his chest. Brantley kneels next to him.

"Gonna make it, Gus?"

The old man nods but says nothing.

"Gus?"

The old man inhales and his hands clutch his chest as he frowns slightly.

"I'm fine."

"You're not. Can you breathe all right?"

Demarais nods and Brantley helps him struggle to his feet, then leads him [to a] wood crate near the door. Wilkes watches silently. This guy is still Brantl[ey's] brother-in-law, ex- or not. Family. Hitting him was unwise.

"Is he okay?"

"Should he be?" Brantley says. "Let me smash you in the chest and you tell m[e."]

"I mean, is he going to be okay?"

"I'm going to take him back to town. Then we'll—"

"No," Demarais interrupts, "I will drive myself."

Brantley shakes his head. "You could be bleeding internally, Gus."

"I am driving myself. You should both leave the woman alone."

Wilkes laughs. He doesn't know what else to do. It may have been stupid to [hit] the old man the first time, but with every new statement, slugging him makes m[ore] sense.

"Enough," Brantley says, perhaps sensing the next assault. "I didn't sign on [for] this shit."

)emarais, with no one in his way, takes another deep, painful breath and hobbles
the doorway. Moments later the sound of Demarais's snowmobile breaks the
:nce and Wilkes gets to his feet.
You're just letting him go?"
I know where to find him later if you'd like to 'question' him further," Brantley
s.
Vilkes drapes an arm across his wife's shoulder and stares straight ahead: he
i't look at her. He has already forgotten the plan to dress her.
Help is coming," Brantley says, more to her than to Wilkes. "I'm going to bring
:k some paramedics for transport. They'll know what to do."
here's no apology from Brantley for the unceremonious treatment. Maybe it's
late for that.
How long?"
Ie looks at his cell phone and shakes his head.
Soon. You keep the fire going. If anybody comes by, try not to hit him."
Brantley gets as far as the door, then turns around.
Just so you know, I like these people more than I like you, Wilkes, and now I'm
una be the one who brought them trouble."
econds later the sound of the snowmobile is swallowed up by the daunting
tness and he's left alone with the muffled crackling in the stove and the near-
nt breathing of his wife.
Ie adds some pellets to the stove and begins to pick up her clothes, but he knows
t the blanket is keeping her warmer than anything else will. And he's afraid that
noving the blanket will show him damage he doesn't care to see. Item by item
lays the apparel on top of the blanket.
The kids," he begins, conversational, chatty. "Well, Brett is mad most of the
e because he doesn't want to admit that he misses you, but James isn't so cool.
can't fake it yet. When you get home, they'll be fine."
Ie looks for a response, especially to the boys' names. He thinks he sees a nod
rushes ahead.
Everybody needs some time away," he sputters. "But this is taking a good thing
far, isn't it?"
Ie forces a smile. A bad joke. Maybe she gets it. Maybe she is past conversation.
he blanket moves. Underneath one of her arms disturbs the stillness.
Keira? Do you want me to dress you?"

Her breathing seems irregular, as if she has been storing some, saving it. S moves her head slightly, not enough to constitute even a gesture, but maybe th remains some understanding, some awareness, some sensibility. Her lips p slightly and a sound spills out, then words themselves.

"I won't go back."

"Keira, you can't stay here. It isn't...it isn't safe."

He immediately grasps the absurdity of his words. It had been safe before arrived and assaulted an old man.

"I mean it's cold, dangerous." He calls her by name again, assures her that h is coming. "We'll all be home soon enough," he says, echoing words she already failed to respond to. If he keeps saying it, then maybe—"

Her head shakes slightly. It can mean anything, but he refuses to believe it denial.

"Yes," he says. "We'll be out of here in a few minutes."

"No," she says, a raspy exhalation. It sounds angry. Where does that emot come from when she hardly has the strength to breathe?

"Let's just...wait then...."

What will you do if you find her?

He remembers some syndrome he's heard of but can't remember the nam some bizarre situation when the victim falls in love with the kidnapper. Th what's happened here, he thinks. His wife has seen Demarais as the holder power, of warmth, of safety, and given herself over to his control. Once he gets out of here—

But he knows that in this case anyway the theory is absurd. Auguste Dema didn't come to New York and abduct Keira Wilkes and drag her north to Nuna where he held her against her will. He didn't give her a new name, force he choose death. Even if Wilkes doesn't want to face the truth, he knows that Kei here because she wants to be.

He notices some movement and considers she might be merely shivering.

"Do you want some of your clothes on?"

He's decided to act regardless of her answer. He peels back the blanket, afrai what lies beneath. Her breasts, her stomach, her thighs—the skin color is faded there is no necrosis. By force of will he ignores the extremities and tries to slip underwear over them, over her toes and feet already darkening, already lost to cold. He manages to get them past her knees and feels foolishly relieved when garment covers her enough to render her basically decent. He struggles with

and then some fleece he has never seen before. Maybe she bought it from
itok, or maybe it was part of a plan hatched long before, a scheme assembled
plotted in the comfort of that beautiful home he had worked all those long
s to buy. His anger, that emotion McNally had attributed to him, swells again.
hakes free of it.

er body is intact: no blood, no bruises. This Demarais has not beaten her or
ed her. He finishes dressing her, then gently lays the blanket over her
lders again, tries to move her arms under it. He catches a glimpse of her
ers: there is a hint of a lurid maroon near the knuckles, but the tips are black.
looks around, finds mittens, covers the damaged hands, then straightens her
ing as best he can. Demarais saw her naked, but at least the medical people
find her sufficiently clothed.

omeone will be here soon," he says, propping her up against him, pulling the
ket tight. He is shivering too; he hadn't realized that he too was cold. He can
breathing. If she can just hang on—

e first faint sounds of a motor revives him.

ear that? They're coming."

e shakes her head; this time it isn't the cold or some spasm. Her lips part again
her breath turns into a murmur, almost words, mumbled and unclear, and
gh he thinks the final word might be "die," he can't even be certain of that, or
esn't want to be.

ou aren't going to die," he says. "Not here."

e sound of the engines grows louder and, within minutes, Brantley bursts in
two workers in what appear to be prison-detail-orange jumpsuits.
ediately they set about wrapping the woman in a thermal blanket, getting her
en, laying her on a gurney, and rushing her out to a large vehicle with tractor
s for wheels. In minutes they're gone and Wilkes races toward his snowmobile
llow them.

antley stays behind.

ou go with her," he says to Wilkes. "I'll tamp out this fire. No sense adding
to your list of crimes."

alf-dozen clinicians race at triple speed through the Repulse Bay Health Center,
atypical beehive of this leisurely community. All attired in faded teal scrubs,
y seem immune to the cold that seems to have inhibited everyone else. And
ugh there may be a hierarchy of doctors and PAs and nurses, they all look the
e to Wilkes: all of them earnest, intent, eager to reclaim a life which, it seems,
owner no longer wants.

staffer leads him into a small lounge with several straight-back chairs in it,
hurries out. A tinny speaker rasps out some inappropriately jaunty bluegrass
le a fluorescent tube flickers in one of the two fixtures. Brantley has come and
e and given no indication of returning, probably having endured enough drama.
in Wilkes is alone in a waiting room wondering about his wife. It's LaGuardia
x without the upholstery. He wonders if Brantley's promise to fly him out of
e still holds.

n Inuit woman enters quickly, her expression placid, her voice so soft that
kes must strain to hear. He stands and looks at her badge. Ilisapie. He's unsure
ther or not to shake her hand, unsure what Inuit culture requires or forbids. He
ps his hands behind his back.

Your wife is very ill, Mr. Wilkes. I'm sure you know that."

e shakes his head. Ill? The word is all wrong. She hasn't contracted some
municable disease, developed some chronic ailment. Dying of exposure isn't
nor is being lured to her death by some lunatic seer.

ll?"

Her body temperature was critically low when she arrived—nearing twenty-
degrees."

he response frustrates him further. "In English?"

Low eighties," she says, ignoring his curtness.

e gathers himself. There is no reason to be disagreeable to the medical staff.

She looked," he says, softening his tone, "she looked...fragile, bluish. She was
lly breathing, but she was, right? Breathing?"

She has a heartbeat. She is breathing. We are helping that a little."

Can I see her?"

We're trying to warm her. In a case like this—"

So you're used to this. You know what to do."

Ilisapie nods, but without enthusiasm. Wilkes was hoping for more.

"We know what to do. We have to work from the core outwards. Her heart lungs have to be warmed first, if possible. Yes, you can see her."

"Her extremities. They looked bluish."

"It's more important now to keep her organs functioning."

"But you can do that, right? And she'll recover?"

The doctor motions for Wilkes to sit and takes a seat across from him.

"There are many risks, Mr. Wilkes. Rewarming can induce arrhythmia disrhythmia and once that begins, there's no way to guarantee returning the h to a normal rate. And the extremities, her toes and fingers, even her hands. With blood flowing to them—"

"But you can save her. That's what I'm asking."

He envisions her with prosthetics and finds the image disturbing, but his m flashes immediately to uplifting stories of soldiers returning from the Iraq with horrible injuries and then five, ten, months later, bicycling and skiing competing in triathlons. Wilkes can be patient, of course, make things easier her, maybe hire full-time nurses and rehab workers. She'd still be a mother to boys. The images flash through his mind so quickly that they prevent others fi worming in, but he knows they're out there and he knows he'll have to pay atten to them.

"That level of cold," the doctor says, "when it slows the heart that much, it sl the blood supply everywhere, even to the brain. We're not a sophisticated med center here, and we can't run complex neurological scans, but there's always a of damage...of permanent damage."

"Brain damage?"

"There's always that risk."

"Irreversible?"

"We've all seen medical miracles, but most of them really are miracles. Fro scientific point of view, the outlook is not promising, but as I say, we don't kn that, not yet."

"She was in that plane that landed in the river."

"I read about that."

Wilkes is hoping this Ilisapie will see the connection—one miracle engende another. But she doesn't work that way.

"Anyway," Wilkes says, "she recognized me before. She knew who I was. If brain isn't functioning—"

There is some brain function."

That's what I'm saying. It's not hopeless."

Wilkes sounds like a child who hasn't received the birthday gift he wanted but needs assurance that there'll be another gift the following day, every day. Ilisapie, though, won't acquiesce. Whether it's caution or cowardice, the approach doesn't sit well with Wilkes. If this backwater physician can't figure out what to do, there have to be other options.

Can we get her to a...better hospital?"

He chooses his words carefully. Better. Not more modern. Not larger. Better. The word is calculated to demean this woman, this facility, this town, this territory. It's a wholesale indictment of this country of quaint villages and airfields and hospitals in a strip mall. But if Ilisapie is insulted, she masks it well: she's there to answer questions.

If we medevac her out it may be half a day. We don't have that kind of time."

Make arrangements anyway. Take her someplace that can treat her correctly. I'll pay for whatever it costs."

I understand," the physician says. His reprimand, his denigration of what she does, has not affected her. "It may be a while. You can see her if you'd like."

After Ilisapie's diagnosis, he isn't sure he wants to, but rather than appear callous he silently follows her down the short corridor and into a small, dimly-lit, surprisingly cool room. Three staff members operate various machines he doesn't recognize but one he does: a ventilator. A fourth staffer seems to be doing nothing but monitoring the readouts, occasionally shifting the blankets that cover the torso. The arms and legs appear to have darkened, and any doubts Wilkes has about Ilisapie's prognosis vanish. His wife will be, already is, disfigured.

He accepts the term, allows it to repeat itself in his thoughts. Disfigured, yes, but alive, a wife and mother still. For better or worse, wasn't that the deal? Wasn't that always the deal when you took a chance that the person you married wouldn't someday give it all up, wouldn't vanish without a warning and take some secret along with her? And didn't she take the same chance with him? Besides, who understood risk and regret more than a Wall Street executive, one who had heard a hundred stories from a hundred investors whose grandfathers "could have bought IBM in the 50s." Well they didn't. Too bad. Wilkes was the kind of man who did. His risk had not worked out. It happened sometimes.

But whatever philosophical monologue is occurring within, his discomfort is apparent, and soon everyone else in the room looks equally ill at ease.

"I don't want to be in the way," he announces to no one in particular. Ilisa
takes his arm as if to guide him out, but he pulls back, leaving her alone with
colleagues to work the miracle they have already admitted is doomed to failu
By the time Brantley returns, Wilkes has run the gamut of scenarios, played out
the solutions while the pilot has been on his own rescue mission, trying to convir
Demarais to get checked out at the hospital, just in case.

"Wasted breath," Brantley says, still angry at Wilkes and now also at his brotl
in-law. "He says he's fine."

"I wasn't sure you were coming back."

"Did you hear what I said? Gus says he's fine. That should make you feel bet
You could have killed him."

"I just lost it."

"And he probably had a lot to do with it, but you can't go around punching
men. Jesus."

Wilkes tries to look relieved that Demarais is all right, but he doesn't care.

"I want to get my wife out of here," he says. "Now."

"What do you mean get her out?"

"She needs a real hospital. These people, they can't help her."

"Did they say that?"

"Not in so many words, but this place is really—primitive."

"Do you know what that involves, moving a patient?"

"I'll pay."

"That's not the issue. I can fly her anywhere, but without medical facilities
the plane, there'd be no one to help her if she needed it."

"It's better than just sitting here."

"No it isn't. She needs medical help, not two amateurs at 10,000 feet."

"Then we fly the staff too."

"Where? You've been in my plane. It's an old kite with some seats and a hea
and you know how the heater works. Where would you put all the life-sav
paraphernalia and the people to operate it?"

"Then we get a bigger plane."

"This isn't New York. There aren't hangars filled with standby planes read
fill in. Who's looking after her now, Ilisapie?"

"Yes."

"Liz. She's very good, the best."

"Liz?"

ust a nickname. She's a *Qallunaat*, not a native."

'ou know, I don't give a shit anymore about their words and their onounceable little language. This is the twenty-first century, for Christ's sake.
't they learn to speak English?"

isapie speaks English."

know. I talked to her."

only meant that she's from Montreal."

.nd that does what? Give me confidence?"

. gives you the option of speaking to her in French. Aside from that, she may
: a better idea of how we think."

Ve? You mean civilized people?"

antley exhales loudly.

know this can't be easy. If you don't want to talk—"

.ll right, I know what you mean. But she was painting a pretty bleak picture of
ything and I think she wanted me to say, go ahead, pull the plug. Is that what
mean by civilized?"

hat doesn't sound like her at all."

o you're on her side?"

didn't know there actually were sides, but she's respected here. I think your
is in good hands, the best hands."

•emarais is respected here too, isn't he? Respect seems to have a fairly low
hold."

•emarais is respected more for longevity than anything else. He's a throwback,
lisapie—"

eah, she's a real doctor from a real city. Now if she only had a real hospital."

:ople die in real hospitals all the time. And before you start condemning this
ity...never mind."

'hat?"

n not trying to be insensitive, but your wife chose Repulse Bay. She didn't run
> Los Angeles or Chicago or Tokyo, all places with big hospitals, all places
e the environment is less hostile. None of that is Ilisapie's fault. Let these
le try to help her. I'm going to find someone to take a look at the old man."

ou said he was okay."

e wouldn't tell me if he wasn't and I'm not an expert."

:sus, I only punched him in the shoulder."

ou weren't being merciful. Your aim was bad."

Brantley disappears through a set of doors and the room goes quiet again. clock on the opposite wall has no second hand so Wilkes must trust the inexor passing of time just as he trusts that team of medical personnel to be doing best. Alone in the waiting room, he reexamines his behavior: his need to e recompense from Demarais while delaying care for Keira.

Keira. He can no longer say the word without thinking of the other name she acquired somewhere. Sylvy. It seems more than an alias, more than s whimsical disguise to hide her whereabouts and her identity. In Baker Lake told Deidre her life story. You don't do that when you're hiding.

Sylvy then. He searches his memory for someone with that name. A charact a novel or movie? A friend he didn't know about? The mother of some chi James's class? Is it someone he knew, maybe from his own childhood? Th nothing.

It's a pretty name, a child's name. Keira was never one of those mothers pined for a daughter, at least not openly. She had given him two children, ag with him that there would be no more. Maybe that discussion should have revisited, but she never broached the topic, and he, their lives comfortable orderly, never chose to alter them. What if, though, what if there had been a before? What if somewhere in Keira's shadowy history, of which Wilkes seer know so little, what if she had had that baby, then maybe given it up for ado and obsessed over it all these years, dividing her love for him and Brett and J with some lost entity from her past. Or was there an abortion, a stillbirth, s tragic turn of events?

Brantley's return shakes him out of his surmise.

"Gus has a sprained wrist."

"What? I didn't hear you come in."

"You were dozing. Gus has a sprained wrist. He caught himself when he f when you knocked him down. An intern wrapped it. He'll be all right."

"Look, about before—"

"Believe me, these people are efficient and well trained. And trying to mo sick person on an unequipped plane would be nothing more than murder."

"I know. Really, I do. What did Demarais say?"

"He understands your anger, but he doesn't know why you're angry with hi

"God knows what he was doing up there with her—with a naked woman conscious—one who couldn't fight back—who he could leave for afterwards."

I don't believe that for minute, and I don't think you do either. My sister married oofball, not a pervert. Maybe she'd have been better off with a pervert, but it n't work that way."

Wilkes paces a few steps, then comes back and sits near the pilot.

"You can't stay here, right? You have flights scheduled?"

"I have to leave at first light, but I can come back."

"For the body."

"I didn't say that."

"But if it comes to that—"

"If it does, I can't transport her anywhere legally. I'd risk the hop to Baker Lake, from there, well there are rules about transporting—human remains."

The term stops them both short.

"Sorry," Brantley says.

"You said there are rules. What are they?"

Brantley hesitates. "We don't have to get into this now."

"I just want to know."

"Then let me worry about it. Did they let you see her?"

"They did. They're...doing things. What's it like outside?"

"Do you really have to ask?"

"I just want to get some air. A minute or two."

"Air we got," Brantley says as Wilkes moves toward the double doors, zipping the anorak he hasn't bothered to remove and pulling on his hat. Outside he misses the possibility of bears and wolves and any other animals that might do harm, but in seconds he is shivering and he hears a door close behind him.

"pie.

"Stay close to the building and you can survive for a little while anyway."

"I just needed some air. Did something happen?"

"No."

"In a bigger hospital? Could they do more?"

"I've worked in bigger hospitals, Mr. Wilkes. The techniques, the protocols, 're the same."

"But the equipment?"

"For specialized treatment it would make a difference—burn victims, heart ents, some cancers, but for exposure, we're as good as anyone else, maybe er than most. We see a lot of it."

"The end is always the same, too, isn't it?"

"It's not the time for that, but I think you know you may have to make a decisio

"Sooner or later?"

"Sooner than later," Ilisapie says.

Wilkes the financier admires Ilisapie's honesty, but Wilkes the husband offended by it.

"What about all your free health care?"

"We aren't charging you."

"Well, in the states people complain that they're getting thrown out of hosp beds because they're too expensive. Now you're doing the same thing to my w I mean what's the sense?"

If he has struck a nerve, she doesn't show it.

"Come inside," she says, opening the outer doors. Even in the near-darknes the vestibule he can see a quizzical look on her face. His comments have made sense, he knows. But he's not retracting anything, not in this place.

"We don't need her bed, Mr. Wilkes, believe me, but after we get her temperature stabilized, we can't do much more for her. We'll move her to our facility, same building, just down the hall. She can remain there until the cas resolved."

"Resolved."

"It's not a euphemism, Mr. Wilkes. Cases are resolved when people choos resolve them."

Calmness. Professionalism. They're his qualities too, or they were when manned a desk in Manhattan. When clients kick and scream about a tanking st or an abysmal Dow, he calms them with facts. Ilisapie is doing no less and approach is the same. Wilkes wants to like her, but until she can guarantee wife's full recovery, that's impossible.

"Doctor, I know you're trying to help. I just need a little time."

"But standing outside on a night like this will make you a patient, too. Why d you look in on her?"

She holds a door for him, but he waves her off.

"Another minute or two," he says. He owes her a thank-you but the words s in his throat. What has he to thank anyone for? The opportunity to witness the vestige of life slip out of the woman he remembers even now as vibrant and ac and beautiful? Is he supposed to evince some gratitude for the opportunit observe her death? He said his goodbyes in a dilapidated shed in a place even n remote and forbidding than the town itself. Who does he thank for all that?

Ie looks up to find a dizzying number of lights overhead. A thousand miles from
 nearest city, with no urban glow to interfere, there appear to be more stars than
 ces between them. Maybe the scientists are right about the numbers—
 ions—or maybe they've underestimated. Billions, not an incomprehensible
 ure to a man who works with numbers all the time. But could there be other
 ets of life that truly are incomprehensible? Could a blathering Inuit fakir,
 irvoyant, seer—whatever the hell Auguste Demarais wants to call himself—
 ld such a man possess some arcane power that allows him knowledge,
 areness, sensitivity? Billions of stars, most of them a mystery. Billions of
 ple, why couldn't some of them be a mystery too? Like Keira? Like Demarais?
 e Sylvy?

 ack inside he finds another person in the waiting room, a boy who cannot be
 re than twelve staring straight ahead from a chair in the corner.

 His father," Brantley says, "fell at home and hit his head."

 And his son had to bring him here?"

 I think the wife may have arranged the accident. There's a history in that
 ily."

 You know him?"

 Seen him around."

 Do you know everybody here?"

 The population is pretty static. Have a nice chat with Ilisapie?"

 I may have been a little brusque with her."

 Brusque?"

 Rude."

 She's a doctor. She sees a lot of distraught relatives and they're not always
 ite. I'm sure she understands."

 I should apologize."

 I already did."

 You?"

 She looked sort of frustrated when she came in so I told her you were an asshole.
 t's based on a small sample size, of course, but I feel confident."

 Wilkes smiles. The expression doesn't come easy, but he owes Brantley at least
 t much.

 I know you didn't do that."

 Words to that effect. She wants you to make a decision, right? It's hard to decide
 everyone."

"Everyone?"

"Yeah? For yourself, obviously, but for your kids, for her family, for the hospital workers, for me, especially for your wife. My dad used to say it was fun being an adult. It didn't take me long to figure out he was right."

"But I make decisions every day, and millions of dollars change hands on say-so. I just hit a key and it's done. I never look back—you can't—you're alwa talking to the next client or looking at the next deal or analyzing the next trend.

"Too bad you can't do that here. Listen, I can leave if you want to think t through."

"No, no. Maybe it's better to think out loud."

Brantley stretches out in a more comfortable position.

"Start thinking. I'm listening."

A young man in a teal uniform comes in, says something to the boy, then leav

"That kid," Brantley says. "He's probably going to be here for a while, and l probably done it before. How many times do you think he's seen his father sm his mother around, seen her retaliate? This is probably a refuge for him, m peaceful than his home."

Wilkes hears him but pays little attention. Keira is not going home—ever. ! will never see her room again, her clothes, belongings, all the minusc possessions that constitute a life. And her husband, kids. The finality of it ma him shudder.

"Still cold?" Brantley asks.

"Trying to come to grips," Wilkes says. "Trying to think the way Ilisapie wa me to think. She knows it's just a matter of time—and not much time either. W if we had the funeral here? I mean not a funeral, just a burial?"

"What about your kids?"

"I can get them up here. They can travel with Keira's folks. They could be h in two or three days."

"Be better if they walked."

"What's that supposed to mean?"

"In two or three days," Brantley says, "the ground is going to be just as froze it is now, and it'll stay frozen until June. There are no burials in Nunavut in winter. There's cremation but—"

"Not for Keira. She didn't believe in that. Neither do I."

"Then it's home, I guess."

"Jesus, what happens when people die up here?"

he bodies are stored. And the graves themselves, once they're actually dug,
hallow, what with the permafrost and all. I'm not trying to make things worse,
you have to know these facts. Like my dad said, being an adult—"
What would you do?"
Uh-uh. This has to be your choice. I can give you facts, that's it. Maybe you
d talk to someone here at the hospital. They don't have a counseling staff but
 deal with loss all the time."
hey don't know me. I'm just some, what's that word, *Qallunaat*."
hat word is for people who live here but aren't Inuit. The word for you is
or, but these folks'll help. That's why they're here."
ilkes kneads his forehead, trying to augment the flow of blood to his brain.
m not asking for advice," he says, "but I want to do what's best for Keira first,
 I'll worry about the...rest of us."
alk to Demarais."
ou're not serious."
you could keep from hitting him again. He's been here a long time."
nd of course he's a mystic."
e's—something—and we both know it. Hell, my sister knows it. She just
n't want to deal with it anymore. And if Keira is your first concern, then maybe
should talk with the last person who saw her. And I mean talk, not wave your
 around and threaten to kill him."
o you are giving advice."
can take you there."
can't leave Keira. She's on a ventilator. If something happens—"
 she's getting help breathing, that means nothing is going to happen very fast.
lives close by."
ilkes doesn't answer. He wonders if the mere sight of the old man will set him
gain. But worse than that, he is fearful of what Auguste Demarais knows or
s he knows or has somehow divined.
aybe I should remember my wife the way she was, you know, before."
on't you want to know what this is all about?"
emarais told you?"
e wouldn't do that. This doesn't concern me. But I asked him if he'd speak
 you. Now it's your choice."
 I go, I go alone."
antley looks apprehensive.

"I'm just going to listen," he assures the pilot. "Whatever this guy says, I'm going to listen."

"I'm not worried about him, I'm worried about you," Brantley says. "Hit again and you'll probably learn the Inuktitut word for lynch mob."

"Is there one?"

"There will be."

marais's house is little more than a large squashed carton with some smaller
:ons attached. All manner of jogs and angles lie beneath roofs of different slants
 (probably under that snow) different colors and materials. In the front are two
icrous window boxes.

/ilkes knocks on what appears to be the front door, pressing himself against it
:scape the weather. Demarais nudges it open and a wan glow, like a bar at
;ing time or just after, escapes into the darkness. There's barely sufficient light
ee the face inside, but Wilkes perceives no fear or apprehension despite what
urred hours before. The old man looks curious, maybe, but nothing more.

 just want to talk," Wilkes says, shivering. His quick pace from the hospital has
t the blood flowing; now, standing in one spot even for a few seconds, he is
nediately vanquished by the cold.

What else would you want to do?" the old man asks, as if there has been no
ory between them, no anger, no argument, no physical violence. "You come

/ilkes follows him through an essentially unfurnished living area and into an
n more spartan kitchen. Extending down from a cracked ceiling is a glaring
ure the size of a basketball with a chain extending almost to the table below it.
 room reminds him of childhood visits to his grandparents and that tiny kitchen
neirs: the undersized bright-white refrigerator with always a vase of flowers on
 an electric range with comically oversized coils, and their one concession to
dernity, a dishwasher on wheels.

emarais doesn't appear to have made even that concession.

You can sit," Demarais says. "And we can talk. I was going to have some tea.
you drink tea?"

Sometimes."

emarais moves slowly toward the sink and fills a kettle. His motions are
ing, painful; and Wilkes, aware that he has aggravated the situation, can barely
ch him without wincing.

 can go back to my room and get you something for the pain," Wilkes says.
pirin or Advil, something like—"

hey give me diarrhea. I don't take them. Tea will help."

Wilkes wants to remind him that tea is a stimulant and probably the last thing injured person needs, but he hasn't come here to argue or to make pronounceme that Demarais will merely ignore.

"Thank you for seeing me," Wilkes said. "I want to apologize for...before."

Demarais sits opposite Wilkes. The day's events have not blunted his candor

"Your wife. Has she passed?"

"The doctors are treating her."

"This will be the worst day of your life, Mr. Wilkes, the worst day you will e have. When you think about it, and you will forever, you won't even remember name."

"Maybe. Tell me what you know about Keira."

"And if the answer is words you don't want to hear? Brantley is not here protect me."

He raises the objection with as close to a smile as he can muster.

"I just want to talk."

"And listen? That's the hard part. Anyone can talk."

"Yes, and listen."

Demarais looks at the tea kettle. A few wisps of steam rise from the spout. tightens the cinch on his long flannel robe.

"Not ready yet," he says, then looks down as if he suddenly discovered the ta "What I know and what I think I know, it all blends together sometimes."

"You say you have dreams. When did they start?"

"I can't even remember, it's been so long."

Wilkes counts back to the crash on the Hudson.

"Was it last week?"

"It was years, decades maybe. I can't remember when I didn't have them."

"And Keira—Sylvy?—was in them?"

"Someone was in them, I didn't know a name. Sometimes I didn't even see face. It was a young girl at first, and she got older as I got older, as time went I always wondered if she was really aging or if it was only me, that I had seen so often and she seemed so familiar that I was adding years to make it all logic

"Somebody in Baker Lake said my wife was with somebody. Was that you?

"I have friends in Baker—old friends. I lost track of them when I was marr but now—you met Jane? My brother-in-law introduced you?"

"He did."

She's a good person, but she shouldn't have married someone like me. I let her so that she could find someone more—more stable, younger too. You are probably her age, but not you either."

Why not?"

Because you wouldn't love her."

And you do?"

Of course. I would not have married her otherwise. But yes, I was in Baker last week. I went because I felt that this woman was there and thought I could save her. I knew that once she came here to Repulse she would never leave. I wanted to stop ."

But you brought her back here anyway?"

We talked. She was very sad. She didn't want to leave you and her children. She d you had tried to make a perfect life for her."

Nobody gives up a perfect life."

Because there is no such thing. Even when we come close, we give it up. In ur mythology, your Adam and Eve, that's what they did. You lament their ision and blame them, but you forget that everything is temporary. How do you ow they didn't wake up the next morning, see clouds for the first time, and rvel at the sunrise? Perfection isn't supposed to last. Same with misery."

he tea kettle emits the slightest whistle. Wilkes motions for Demarais to wait.

When you were married to Jane, did you have visions of Keira?"

Not the way you think. Your wife is a beautiful woman, but to me it was erent. Jane was my wife. My feelings for others will never be the same."

But in your dreams—"

Yes, she was there, always in trouble and always afraid. Even in Baker, she ted to be farther away—from—home. And there are so many men with planes will fly anyone anywhere. I found her a good pilot, one that I could trust."

Brantley?"

No. That would have been too complicated. Besides, I pleaded with her to go k home."

Why didn't you try to notify someone?"

Your wife is not a child. I didn't understand what she was doing or what she ted, but it wasn't my place to stop her."

emarais's voice has gradually become subsumed by the now-raging tea kettle. old man pushes himself to his feet and pulls two teabags from a box on the nter, dropping one into each cup.

"I have some crackers if you—"

Wilkes politely refuses, then both men watch the tea steeping as if it were so
science experiment requiring close observation and documentation.

"If you leave the bags in too long," Demarais says, "the tea will be bitter."

They watch in silence for a moment more before the old man removes the b
and walks to the sink, dripping an amber trail on the floor. There are other sim
marks, all dried.

"Sugar? Milk?"

"No."

"Sometimes I add a little whisky—"

He pours in a small amount.

"If you'd like," Wilkes says. "Not for me. When she got here to Repulse, w
happened?"

"I took her to the hotel and found her a room. She had some clothes with her,
many, but she had bought some things in Baker. I wasn't afraid of her going
and freezing. She seemed to know what she was doing."

"Did you stay?"

"I got her settled in, told her about the town. I thought I was supposed to tal
her, learn about her. I even thought I was supposed to save her, that some gr
plan in the universe brought her to Repulse to be rescued. I drew a little map
her, told her where I lived in case she needed anything. I even gave her Brantl
name, someone to fly her back. Then I left her there."

"There?"

"In the hotel."

"And that was all?"

"You should be more candid in your questions. I don't have sex anymore. J
and I stopped a long time ago and I never had the urge to go about it with someb
else. It's too difficult. Too demanding."

Wilkes feels inexplicably relieved, as if some act of abstinence will m
everything normal. Demarais smiles.

"That makes you feel better. Why?"

"I didn't want her to be intimate with someone else."

"Sex isn't intimate. Men pay whores for sex, even here in Repulse. If you
better that's fine, but it isn't important. Her sadness, though, that was importan

"You already said she was sad, but you didn't say why."

ome people get that way near the end of their lives, not because they're afraid
ing, but because they aren't going to do all the things they wanted to do; others
ze they didn't really want to do them anyway. With your wife it was something
 like she had already been as happy as she would allow. I think you gave her
e of that happiness. What more can anyone do?"

ou make it sound like she had some kind of limit, like she could have some
e amount."

es, a limit. I didn't think of it like that. Drink some tea. You'll feel less angry."

m not angry, but there are things you aren't telling me and I need to know
."

Ve are seldom the best judges of what we need to know."

ilkes stirs the tea and forces a smile.

ou're laughing," Demarais says. "At me?"

a way. You say infuriating things that make me want to hit you."

ow you're coming to know yourself."

nd there's another one. How long were you and Jane married?"

marais shrugs. "It was a much longer marriage for her than for me. I'm not
 to be with, I know."

hen stop philosophizing like some, some Arctic Buddha and tell me what you
v. Did Keira dream of you?"

he didn't know me at all, until we started to talk. She told me about Deidre, a
g girl in Baker."

met Deidre."

our wife said it would be wonderful to live like that, alone and isolated with
ne to bother her and everyone to worry about her. Those shacks by the lake,
ound them appealing."

nd of course you told her there were some right here."

said ours were worse, more remote, more dangerous. Yes, I told her. She could
 asked anybody and learned that. She told me she was going to walk there."

ut you offered to drive her, like a good Samaritan."

ou'd have said no? You'd have let her die somewhere on the way?"

would have talked her out of it."

ell me what you would have said, Mr. Wilkes. What would you have said that
adn't already thought of? All I knew was if I let her go off by herself, she'd
or sure. Maybe someone would find the body and maybe not. It might not be

until summer and by that time some wild animal would make sure she was n
found."

"You could have called somebody."

"And done what? The most I could have done was find her in one of those pl
and have her arrested for trespassing, but even then, who would press char
And when she was released, then what?"

"So you're not accountable, I get it."

"In my religion we're all accountable. In yours too."

"I don't have a religion."

"You live in a Christian country. You don't practice Christianity? No or
accountable when a life is over, but before that happens we all are."

The light that hangs above them flickers slightly, then blazes again. Outside
wind has increased and begun funneling cold air under the doorway behind Wi
It was dead calm when he stood outside the hospital, now the return trip wi
unpleasant. Too short to be dangerous, but long enough to be uncomfortable.

"Where you dropped her off—"

"I got the stove started, found her fuel and blankets, even a bag of coffee a
pot. I tried to tell her that she could stay with me, that I would take her up i
again the next day. Sometimes people will have a vision of the end and ch
their minds."

"But she said no."

"She told me to come back today and she would decide."

"Did you leave her?"

"Yes. She is an honest person. We talked for a while and then I left."

"Talked about what?"

"She told me about the plane crash and the rescue. Said she was in a daze f
of it. She had argued with someone in the airport—"

"And someone named Em? Did she mention that too?"

Demarais shakes his head.

"But the next day, yesterday, I came back as soon as there was light."

"And found her naked. Did you touch her?"

"I put another blanket over her."

"You know what I mean."

"You worry too much about the insignificant, her nakedness, an old boyfr
me. The stove was almost out. Her clothes were next to her. I don't know how
undressed in the cold. I'd have been shaking so much—"

How long can someone last in those conditions?"

"The younger you are, the longer your heart can hold out. But going through that initial pain...unless she had medication, drugs, pills—?"

"She didn't. What do you mean the initial pain?"

"I don't know. Are you finished with your tea?"

"You live here. You've seen it. What would it be like, the pain?"

Demarais cups the ceramic mug as if trying to warm his own hands.

"There would be discomfort first of course, like anyone who was cold. Then shivering."

"You're stating the obvious."

"I'm not. I mean shivering so violent that bones can break, ribs can snap. It can tear muscles and tendons. I've seen it. Bodies can become twisted and contorted."

"Keira didn't look like that."

"I don't think she would allow it. Why do you want to hear this?"

"After that, what?"

"Head pain. Awful head pain. The circulation slows down so much that the brain has to go without. Eventually it stops—everything stops."

"Everything?"

"Once the brain is asleep, the body doesn't know cold anymore. So at the end, it's just warmth and quiet."

Wilkes has known people who suffered for years before dying, who spent the better part of their old age in some neurasthenic state surviving via tubes and machines and the assistance of strangers trained to use them. An uncle with a body riddled with cancer and the father of a co-worker burned in a fire. Both had hung on for months in crippling agony mitigated only by morphine. Maybe Keira was escaping a worse fate.

Demarais adds a few more drops of whisky to his tea, then leans across the table and looks his visitor in the eye.

"There's more. When she was a child she got angry one day and did something childish, and someone died."

"Who?"

"Another child."

"She never told me that."

"She was a child—"

"She still would have told me. Or her parents would have told me. You can't keep a secret like that. Someone would have—are you sure that's what she did?"

"Of course not, but she is. There was a birthday party," he says, and lays out
story Keira has confided in him, filled with sharp detail and precise descripti
Wilkes is silent throughout and even silent for a moment after Demarais finisl
Outside the wind has dropped off again and the only sound is the rumbling of
compressor in the ancient refrigerator.

"I'm sorry," Demarais says. "That's what she said happened."

"But it was an accident. A prank. Nobody killed anybody. Didn't you tell
that?"

"What we believe ourselves can never be replaced by what someone
believes. I think you know that."

"But we can change our minds. Jesus, an accident—her life revolves around
accident that happened thirty years ago? My life, the kids', everything beca
some girl tripped and fell and hit her head? And everything since then has be
what? An act? Something, fake?"

"She was glad the girl died. She didn't like her."

"But she didn't kill her. Kids can be mean, want others to get hurt. It's just ki

"She said she was glad."

"It doesn't matter. It was still an accident."

"From our viewpoint."

"From anyone's. Did she tell her parents?"

"She was told not to talk about it."

"Her parents said that?"

"They told her talking about it would only make it worse."

Wilkes takes a deep breath and stares at the light fixture. It's ugly and dirty
inside it are bulbs of different wattages. It's a joke, a fucking joke like Dema
himself, like Nunavut, like the marriage he'd been part of and the woman
shared it. Too bad Demarais hadn't just let her go wander off toward the outs
of Repulse by herself, let her just die a mysterious, anonymous death. He cc
have mourned a loving wife, not some vision of a woman who never really exis

"So that child. That was Sylvy?"

Demarais nods.

"Wait here," he says. "One minute."

Demarais goes back into the living room, then returns and lays Keira's lice
on the table.

"I wasn't going to keep it. I just forgot. And this. This belongs to your wife,
says, unwrapping some newsprint to display a piece of amber-shaded ivory in

pe of some sleek animal, akin to the hood ornament of a Jaguar. Through its
k, just above the front shoulder, is a hole through which has been threaded a
ce of rawhide, long enough to fit comfortably around someone's neck. Demarais
les it toward Wilkes. "It's an amulet."

What animal is this?"

A polar bear."

Wilkes smiles. "Is this more Inuit humor?"

To this artist the bear was sleek and fast. Take it, leave it with her."

Why? Is this some magical, spiritual?"

It's just a polar bear."

hey are silent for a moment as the wind again rattles past, then just as suddenly
ps to calm, only to gather again.

The child that died, why does my wife have to suffer for that?"

In our world there is evil, the tuurngait, and they make us pay every time. Even
ve have done nothing wrong, they make us think we have."

Conscience?"

Yes, but guilt and fear too. Your wife felt a similar responsibility, and nobody
ld remove it from her. Not you, not your sons, not a good home, nothing."

But after thirty years? Why now?"

That I don't know. It's going to begin snowing soon and Brantley will not be
py when he has to fly in it. You should hurry and be with your wife."

Is that a psychic forecast?"

I have a weather radio. Take the amulet."

Wilkes pockets it. "If you have to pay a doctor or anything for your wrist—"

Save your money," he says with a knowing smile. "My brother-in-law will be
ing most of it anyway."

Thank you for the tea."

Demarais nods. "Just now," he says, "you felt rage and overcame it. It will not
he last time. You know that, don't you?"

I think so."

If she does not survive, will you take her back home to America?"

I don't know yet."

Your children, they'll want to see her, but not like this."

And you think she should stay here."

She should stay where she belongs."

Until a few weeks ago that was—home, with me."

"No one can know a woman like her husband. You'll make the right choice."

The words sound like a suggestion, but they resonate with indictment: Wil doesn't know his wife at all. Demarais understands that. So does Brantley. And t high school girl in Baker, and even McNally still cashing checks back in N York. Everybody knows. For Wilkes to be called upon now to make this fr decision is ludicrous, but no more ludicrous than his resentment toward Demar The old man saw her naked, but in truth, everyone saw Keira Wilkes naked everyone except her husband.

"Walk back quickly," Demarais says, pushing open the door. There is handshake or other nicety. They are simply two men who talked and finish talking.

In the waiting room at the Health Center, Brantley is dozing lightly but awak when Wilkes arrives.

"Everything okay?"

"He's fine," Wilkes says. "I'm going in to see Keira."

"I'm just—resting. Nobody said to get you."

"Keira's going to die. Do you think she should stay here...afterwards?"

"Afterwards? You mean be buried here?"

"Yes."

"That was Demarais' advice?"

"I think maybe it's mine."

"What about your family?"

"Keira's my family too," he says, and hurries toward the patients' corridor.

e sterile procedure is occurring and Wilkes waits in the corridor, making
mfortable small talk with one of the nurses. She's from a small town in
bec, almost two-hundred miles from Montreal. Another Qallunaat, apparently,
e's unsure whether the word is derogatory so he thinks better about mentioning
e hands him a surgical mask and leads him inside.
's a precaution," she says, "for anyone whose skin has been compromised."
mpromised, a more genteel word than ruined or destroyed, but there's no
g the meaning. He's seen Keira, though, so a euphemism serves no purpose.
he can probably hear you," the nurse says, then makes an obvious, but still
izing, distinction between hearing and listening, and another between
ning and comprehending. Then, having exhausted all her caveats, she drags a
closer to the bed and rushes out.
r a moment Wilkes remains standing and says nothing, simply listens to the
murmur of the machines that are keeping Keira alive.
extraordinary means, he says to himself. He's seen enough living wills to
the term. He and Keira have made no such provisions. They're barely in their
es, for God's sake. Who can fault their certainty that they could go another
de or two without thinking about choices like that? Other situations should
occupied their thoughts: choosing schools for the boys, sweating out Brett's
r's license, guiding them through first loves and first heartbreaks. Their own
ality was never on the horizon. It should have been.
missed something," he says, his face inches away from Keira's. "Tell me what
s."
looks around. He doesn't want anyone to hear the angry edge in his voice, but
esn't seem able to file it down.
ou had no right to leave this way. None."
balls up the mask and shoves it into a pocket, then for a moment or two
tly watches the monitor flashing numbers behind her, signs of life, little more.
egrets what he said, but if he hadn't told her, that would be one more secret
een them, one more of God knows how many.
wants to touch her, and though he doesn't shrink from the thought of it from
queamishness, he is afraid her skin might actually break. He lays a hand softly
r bare shoulder, convinces himself she is listening

"That day you flew out with the boys," he says, "maybe if I had been the
could have been different."

He lets the words register.

"The boys miss you. I don't know what to tell them. I don't know if they're r
for the truth and I don't even know what the truth is. But they're okay, and th
be okay until you're, you know, ready to come home."

A lie, exactly what he wanted to avoid: they aren't okay and she isn't co
home. That realization doesn't stop him, though.

"They enjoy being with your folks. It's like a vacation for them. They're alr
tired of me."

She stirs slightly. A response? An involuntary contraction? He doesn't know
he repeats himself, calling the boys by name each time, adding inconseque
details about homework and grades and school buses and snacks. He mention
parents again, her sister Hayley, adds other relatives, tries to emphasize the
to whom she feels close, avoiding the others. He mentions Valentine's Day
fabricates a white lie about already having ordered her roses. The lies come e
as he plays out the year: it'll be spring soon enough and there's her garden to
to and plans to be made for the summer. As the fantasy gathers strength he a
full month at the Cape or Nantucket, no more piddling two-week vacation fo
Wilkes family. She stirs again. Some miracle is about to occur, some dea
resurrection right out of a Victorian novel or a mawkish screenplay. Or m
there'll be nothing more than a revelation where he learns everything. Who
those evil spirits Demarais was talking about? The tuurngait? Maybe they'll re
her and give her a voice to clarify everything. Maybe if he waits.

Nothing.

The silence renders him almost manic. He talks more feverishly, rapidly, his
and volume increasing as if in inverse proportion to her diminishing moven
and slowed breathing. She is hurtling farther away as he resolves to pull her
It's a struggle he can't win.

He leans close again and lowers his voice. One last try.

"Demarais says you came here to die. Tell me why you did that."

He can hear breaths, one quietly following the other, but he can see no risin
falling of her chest. The motionlessness, the pallor, the silence. This isn't K
this is some representation formed out of the cold to distract him while his
recedes from his sight. He lifts his hand from her shoulder, then moves back.

The door swings open and three staff members enter.

I thought she moved a little when I mentioned our sons," he says. He's given up the miracle but hasn't lost hope. The two feelings seem contradictory and he's quick to add, "Do you think she heard me?"

"It's likely," a nurse says, a man about Wilkes's age.

"I...uh...was talking and...that mask..."

The nurse waves off his concerns. The mask is protocol only.

"I need to check some dressings," he says. "You can stay if you'd like."

"But that movement," Wilkes repeats. "If she can still move a little, respond you know—"

"I know you're looking for encouragement," the man says, "but right now we have to keep her alive. We'll let the doctor handle the rest."

"And the possibility of brain damage?"

It's not the question to ask the duty nurse and Wilkes knows it even before the words escape.

"I can't," the man says, carefully lifting a blanket from Keira's chest. "I'm just not qualified to make that judgment. Your wife has age going for her, of course, but time of exposure and temperature, those are hard to overcome. I wish I could be more helpful, more optimistic."

He points Wilkes to a supply closet across the corridor. "A coffeemaker inside, do yourself, take some to your friend." When Wilkes returns to the waiting area with two cups, Brantley is dozing again, his cell in his lap. He bolts awake when Wilkes arrives and immediately reaches for his anorak.

"I gotta leave. I have to make this run. Promised someone."

"But you'll come back, right?"

"Tomorrow, this time, maybe earlier. I'll be here."

"What if...nothing happens by then?"

"Then we'll figure something out. There's a room at the airfield where I can sleep a while. Maybe you should do the same?"

"You can use my hotel room."

"Nope, I've done this before. You use it. Get some rest."

Wilkes hands him the extra coffee and Brantley moves toward the door, then turns around.

"Worse comes to worse there's my sister. We do actually like each other. She'll help."

"I'll be okay." He isn't sure if he's reassuring the pilot or himself.

He paces the room like an expectant father, a grim irony. The nurse glance
and Wilkes shows him the coffee cup.

"Good," the man says. "You found it. You can go back in if you want."

"I was wondering. Is Dr. Ilisapie still around?"

"She's five minutes away."

"I mean if Keira took a turn, could the doctor be here?"

"Yes."

"And...do you have a minute?"

"Of course, what is it?"

The man does not sit. He may have a minute, but little more.

"I understand," Wilkes begins, hesitant, "that when someone dies here, you c
bury them, right?"

"June 5."

"What?"

"The day is stuck in my head. We have a weather-watcher who predicts the th
It's just an average, really. But this year, he says, June 5."

"And until then?"

"We store the remains. Sometimes for a visitor the service is held right after
passing and the family doesn't come back. Even the burial is private, unadverti
It just happens. Sometimes the family returns and there's a ceremony. It's u
them."

"So with Keira, if, you know, the worst happens, you would store her?"

"You could come back for a service, or have the service here and the burial c
take place when the ground was right."

"June 5."

"It's just an estimate," the nurse repeats, his voice apologetic, as if he v
somehow to blame for the frozen ground. "I'll be around in case you need
doctor."

Wilkes smiles.

June 5.

Their wedding anniversary.

In the lobby the shock slowly overspread him. It isn't what shock is suppose
do at all: it should stun, astonish, paralyze. And it should have occurred earli
that ramshackle building on the perimeter of town, on the perimeter of life it
But now it keeps building, piling on, rising. Maybe the pace, the cold, the inf
desolation of the landscape; maybe they don't allow for reasonable and expe

man reaction. Or what he calls shock is nothing other than a crushing and suffocating depression.

He wants to call McNally but his cell is worthless. He tracks down the same nurse yet again (his name is Herman; his ID badge is finally visible) who shows him a phone and gets him an outside line. "It's for emergencies," he says. "If a call comes in, you have to hang up."

Wilkes dials McNally's number and hears a groggy hello.

"You said call anytime. Just checking in."

"So you found her."

"How do you know?"

"Your voice. And there's more, right? And it isn't good."

"She's alive."

Wilkes hears an audible sigh.

"Alive," McNally says. "So I was right. I told you—"

"She's very sick. She's dying."

"Shit."

McNally can be flip, cynical, sardonic, even funny. Anger doesn't sit comfortably with him, renders him momentarily silent.

"We found her yesterday afternoon."

"Man, I'm sorry. Goddamn it!"

"I'm just, you know, waiting."

"Where are you?"

"A hospital in Repulse Bay."

"Repulse? If I were naming towns—" He stops himself. This isn't the time. "What happened to her?"

"The cold. The elements."

"Cases like this, runaways, whatever—Did you say the elements?"

"She just got herself into a bad situation. The cold up here is overwhelming. The doctors don't think they can save her, and even if they did, she'd never be the same."

"Those doctors up there—primitive, probably backwards—"

"They're fine. The hospital here is good. Everyone is doing what they can."

"Sorry, man. Fuck it all, I told you she was okay when you first hired me. I was right."

"And she was then. She told someone she came here to...to die. I didn't want to believe it, but I think it's true."

"Is this a criminal case? Is someone responsible?"

Wilkes would love to blame Demarais, an easy target, an old coot with we
ways and bizarre mannerisms who wielded some occult power over her, lured
there, then became an eyewitness to Keira's last self-destructive acts. But Demar
isn't the villain here.

"This was beyond us," he says. "You understand your business; I did
understand my wife."

"I know what you think," McNally says. "A PI searches for a missing pers
who turns up dead. Shit happens. Well maybe it does on TV, but when I searc
find them. Maybe if I had come with you—maybe my wife was right."

"You'd have been one more witness, nothing more."

Wilkes explains the complications involved in death and burial in the Arctic, a
McNally, though he hardly says a word, expresses his frustration and discomfit
with an ongoing series of guttural sounds and the occasional epithet. But he list
well, and at the end Wilkes is sure he grasps the situation.

"So you have a decision to make."

"I know. I have to ask you something. What would happen if I didn't
anyone?"

"You just told me."

"I trust you. As far as everyone else is concerned, she disappeared and I follow
her into Canada and never found her."

"Wilkes, listen. This is a bad time to have to make a decision on anything,
alone something this serious. But don't make the wrong one."

"I don't know what the wrong one is. I can tell people she disappeared
happens. It did happen."

"But you found her. Do you know what kind of trouble you'd be asking for?"

"No one knows about this except you."

"So you were what, invisible when you crossed the border? In my line of w
that skill would be invaluable."

"Plenty of people saw me, but they're locked away in the Arctic. Repulse Ba
not Montreal. No one is going to bump into these people. Most of them didn't kn
I was looking for my wife, only that I was looking for someone. They have a l
weekly newspaper filled with wolf warnings and polar bear relocations and min
complaints and pot luck suppers. Nothing that ever happens in Fairfield Count
going to wind up here, not unless we get an influx of wolves back home."

"How about video cameras?"

"In Repulse Bay? It doesn't matter."

does matter. In the old days of security tapes, they really were tapes. You them and erased them and used them again. Now they're digital, so why erase ? Storage is cheap and efficient. Your face could end up on a flash drive for a red thousand years."

e'll all be gone by then."

ut you're there now. Do the police know you found her?"

e have EMT's. They brought her in."

don't mean the Mounties. I mean cops, in Wilton, in the city. What about that tive, that Staubley? What are you going to tell her when you're home and rently no longer searching?"

don't know. It's all just happening, just a thought. Anyway, it's none of her damn business."

cNally has pushed him far enough to pull back.

kay, I understand," he says. "Why don't you get things squared away up there then we can worry about the legalities. Can I just tell you though, you're going ve to sign off on things, forms, legal documents. Your signature will be your . How many times are you willing to lie?"

m not concerned about that."

et concerned. A man whose wife dies goes on with his life. It may not be the e wants, but he can make it into something. And his kids, if he has kids, reach understanding, adjust, get by. Understand?"

es, what—?"

ut a man whose wife goes missing and stays missing and becomes part of an solved situation. That man has nothing, and his kids keep watching the door e their lives go by, and they get angrier and angrier every time the doorbell and their mother isn't ringing it. This scheme of yours is the worst of both ds."

didn't think of it that way."

know. If the local cops find out that there's been some kind of foul play and I about it, do you know what that makes me?"

n accomplice?"

n accessory after the fact. I don't want to be an accessory after or before or g. I don't want to be an accessory at all. Tell me how you found her."

ow much time do you have?" he asks, and skims the details, soft-pedaling the bility of her being "with" someone, but leaving out nothing else, including tercation with Demarais.

"And you actually hit this guy?" McNally says.

"I lost it. I apologized."

"I'd have done the same thing. Is he going to sue?"

"He's like a—I don't know—kind of mystic. I don't think money means muc
him."

"If he needs fuel to heat his house and do all the things you need to stay
when it's a hundred below, money means something."

Wilkes tries again to explain Demarais's spirituality, some sort of prim
quality that allowed him a clearer understanding of the world. The mor
explains, the more Demarais sounds like a noble savage, a throwback to s
centuries-old Cooper novel, an accumulation of clichés that doesn't even ring
with Wilkes. Yet, it's pretty accurate.

"And then Brantley," McNally says, "the pilot. Maybe he'd like a nice settle
to keep silent."

"He's not like that; besides, isn't he an accessory too?"

"He's done nothing wrong, yet. I know I'm giving you a hard time. As a, I
know, fellow human, I'm sick about this. As a PI, I can't give you legal advice
our lives are filled with contacts and witnesses, none of whom would ever
you a second thought until some uniformed agent waves a picture at them and
'Ever see this guy?'"

Wilkes knows the answers.

Yep, saw him in a bar in Saskatoon. He was looking for action.

He was checking out my legs on the plane.

He was in here buying clothes.

He looked at a piece of artwork.

Already the trail is long and obvious and replete with witnesses who can
him in a myriad of locations at various times.

"You haven't broken any laws," McNally says. "That's a good thing. Be
that, I don't know how I would ever handle what you're going through, just l
the woman I love in an instant. And I really and truly don't want to make t
worse. But at least let me touch base with the locals back here, maybe tell Sta
your wife's not missing anymore. You're just updating what you told them a
ago."

The nurse waves to get Wilkes's attention, puts a hand to his ear to mimic a p
conversation.

"I have to get off," Wilkes says. "Do whatever you think is right."

Think everything through," McNally says. "Make good choices."

Wilkes reclaims his seat in the waiting room. He had misjudged McNally, assuming that maybe because the PI dealt with sleazy characters, swindlers and rats of all shapes and sizes, he could turn a blind eye to this seemingly innocent deceit. Another miscalculation.

He pulls on the anorak, yanks the hood over his head, slides quietly past the main desk, unmanned at this hour, and exits into the night. With his hands buried deep in his pockets, he walks. He has no destination. He wants to feel the freezing air catching in his throat, to experience that elemental fear that only the most hostile nature can instill. He focuses on the lightly falling snow, at first, then the streetlights, then nothing. His mind shuts out the cold because it can, just as Keira shut out life. No more than a hundred yards from the hotel he wills himself to turn around and wills his legs to move, to run. He stumbles once and catches himself, then stumbles again and falls, landing on hands he has quickly extracted from his pockets. To an insomniac staring out a window, or one of those ubiquitous video cameras McNally mentioned, he's a drunken man weaving a path home. He envisions Keira sitting in that shack with a blanket around her, naked before Marais found her, naked in cold that he would not have been able to fathom only days before. Brantley said that freezing to death occurred in stages, the final one resembling a morphine high. But getting there, the shivering and the pain and the knowledge that your life was being forced deeper and deeper inside until no vestiges of it remained on the surface, how much more agonizing could death be? And she had chosen that over a life with him, with her children.

"It's Sylvy," she says when he asks yet again. "I killed her. I don't want to kill again."

"It was an accident. Like a plane landing in a river. So many people could have died but didn't. Accidents. Luck. That's all it is."

"I hated her. I was glad when she fell."

"That's different from making her fall. Kids can be mean. Brett is always pushing his brother. It doesn't mean anything."

"I never thought of it like that."

"That's what kids do. You and Hayley. Brett and James."

"Maybe I was wrong."

"You were. Yes. Now you'll come home."

"I'm too tired. So are you. I can see it. We should sleep."

She's right. He is tired. And why shouldn't he be—racing from town to town
a strange country, relying on strangers to help, living in stark rooms in ugly hot
grabbing a meal when he can. He's exhausted. He should sleep. And he woul
he could stop Keira from yelling his name.

But it isn't Keira.

"Mr. Wilkes!"

"I'm trying to rest," he says. He's angry, but it isn't Keira.

The voice is louder, right in his ear.

"Stand up. Now!"

He knows the voice. Ilisapie. His mind gradually clears. He isn't talking to Sy
he isn't talking to anyone. He's on the street where he fell the second time and ne
got to his feet. Now, panicked, he does. He leans on the doctor and together t
drag each other to the door and stumble inside.

He looks at the clock. He has been outside less than five minutes.

"You're okay," the voice says.

Ilisapie. She wears jeans. A heavy brown sweater. Her hair is pulled back
someone who has just been awakened but must appear professional and invol
A red anorak, unzipped. She's come from home probably after being rousted f
a pleasant sleep in a warm bed, maybe with her husband, maybe with kids in
next room. He doesn't know much about Ilisapie because he has never asked,
there is little mystery about her presence.

"Is she gone?"

"Yes, Mr. Wilkes. I'm sorry."

"It's what she wanted. What time?"

"Pardon?"

"What time? What time did she die?"

"Four-fifteen."

"Central Time. Five-fifteen at home. I want to remember the time."

"You'll have the certificate when—"

"Another decision I won't have to make, isn't that right? You would have t
to talk me into pulling the plug and I would have said no. I would have ha
decide, but now I don't. Keira decided for me. She decided everything."

Ilisapie nods. "Did you want to see her?"

"I'm shivering."

"Shivering is good," Ilisapie says, and leads him to Keira's room.

28

5 a.m. CST, for the record.

he nurse stands in the doorway, hands at his side, waiting. Someone has just wed coffee and the aroma contends with the pervasive smell of antiseptic sprays food cooked long before. The occasional brush of wind against the window turbs the quiet. All part of the final scene Wilkes wants to remember, though he er really understood the play.

It was peaceful," Herman says. "She just stopped breathing."

Could you have resuscitated? Adrenaline?"

And atropine, yes. But your wife's heart was badly damaged."

And her mind?"

I don't think she felt pain at the end."

Vilkes nods. He knows they did the right thing, like Jasmine in the airport that ht, and McNally letting him go alone, and Brantley and—Jesus, everyone does right thing and everything turns to shit anyway. He wonders if there was one take, one omission, one final failing, but he remembers McNally's admonition ut remorse, that it's a phony emotion. Maybe that's true: as futile as it is to beat self up over actual mistakes, it's even worse to do so over imagined ones.

ater come the paperwork and forms and an official cause of death, but Wilkes y half listens to what follows. His head throbs, the pain centering itself behind eyes but radiating everywhere—his neck, his shoulders, his chest. A rush of tigo comes and passes and he forces himself to his feet, trusting the floor to be re though he can't feel it. He holds onto a table for support.

I'm going back to the hotel," he says to Ilisapie.

It's bad out now. The wind. I'll have someone go with you."

le refuses. He wants to sleep, not because he's particularly tired, the fatigue he s will not submit to sleep, but he wants to be alert and awake later. Decisions be required and he will have to make them before Brantley comes back. Nally scoffed at the plan never to tell anyone what happened, to relegate Keira "missing" status forever, but Wilkes has not given up the idea entirely. There e been precedents. Once when he and Keira were traveling in the West, they rd the story of a Wyoming schoolteacher who went for a run in a forest one rnoon and was never seen again. That very day, in front of witnesses, the nan had argued bitterly with her husband, but in a western forest that seemed

to stretch out forever, her body had never been found. How much more vast w
the expanses of Nunavut. How much more desolate? Who could ever doubt tha
person could be lost here, lost and never found? And who would ever hold Mar
Wilkes culpable?

But here of course there were the doctor and the first responders and Demar
and Brantley (and back in Baker Lake, Deidre and Manitok) and God knows h
many others whose path Keira crossed on her way to this death. McNally v
probably right: secrecy is not a viable option.

And Ilisapie was right. The weather has deteriorated. Wilkes carefully walks
the hotel and, at the entrance, senses someone a few paces behind. Herman
followed him.

"Just wanted to make sure on a night like this," the nurse says, then turns quic
back. Does he mean the weather? Isn't every night a night like this?

In the room with every light blazing, Wilkes dozes, but before even a hint
daylight nudges the southern horizon, he returns to the hospital. Ilisapie is g
and he speaks with a stolid Inuit woman named Olanna whose overwhelm
accent masks an excellent grasp of English. There is some more paperwork to
out, forms that Wilkes sleepwalks through. When he asks about local burial,
June 5 date surfaces again, like a mantra.

"That's our anniversary," Wilkes says.

"This winter has been very bad," Olanna says without acknowledging
unfortunate coincidence, "and not much snow, nothing to insulate the grou
Maybe June 5 is too early, but I have to write it."

"Until then, what?"

"Come," she says. "I will show you."

In a small fenced off area behind the hospital sits a mustard-yellow box-
whose sides are slatted like an old railway cattle car. In the center is a sliding d
double-padlocked.

"Until late March, we store remains waiting for burial," Olanna says. "It's co
outside than we could ever produce with normal refrigeration."

"And after?"

"In the hospital we have a small morgue. It's...small. We do what we can."

Wilkes tries to probe her eyes, but she looks away. Images of dead bo
doubled up in some makeshift freezer, of Keira lying next to someone, or ur
someone, overcome him. It seems barbaric, another form of primitive desecrat

'ou have misgivings," Olanna says. "It's a body though, and the spirit has
idy passed on."

's my wife's body," he answers, struggling against his own anger.

nd I understand," she says. "Some would say that in your tradition you also
ie the body when you embalm it. There is a body and a spirit. We protect the
but never defile the spirit. That happens only when people are alive."

r words sound so much like an accusation that Wilkes wants to defend
elf. He hasn't defiled anyone's spirits, least of all Keira's. But Olanna is merely
g her job, nothing more, and Wilkes remains calm as the two of them stand in
old near the truck.

Vhat will you do then, Mr. Wilkes?"

want her to be treated as if she were home."

hen you must take her home and have an American funeral," she says.
ie."

e leads him back inside.

en, sometimes fifteen thousand dollars, isn't that right?" she asks.

or a funeral? Yes."

nd this is for someone already dead?"

Je do it to show respect."

or each other. The dead can't understand or appreciate it."

Vhat about the spirit, the one you say has passed on?"

think they would be amused, but they would be happier if you carried good
ghts, honored their memory and not their grave."

r face is kind, strangely soft in this unforgiving environment, and her smile is
e but genuine. Wilkes does not want to argue with her, but he isn't sure she
rstands.

agree," she says. "There is something barbaric about leaving a body out to be
ged by animals or rot in the air, something that speaks against us as humans.
f we protect the spirits of people while they're alive, and protect their remains
they die, isn't that enough?"

Iaybe we do the same thing in different ways," Wilkes says.

you were my husband," she says, broadening her smile, "I would want you to
for me this way, even though I disagree."

hen why would you want me to?"

ghting for her like this: in a way you honor her spirit. Brantley. He is your
?"

"You know him?"

"Everyone knows Curtiss. He's a good man, but you must tell him. He prepare the plane. There are rules and legalities, even up here. We may have own territory, but we are still Canadian and our nation has laws. He will k what they are."

"I'm not trying to be difficult."

"On this day you have the right. Let Brantley worry about details. You will him plenty of money to do it, of course. As I say, we all know Curtiss."

Wilkes forces a smile.

"You're the second psychic I've met today."

"Anyone would know what you're thinking. This awful day, you must let o share some of it. You have children?"

"They don't know yet."

Olanna frowns.

"I know," he says. "I'm going to tell them."

"And they will help you?"

"We'll help each other. Right now I just have to leave this place."

Olanna turns and leads him back indoors, then grasps his arm.

"This is not a place of death," she says. "This town, this region. I don't wan to remember it that way. There is life here too."

Wilkes nods politely as she leaves, but he sees no life in Repulse Bay. trappings of a normal town don't matter, not when the cold overwhelms e space, violates every sanctuary, jeopardizes every life.

He calls Keira's parents. He expects shock and disbelief, but there is none. Eason cries softly in the background while her husband gathers the details—d that omit Demarais and the miserable shack where their daughter died accident, Wilkes says. Visitors here underestimate the cold and get themselves trouble, get caught away from shelter, lack basic survival skills. He sells the effectively because it contains several fragments of truth, and the Easons neve the overriding question: Why in the name of Christ was she there? He asks to keep it from the boys and hopes they will honor the request, though he kno will be difficult.

He leaves a message for Andy at work, gives his assistant the same ske account. He wants no return call. He'll be in touch.

He reaches Brantley, still in Winnipeg.

know the options," he tells the pilot. "I saw the van where they store the bodies.
taking her home. You said something about an air tray?"
That's gonna involve some plane swapping. I'll get a King-Air. It's faster,
ger."
I'll pay the difference."
The guys and I, when we swap, we swap evenly. In the end it's a wash."
I'll pay the difference. Now this bigger plane. You can land it here?"
There are certain things you can still trust. This afternoon then. Late."
When he sees Ilisapie again, he mentions the conversation with Olanna and asks
king the body home is the right thing.
try to give medical advice only. I'm not much good at other stuff. Now Olanna,
s old school in some ways, but she's a Christian too, a convert, like many of us.
ne are choosing cremation now. That never used to happen."
But all those Inuit beliefs about respect for the spirit?"
There is no right answer here, Mr. Wilkes, no perfect solution. There's only you
your choice. You can only do what you've already done: ask, get opinions,
e a decision. When your pilot gets here, we'll be ready."
Olanna said that Repulse Bay is not a place of death. She wants me to have
itive thoughts about it. I don't think I can."
don't think so either," Ilisapie says. "Olanna takes pride in her town, her
vince. We all do. Her intentions are noble, but for you too much has happened,
much to erase. When you return to life—and you will—it will have to be
ewhere else.

antley lands the bartered King-Air at sunrise the following day, without the aid
a permanently manned control tower or runway lights or any of the aviation
provements that allow for planes to travel from place to place without killing
ir passengers and crew. And Brantley has flown four other fares in from
nnipeg, two young Inuit sisters, a middle-aged man from Vancouver, and a co-
worker from Baker Lake.

Manitok.

I'm so sorry," she says, touching Wilkes on the arm. "I thought there would be
ifferent outcome."

I did too. I'm glad you're here...but...why?"

Your PI called," she says. "Mr. McNally. He thought you needed help with
ngs and he didn't think he'd make it in time. I called your pilot here and he made
op."

What about your job? What about the cost?"

Paid for," Brantley says. "McNally's credit card. Round trip."

Wilkes is astonished. "Why would he do that?"

Failure," Manitok says. "He blames himself for what happened and this is some
nement. Failure makes us better people. As for the co-op, I can always find
neone to cover for me. What needs to be done?"

Everyone has been good, though—at the hospital, in town."

He chooses to omit Demarais from the equation, but even with him there has
n a lessening of tensions, a reconciliation of sorts.

If I can help," Manitok says, "I will. Otherwise I'll stay out of your way. I know
ne folks in town. I'll tell them I wanted to get away for a day or two."

Wilkes smiles. "Where I live, people go south for a day or two in the winter, not
th."

You aren't *Inuktitut*," she says. "Now how can I help?"

We can start with breakfast," Brantley says, "but we need to unload the air tray."

he term may be new to Wilkes, but the apparatus isn't: a pine box, simple and
itarian. For generations objects like this served as a final resting place before
ple felt the need for more ostentatious displays, or some need to postpone
y's inevitable moldering. Even today, Wilkes knows, it remains a symbol of
overishment and anonymity.

"Nicer on the inside," Brantley says as they drag it out of the plane and secur
to a sled behind a snowmobile. "Most of all it's solid and secure—and tempora
We get to Winnipeg and we go to a real funeral home."

Wilkes turns to Manitok. "Sorry you had to ride up with this."

"Just a box," she says. "For now."

Brantley pays an airport gofer to haul the air tray to the hospital while the th
of them walk to the *Naujat* and Wilkes fills in some details from the previous da
Manitok knows almost everything already. McNally has been a go
correspondent.

"Tell you what, though," Brantley says to the woman. "It'll be good if you
help us with the medical examiner. Olanna can be difficult."

"I spoke with her already," Wilkes says. "We're good."

"But by now she has heard about the fight. You may not be so good today."

Manitok's eyes widen. "What fight?"

"Our friend here," Brantley says. "He and a local man had a little...scuffle."

"A local man? The one Deidre told me about?"

"Probably. He and I talked it out afterwards. He's okay. We've reconciled."

"Get ready to reconcile again," Brantley says. "Olanna might work easier v
someone else who speaks Inuit."

"Then I can help," Manitok says. "Good."

She smiles at Wilkes.

"You surprise me. You seem so, so orderly. I can hardly imagine you in a fig
"One punch," Brantley says. "Let's not make this too dramatic."

"If this were Baker Lake," she says. "Everyone would know within the hour.
sure it's the same here.

Brantley smiles. "I'd check my pancakes for ground glass before I actually
them."

"Our people would never do that," Manitok says. "But they would kick your
Where is this Olanna, Mr. Wilkes?"

"She'll meet us at the hospital. And could you call me Martin? It seems friend
And it appears I need friends."

"You do," Brantley says. "And incidentally, just so we're clear on this, you
friend comped the air fare for Manitok."

"I know that."

"And only for Manitok, Martin."

e subsequent meeting with Olanna is businesslike and efficient. If the woman
ors any grudge over Wilkes's mistreatment of Demarais, she doesn't show it.
produces a loose-leaf notebook, removes a few pages, puts them on a
oard, and hands it to Wilkes.
Vherever there's an 'x,'" she says. Seconds later she's gone.
ilkes shakes his head.
Vhat did I just sign?"
release," Manitok says. "You just absolved her from the responsibility of
ng for your wife's remains. By the way, she knows."
bout Demarais?"
can tell. Just like the waitress."
ilkes shrugs. "Then it's lucky we're through with her."
only," Brantley says.
leads the other two back to the panel truck where Olanna waits with a key.
n Wilkes envisions bodies piled high, stuffed together in some sacrilegious
ay, but the truck is empty save for one white bag. It's primitive and repugnant,
t isn't, despite his revulsion, disrespectful.
ou have to identify," Olanna says, her voice flat, neither cordial nor hostile.
antley puts an arm on Wilkes's shoulder. "I should have warned you, but I
t want you to agonize in advance."
s okay. I saw her in the hospital. I can do this."
can, and he does, but he's shocked by the transformation. Only a day before
vas a person whose body had been ravaged by the cold. But now she's hardly
son at all: her face hollow, the definition gone, the color a uniform pallor.
alming may be anathema to the locals, but in the world he's accustomed to,
necessity.
chokes back the bile rising in his throat but forces himself not to look away.
must ask you some questions," Olanna says.
lkes is silent. Manitok steps between them.
his kind of thing is difficult for him."
he spirit is gone," Olanna says. "There is nothing here."
here is nothing but bones in the ground where the stone men stand watch, but
ave respect."
s not the same."
is spirituality is different, that's all. His isn't wrong."
ut he must identify."

"This is Keira Wilkes," Manitok says. "I met her in Baker Lake last week she told me she was coming here."

"Are you related to the family?"

"In the same way you are."

She gently takes the clipboard out of Olanna's hands and asks where to Wilkes only half watches. Olanna zippers up the bag.

For the next few hours Wilkes remains a witness more than a participant. Manitok watching him, he packs, retrieves his ring, and waits while she do checks the room lest he's forgotten anything. He settles up at the desk, then hi cab for the short ride to the airfield because he can't endure the thought of wal another yard in that town, or hamlet, or whatever they chose to call the godfors place. The closer he comes to leaving, the faster things happen, and for that grateful. If he can make everything a blur, maybe the day will come whe forgets the particulars: how Keira looked, how he dreaded the journey west with this grim cargo. Maybe Demarais will be proven right. This will be the v day he will ever have and everything afterward will climb upward. He thin the wheel of fortune from medieval times; maybe this is the bottom.

Manitok will fly back to Baker Lake with another pilot, one whom Bra knows and trusts. Wilkes will be Brantley's only passenger. The air tray will c as cargo, no matter how callous the designation.

"I feel like some big business executive," Manitok says, "flying 500 kilom for a meeting, then turning around and flying back. Is this what you do, Mart

"I've done it, but after a while you wouldn't like it much. Thank you for d this."

"I'm glad I could help a little. I won't tell you I'll see you around. I don't you'll be headed back this way."

"Probably not."

He extends his hand to shake hers but she hugs him instead.

"You and Brantley here can shake hands. Not me."

Wilkes smiles.

"Have a safe trip. Have you thought about a new name?"

"You remembered?"

"Yes. Any contenders?"

"I don't think so. You get used to a name and it becomes you, or you becor Either way, I don't think I want to change just yet."

So when I send a Christmas card to the co-op and write Manitok on it, you'll
it?"
Solstice."
What?"
We celebrate the solstice too."
You said the summer solstice was one big party. Winter, too?"
Any excuse, I guess."
But isn't that the shortest day of the year?"
And the darkest, which means of course...."
..that it can't get any darker. I understand. I don't think I can find a Happy
stice card in the Hallmark store."
 carry a dozen different ones. If I had the space, I'd carry more. I'll send you
."
You don't know my address."
You left a trail, Martin: credit card receipts, hotel registers. I'll send you a card.
l if you start looking now, well, you've got most of the year to find one. Buy a
ch. Confuse your friends."
She's right," Brantley says. "The winter solstice is as good as the summer, just
 nudity. It's that forty-below feeling that keeps people from disrobing. Come
I have to get this plane home."
Wilkes hugs her again, this time with less reticence.
See you 'round," he says, forgetting her comment that he probably wouldn't,
 climbs into the plane.

*****

quiet ride under a clear sky.
crosswind occasionally waffles the wings slightly, but the King-Air seems so
h more substantial that the bumps go unacknowledged. Hours later a hearse
ies Wilkes from the airport in Winnipeg to the Sanderson Funeral Parlor a few
ks from the Red River, while Brantley retrieves his own plane and finagles a
 to the funeral parlor.
made some inquiries," the pilot says. "I can get you on a redeye tonight if, you
w, these people are ready."
s there any place you don't have connections?"
m solid north of the border. In the U.S., you're on your own."

They find a restaurant nearby, recommended by one of the staff at Sanderso
and in the seemingly mild Winnipeg evening with the temperature hovering ab
freezing, walk the few blocks without fear of dying from exposure. Neither ma
very hungry, but they have time to kill and the liquor is soothing. Brantley, with
a another eastbound flight until the following afternoon, puts away more than
share of Scotch, a fact that leads to several mildly inappropriate tales told at equ
inappropriate volume. None of the other diners seem annoyed; in fact, the sm
far outnumber the dirty looks. It's a release for Brantley: the failure isn't his,
was merely an observer, but the residue has rubbed off. For Wilkes it's differ
His life has collapsed in ways he cannot even begin to imagine, and he has
doubt that, even if this is the worst day of his life, other unforeseen agonies
ahead.

Agonies and formalities. He uses his cell phone to make a money transfer: a g
faith payment of $3,000 to Brantley who, not yet inebriated, scribbles a receip
the dessert list and promises that a bill for the rest is imminent. Wilkes doubt
will ever see it.

Just before midnight the Sanderson hearse takes the casket to the airport wl
it's loaded onto a Newark-bound 737, one stop to Toronto. It's the same path K
followed west, but there's little of coincidence in the fact: the way to wes
Canada inevitably passes through Toronto. The two men watch from the term
before Brantley, eschewing any long goodbyes, shakes hands with Wilkes, wis
him luck, and walks away. To an outside observer the exit seems indifferent,
both men know that failures cannot be couched in pretty words.

Half-dozing on the plane, still feeling the effects of the gin, he remembers
humorous references to the Great White North when he was a kid. Two comed
had poked terrible fun at Canada, every sentence ending with an obligatory
while they sloshed unimaginable amounts of Molson beer and centered their l
on doughnuts. But their imagined Great White North, as great and white as it m
have been, didn't extend as far into the Arctic as Baker Lake and Repulse Bay
had heard a few eh's, of course, and seen some beer consumed, but Nunavut
not Montreal or Toronto or Vancouver or any other cosmopolitan city to
lampooned; and maybe because of its vastness, or its darkness, or the nights it s
shimmering under the splashy Aurora, Wilkes understands it as little now as w
he first stepped off that plane in Baker Lake.

He knows some of the *Saqiyak*, the oral history, and he is pleased at his
willingness, facility, even with some *Inuktitut* words, words like *Saqiyak*

ktitut. In the margins of the airline magazine he scribbles some of the symbols remembers—letters, pictographs. He doesn't know what they mean or stand for, at another time maybe, in another universe, he might like to learn them. But these are just vagaries: he fears that the answers to all his whys lie not within Arctic Circle, not under that almost solid white canopy of celestial objects, not the abandoned hovels outside Repulse Bay. They lie, instead, right inside that ely extended Cape on the half-acre lot in Wilton where his children eat and play sleep and grow, and will continue to do so with or without a mother. That ne, the one Keira had decorated so assiduously, had special-ordered furniture, ticulously gathered wall hangings and lamps, had fussed with and overseen ry iota of decorating. Why had she done all that just to relinquish her life on a im?

t's midnight, only 11:00 back home. He phones McNally.

On my way home."

About time."

Thanks for what you did."

Lynne made me do it."

For whatever reason."

Did she help, this Manikot person?"

Manitok. Inuit, not Italian. Yes she did."

Well then it was worth the million dollars I spent."

You got away cheap. What does your schedule look like?"

I'll wait for the phone to ring. It always does. Why?"

I need you to work for me."

I'm working for you right now. Again. Second time."

Something happened back there, or here, and I don't know where to begin. narais told me things. He talked about a young girl, a child. Someone named vy."

What about her?"

I don't know."

Well, that's enough to go on. Give me a minute or two to pull this all together."

know that's nothing, but maybe you can make it into something."

Did you ask Keira's parents about it? About her?"

Why would I do that?"

Why wouldn't you? Maybe they know who she is."

'm not sure if they'll tell me."

"I'll get on it. And listen. You need to set limits. We both need to. Sometin
answers escape us and we either live with that or we go crazy. Or in your ca
broke paying a PI. I'm honest enough to tell you when I think we're at a dead e
but—now listen, this is the important part—you have to be willing to accept it.

"Doesn't this contradict your profit-making philosophy?"

"It's a little-known part of my paradigm. It allows me to live with myself."

Wilkes smiles. "You mean with your wife."

"That too. I don't tolerate failure very well, but does anybody really give a s
anymore what happened to Jimmy Hoffa? You have to recognize lost causes. T
thing is, though, your wife. I was supposed to find her. Tell me more about Sylv

"I don't know any more."

"Okay then," McNally says. Wilkes doesn't need to talk any more. McNally
already, or maybe still, on the clock.

limos in tandem cross the GW into the city, follow the Cross-Bronx eastward,
swing north onto the Hutch. A half hour into Connecticut they separate: one
sporting Keira Wilkes's remains to the Bellman-Smith Funeral Parlor in
tport; the other bringing Martin Wilkes home. The sun has barely risen and
ong shadows remind him of Baker Lake and Repulse Bay, but the biting cold
been left behind. There are lights on in the house.
o early for the kids. His in-laws then. They knew he was on his way and have
the coffee on for hours. His father-in-law, still in pajamas, sits in the sunlit
g room, a cup of coffee on an end table. Keira's mother is fully dressed in what
to be called a pants suit. Wilkes doesn't know if the designation still applies.
mood comprises less sadness than concession and defeat. He has failed to
back their daughter. That much they know and accept and maybe even honor
ffort. But he has also failed to keep her out of harm's way, to provide a life
lid not want to renounce. He is certain they will never entirely forgive him for

he kids are still asleep," Mr. Eason says.
figured. I can get Danielle over here and the three of us can run over to the
ral home."
ilkes gets the answer he wants: no. The Easons will "visit" later, but they'll
for Brett and James to awaken.
nd I want the boys to go to school today, even if it's late. They have to start
ng their lives back. If you could drive them. Do they know?"
ey know only that their mother is missing, and that their father is due home.
afternoon, Wilkes says, he will tell them the truth. Keira's father nods and
off to dress, but her mother says nothing more. Wilkes wonders if he is
red to fill in the silences, but how? They're all in mourning. They're all
ng. What does one say that diminishes the misery without dishonoring it?
least, removed from the suffocating cold of Nunavut, he feels capable of
ng decisions again. At Bellman-Smith's he selects a tasteful but brief obit. The
. Few details. Calling hours. He won't be going into detail about cause of
. Died after a brief illness is misleading, died suddenly is closer, maybe, and
accidentally: well that's just a lie. Whoever Keira Wilkes was before that plane
aGuardia vanished that afternoon, not a week later in Canada. But it isn't the

role of an obit to be cryptic or clever or philosophical. And he has always dete
as did Keira, the long and flowery eulogies about beloved wives and lo
mothers and resting in the bosom of some supreme being. These were things
told a person when she was alive; you didn't share it with others after she was g

In the end, he opts for simply died unexpectedly and inserts the date v
Ilisapie gave him the news. Ilisapie. The name already seems alien now that
back in the realm of Bellmans and Smiths. The rest of the obit is boilerplate
Wilkes makes certain all the names are spelled correctly: the boys, of course,
Keira's family. Calling hours, burial plans--all that will be in the next c
editions, allowing friends and relatives a few hours to plan for an evening v
and, if they choose, the following day's funeral. No church. No priests or mini
or rabbis or shamans. He owes her that much.

At home with the boys in school he fills in details, editing on the fly, omi
Demarais and replacing him with a passerby, omitting Keira's nakedness, omi
the conversation with Deidre altogether: if their daughter truly wanted to die,
should her parents be shackled with that burden? He considers what McNally
about Sylvy—did you ask her parents?—but this seems neither the time nor p
To them Keira will forever be the daughter who ran off to a harsh and unforgi
place and died there.

The boys, though, that will be different. That afternoon when they arrive h
he'll be there to rescind all the optimism of the previous week, all his exampl
people who disappeared and then just showed up again, all his assurances
grownups make mature choices. He left them with thoughts of an eventual re
to normality, of becoming, again, just another family. Now he will have to ex
to them a loss beyond reckoning, explain to them what he cannot expla
himself. In the intervening hours he makes some calls, reaching only a cous
Cleveland. Everyone is at work and he leaves a message asking that they get
to him. It's doubtful they will. His tone betrays the reason for the call, and tl
phone each other to find out what happened before they phone him. The Ea
leave for their own home, to get things in order, they say. Wilkes does not diss
them.

He riffles through the mail, separating the pieces addressed to Keira and pu
them aside. A detailed account of the river rescue dominates Newsweek, a
number of related articles satisfy the need for human interest. The surveil
video has become iconic; the rescue, a legend; the crew, folk heroes. Wilkes k
there are details he might like to know, but they won't answer his questions a

ıses to read about it. It has not been a miracle for him. Just after eleven he pours ıself what he used to call a double. It's become his new standard. He drinks it ckly, then stoppers the bottle. He can't be showing up drunk to pick up his sons, he can't be adrift in the hazy anesthesia of alcohol while the boys face tragedy h no similar crutch. His task transcends bearing bad news: he must also ntain the dignity of the woman who was, who is, their mother. To do that ectly, and to sit behind the wheel and carry his sons safely: one drink, no more.

 hot shower removes the residue of terminals and tarmac, and he chooses an fit he might wear to work. Presenting news like this demands protocol. A phone dismisses his sons early, and at 1:00 he sits apprehensive but sober in his idling outside the main entrance to Franklin Elementary, staring blankly at the "No ıding" sign. No one is around to enforce it. A school monitor opens the main r and escorts Brett and James to the curb where Wilkes is forced to produce ıtification.

Sorry," the monitor says, a young woman who probably serves double duty as ıide. "It's protocol since Columbine."

3etter to be safe," Wilkes says as his sons pile into the back seat. He's glad for diversion, hoping it will provide a topic of conversation until they get home. doesn't.

Grammy said you were coming home without Mommy."

'ilkes bristles. Grammy wasn't supposed to tell them anything. Then again be they asked if Daddy was home, and the only logical question after that one ıld involve Keira. So okay then, let that go.

Yes, she was right."

You still didn't find her?"

ill. There's a hint of exasperation in the word. He's no more than five minutes ı his driveway, but he can delay this no longer, not after all that had happened. pulls into a service station and past the pumps, then turns around to face the s.

Mommy isn't coming home. She got very sick and the doctors couldn't make better."

e looks directly at Brett as the words stream out and the older boy, who does need to puzzle the meaning, pounds the door panel next to him. James looks zical. Does that mean they'll find new doctors who can do a better job? Does ean she's still sick? Wilkes knows what must come next: an innocent question

from the younger boy followed by a sarcastic comment from the other. He c
allow an argument to aggravate an already untenable situation.

"James," he says, "Mommy didn't get better. They couldn't make her bet
Sometimes people get so sick that they just die no matter what the doctors try
do. Like when your Uncle Frank was in the hospital and all the doctors were th
but he still died."

Wilkes searches James's eyes for recognition, realization. They come slowly
they come. There are no tears, though, and that surprises him until he sees
Brett's eyes have gone crimson, though by sheer force of will he doesn't rub th
For James the same release will come soon enough. They drive the rest of the
home in silence.

Wilkes sits the boys down in the kitchen, where family business is discuss
Everyone has to pull together, he says, they have to honor their mother's mem
by being good to one another. He's earnest and reasonable, but it all sounds like
much bullshit, a political speech made in the aftermath of some tragedy or disas
And maybe it works with a huge audience empathizing with the suffering—ma
Reagan after the Challenger disaster, or Bush after 9/11—but on a personal le
such philosophizing is transparent enough for even a six-year-old to see throu
It's a pep talk and little more, but that that realization doesn't stop him.

"Now there are things we have to do for Mommy," he says. "We have to p
out something for her to wear."

"What's she wearing now?" James asked.

"Well," Wilkes says, "you know like jeans and stuff. Not really dressy. We h
to make sure she looks really nice."

James shakes his head. "I don't want people looking at Mommy."

Wilkes nods. "Well, that's okay too. We can just...make it more private."

He doesn't want to introduce the concept of a closed casket into the conversat
or a casket of any kind. Both boys have been to funeral masses, but never
wake. Wilkes asks the boys for questions he might be able to answer, ma
questions about death that he has pondered since Keira lay dying in that hosp
in Repulse Bay. Brett has wrapped himself in his always reliable cloak of sile
but James has not acquired that yet.

"What if you die too?"

"I meant questions about the funeral."

"But what if?"

It's 2009," Wilkes says. "Remember I told you that in 2019 you could drive a
 and you said that'll never get here? Well, think of 2019, and in 2025 you'll have
b like me and earning lots of money, and I'll still be here. So when 2025 gets
e, you can ask me that again, okay? Same for you Brett."

Brett does the math but for whatever reason doesn't share the obvious answer
 their father will then be pushing 60, several years older than their Uncle Frank
en the doctors found the tumor that killed him and brought the boys to their first
eral.

What we need to do now," Wilkes says, "is to pick out some clothes, huh?"
For Mommy?"
And for you. Come on, we're taking a ride."

He ushers the boys back into the car and they take the Merritt north to a mall in
dgeport where he settles on a blue blazer for each of them and some clip-on
, new shoes and dark socks. They are docile and unusually patient during the
cess; he has promised McDonald's on the way home. Only later, well into the
ning, do they attend to Keira's outfit. Something red of course: he reminds the
s that it was her color. Wilkes lays out three dresses and James points to the
dle one, wool with a round, modest neckline.

Thanks," Wilkes says. "Mom would want you two to make that decision."

he boys move toward the door. Brett stops.

And the cross," he mutters, his voice broken and halting. "She always wore
."

lone in the room, Wilkes stares at the ensemble, then sits on the bed and
oths the dress slowly. This dress once surrounded her, he says to himself, clung
er, touched her shoulders, her hips, her legs. He can almost feel her in it, smell
, hear her breathing. Not the Keira in the Repulse Bay clinic but the Keira of
ations and galas and weekends in the city, of holidays and movies and
ntaneous trips to Broadway, ticketless but hopeful. The Keira who would tease
 and tempt him and, at least one time when they were already late for some
ner party, allow him to gently remove this very same dress, toss it recklessly on
air, and make love to her.

ut now instead of making love he is weeping. He has been in control until this
y moment and he will be again. But for now the finality of death, what he could
 explain to his son, overwhelms him. He wishes it were 2025 or whatever year
sed to mollify James so that he himself could have his final wardrobe laid out
 him. He gathers himself, ashamed of his weakness: after 9/11 thousands

endured this and went on with their lives; and with Iraq and Afghanistan aflar
more suffer every day. But as always, the generality pales next to the specific. I
is not some faceless name in the papers; his boys not a grieving family on televis
he can turn from with a click of the remote.

He lays the cross necklace on the dress, then calls the boys back.

"Best I can do."

"Mommy always wore a fleece in the winter," James says. "What if it's cold?

"We can bring one."

Brett says nothing. He knows the question is stupid, but apparently realizes t
may not be the time to proffer that opinion.

"I feel sad today," Wilkes says. "Do you feel sad?"

"I miss Mommy," James said. "Who's going to make dinner tomorrow?"

"Well, we'll have to learn to cook, I guess. We can do that, right?"

If James agrees, he doesn't show it.

"And pick us up at school?"

"I can do that without learning. I can work from home some days and be the
And there's always grandma and grandpa, so you don't have to worry."

James nods. He still isn't convinced, but to Wilkes the boy seems to have stop
pondering his own mortality at least.

"Anyway," Wilkes says. "It's okay to feel sad. I think Mommy was sad too w
she left."

Brett begins fumbling with his hands, his face deepening in color. His sile
explodes into a curt question:

"Did Mommy kill herself?"

At first Wilkes isn't sure he heard right.

"What? Kill herself? Of course not."

The answer is too fast, too reflexive. Maybe James accepts it, but Brett does

"How do you know?"

"She talked to people up there...in Canada. She was looking forward to com
home, she just didn't understand how bad the weather...how cold it could
Mommy would never do that to herself."

"But it was in the newspaper."

The suddenness of the words is overpowering, but he is more baffled t
shocked.

"What newspaper?"

"I don't know. My teacher told me."

Mrs. McDonough?"

Some other teacher. She works in the office. She said that if I wanted to talk to someone about it, I should tell her."

She said it right out loud? In class?"

No, just to me. In the office. I guess she isn't a teacher."

She had no right to do that."

But it was in the paper. I think other kids saw it."

What paper?"

I told you I don't know."

Sometimes newspapers are wrong. That's not what happened to Mommy. I'll make sure they print an apology."

He hustles the boys out of the room and gets on line. Nothing in the *Times*, the News, the *Post*. It seemed unlikely that Newsday would break a story this remote, but he checks anyway. Bridgeport, New Haven, Hartford. Nothing. He Googles Keira's name and finds little more than early reports and a reference or two to some school committees. Page after page--all the same, but McNally's derision of journalistic integrity reverberates and pushes him. Just when he is about to give up, he finds it: a blog that calls itself The Westprint: "Missing Local Woman Thought to be Suicide."

The article is hardly about Keira at all: it's about women who find themselves overwhelmed by time and place and circumstance, women who run off and leave families behind. Well-researched and more than likely accurate, it reads like a B-plus high term paper, filled with erudite allusions but crippled by sexist stereotyping and sweeping generalities. Occasional hypotheses like "a similar panic may have overtaken the local missing woman" and "suicide is often the logical outcome of such episodes" make it clear that someone considered Keira a suicide even before she was declared dead.

And one of the sources when it came to the reporting and follow-up and resolution of these cases? Detective April Staubley.

"That miserable fuck," Wilkes says, maybe a little too loudly, though his breach of propriety doesn't keep him from repeating it...slightly louder. He calls McNally. The PI concurs.

:he wake, a steady stream of mourners keeps Wilkes occupied, trying to match
ies with faces and keeping family relationships and friends straight in his own
d. A contingent from Tolliver & Byrne arrives en masse, a few hours after the
very of a tasteful though oversized basket of white lilies. Wilkes has not made
"in lieu of flowers," request, having no charity in mind to whom well-wishers
ht donate. Had he wanted to be more forthcoming, he might have redirected all
good intentions to the hospital in Repulse Bay or the College of the Arctic. But
er request would have engendered countless questions he does not want to deal
1. He decides he will check the registry later, find out the mourners' names,
< for the elusive Emil, Emile, whatever.
here are tears and the occasional outburst of emotion, but among the visitors
√ the discreetly attired Sandy Qualling seems least able to maintain any
1posure. She weeps continuously until the rest of the T&B contingency leads
out. The procession through the viewing room is steady but never what anyone
1ld call overflowing, and at 9:00 p.m., the posted conclusion of visiting hours,
1ne is left except Wilkes and his boys along with the Easons, Keira's sister
·ley who has flown in from Salt Lake, and a cousin from New Hampshire who
. for directions to, as he puts it, any nearby motel. Wilkes provides them
ingly: he isn't ready for a houseguest, especially one who has opted for tattered
·s for mourning apparel. Hayley has taken a motel room too, either opting out
.n invitation by her parents or, more likely, never having received one. The
·rs were never close and Wilkes hardly knows her, but their physical
ilarities are disconcerting, even more so, he assumes, to Brett and James.
·ett was three the last time Hayley was back east, and then too for a funeral.
she smiles and calls them both by name, tells them how wonderful their mother
, how important it is to have brothers and sisters. It may be false, contrived,
oted, but she's a stranger to him and he can't envision any way she'll ever be
of their lives.
ut in the lobby voices swell somewhat until the Smith half of Bellman-Smith
ppears from Wilkes's sight. Seconds later calm returns.
·robably a fender bender in the parking lot," Wilkes says to the boys, though
haven't asked. "So many cars in and out of these small parking places. We
ıld say goodbye to Mom for tonight, huh?"

Neither boy is deceived by the euphemism, nor is either heartened by prospect of repeating the same process the following morning. Brett says nothi but he looks lost and defeated, his control gone; James needs assurance that lights will remain on all night so that his mother isn't forced to lie in the d Reminding the younger one that a closed casket allows no light anyway would futile, if not plainly cruel. Bellman assures both boys that the room will never dark, then retrieves their coats because, as he puts it, "it's freezing out."

Wilkes knows it isn't, his notion of the term having been forever modified, he lets the harmless hyperbole go unchallenged.

"What was the fuss before?" he asks.

"Some argument," Bellman says. "My partner took care of it."

Bellman's face divulges nothing, neither anger nor surprise, as if a dispute in parking lot of a funeral home is pretty much de rigueur.

"So it's settled?"

"I believe it is. Now, I have made arrangements for the morning. You'll be h around 8:45? Is that going to be suitable?"

"Yes."

"There'll be a brief service and if anybody wants to say a few words, you or boys or someone else, that would be the time. You can let me know in morning."

"Should we? Should I? Say a few words, I mean?"

"It's entirely up to you and what you feel comfortable with. I will make sc comments anyway, somewhat generic, but the information you provided will m it personal. I always feel there need to be some words of departure. But y personal involvement is entirely up to you. And of course I can remain silent if you wish."

"You should say something, Dad," Brett says.

Wilkes is surprised: the older boy has been practically catatonic all even hardly uttering a syllable.

"Okay," Wilkes says, a little too breezily perhaps. "I will."

Bellman makes a note in a small book. "Why don't you give me your car l and I'll have your vehicle brought around."

Wilkes is still curious about what occurred outside, but he's had enough braving the elements. Later at home he calls McNally, a late arrival at the w who waded through the line with everyone else, remained for a short w afterwards, then disappeared.

I just wanted to thank you for coming. That was thoughtful."

No problem. Did everything go all right?"

Yes."

That's good then," McNally says, but he sounds unsure.

Did you find out something...about Keira?"

Oh no, nothing like that."

Then what?"

And Wilkes senses immediately. The minor argument in the parking lot involved Nally.

What happened outside the funeral home?"

Outside the funeral home?"

You sound like one of my boys repeating a question he doesn't want to answer. at happened?"

Nothing much. I told Staubley she wasn't welcome. She wasn't, was she?"

Do you always ask afterwards?"

I'm asking now."

No, she wasn't, but if she had been there, I'd have dealt with it. What did she to you?"

She gave me a civics lesson, reminded me that a funeral home becomes a public lding during a wake."

But she didn't come in."

We talked for a while. She said she wasn't finished pursuing this—this case. kept calling it a case. Well, fuck I know what a case is and this isn't one. I'm for enforcing the law. It's not that."

I'm sure police everywhere will feel better when they know."

This woman, though, she's got this bug up her ass—"

And you told her that?"

phrased it differently—maybe—I'm not sure. Then of course she said that my olvement in wrongdoing would make me an accomplice. She thinks you knew along where your wife was and you wasted their time filing a false report."

already had that conversation with her."

'd expect to have it again. I asked her about the Westprint article. She seemed rised. I think that's when I asked her how she planned to spend her suspension. ggested volunteering at a soup kitchen."

Not too many of those around here."

"Oh yeah, the gold coast. Listen, I know you don't want to talk shop tonight, I'm still working for you. You know that, right?"

"I know that. I know you feel bad—"

"This hasn't worked out the way it was supposed to, but I'm not done."

Well before 11:00, Wilkes has gotten both boys off to bed, though neither is ev close to sleeping, nor is he. He fills a glass with ice and pours the gin with measuring. Two fingers of gin and the late news have been, in the past, a sure sedative. The only difference now is that Keira will not descend the stairs a remind him it's late, that it's time to come to bed.

Despite the gin he's still annoyingly awake when car headlights illuminate driveway. With so many relatives and friends around, it could be almost anybo He peers through the curtains and sees a blue Camry, then pushes opens the d to forestall the noise of a doorbell.

"Arrest me," he says, extending his hands to be cuffed. "Private intoxication. you can drag me outside and make it public. Your call, detective."

Staubley, as always dressed in her seemingly ubiquitous leather, allows a t smile.

"I'm off duty. May I come in for a moment?"

"Breakfast isn't for another seven hours. You know that, right?"

"I just want to talk."

"What'll happen if I say no? Does it take long to get a warrant or can download one from the Internet? Or maybe your reporter friend from Westp can drive one over."

"I can just stand here if you'd like. It won't take long, a minute or two."

"Well, God knows I've got that. Come in out of the cold."

She takes a step over the threshold. He holds out a hand to stop her.

"My kids think their mother killed herself. Do you know how they know t Somebody read it online in what passes for a newspaper these days. How did happen, detective?"

He lets her pass then closes the door behind her and takes a position near staircase, a hand casually resting between two balusters, the glass on one of steps. He isn't planning to forgo his drink or to sit, or to provide any comfort her.

"I just wanted to tell you," she says. "I never gave them that information."

"You were quoted."

"I never spoke to that reporter."

ccording to Detective April Staubley, the disappearance, etc. I saw it."

Ir Wilkes, believe me, that reporter never spoke with me. He talked to

eone at the station, found out I was working the case, then asked some general

tions about situations like this."

here is no case. There never was a case."

didn't come here to argue. A disappearance is always a police matter."

ine. Next time send people in police uniforms, not some lady in a blue sedan."

Vhoever came would have asked the same questions, done the same things."

nd came up with suicide?"

es, as a possibility, along with abduction and desertion, even amnesia and

r...conditions."

hose weren't mentioned in the newspaper."

Ir. Wilkes, it's hard to censor what's out there: idiots can pretty much say what

want as long as there are other idiots there to listen. Still, we were careless. I

careless: if I could print a retraction, I would. If I could prosecute the jerk who

e it, I'd do that too. We can issue a release saying that the investigation has

concluded, that there is no indication of foul play, but no one cares for

ctions. Look, if you want, I can explain it to your kids."

ou? I don't think that's going to happen. Maybe an apology, though."

can't apologize for accidents or for mistakes others have made."

ow about being sorry it happened? Can you manage that?"

es."

ecause sloughing off your job to someone else really is your mistake. And

ng a scene in the funeral parlor parking lot, is that on your list of things you

pologize for?"

our PI, McDougal—"

IcNally."

hatever, he was spoiling for a fight."

e doesn't handle failure very well. He's still pissed off because he was

osed to find my wife before she died—which is kind of what I wanted too."

lets Staubley absorb the jab before continuing.

lon't think you'll be bumping into him in the future, though he is still working

e. So if you're going to continue this harassment—"

orking a case, exhausting possibilities, finding evidence, considering and

nating suspects—none of those constitute harassment when they're done—

ctly. Anyway, as I told you, this case is no longer being actively worked."

"That's not the same as being closed, is it?"

"We can't close it this quickly. It's protocol."

"It's semantics. But if you're not actively working, then don't worry a[bout] McNally, or me, or my kids."

"As long as you know." She takes a few hesitant steps toward the door[.] Wilkes, noticing something in her tone, stops her.

"You're in trouble for this, right? For letting that story slip? For letting s[ome] hack discuss an ongoing investigation?"

"I have some explaining to do. We're a small department. We can't dis[miss] mistakes by blaming some faceless subordinate. We all know each other and [this] one's on me."

"And the guy who leaked the story."

"College kid, intern, part-timer. Good guy but inexperienced. But that's o[n me] too. I'm sorry for your loss, Mr. Wilkes, and the offer to explain this to your [kids] still stands."

This time he isn't so quick to dismiss the offer. There is something sincere i[n her] admission and at least she's embarrassed if not contrite. Their goodbyes bord[er on] cordial, but once she's gone, the gin is far less effective a sedative than W[ilkes] hoped. He lasts through the news and most of the hour-long SportsCenter [that] follows it. Somewhere along the way, though, the liquor kicks in and W[ilkes] awakens later to a TV still flashing images and the word mute on the screen[. He] turns off the set and steadies himself on the couch arm. Brett is sitting on the s[tairs.]

"The TV was keeping me awake."

"I'm sorry, I fell asleep. I didn't realize it was that loud. You okay?"

"Sure. That thing you're supposed to write for Mom? Did you do it yet?"

"Thought about it," he says, slurring out the lie. "I was thinking I would jus[t say] a few words, you know, without writing them down."

Brett nods, but he looks disappointed. Wilkes picks up his glass, now filled [with] tepid water only, and brings it into the kitchen.

"You don't think that's a good idea?" he asks.

"My teacher says you should always prepare. I want you to say somethin[g about] Jamesy and me."

"Sure," Wilkes says. "Like what?"

"Well, sometimes I was bad and I got mad at Mommy. And Jamesy was [a] jerk too about picking up toys and brushing his teeth. I know we made her m[ad]

But that...that's what mothers and fathers do. They get mad and then they forget
ut it. I'm sure she forgot all those things."
But can you say that we're sorry, you know, at the funeral home. Just so other
ple know."
Sure. I may not say it exactly that way." He forces a smile. "I don't want a lot
trangers thinking you and Jamesy were bad."
Even if we were?"
You weren't. She loved you both. She never stayed mad at you, so she wouldn't
it you to stay sad like this."
rett is unconvinced.
But you'll say something?"
 will. And maybe your teacher is right," Wilkes says. "Maybe I should write
e things down, you know, to make sure I don't forget."
rett's face brightens a little. "That's a good idea."
Come here," Wilkes says, and hugs him. It is an uncharacteristically
ntaneous gesture, but Brett, if he feels surprise, does not show it.
You should try to go to sleep now," Wilkes says, still feeling groggy and
ating nothing more for himself than to get some sleep too. But instead he ushers
tt up to his room, waits at the door to flick the light switch (the boy is past the
ing-in stage), and heads down to his laptop. He has made a promise: now he
a eulogy to compose.
e knows it can't be one of his investment presentations where the newbies stare
im in admiration hoping to achieve his stature (and salary) someday, a meeting
re it doesn't matter what he says as long as the numbers at the bottom are
iciently black. In the funeral parlor, with Brett hanging on every word and
es probably doing the same, he will have to speak from the heart and do so
out charts and graphs and statistics. It won't be a call to action or a rallying cry
dreamers of seven-figure salaries. Instead it will be the last words ever spoken
licly about Keira Eason Wilkes: a summary of forty years and a marriage and
children and a death that came without warning.
o anecdotes. No cute stories. He wants the ceremony to be serious but not grim,
ts his sons to respect death but not fear it, to treat it as they treat life, even
gh, at that moment, at least, Wilkes himself feels no more than an overriding
ed and contempt for it. He taps out a few sentences, saves the file, and again
 asleep on the couch. Just before dawn he phones the funeral home and reaches
man's cell.

"I want my wife cremated," he says. "I don't want a graveside ceremony eit[
Is it too late to make those changes?"

Bellman, at five in the afternoon or five in the morning, sounds the sa[
Everything can be altered according to the family's wishes.

"Sorry to call at this hour,"Wilkes says, "but I just..."

"Choices like this take time, and we seldom have enough," Bellman s[
"Changing your mind or being uncertain is common."

"I still want a headstone and a place where people can visit."

"A memorial to Keira. I understand. And if you'd like, maybe tomorrow or
day after, you can choose a suitable repository for the ashes, if you'd like to h[
them."

He does want to have them, though he isn't even sure why, not at this time of
morning, or this time of his life. Her parents will object, maybe not openly
privately. His sons don't have to know, not yet.

At the funeral home, he allows everything to progress normally. Bellman ta[
care of the rest, mentioning in an efficient and undramatic manner that there
be no procession to the cemetery and no graveside ceremony, what with
weather being so unpleasant. It's a matter of perception: thirty-five degrees
cloudy would be beach weather in Repulse Bay.

But no one complains and Bellman calls Wilkes forward to speak. He str[
confidently to the lectern, a veteran of reports and presentations to big
audiences than this. But the boys being there changes things.

"Our sons Brett and James," he says, a single note card in front of him, "v[
everyone to know how much they loved their mother, even when they gave h[
hard time."

There are some subdued smiles. Wilkes looks at the boys. They seem okay [
his words.

"They loved their mother. Of course, I knew that, and Keira knew that, bu[
important that all of you know that too. As for me, I think I gave her my shar[
hard times too, but she was the best person I ever knew, and whether she's [
with us or not, that will never change."

He looks at Brett again and receives a silent approval. James, less compo[
fixates on the coffin as Wilkes' speech becomes more impersonal: he tha[
everyone for coming, for their expressions of sympathy, for the flowers. He [
a few unprepared comments and retakes his seat. Bellman invites the mourne[
a reception (originally lunch, now brunch) for friends and family at a West[

taurant and says in his perfectly cryptic inscrutability, "Burial will be private, at
 discretion of the family." Wilkes's eyes search the corners of the viewing room
avoid contact with his in-laws. Neither Brett nor James deciphers the true import
the pronouncement.
Before the room has even cleared, Keira's father approaches him.
Was this our daughter's wish?" He seems more quizzical than confrontational.
I don't know."
I know she said once that she would never want to be cremated," Eason says,
ispering the final word so that the boys do not hear it. "Is this what we're doing?"
Yes."
When did she change her mind?"
Wilkes tries not to laugh. When did she change her mind about what? being his
e? being the boys' mother? remaining a part of the world?
He forces back the swelling anger: he does not want to fight that emotion today.
We talked a few times about how cemeteries took up so much space and maybe
as time to do things differently."
here are facets of truth in the explanation, at least in Keira's case. She usually
de the ecological arguments and Wilkes opposed them. Still, it's not really a lie.
His father-in-law shakes his head. "Our daughter wasn't usually that socially
scious."
She was on a lot of committees."
he answer sounds so lame that Wilkes immediately looks about to make sure
one else has heard it.
Or maybe," he says, taking both his son's hands. "She just changed her mind."

the click of a ballpoint and a signature on a credit card restaurant receipt, the
y and uncertainty of the past two weeks come to a whimpering end.
l that's left now, he says to himself, is the rest of my life.
home he opens a few sympathy cards and pores over the registry book from
man's. He will have to dash off some thank-you notes and maybe make some
. The Easons are back home. Hayley is already at Westchester County, waiting
ɔard a westbound flight. He envies her ability to escape. As for the casual
in, he never made the church service.
the evening McNally calls.
ias Staubley bothered you anymore?"
r a PI who must rely on a certain amount of deception, McNally can be, at
s, painfully transparent. This is a pity call from someone who understands that
ight is more dismal than the one of a funeral, when well wishers have returned
eir lives and the bereaved are supposed to do the same.
taubley? She won't be doing that. I'm glad you called though."
eally? I don't get that response very often. How are you holding up?"
's all very weird."
nd the boys?"
make sure they talk when it looks like they want to. Brett of course will tough
: or pretend to. With James, I don't know. Everyone I talked to today said kids
esilient. They couldn't all be wrong, could they?"
ould, probably are. What about you?"
n sad. I'm angry. I'm confused."
runk?"
ot yet."
ant some company?"
ou gonna drive an hour to babysit a—Jesus, I'm a widower. What a fucking
."
ie wife is at a movie with her college gang and I'm tired of watching
ɔtball. Tomorrow I have to report in to this woman who thinks her husband is
ing his sister."
ɔu mean her sister."
vish I did. See you around 8:30."

Wilkes tells the boys that they're having company. The timing surprises th
but if this is like most adult company, they won't be affected in any way. Ex
McNally isn't like most adult company: he arrives with four hot fudge sundae

"Nothing melts in the trunk," he says to the wide-eyed boys. "If you're lac
intolerant, scrape away the ice cream and eat the hot fudge."

They aren't, so Wilkes doesn't remind the PI that hot fudge would be just and
culprit. For a while, at least, the rigors of the last few days are shunted aside.

"Someday maybe Lynne and I will have kids," the PI says when the boys
been gently hustled out of the living room.

This time Wilkes remembers. Lynne is his wife.

"It's never too late."

"Sometimes it is. We're pretty stuck in our lives and we're getting older. I
your two guys, though; of course they're all broken in and everything. That w
be the tough part."

"In the beginning. There's more tough stuff after, but the sundaes helped. Th
for doing that."

"You can't be doing feel-good things at a time like this, but other people
And if they think I'm an asshole for bringing them ice cream in the midd
winter, it'll just be something they agree on. Now that drink I came for. O
know how you pour. I don't want to run off the Merritt reeking of gin."

"Is that why you drove all the way up here? For a drink?"

"Have to check on my clients, and you're still a client."

"Even if there's no case?"

"Even if. One drink. A single. Do I have to watch you measure?"

"Probably."

Wilkes fills a single jigger and splashes it over ice, then adds a few more d
In the dining room McNally mentions his new case, discreetly avoiding name
locations. And he talks about investigating in general, how it was
romanticized on television, how its portrayal has evolved, how technology
advanced it and rendered it almost superfluous.

"Everything's on record these days," McNally says. "You got a GPS to track
and a cell phone to locate you. Every call you ever make is recorded and st
Somewhere someone knows how many times I've ordered Chinese, which
illegal, but it doesn't take a skilled investigator to figure out. Somehow sitti
your bedroom with a laptop solving crimes seems mundane."

"In my job, I never have to appear on the trading floor."

But managing money, I don't think amateurs can do that."

Really? Watch the ads on TV. Someone thinks it's doable."

McNally raises his glass. "To better days," he says. "Now tell me more about
r psychic."

Demarais."

The old guy. You said you half believed him."

We sat in his 1935 kitchen and drank tea, his with whisky. Maybe he isn't nuts.
 up there, I don't know how to explain it exactly, there's this pervasive sense
of weight, like the cold keeps pressing down on you until you feel you're going
uffocate. Maybe in that old house, away from that cold, I felt safer. Felt like
rything was normal."

The reason I asked about Demarais...."

You found something."

've been poking around under rocks."

Did you dig up my yard?"

'm not some local constable. Maybe I'm not being clear. What I mean is, I need
ook at you, you and Keira."

thought you did that."

did. Are the boys sleeping?"

No. I'm holding them out of school tomorrow. Let them have the weekend to
 of normalize. Besides they're all hopped up on the sugar you brought them."

That's why I wouldn't be a good father. Been crashing on the couch?"

How'd you know?"

just do. That'll probably stop in a little while."

e doesn't share with McNally that he has considered buying a new bed,
ewing the idea only when he realized it's merely one component in a larger
 of furniture, one that he cannot arbitrarily dismantle. And what would he do
? Preserve the room in its current state and never use it again? Padlock it and
ntain it as a museum or shrine? He refuses to live in a gothic novel: he will
 e back in when the sting has begun to dull a little.

 o these rocks you poked under—"

We can wait a day or two if you want," McNally says, "I do have that other case
s about over. I had one of my camera people get some pretty incriminating
s—"

You have camera people?"

"A few. And a videographer. Wasn't incest after all. The guy was screwing
sister's best friend. His sister was just the middle man."

"Like a pimp."

"Who apparently worked cheap, but apparently a video is on the Inter
somewhere. Nice family, too, before this happened. Right now it's just a quest
of reporting out. But about Keira," he says, pulling a small pad from his b
pocket, "I have notes. I wasn't sure you were ready for this sort of thing so soo

The hesitation unsettles Wilkes.

"This sort of thing?"

"I could tell you that the truth is always best, but that would be a lie. Usually
truth sucks."

Wilkes hears the boys playing upstairs. Nothing raucous or wild, just play
returning to a semblance of normality. Wilkes can point himself in the sa
direction, or he can settle in with McNally to find out the truth which, as the
already stated, usually sucks. He pours himself another gin.

"An affair? Was my wife—?

"Nothing like that. I poked around in Greenwich a little," he says. "Keira g
up there."

"I know that. I told you—"

"Except she didn't. She was born somewhere else, wasn't she?"

"Right, Hamden or Haddam, I never got them straight."

"Maybe you should have. It was Hampton. Her father worked in Rhode Isl
over near Providence, some aerospace company that folded up in the nineties a
he left. He got out before they went under. Got himself transferred to New Ha
then switched jobs."

"Keira once said he took the job as a last resort. They wanted to live near N
York but the jobs were scarce and they were just starting out so—"

McNally holds up a hand.

"I know the story. You told me and they verified it. Or vice versa. It doe
matter. The point is it's a good, verifiable, substantial story. 'Cept it ain't true."

"You just said—"

"That it can be verified. Right. It can. But you know the devil and the det
How long did they live in Hampton?"

"I don't know exactly. They came back this way before Keira started school.
they had her right after they were married. Three, four years maybe? What do
mean he got himself transferred?"

You don't want to know the what, you want to know the why."
Well, you're making it sound insidious. People get transferred all the time."
He took a 30 percent pay cut in 1980. He was earning 70K. Let me put that in
spective. That's about $250,000 current buying power, maybe more. He gave
a third of that to be closer to New York."
They were tired of living in the boonies."
McNally flips open the notebook and thumbs through it, stopping at a small
oto of a white colonial, attached garage, a breezeway, nicely landscaped, well
back from the street.
This is their house in the boonies. Just over an acre. It sold in 2005 for just under
thou. Not bad for the boonies, huh?"
So when they sold it," Wilkes says. "They must have recouped the loss of
ary."
They took a beating on it. Wanted to sell fast. They didn't exactly give it away,
it was way underpriced. Here's the place they moved into."
McNally shows him the Easons' current home, a modest ranch.
Been there, huh?"
Of course."
Now that house, it's nice enough, and it's closer to the city, and it's on the gold
st. Maybe all that's worth a big pay cut and the bath you take on a home sale."
But his job—"
Eason was scheduled to be transferred anyway, either Stamford or White Plains.
and I could have been neighbors. So why the hurry? Of course, sometimes
ents move because they want their children to have some stability in their
cation, maybe start and finish in the same school system. Think that might have
n a factor?"
They never mentioned that but—"
Look at this," McNally says, rifling through the notebook to a folded sheet of
y paper with almost unreadable print.
Keira Eason's report cards from Fairland Elementary in Hampton. Four years
hem. They didn't issue them in kindergarten."
That's impossible. They moved here before she started school."
The copies are hard to read, but the name on the top isn't. Think there were lots
Keira Easons bouncing around over there?"
Wilkes feels as if he has just finished a workout. His breath is coming hard and
an feel moisture on his forehead.

"I don't understand. What does this mean?"

"It means the time sequence is wrong. That they lived in Hampton longer th[an] you thought."

"But why lie about that?"

"Because a girl named Sylvia Reed lived across the street from the Easons bef[ore] they moved. Keira never mentioned her?"

"No. Did you...talk to her?"

"That would require special skills. She's been dead for thirty years. I'm j[ust] wondering if ever, in the course of normal conversation with your wife, [her] parents, at a family get-together—"

"That's what Demarais said—a young girl died. Sylvy. The guy was right?"

"That doesn't make him psychic."

"It doesn't make him wrong. How did she die?"

"An accident on her tenth birthday, actually the day before. One of those horr[ible] stories you hear about where a kid—"

"What kind of accident?"

"I got clippings at home here but I'll save you the trouble. Her folks threw h[er] party. The girl fell backwards on some concrete steps, hit her head and died. It t[ook] a while to realize she was missing and a while longer to find her. EMTs clai[med] that if they had been there right away—you know, if she had fallen where some[one] had seen her—she'd have been okay. 'Course they don't know for sure."

"And Keira knew her?"

"Lived across the street. Never mentioned it, huh?"

"Never. If the girl was ten, then Keira—"

"They were in the same grade at the same school. Childhood trauma and [all.] Probably didn't want to relive it. That's understandable. Of course, Keira wa[sn't] actually invited to the party."

"How do you know that?"

"I investigated. Remember? That's what I do. State police have pretty g[ood] records and they interviewed every child there. Keira Eason was not on the [list.] Now I don't know if your wife and the victim were friends. The girl's folks s[ay] they sometimes played together."

"But if she wasn't at the party, what's the point?"

"The Reeds, the girl's parents, they live in the same house after all this time. [You—"

Wilkes has been anticipating a startling conclusion, or at least some pithy tag[line] that will make everything suddenly logical. There is none.

hat's it? They interviewed Keira's parents?"

hey interviewed all the neighbors, just in case."

Vhat did they say?"

here were no individual attributions. Nobody at the party had seen anything.
 as hell nobody across the street did. But at least, you know, if you want to ask
at it, your in-laws should have some recollection."

ilkes shrugged. "And what do I do with this information?"

cNally smiles. "My position is always the same: I tell you what you need to
v. What you do with it is up to you, unless I find evidence of a felony. I can't
wink at that. But this notebook, this is yours. Maybe you'd like to share it, you
v, with your in-laws."

ou mean leave it lying around so they can find it?"

ow you're beginning to think like a sleaze. I like that. Am I going to have to
y about competition?"

don't think I can do this kind of work."

hen I won't worry. Listen, you remember that incident in Fairfield just before
stmas? Man and his wife were broadsided by a truck, rolled over a number of
s, walked away with some scratches and bruises. Witnesses called it a miracle,
ared there was no way they could have survived. A month later the man
ped that same wife in the chest thirty-three times. Thirty-three! I heard he
e one knife in the process and finished with another which he then used to cut
wn throat. Old married couple. Never a problem. 'Splain me that."

don't see the connection."

hese miracles of survival. I don't know if they're good things after all."

on't even go there. If that plane hadn't floated—"

know. I know. Your kids were on it too. We just don't always know what's
ng next. Anyway, now you have...something. I'm still going to poke around.
 just for the record, I never said Keira wasn't at the party. I said she wasn't
ed."

ou think she crashed it?"

arents had cameras, lots of pictures. Apparently she wasn't in any of them. No
emembers talking to her. The Reeds knew her and claim not to have seen her.
ss she was a ghost—"

ut you still think she was there."

ook at these report cards. Everything exemplary until fourth grade, a general
 off. Her teacher wanted to speak to the parents. What happened to her?"

"You think it was the accident."

"I think it's likely. Maybe it was being close to something traumatic, or m
she was closer than anyone knew.

Wilkes studies the papers in detail, looking for any notation that will su
McNally's theory. But the numbers and letters are right there. The girl who
through the school in exemplary fashion vanished. Kids can be sensitive. W
has two boys to prove it, but being in the proximity of an accident, even
involving a friend, shouldn't have altered her personality so drastically. Th
more, and if McNally isn't saying just what, it's bad.

"Finish up," Wilkes says.

"What?"

"Finish up. You have something to add right?"

"There's a difference between conjecture and fact. These photocopies—"

"You think she had something to do with that girl's death."

McNally shrugs. "How could I have any idea?"

"That's all you have is ideas, for Christ's sake! Don't leave me with this hi
report unless you think it points to something."

Wilkes isn't angry, but the idea that Keira was somehow involved is
unsettling. She might merely have seen the police arrive—witnessed the hys
and fear and chaos—watched the girl being carted off—learned later that she
All that made just as much sense.

Of course kids did things in childhood that they never admit to later, comm
little indiscretions that seemed heinous at the time but which might have bee
fact normal, or typical, or most likely just tiresome. When he was twelve, M
Wilkes spent a summer watching his friend Josh Hansen's aunt sunbathe to
The woman was probably no older than 30 and had what Wilkes would now
pretty good figure, though back in the simpler world of childhood indiscretio
had nice tits. Josh would simply call Marty and say something cryptic like "
out there," and he would race over to "play catch with Josh," sneak through a s
in some hedges and find a space in the pool fence to best observe the show
some days she would lie on her stomach and they'd see nothing other than a
seconds when she might stand to slip on a cover-up and the breasts disapp
too quickly to be worth the wait. But on the good days, when they could ga
leisure with their hands mashed between their legs, the show was amazing. I
all stupid childhood behavior, but embarrassing enough so that Wilkes neve
to Keira hey, did I ever tell you about how my friend and I used to jerk off—

o if Keira had concealed her little secret episode from him, if it pained her, barrassed her, mortified her, even sickened her, how could he fault her for it? course, Wilkes never colluded with his parents about Tommy's aunt's little w, or swore them to secrecy because he was playing the voyeur a few houses y every sunny afternoon. So Keira and her parents had to have shared this ret. The Easons might have moved away because there had been an accidental th in the neighborhood and their daughter could no longer bear to look at the se. Or their involvement could have been less innocent.

'll talk to her folks," Wilkes says finally.

3etter you than me," McNally says. "We should talk to the boys too. I want to w what happened at the airport before they boarded."

Shouldn't you have found that out first?"

didn't think it was important. I was always tying together the crash with the ppearance. Now I'm not so sure. How about if you tell the boys I'm going to e by again and that you and I have things to talk about. Make it seem nportant, like they don't even have to be there. I'm not going to question them, they may remember things they don't even know they remember."

t's a lot of driving for you, isn't it?"

t makes me feel like I'm working. Can we say tomorrow night, around 6:00?"

Ve usually eat around then."

Do you all like Chinese?"

The boys do, I'm more of a—"

Good, I'll bring Chinese. Six o'clock."

3ut if I have to broach this with my in-laws—"

You don't have to yet. If they kept the secret for thirty years, another day won't ter. Relax. Take the boys somewhere fun. Stop drinking. Do some work in case want to have a job after this is over."

So you do think this will be...over."

Everything ends," McNally says. "Other people out there are waiting to write checks."

ere's no such thing as a normal afternoon anymore. The family of four is now a
nily of three, and nothing can take place without the nagging awareness of a
son missing. Routines exacerbate the difficulty. A dinner table set for three, the
pty front seat in the car, the nighttime rituals: all contribute to the sense of
eality. Restaurants don't help. Asking for a table for three is jarring, and so fast-
d places that don't ask "how many sir?" provide the only sensible alternative.
en Keira was alive they would see families like this, a father with his children,
l always surmise divorce, weekend custody. They never once considered he
ght be the one surviving parent. Now Wilkes wonders if people watch him in
same way, curious as to how he murdered his marriage. If he stood up and
nounced that his wife was dead, would that turn their smugness into shame? Or
uld they ask how and make things worse?
McNally arrives the following evening with enough food for a family reunion:
shopping bags from an unidentified restaurant whose name he refuses to
ulge. "Nothing personal," and he winks at the boys who are well occupied with
on chicken and some crunchy items that could be just about anything, animal
vegetable. "I'm not giving you the name. I don't want you people hanging around
in my area."
McNally is like a lot of men who don't have kids: he's really good with kids.
ce they aren't part of his everyday life, he treats them like a diversion, which
y are, and which he is to them. He can be funny, flip, maybe even a little
fane, because in an hour or two he'll be gone and the real job of raising children
l revert to their father. And Wilkes is fine with it; anything to make his sons'
s less grim is welcome, even if the respite is short.
nd like most PIs he possesses an endless skein of anecdotes: cautionary tales
ut people who did something wrong and then compounded the problem by
ng to keep it from him. The seamier details he excises from the narratives,
ping their rating at PG (the cheating sister-in-law/pimp will not be part of the
ning's program), but extortion and embezzlement hold starring roles. James
be a little too young to appreciate the nuance, but he grasps the overall:
eone is telling funny stories and everyone is laughing. Even Brett, if not
ctly mesmerized, is fascinated by the little incursion into the world of

subterfuge and crime. When he asks if you have to go to school to become a priv
investigator, his father cringes and McNally feigns offense.

"Truth?" he says. "If you do poorly enough in school, let me know. I'll find y
work."

After a half hour they've hardly made a dent in the food, but Wilkes dumps
fortune cookies on the table. There are six of them and the surplus requires choic

"Can we say it out loud?" Brett asks, cracking his open. "Or does that ruin it?

"If it's a wish you have to keep it secret," McNally says, "but these aren't wishe
He opens his, stares aghast."You will meet a tall dark stranger. Uh-oh, that sho
pretty well piss off my wife."

He balls up the paper and tosses it on the table. Brett's says he will soon co
into money and James's, as if some perverse fortune-writer knew it would end
in the hands of a six-year-old, contains the word refractory.

"Just don't be it," Wilkes says, before offering a fuller explanation.

McNally laughs. "Good thing your father's here," he says to James. "I'd ha
needed a dictionary."

James laughs too, though his dictionary contains mostly pictures. Wil
produces two mugs of coffee and pours the boys some milk.

"What about your fortune, Daddy?" James says, pointing to the unopened coo

"Do you know what a fortune is?"

He doesn't.

"It's when someone tells you something is going to happen before it happens

The younger boy accepts the explanation, but until Wilkes opens the cookie,
cannot proceed. When he does so, he can do little but smile at the snippet of t
paper and the faded blue lettering.

"Read it," James says.

Wilkes nods.

"Your artistic tendencies will save you."

McNally shakes his head.

"You're an artist?"

"If there's an opposite of an artist," Wilkes says, "I'm it."

Brett scoffs. "That's dumb. Open another one."

"Only one fortune a day," McNally says. "You guys probably have homew
to do, huh? You don't want to hang around with us old people."

The comment produces the expected groan, and McNally, suddenly someho
charge of the parenting, relents.

an I ask you guys a question about that day in the airport?" He looks at Wilkes.
hat all right?"
ilkes's expression provides tacit approval.
o when you were at the airport that day," McNally says. "Before you took off,
it crowded? Were there a lot of people around?"
Ve had to wait in line," Brett says. "Twice."
o check in, then to go through security, I'll bet."
ett nods. James isn't quite sure, but he remembers the beeping machines and
guards.
nd your Mom was talking to some guy?"
or a little while."
an you remember if it was after the first line you waited in?"
think it was after," Brett says, and inexplicably looks to his brother to verify.
s's expression tells him nothing.
oes it matter?" Wilkes asks.
there's video, it does. And there should be records of who went through and
. Someone would have scanned the boarding pass. We can bracket the people
re and after Keira, maybe get a hit on something. James, can you describe the
?"
course he can't, but McNally is clever enough to know that if he asks James,
will volunteer.
e wore glasses on this thing around his neck," Brett says.
ike a strap?"
eah but yellow and stupid."
hat color were the glasses, the frames?"
don't remember, but they were big."
as he taller than your father?"
bout the same I guess. Skinnier. Bald."
ald? Like no hair or some on the sides?"
o hair."
ustache? Beard? Big nose? Clown shoes?"
nes, still obsessing over McNally's initial question, misses the joke, but Brett
n't and, out of character, explodes in laughter.
one of those," he says, trying to catch his breath.
o you remember anything they said? Did your mom introduce you, tell you
an's name?"

"Nope."

"What did they talk about?"

"I dunno. It was noisy there."

"And then what, you got on the plane?"

"She pushed us ahead like we did something wrong but we still waited."

"This bald guy, did he get on the plane with you too?"

Brett shakes his head, but the truth is, and he admits it seconds later, he do[es] know. He never saw the man again, but there were so many people on the p[lane] that he had no way of knowing what ever became of him. McNally tries to [be] pleased, but Wilkes knows that just a little more precise information might m[ake] a difference, something identifiable other than baldness and average height.

"You guys have been a big help," the P.I. says, beaming like a mall Santa. L[ater] after the boys have been shuffled off to their rooms, he's more candid. "Just so [you] know, those airport videos, I doubt if they'll be helpful at all. Even f[ace] recognition software doesn't always work. But there are records and scans [that] we—I—might be able to find who went through security before and after [your] family. It would be a name—if you want a name."

"She didn't have a double life. She wasn't having an affair. Yes, find the na[me]."

"But she had secrets."

"We all do. Find the name. And I want you to tell me when you learn thin[gs] you do, no matter what they are."

"The evil that men do," McNally says. "It lasts for years."

"That's not exactly the quote."

"It's close enough. A lot of men whose wives go missing. They want them [back,] but there's an element of vengeance too."

"Keira's dead. What kind of vengeance do I get?"

"But before she died, did you miss her more than you resented her for leav[ing?]"

"Does that matter?"

"It will when we find out the truth, if we ever do. Are you still angry?"

"Even if I am, I still love her. And if it's the worst, tell me the worst."

McNally shrugs and looks around the room.

"I know this is none of my business, but what did you do with her ashes?"

"How do you know about that?"

"That you had her cremated? Jesus, Wilkes, your friends and relatives a[re] going to make an official inquiry, but you knew I would. What did you do [with] them? I didn't see an urn on the mantel when I came in."

We don't have a mantel. They're in my closet. I don't like that public display of es. It's vulgar."

So the boys don't know?"

No. They wanted things in the casket and I didn't want them to know everything uld be burned."

Things?"

James put in a red Candyland token. It was the one Keira always used."

Not to be crass, but I've played that game with a nephew. The entire game uld be burned. Are you planning to have a headstone?"

Eventually. Why do you care about her ashes? You're not the sentimental type."

I still respect death. Are you going to scatter them?"

When this is over, however it turns out, maybe I will, either in Long Island nd or in the woods out back near her garden. That'll be fine, but not yet, not en I don't know why."

You may never know why."

And that'll be okay as long as I can say I tried to find out—or you tried."

fter McNally leaves Wilkes finds the "tall dark stranger" fortune balled up on table. He opens it and reads the crinkled letters.

our heart of gold will win you friends.

Wilkes smiles. There's far more truth in McNally's than in his own.

utines: Before January 15 they dominated Wilkes's life, gave it order and
ostance. He needs to reestablish some of them. On Monday he'll meet with Byrne
d work out some new work schedule, and he needs to reconfigure Danielle's
by-sitting calendar, learn just when she can work. The Teggs down the street
e apparently forgiven him for sicking Staubley on them and have offered to
vide the occasional ride to and from school, even a haven for the boys when a
er is unavailable. Ginny Tegg told him at the wake that she works from home
ilkes didn't know she worked at all) and would be happy to help. Hers is the
d of overture he would ordinarily have rejected out of hand, but ordinary,
tomary, normal, all those good words reside somewhere else these days. He
epts, offering what he knows would be a fair day-care rate. Predictably, she
uses any payment.

nd there's Sunday dinner with the in-laws. A quick ride down the Merritt, out
he house for a while, everything helps. But it turns out that Sunday dinner with
Easons adds little to the normalizing process. Too much of what McNally has
rned demands an explanation.

was talking with someone from Hampton the other day. That's where you used
ive, right?"

e poses the question naturally and without fanfare. Dinnertime chatter, bland
innocuous. Inoffensive. The obituary said as much.

We lived there for a very short time," Eason says quickly. "Who was it you
?"

ust a client. Actually the husband of a client. How long did you actually live
e?"

And you're sworn to secrecy?" Eason says, eyebrows raised. "I mean about the
e?"

t's confidential. It's a client."

The husband of a client."

eira's father sounds like a TV prosecutor who has finally discovered the one
ial flaw that breaks down the defendant's story.

ame thing," Wilkes says. "Same confidentiality."

A tentative response. Eason shrugs, sips at his wine, then mentions something
the boys about February vacation. Wilkes, not ready to concede, throws up a sm
impediment.

"What do you mean for a very short time?"

"Are we still on that confidential material?" Eason asks, his tone still genial
his eyes flickering slightly. Mrs. Eason begins clearing the table and Wilkes
certain that her husband will volunteer to help, to find an escape route for hims
But that kind of avoidance doesn't matter, not this time. For years Wilkes has be
willing to accept the nebulous family background, to accept their having spru
full-blown in Greenwich twenty years before, as if deposited there by so
intergalactic travelers. And even today Wilkes doesn't require an extensive fam
history, just a simple answer: what constitutes a very short time?

"That was long ago," Eason says.

"Just curious," Wilkes says. "This guy was going on and on about wha
wonderful place it was and I wondered why you left."

"Job opportunity," Eason said. "You know what that's like. You live near
City for a reason."

"Absolutely. When did you move?"

The same question in a different format. He knows he's pushing it, but he
tell when he's being lied to. Clients have done that to him: lied about the stupic
most inconsequential matters, some $1000 savings account, a few stocks th
grandmother gave them, the amount they spend on liquor every month, facts
in the overall pattern of existence mean nothing. And now Eason is doing the sa
thing, except this time Wilkes already knows the answer. He just wants to kn
why.

Mrs. Eason yells from the kitchen, "A year or two. Who wants coffee?

"So her sister never lived there, in Hampton."

"We were gone before Hayley was born," Eason says, "though she may h
been on her way."

"May have been? I'd remember if my wife were pregnant when we moved."

He laughs and looks at the boys. Clearly they have no idea where this is go
or why. They're hanging around for dessert, the chocolate cake on the buffet beh
them.

"Reason I asked," he says loud enough for his mother-in-law to hear
understand there was a terrible accident in Hampton about twenty years back. L
girl was killed."

m sure it's true," Eason says. "People come home from those casinos at all
s and they've had a few too many—"
hose places were there back then?"
ilkes has already checked: they weren't.
guess so."
egardless, it wasn't an auto accident. The little girl died in her home."
s mother-in-law returns, shakes her head. "I'm sure the boys don't want to hear
hing like that."
course she's wrong: the story has already piqued their interest.
What kind of accident?" James asks. Brett, too cool to pose his own question,
now enjoy the answer without deigning to participate.
was at a party I guess," Wilkes says. "A little girl fell and hit her head. They
her to the hospital, but it was too late."
mes looks surprised. "She died?"
m afraid so."
rs. Eason frowns at Wilkes. "Honestly, is it necessary to frighten the boys?"
m not frightened, Grandma," James says. Brett feels no need to involve
elf in any disclaimers: nothing much frightens him anyway. Wilkes is tempted
k just how much more frightened they could be having recently endured their
mother's funeral and survived a plane crash. But there is shared grief at that
. The Easons have lost their daughter, and Wilkes has no desire to be sadistic.
nyway," he says, "I was just wondering if they lived near you. I mean I know
's a lot of land out there but—"
he lived across the street," Mrs. Eason snaps.
r husband exhales loudly.
e sudden admission unsettles Wilkes, upsets the natural sequence under which
s been laboring. He expected a further extraction of information in dribs and
: the town, the neighborhood, the street, the house. They have done it all for
leaving him feeling disorganized.
y God," he says, the words false-sounding and forced, like the response to a
ise party he'd helped plan. "That must have been awful. Was Keira at the
?"
e didn't live there at that time."
eah, of course," he says, tap-dancing now. A moment before he had a script
plan: now he has neither.

"But sometimes you make friends in a town, maybe come back for a birthda
something."

"I doubt if we'd drive two hours for a little girl's birthday party."

"Could have been anyone's party. Could have been a neighbor."

"But you said a little girl was killed."

"I guess I did. Anyway, this man I talked to, he remembers Keira. Could
have been in daycare together? Something like that?"

Mrs. Eason shakes her head like a dog casting off fleas. "How could we poss
know?"

The boys may not grasp evasiveness, but they recognize admonishment: th
usually on the receiving end. James begins to fidget and Brett, satiated on one p
of cake, excuses himself and goes into the other room. James follows.
somewhat mesmerizing tale of a party and an accident and death had kept t
interested, but now this reminiscence is just boring.

Except to Wilkes. He knows his in-laws are lying. He just doesn't know wh

"It was that girl's birthday, the one who died. She was ten."

Mrs. Eason leans back and puts her hands in her lap.

"Keira wasn't invited."

Her husband shakes his head rapidly, a warning issued too late.

"She wasn't invited?" Wilkes repeats. "Well that was fortunate, I guess. Did
know the people?"

"I told you, they lived across the street."

"You hadn't moved yet."

"No."

"Well, we have some neighbors across the street that we hardly know.
understand—"

"We knew the Reeds," the woman says. "Their daughter, I hate to say this
her being dead and all, that child was a brat and we didn't want Keira playing
her."

"So they didn't invite Keira? Wasn't she popular?"

"That's a terrible thing to say. Keira had lots of friends. The truth is..."

The words immediately put Wilkes on guard. In his experience people who
to lie usually begin by indicating what the truth is. But he evinces no suspi
just lets her go on.

"...Keira was invited. We didn't tell her. Then after the accident, we moved
just didn't want Keira to grow up with that...that specter of death across the st

Specter of death?" Wilkes asks, and he almost laughs at the image of some
sory death's head hovering over the house. But Mrs. Eason isn't backing down
v that she's made her admission of guilt, or collusion, or whatever it is.
Every time I looked at that house I remembered that little girl...."
Sylvy."
Yes, and I knew Keira was doing the same."
Did you talk to her about it?"
Of course, and she seemed all right. But sometimes, as a parent, you know
erent. I don't see why you had to bring it up. Our daughter is gone and this isn't
 of those nice things her father and I would like to remember from her life."
The man from the airport, maybe he was at the party?"
What man? What airport?"
The client."
The husband of the client."
Yes. Could he have been at the party?"
Of course. If you can't provide a name, anybody could have been there."
ason's patience is wearing thin but Wilkes won't let go now.
And maybe he remembers Keira."
f he does he's wrong," she says. "Or his memory is playing tricks on him. We
remember events from our childhood, but we can't always remember the
uence. I'm sure if you wanted to dredge up all the misery for that poor family
 lost their daughter, you could have that investigator of yours go back and
stion them. They probably kept a list of people who were there; and if they
't, the police did. Keira's name is not on any list."
hat phrase buried in the middle—that poor family who lost their daughter—it's
just the parents of Sylvia Reed: it's the Easons too. Wilkes can't tell if it's a
ulated attempt to terminate the discussion or merely an effective use of
guage, but whatever the intent, he backs off.
f she wasn't there," he says, conceding the point though he is no more
vinced than he was when he started. "Then there's no sense pursuing it."
me deceives in awkward situations, and what Wilkes believed later to be a
sequent minute of quiet was, in fact, no more than a few seconds. And he isn't
 just how long after that he's in the car driving the boys back to Wilton, where
hen must somehow make the Sunday evening as normal as possible. School
orrow, homework, clothes, alarm clock. It's the first time he's starting a week
out Keira and the entire routine is absolute misery. When either of the boys

moves too slowly or fails to follow an order to the letter, he points out their gene
inability to get things right. The unfair censure grates on him, but he lets it conti
until they seem sufficiently bullied, then couches an apology in the hint
something special for next weekend. He doesn't know what, but he has five d
to figure it out.

When the house quiets again he riffles through the morning Times. The hyst
over the Miracle on the Hudson has died off and he can find but one article on
crash. The news cycle has begun anew, or maybe more correctly has come bac
the starting point. The economic situation has worsened and the market contin
to fall. One expert says there'll be a rebound in the fall, but Wilkes, who has p
scant attention to anything outside himself, recognizes the incipient signs o
recovery. With no one there to read the magazine and book review, Keira's Sun
pleasures, he folds the paper into a neat pile and lays it on the coffee table. F
moment he considers sleeping in his own bed, but that can come another ni
especially since the blanket he's been using still lies there neatly folded on
couch.

When the phone rings, he assumes it's McNally, but the caller ID display
name, Tegg.

"It's Ginny," she says when he answers. "I hate to disturb you so late."

"No problem. I'm still awake." He anticipates the reason for the call. "1
Gomez girl is going to take care of the kids most days so—"

"I didn't call for that," she says. Since that morning she stood outside in
running clothes and confessed her role in some secret letter, they have talked li
which is to say no more or less than before. "That was a nice eulogy you gave.
made people cry."

"I was just repeating what the kids wanted to say, but thanks. And thanks
coming, you and John."

"You're welcome. I just wanted to tell you there was a car at your house
afternoon and I think somebody put something in your mailbox. It's probably
important, but, well you know. With the burglary and all."

He does know. The previous autumn, just one street over, a break-in
occurred and made everyone more wary.

He thanks her, tells her he'll check it out, makes a few customary inquiries a
her husband and kids, and accepts an invitation to bring Brett and James by
dinner some night when their schedules coincide.

"And you too," she says, laughing discreetly, cautiously.

He thanks her again, hangs up, then switches on the porch light and checks the mailbox: the cover is partially open and resting atop a large manila envelope. No return address, no address of any kind.

He remembers the Unabomber and the anthrax scare of years back, but neither memory stops him from ripping apart the seal. Inside there's a grainy surveillance photo: Jesus, it's Keira and it looks like an airport. There's a bald man standing next to her and they appear to be talking. He can see blurs in front of her and assumes they're Brett and James. The time stamp however is much clearer: January 15, 2009, 12:21.

Attached to the photo is a Post-it note neatly printed in red: MICHAEL CLIFTON, OAKDALE, N.Y.

He has never heard the name, but McNally is on the job. He races for the phone and calls him.

"I can't believe you got that picture and drove it all the way out here."

"What are you talking about?"

"The surveillance from the airport. You hacked in and got it?"

"I got nothing from TSA," he says. "There's a lot of concern about invasion of privacy lately and I didn't have a good enough reason for access. And I'm not a cop or fed. It wasn't me."

"Then how did I get this?"

"Good Samaritan? Guardian angel? What'd you say this guy's name was?"

"Michael Clifton. Oakdale, New York. I don't even know where that is."

"It's out on the Island, near Islip. Pretty upscale."

"You've been there?"

"Never had a client there, but I've been by it."

"Well, if this isn't from you, then where did it come from?"

"Dunno. Don't look a gift horse and all that—"

He phones Ginny Tegg again but her husband answers.

"Sorry, John. I know it's late. Could you ask Ginny, she called before, what kind car dropped off the letter at my house today? I mean, if she got a look at it?"

"Sure, but she's pretty typical. Not real good at recognizing car brands."

Wilkes remembers immediately why he dislikes John Tegg, then hears some chatter in the background and finally Ginny's voice on the phone.

"It was light blue, four doors," she says.

"Did you see the driver?"

"It was a woman."

"Wearing leather?"

"Could have been, yes."

"Thanks. And tell John you know more about cars than he thinks you do."

Wilkes looks at the photo again. He doesn't know any feds but he does know cop who drives a blue Camry. With the phone still in his hand, he fishes her ca out of a basket in the kitchen.

"Martin Wilkes," he says when she answers. "I wanted to thank you for t photo."

"What photo?"

"From the airport."

"Sorry, Mr. Wilkes, I really don't know about any photo."

"Someone saw your car."

"I merely stopped by to see how things were going. Nobody seemed to be hom

"It's a security photo, from a video I guess."

"My God, Wilkes, if I ever accessed a security camera, then gave the result a private citizen, I could kiss my career goodbye. You know that, right?"

So she's done this off the books, broken protocol, taken a risk.

"Let me ask you this, detective, is it about as bad as officially leaking an incor cause of death to a website?"

"In the same ballpark."

"Would one breach of propriety balance off the other?"

"In some candy-cane world, maybe. Is there anything else?"

"Do you have a red pen?"

"Red barrel or red ink?"

Wilkes smiles.

"Got it. So, do you want to know how things are going?"

"Sounds as though you're getting by."

"I am."

"Good. Stay safe, Mr. Wilkes. With information comes responsibility. You kn that, right?"

"I do now."

But he doesn't: he has a name, a photo, a partial address. He has no idea wha do with them.

is not a name.
ere is no Emil or Emile any other combination of letters beginning with em.
n is simply em, the phonetic spelling of the thirteenth letter of the alphabet,
ame letter that begins the Michael half of Michael Clifton. Brett told him the
ious night, told him without ever knowing it, asked how a dash was different
a hyphen and sent the two of them on an Internet search for punctuation. They
d dashes, and somewhat longer en-dashes, and finally, the em-dash—as wide
e letter m.
never knew they had names," he said to his son, hardly able to subdue his
tion. The next morning Wilkes awakens to a fresh snowfall, just enough to
the roads and close schools. Five full days have elapsed since he received the
lope: five full days of trying to make life bearable. It isn't working. He's
me a veritable shut-in when the kids are in school and can think of little to say
yone, even the loquacious and bubbly Gomez girl whom he has known
er. He's drinking too much and blowing off work on the slightest whim. He
even mourn effectively because the anger keeps returning and he never
s what will reignite it. He fantasizes Keira's miraculous return, but whenever
es so the episode terminates in anger and recrimination. So far he's done a
job of keeping his feelings hidden from the boys, at least he thinks so.
ally figured it out quickly enough, but the boys are young, naïve, unaware
anyone could resent someone who died, let alone their mother.
d he's been sitting on Staubley's information for a week. The cop stepped out
unds to give it to him and he's done nothing.
en the snow stops falling, he phones Danielle Gomez. She'll gladly be there
o'clock: it's a snow day for her, too, though the cancellations may have been
and the roads already look more than navigable. The TV is filled with
nitions not to drive, but Wilkes ignores them and, as soon as Danielle settles
eads south on the Merritt. As often occurs, snow in Connecticut is a slushy
ire closer to Long Island Sound, and the roads and sidewalks in Islip are far
treacherous. Well before noon he's searching for Michael Clifton's condo.
ally was right—Oakdale seems tony enough—but Clifton's complex is not
and, with most people off at their jobs, finding a place to park is not an issue.

Clifton himself could be at work, but an Internet search revealed him to
software engineer, one of those work-from-home occupations—maybe.

And even if he isn't at home, at least Wilkes has done something, made
ninety-minute trip, accepted the responsibility that, according to Staubley, is
obligation.

"Mr. Clifton?"

Wilkes is so surprised when the door opens that he forgets the man's first na
but this is the guy that Brett described. Thin, bald, a pair of glasses draped aro
his neck, held there by some yellow braid.

"I'm Martin Wilkes. We've never met, but you know my wife Keira, K
Eason. I think you went to school with her."

Clifton looks wary, but he can hardly deny the fact.

"I did, a long time ago. And I saw her at LaGuardia a few weeks back. She
on that plane that went down, right?"

"In the Hudson? Yes."

"Jeez, I thought so. That was really something."

"A miracle, if you believe the papers. I wonder if maybe we could talk
minute. I'm not selling anything."

"I wouldn't imagine you were. Come in."

A woman in athletic shorts and a black t-shirt appears in a doorway be
Clifton. She cups an oversized stainless steel mug in her hands.

"I was just going to work out. Who is it, honey?"

"The weirdest thing," he says to her. "Remember I told you how I saw
woman at the airport, the one I went to elementary school with, and then her
landed in the river? This is her husband...Martin is it?"

"Martin Wilkes," he says.

"Suzanne," she says, then adds with a hint of accusation. "Was my hus
expecting you?"

"No, and I'm sorry about just dropping in. I just—I work in the city and
the accident I don't get many chances to take care of personal things. I just to
chance."

"You live on the Island?"

"I live in Connecticut."

The wife moves closer. "This isn't exactly on the way home."

Her husband may be okay with a drop-by, but she's on her guard, cautious. Keira is the same way, though: dusting, vacuuming, straightening. They all had to be completed before a guest could arrive.

"Honey," Clifton says, cajoling. It's something he appears used to. "Let's see what the man wants."

"Sure," she says, then shakes her head as if this sort of thing happens all the time and she's sick of it. Before she can learn *what the man wants,* she's gone. When Wilkes hears no exercise equipment, he envisions her in another room calling the police, but Clifton motions him to follow and they step into a solarium filled with potted plants and gardening tools, a room rife with dampness and the dark smell of humus, out of place in mid-winter. Some snow clings to the roof, sending feeble rivulets down the sloping sides.

"Rushing the season a little, like I always do," Clifton says. "Be starting the seeds next month. Can I get you a drink? Coffee? Anything?"

Wilkes would love a gin, just to take the edge off this uneasiness, but that's a message he doesn't want to send and he turns it down.

"I'm just wondering," he says. "How did Keira seem that day in the airport?"

"Nervous. At least I thought so. Sometimes people get that way before boarding. Unless maybe she was clairvoyant."

"Do you remember what you talked about?"

"If you were a kid in Hampton in '79 you only talked about one thing: the party."

"Where the little girl was killed."

"Sylvia Reed. Yes."

"But Keira wasn't at the party. Why would she want to talk about it?"

"Everybody talked about it. There were meetings in school, they brought in psychologists to talk to the kids. It was a pretty big deal."

"Is there any chance you could have been mistaken about Keira? Could she have been at that party and you just didn't see her or don't remember?"

"The funny thing is I thought I did see her, but there was so much confusion that when I was told she wasn't there, I didn't question it. Of course these days I can't remember where I parked my car."

Wilkes has not come here for small talk, nor does he wish to be cordial; but there is something engaging about Clifton and he allows himself a smile. Clifton returns

"The truth is," Clifton says, looking at his gloves, "I thought Keira was pre
and I guess I liked her, you know, the way little boys like girls. But her fam
moved away. I never saw her again until…whenever…January."

"And you recognized her."

"I did. I'm pretty good at that."

"And after the party that day, the police questioned you?"

"My folks did, and then my folks talked to the police. I think that's mostly h
it worked. I think now the police might have gotten better answers if they'd g
right to us. Kids lie to their parents all the time, but in that case there wasn't m
to lie about. It was just a terrible accident."

"But you still talk about it."

"You can't control what you remember. Sure I can't get you something?"

"I'm sure," Wilkes says, and watches Clifton pick up a miniature rake and p
at some soil around a potted plant Wilkes does not recognize. In his green p
flannel Michael Clifton looks more Vermont-rural than Long Island-affluent,
if his recollections contradict the musings of some old snow-blind psychic, is th
any question as to whose story is accurate? Even so, Demarais's words reverber
what we believe can never be replaced by what someone else believes. /
goddamn it all, Wilkes can't help attaching some credibility to the old man v
cared for his wife and seemingly forgave him for the angry outburst that cc
have killed him. If Demarais were here now, he'd at least get to the point. Wil
maybe, can do the same.

"Do you know a woman named Ginny Tegg?"

"Did I go to school with her too?"

"I don't think so. She's a neighbor of ours in Wilton."

"Doesn't sound familiar. Why?"

"She got a letter sometime before Christmas, said something like all these y
I haven't forgotten you."

"An old boyfriend?"

"Here's the weird part: it went to her house but it had Keira's name on
envelope. So Ginny opened it."

"I don't follow."

"Ginny was supposed to give it to Keira, but once she opened it—well—the
was too late."

"I guess she could have still given it to her," Clifton said.

'And think she's having an affair?" Wilkes shook his head. "And then what does

: do with the information? How does she face Keira, or me? We're neighbors.

ends. What kind of person puts a total stranger in such an untenable situation?"

'How do you know it was a stranger?"

I don't. But listen to this," Wilkes says, ignoring Clifton's question. "It was

ned em, just e-m, em. And we thought it was initials or maybe short for Emily,

it wasn't. It's em, the first letter of Michael. I checked. There were no other

s in your class. No Marys, no Matts, just Michael."

You think I wrote a letter to your wife?"

I do."

Do you have it?"

Long gone."

Because maybe there was DNA evidence that would have proven I didn't write

You could have worn gardening gloves."

Why not boxing gloves?"

I'm serious."

I am too. Just ask Keira if I've had any contact with her outside LaGuardia that

, if I ever called, or emailed or—"

Keira's dead."

What?"

Last week. I can show you the obit."

My God, she was fine in the airport that day."

She got sick. It was fast."

Honest, I didn't know. I'm sorry."

lifton looks stunned, and he doesn't appear to be acting. There was always an

side chance he would have read about the missing woman from the plane, but

ie of those articles omitted Keira's name. And the death notice never left

inecticut.

So all this is moot, I guess, but did you write that letter?" Wilkes asks. "You

tell me. I don't blame you for anything."

didn't. Can you sit for a minute?"

If that's your answer then I have no reason to sit."

Look," Clifton says, moving away from the plants. "Maybe we can start over.

iow Keira was upset at the airport and maybe I shouldn't have brought up the

c. But that day, it's part of us."

"Part of you maybe. She never ever told me about it. Apparently she had mov
on."

"We all have, but that doesn't mean we've forgotten."

"Then you haven't moved on. Does your wife know?"

"About the accident? Of course. Kids too."

"A cautionary tale, right? Did you tell your wife you sent the letter?"

"Mr. Wilkes, listen. I am sorry for your loss, and I'm sorry you came all this v
for nothing, but I didn't send any letter. And I'm shocked that Keira never talk
about the party with you. To keep it bottled up like that—"

"Maybe the truth doesn't always set you free—maybe it makes things worse
she had gotten past it before we met, what was the point of dredging it up agair

"I'm telling you, Mr. Wilkes. I didn't send the letter. It's true I feel—haunted
the whole thing, even after thirty years. That day I thought I saw Keira and Syl
both and maybe if I'd said something right away—I don't know. Maybe it v
already too late. But that was my problem, not Keira's. I never once tried to ge
touch with her. Wilkes sees movement out of the corner of his eye. It's Suzanne
the doorway, the mug exchanged for a cellphone.

"Is something wrong?"

"The woman at the airport," he says to her. "She died."

"Oh," she says, turning toward Wilkes. "I'm sorry. I thought I heard you ment
Sylvia too."

Clifton looks sheepish. "Yes, I did." He turns to Wilkes. "Suzanne thinks—
she's right—that the subject comes up too much—that maybe like you saic
haven't moved on quite enough."

His wife, arms folded, seems to be trying hard to look sympathetic, but the ef
isn't successful. Whatever discomfort Wilkes felt traipsing into a man's home a
accusing him of all sorts of mischief is worsening.

"I should leave," he says.

Clifton's wife remains in the doorway.

"It's almost as if," she says, looking at Wilkes but not focusing her gaze. "A
he was married before and the first wife becomes part of every conversatio
don't expect him to forget her, just put her—put things in perspective. This pa
this accident, Sylvia, and now this letter. When is enough enough? When doe
end?"

Now, Wilkes says to himself. It ends now. He fends off the temptatior
apologize to either of them; after all, they've lost nothing compared to him. H

to accuse Suzanne of eavesdropping, but he doesn't know if a person can be
used of that particular indiscretion in her own house. So he's disturbed their
ning, granted, but once he leaves they can carry on with their day and forget
was ever there. He'd love to look forward to the same resolution.

Before he even starts the car, he phones McNally: the condensed version is all
PI needs.

"his Clifton, you believed him?"

"es, but people lie," Wilkes said.

"hey do, but he had no reason to send that letter. If he was working out his guilt
egret or anxiety or whatever was eating away at him, he was working it out
 his wife. He didn't need to open up any old wounds with Keira or anyone
 Make sense?"

"suppose."

"o harm, no foul."

" wasted trip."

"t least now you know who wrote the letter."

"do?"

" you don't, you will—I'd say by the time you're halfway home and too far
g to drive back to Islip—"

"e realization comes much quicker.

"on of a bitch."

"Now, you got it already. What do you wanna bet Michael and Suzanne don't
about that party anymore?"

"is wife."

"re. Got sick of hearing the same story and was probably convinced her
and was still in love with a thirty-year-old memory. Now do what you
Clifton to do, let it go."

"ut—," Wilkes clenched the steering wheel, his knuckles white.

"at possible reason would she have for doing that?"

"ometimes people just get pissed off. If it's any consolation, it
t take Clifton long to figure out what his wife did. Let that be their problem.
e them to their misery."

*****

"When Mommy was young, about your age, Brett, she made a mistak
and someone got hurt."

He's several hours and a couple of gins past his conversation with the Clift
Calmer. Relaxed.

"Who got hurt?" James asks.

"A little girl named Sylvia. She and mommy were playing and Sylvia fell d
and hit her head. Mommy got scared and didn't tell anyone."

"At that party?" Brett asks. "That little girl Grandpa talked about. It
Mommy's fault?"

"It was an accident, nobody's fault. But sometimes we blame ourse
anyway."

"But why did she run away now?" James asks. He couldn't care less a
ancient guilt or regret: he wants answers to simpler questions.

"I don't know," Wilkes says. "But I think if you have a secret all your life,
can make bad decisions."

"Like suicide?"

Brett has not excised that blog post from his mind.

"No. She just wasn't careful and got very sick up there. Too sick."

"Was it cancer?" James asks.

"Something like that," Wilkes says. "It takes all the good things inside you
replaces them with bad things. And then you have too many bad things in
body, and that's when people die."

Wilkes doesn't even look at Brett: if James gets it, Brett does.

"Keeping secrets," he says, lapsing reluctantly into philosophy. "It's li
cancer."

"You told us we shouldn't tell on people," Brett says.

"And you shouldn't if it isn't important. Like if you spill a glass of mi
something and clean it up and don't tell me, then that's not so bad. Or if
brother does that and asks you to keep it a secret, as long as no one gets hurt-

"What about at school? If someone breaks something? Or knocks some
down?"

"Then you should tell the teacher so that nobody else gets hurt."

"How about you, Dad?" Brett says. "Do you have secrets?"

"A few."

"Tell us one, one that didn't hurt anyone."

"But then they wouldn't be secrets."

Just one," James says.

He has plenty, almost all of them involving underage drinking and backseat, sometimes frontseat, sex. All those adolescent indiscretions that he shares with most of the remainder of the earth's population. And there's Millie Hendrickson, Keira's college friend, fantasies and betrayals that can't be sugarcoated. And he ogled Sandy Qualling at work and that woman on the plane. And that secret college fund. Is that an evil secret too? He implied that everyone has them. Does everyone have as many as he does?

"Once," he says, scrounging for a story that doesn't impugn his character. "Back when we had VCRs. Do you know what those are?"

They don't.

"It was a way to record TV shows to watch later. One time I wanted to watch a movie, it was on after midnight and my folks told me I couldn't. So I set the timer and recorded it while they were sleeping and watched it the next day after school."

Brett homes in on the motive. "Were there naked girls in it?"

Not nearly enough, Wilkes remembers. Not even a nipple unless you count the ones on the guy who was trying to undress the big-breasted bimbo Wilkes wanted to see undressed.

"Sort of."

James laughs, though he finds the situation more amusing than titillating. Brett acts like some sort of pre-pubescent sage, his face showing the beginnings of a smile.

"But you see, nobody got hurt," Wilkes adds quickly.

"Do you think you should have told?"

A trap. A yes means the boys can expect to find their father dead too, another victim of a guilty conscience. A no promotes a kind of unprincipled approach to life, picking and choosing truths and falsehoods as convenience dictates.

"What I mean," he says, sidestepping as best he can, "is that when you get older you understand other people's feelings a little better, and you know what's going to make their lives—"

He stops. Bearable—that's the word he wants to use. But how can he when his life has degenerated into a skein of intolerable days and miserable nights? He's drinking too much and blowing off work all the time. He's a veritable shut-in when the kids are in school and he spent this particular morning on Long Island accusing a complete stranger of lying. What's bearable about this, about any of this? He

can't even mourn effectively because the anger keeps returning and he ne
knows what will ignite it. Goddamn her for doing this, for leaving them this w
for not trusting him to overlook some childhood mistake.

"Dad?"

Brett is waiting for the sentence to end, maybe for this little confab to end to

"I was going to say," he begins, controlling his words, "to make their lives oka

"But Mom."

"She made a mistake. She...sometimes even grown-ups don't understand h
everything is going to turn out and then it's too late."

He doesn't want them to blame their mother. It's doubtful that they do anyw
Only he does. But at least he's laid out the facts, or his version of them, and he w
make sure that anytime more questions arise, he'll be there to listen. Answer
them will be a different matter. He doesn't know the answers.

The boys leave the bedroom to Wilkes. He's in there frequently, gather
clothes and pairing outfits for work. He has begun to use the master b
sometimes even the phone by the bed. Yet alone like this, seated in the chair
belonged, unofficially, to Keira, he feels like an interloper. The two of them m
decisions in that room, he leaning on his arm sideways across the bed, she in
chair overlooking the back yard. Conversations about vacations and cars
appliance purchases, trivial exchanges about neighbors and movies and part
they'd all taken place there. Over the years, they came to know that once t
positioned themselves in those spots, it was time to talk. Only once had he bro
that rule—only once had he knelt before her as she sat in the chair, massaging
feet as she sat barefoot in her pajamas, the winter sun having risen an hour ab
the horizon. Massaging her feet, and then her ankles, and her calves, and as
heat grew inside him, methodically up each leg until her breath was coming as
as his, and she had finished even before he could slip off the last piece
clothing—had come in quiet but intense spasms, each more violent than the la

Afterwards she had run a finger around the waistband of her underwear and
with a mischievous smile, "Guess we can burn these."

And he had lain there with his head in her lap until the harsh angle of the morn
glare dissolved, arched above the window. The tastes, the smells, even the fee
the skin and the silk together—the thoughts of that morning would return to
often and always produce in him the same longing, the same pulse-quicke
awareness.

He slides open the closet door. Since he received the ashes from the funeral home
(the director, Bellman, insisted on calling them cremains, a word Wilkes always
deemed frivolous and disrespectful despite its accuracy), he has never opened the
cardboard box, never examined the plain and unpretentious mahogany container
inside. He cannot display it anyway, and anything more ornate would have been
ludicrous. His intention of driving to Sherwood Island and scattering her ashes into
Long Island Sound remains intact. Not too soon, though. Not when he's angry.

At eleven, fully awake and refusing to anesthetize himself with more gin, he calls
Andy Campanella, a calendar program open on his laptop.

"How long before a flight can you get tickets?"

"Six months, maybe more."

"I'm going back north. June 21, to Baker Lake. Do your magic. Same itinerary.
Toronto, Saskatoon—"

"It's saved from last time. That's the summer solstice, isn't it?"

"Is it?"

"Yes. How many tickets?"

He considers the possibilities.

"Just me."

He won't take the boys and he won't even tell McNally. The PI has had enough
of the Arctic. So has Wilkes, and after this final trip, there won't be any more.

36

Martin Wilkes, arriving in Baker Lake at the summer solstice is akin to arriving
iami International and watching the ground crew deice a plane. Nothing makes
sense, beginning with the lake that actually is a lake, filled with small craft
eying for position amidst a few remaining ice floes, nagging reminders of
er times gone by and yet to come. Even on land there remain isolated patches
ow, though unlike the late-season residual piles of New England, these remain
ine, unadulterated by car exhaust and melting chemicals and airborne
ition. Climatological changes notwithstanding, it's still a barren and rocky
scape. It would take more than mild weather to alter that.
repeats his original pattern, checking in at the co-op first where Manitok is
ned.

Ir. Wilkes?"

ou remembered me."

f course. Why are you here?"

hat isn't much of a welcome."

d have prepared a better one if you'd told me."

st have some unfinished business."

/hat a nice surprise," she says. Even the hug seems heartfelt, sincere. He
n't remember the last time anyone was happy to see him.

e looks older, no longer the kid he remembers from only months before, the
g girl who claimed to be older than she looked. Now she looks her age and
es wonders which of them has changed.

nd your kids, you had two sons. Are they with you?"

ou have a good memory. They're home, looking forward to summer...like

Ir. Wilkes..."

ou should call me Martin. I'm not your financial advisor."

artin, this unfinished business. Is it here or in Repulse?"

rought Keira's remains. I think they should be in Repulse Bay."

ee. You were angry when I saw you last," she says.

as it that obvious?"

es. Are you still?"

"At times I am. At times I feel like I knew so little about her that I never e
had a wife. I was never married."

Manitok is in early-morning mode, rushing, fitting in words between custom
but she puts everything down and stares at him, her head cocked to one side.

"I have always spoken honestly to you, Mr. Wilkes, at least I did when
decided to be honest with me. Am I right?"

"Yes, I think so, although how can we know when a person—"

"Stop. Please. I was never married? Those are the words you say to
someone, to get revenge, to let someone know that you despise her. You know
just bullshit."

He smiles. "You've expanded your vocabulary. Isn't there an Inuk
equivalent?"

"Not as eloquent. Don't say things like that. It's like dialogue from a sa
melodrama. If you're mad, say so. Get it out and get it done. She was your wi

"She betrayed me and her sons."

"But for all those years she didn't. Now you can tell yourself those years e
count, that her betrayal undoes everything, but if you meant that, you woul
have come all this way, twice. You'd have put that pile of ashes out by the
and let a sanitation worker take them away."

"That would be disrespectful."

"So you made this trip out of duty, not love, I get that. But I think t
something you tell yourself, not something you feel. Throwing daggers at the c
They're an easy target, but when you're finished, they're still dead and your
hurts."

She shifts backwards a step and scans the co-op.

"Does it bother you that I speak honestly?"

"Yes."

"Good. Then we understand each other."

A woman nudges him aside and drops some bills on the counter. An
follows.

"It's the solstice," Manitok says. "It always means more to do. I thought m
that's why you came back—for the celebration. Your reason is more appropri

"I'll get out of your way. I was wondering, do you ever see Deidre anymore

"She comes in once in a while. She's still Deidre."

"Tell her that I was asking for her. Tell her she can do a lot better than the di
she was with last time."

Your sons, are they Deidre's age yet?"

No."

When they get to be in their teens, let me know how much luck you have with ice. But I'll try to keep an eye on her, maybe tell her you're concerned."

Is there an Inuit word for dipshit?"

The joke is that Eskimos have a thousand words for snow. Based on the guys met, a reasonable sampling, there must be a thousand more for dipshit. I'll ose one."

Do you already have one for me?"

I'm reserving judgment. Deidre's boyfriend, though, he's young. He still has sibilities. Tell me how you will you get to Repulse"

have to find Brantley. Get him to fly me up there. If he isn't around—"

Manitok shakes her head.

You haven't heard then."

Heard what?"

Brantley went missing a few months ago. April. He was coming back from olute up near the pole, supposed to make a stop at Repulse but never showed They never found the plane, wreckage, anything."

Brantley? That's impossible."

It's been months."

But he was so good at what he did. And that plane was like new."

Up here—sometimes those things don't matter."

Wilkes can think of no reasonable reply: the idea that anything untoward could pen to a pilot that skilled and adept, even in the inhospitable Arctic, seems ird. Even if the man played the hotshot and took the occasional risk, even if he d at the impossibility of Arctic survival ("It'll be a small explosion. I don't y much fuel."), he understood the odds as well as anybody and he knew how eat them.

liked him," Wilkes says. "He once told me what would happen if his little cher crapped out. Any injuries at all and he was, in his words, another ropping on the tundra."

He was funny. We all liked him. But this place. Sometimes we forget how gerous it can be. I think every pilot knows that, but it's the rest of us who etimes forget."

owed him," Wilkes says. "I mean he was a friend, not just a pilot. He waited vith me when my wife was dying. Helped me with arrangements and

paperwork and transport and—Was there a memorial service? Anything? I me
what did people do?"

"He had family out west. I think they took care of the formalities."

"And a sister in Repulse. And a nephew. Goddamn it, he should have kno
better," he says, the anger rushing to the surface. "Did they really try to look
him? I mean, the government? Not just a couple of beat-up mounties with a do

"He knew every pilot in Canada. They searched. But up here, they know
causes."

"Don't planes have beacons? Distress signals?"

"Any pilot will tell you: sending out a rescue party usually makes more pec
die. That didn't stop his friends from looking, but they knew the odds too."

"I wonder how hard they tried if they thought it was a lost cause."

He searches her eyes for some hint of prevarication, but this is Manitok.
doesn't play games with words: Brantley is dead, and Wilkes, true to form, has
anger overtake him.

"Daggers at the dead," he says.

Manitok smiles. "See what I mean?"

She hands him a notebook, one page of which is filled with names and numb

"Pilots. Any one of these will get you to Repulse."

He stares at the names, all meaningless. His plan involved Brantley, not s
stranger from a list.

"Jane, that's the sister's name. And Ben. The boy's name is Ben. Jesus,
fucking place!"

Manitok says nothing. Maybe she agrees. Maybe she simply knows enoug
let a person vent without criticism.

He holds up the list of pilots.

"Know any of them?"

"Withers, Callet, heard the names. I think they're good. Are you staying the

"No. Just in and out."

"If you're flying right back, tonight is the party. You may not be in the m
but just so you know. You can add a word for your Inuit vocabulary: *Pigartok*

"That's what the party is called?"

"No, the party is called a *ceilidh*. *Pigartok* means awake all night. Of co
there is no night, but there's a party anyway. You should come. It's an arts fes
with liquor—mostly liquor. If you get drunk enough you'll swim in the lak
midnight. The water temperature is all the way up to two above. Celsius."

"This icy drunken dip, that would be naked, right?"

"Of course."

"Have you ever done it?"

"I never looked very good in a swimsuit so it doesn't matter much. Of course as et older I don't look very good naked either, but I have few reasonable years left. u probably do too."

"My decline is progressing nicely."

"I don't see life that way, all kind of hooked up together on this, this hill going vnward. If anyone should know that, it's you; otherwise that plane crash on the er would have been the culmination of some sequence. But it simply happened. e an episode."

"Episodes are connected."

"In a novel maybe; otherwise they're only episodes."

"Then let's say this: my swimming nude would be an unpleasant episode for all olved."

Manitok smiles and offers to point him toward some of the solstice preparation, Wilkes needs to hire a pilot. On a hunch he tries the Polaris where he first found ntley that morning in January. Nobody looks familiar, but he intimates his need he bartender.

That table," the man says, pointing to a spot near the door. "Two of them."

Neither pilot is heading north, but they know one who is and, within the hour, lkes and two others are squeezed into another Beechcraft with a middle-aged te man named Timmerman on the tedious flight to Repulse Bay. Timmerman ms devoid of personality, but Wilkes remembers how businesslike Brantley at the controls and writes off the pilot's restraint to safety, not hostility. ides, Wilkes doesn't need to talk, he needs to readjust. His plan called for ntley to be his guide and go-between. That idea had evaporated two months ore, but nobody told Wilkes.

f course, in a pinch there's Jane to provide a friendly face, and there's the man se name he never did get right to provide some transportation, and if he injures self somehow, there's Ilisapie at the hospital. But on a day when a light dbreaker suffices and the urgency to rush from one protective shelter to another vanished amid the lengthening daylight, Wilkes seeks out Demarais's house. window boxes, filled with dirt instead of snow, seem just as ludicrous; rwise it's the same place.

There's no answer when he knocks, but seconds later Auguste Demarais emerg
from around some hedges. He's dressed for winter; overdressed in an anorak a
boots, though he has eschewed the hood.

"I was in the back," he says, then examines his guest more closely. "Mr. Wilke

"I wasn't sure you'd remember me," he says, without adding the obvic
clarification: I'm the guy that attacked you last winter.

"Do you want to come in? It's starting to drizzle."

Wilkes follows him into the kitchen and, without being asked, sits at the sa
table, in the same chair as he did before.

"I can make tea," Demarais says, but Wilkes declines.

"Thanks, but no. You don't seem surprised to see me."

"Did you come to surprise me?"

"No. I...I'm sorry about your brother-in-law. He was a good man."

"He was that. We all miss him, Benny the most. Still cries."

"And Jane, how is she doing?"

"They annoyed each other, but she misses him very much. I visit them m
often, try to be a friend. I don't belong there, and we all know it. A man can't
something he's not just because someone else demands it. You already know th

The implication, annoying and presumptuous, reminds Wilkes of why it wa
easy to lash out at him.

"Did you look for him?"

"I'm not—I don't have the talents people think I have. But the search v
thorough and the people did it out of love. He's just gone. Now you, Mr. Will
why are you here?"

"After we talked that night, my wife died. You knew that?"

"I did."

"For some reason, I don't really know why, I came back with her ashes."

"And you don't know why?"

"I guess if she wanted to die here, then this is where she should remain."

"So you do know why."

"My God," Wilkes says, trying to suppress a smile and frustration at the s
time. "You have knack for pissing people off."

"And you seldom say what you mean. You know exactly why you're here.
okay to say so. Now, where will you put the ashes?"

"I haven't thought that far ahead."

"Of course you have. Where?"

hat shack. Somewhere around there."

nd you're sure you wouldn't like some tea?"

ilkes smiles. "I tell you about scattering my wife's ashes and you ask me if I

t tea."

ne has nothing to do with the other. No tea then. Let's go."

e old man takes the controls of his camouflage-painted ATV (Wilkes feels

a character in one of Brett's video games) and the two of them head south past

irfield, then east into the same series of hills and rises where, a season before,

a Wilkes had come to die. In the distance the scattering of jury-rigged shacks

most indistinguishable from its surroundings, no longer contrasted by the

v. If anything they look even more forlorn, more desolate, a situation that does

mprove with proximity. The changing season has roughened the terrain, the

ing winter snows having dissolved into an oozing thaw interrupted only by

occasional boulder pushed upwards, released from its frozen constraints.

es is grateful not to be driving: he'd be a new client for Olanna's burial service

d up in the health center with Ilisapie again.

ey pass the first rise, just past the airfield. A single-engine plane swoops

head and touches down just out of sight. Wilkes thinks of Brantley and how

y times he must have done the same thing, not just here but in Baker, Resolute,

Haven—all these names Wilkes had hoped to excise from his mind but which

nue to reverberate.

y brother-in-law," Demarais says. "I think of him whenever a plane flies

"

ou see things," Wilkes says, more a concession than an admission. "Did you

ion him dying like that?"

o, never. I would have told him to stop."

e wouldn't have listened."

obody does."

marais turns the machine north again and they continue around a snow fence

ast a series of cairns.

ere are animals buried in them," Demarais says. "Family pets, maybe even a

We should leave them be."

lkes has no intention of disturbing them.

lon't even know which shack it was," he says.

now the events of that day anger you," Demarais says, "but I do remember

h one. We'll go slow, roundabout—stay on level ground."

It actually feels like summer, even though the digital thermometer at the airf
read a mere sixteen degrees centigrade. Back in Connecticut, this warmth we
have sent Wilkes scurrying for a windbreaker. Then again, back in Connecticut
temperature has already surpassed ninety degrees twice, both times on Memo
Day weekend, when the beach access was stopped well before noon and cars
of disappointed and angry people trudged home. In Repulse Bay the tempera
never rises to such levels, but even these moderate readings have saddened I
Keira was alive last winter. A person, not merely ashes being hauled out into
tundra.

"Are you all right?" Demarais asks.

"What?"

"I asked if you wanted to take a look inside. Where were you?"

"Just spacing," Wilkes says, unaware that they've arrived. "Yeah, let's go."

Wilkes pushes open the door. There is evidence that the shack has been live
recently. Cereal boxes and canned fruit fill one shelf and other jars and an er
liquor bottle lie scattered about. There is a ragged coat draped over a crate a
faint smell of cigarettes. The stove is cold.

"Someone is using it. We should move on," Demarais says. "We can just ge
a few yards."

"Not here," Wilkes says. He glances about inside once more but refuses to d
on the images that rush back so readily.

They cruise by a few more ATV's before Wilkes sees a crowd gathered i
distance.

"What's going on there?"

"Caribou. It's tourist season."

"Is that what I am, a tourist?"

"An angry tourist."

"My friend in Baker Lake says the same thing."

"You'll get better. You have to; otherwise you don't get to see the caribou."

There's an almost imperceptible wink and the corners of Demarais's mouth
slightly. Is this a smile? A joke from Auguste Demarais? Is he capable of hum

"You're making fun of me."

"Don't get me wrong, Mr. Wilkes. You have a right to be any way you wa
be. But admitting it is a good thing."

"You and Manitok should do interventions. You have the same spiel."

"She must be a wise woman. You're lucky to have found her."

he old man turns the ATV toward the caribou crowd, which is already
persing, and drives past them, across the moraine and through a few rivulets
swollen with snow melt. As the topography undulates more, Demarais slows
pace, but not enough to eliminate the queasiness Wilkes is beginning to feel.
With the sun at their back, somewhere along the way the drizzle and mist have
pped, the colors deepen, the contrast sharpens. Even the distant mountains seem
se enough to touch, close enough to park the ATV and scoot up to the top on
t.

Twenty miles away," Demarais says when Wilkes mentions their proximity.
lieve me."

e points instead off to the right where a figure stands, or what looks like a
re. It might be a statue if anyone is foolish enough to erect a memorial no one
ever visit. As they draw nearer, Wilkes recognizes it, though he's forgotten the
d for it.

know what that is, or I knew—"

nukshuk," Demarais says.

es. I've seen the statues before."

t's not just a statue. It's more than that."

e slows the ATV, almost as if he were showing some reverence for it, then
s several yards away. Stonehenge it isn't: the misshapen rocks seem to have
gathered at random based only on their ugliness. They aren't smooth or
ectly aligned. They don't even constitute a decent ceremonial cairn. And
red as they are with what appeared to be a thick layer of lichen, they look as
ey need a good power wash.

s that what *Inukshuk* means? More than that?"

means something that can appear to be a human."

ppear to whom?"

aribou."

don't want to insult any of your native species, but now I know where dumb
al came from."

ook at the slabs," Demarais says. "Everything is laid out in proportion—a wide
that could be an anorak that a hunter would wear, then a thinner torso, then a
slab to simulate outstretched arms, then the head. To a caribou—"

o a really dumb caribou."

"To any caribou it signals danger. They sometimes altered their foraging pa
to avoid them and the Inuit waited for them along the detour. Maybe the carib
are dumb, but the hunters aren't. Maybe...this is a good place?"

"Just some primitive monument."

"But they're trail markers too. I don't have to tell you how vast this land is. You
seen it from the air, there's nothing for hundreds of miles at a time. But there ha
always been people here, and they needed to get from one place to another
follow the food, the water, the seasons. So they built these."

"*Inukshuks*."

Demarais smiles. He is comfortable in the surroundings, even with an adversa

"You never will make a good Inuit. *Inuksuit* is the plural."

"Kind of a combination scarecrows and road signs. Who takes care
these...markers?"

"They're built to withstand anything. They're permanent. As a monument
someone, you can't do better than that."

"But they honor nobody, just legend and myth. At home there's a real monum
with her name on it."

"This marker, so close to the village, maybe it honors a loved one who died b
or hunted nearby. I think something important happened here."

"So it's a place of honor."

Wilkes tries to examine it from a different attitude. It doesn't grow prettier v
close inspection, but the longevity and durability impress him. Polished headsto
in nicely manicured cemeteries have greater appeal, geometric perfection, intri
carvings, moving inscriptions, but nobody ever attributes any function to them
one asks how they'll perform over the next decades, centuries, millennia. T
don't save lives or guide travelers to safety or provide a livelihood for people
survive by the hunt.

For the first time he feels some wonderment at the place. Maybe it's becaus
is no longer consumed by the search for his wife and the concomitant need
survival. The immensity and the strangeness, so far away from everything fami
affects him differently now.

"To last that long," Wilkes says. "That's impressive—I guess—those what
they are."

"Call them stone men, it's easier."

"I've already done that. My sons told me to."

ur boys," Demarais says. "Why are they not here?"

"We had a funeral at home. The boys saw that."

Demarais nods. If a mere body motion can be an indictment, the old man has mastered the skill and Wilkes doesn't miss it.

"So you think this is wrong then?"

"This?"

"Yes, this, scattering these ashes without her sons here."

"I don't know your sons. You're the best judge of where they should and shouldn't

"But someday you should tell them. Do they know about that little girl's death?"

"I told them about the accident."

"But you know it wasn't an accident."

"I'll never know for sure."

"But your wife knew. She kept that secret all those years. How many years will keep yours?"

"I get what you're saying. I do."

"To 'get it' is different than to act on it. I am only pressing you because I think have lost your desire to strike me again."

"Not quite."

Demarais taps a cigarette from his pack and lights it.

"When I was young," he says, "my father told me a story about a man named aq. When this Itigiaq died all his friends stood around and told stories about , and they were all different. It was like they all knew separate people with the e name. His friends had liquor and toasted him and each other and then, as the t went on, fought about what stories were true: what people he liked and didn't , what he had done and not done. Everyone got drunk, there were fights and ple got hurt. In the end they agreed never to talk about him again."

"But he was already dead."

"His spirit wasn't. Nothing remained except his lies."

"Then what happened?"

"What do you mean?"

"Well he's dead and buried, if it isn't winter of course and he doesn't have to wait the thaw, what else bad can happen to him?"

"I think you know the answer, Mr. Wilkes. You don't accept all this spiritua
and yet here you are, thousands of miles from home, with a box of ashes you n
to scatter in just the right place. I think you understand my story better than
want to."

Wilkes nods, then gathers in the scene again. There is nothing beautiful abou
nothing ugly. He remembers Leo in that unpronounceable art gallery in B
Lake, Leo who found Americans' fascination with lighthouses to be so amus
He called them insignificant and common, like this place, like these stone mer

Demarais puffs casually on his cigarette.

"As you Americans like to say, it's your move."

"Right here then?"

"If this is the place." Demarais starts to walk away

"Where are you going?"

"Thought you needed some privacy."

"No, I want a witness. Besides, you can't have a ceremony with one person."

Demarais stops as Wilkes removes the box from the duffel bag. The fun
director advised him to spend less if he planned to simply scatter the ashes. Des
that, Wilkes opted for the larger one, the pricier one—lining, integrated l
heavy-duty hinges, brass nameplate forever to be unengraved—little accesso
he didn't know existed from an industry he didn't know existed. And now he wo
scatter the ashes a thousand miles from home in a place Keira had, for want
better word, chosen. But Demarais's words—*something important has happe
here*—resonate, make it suitable.

He unlocks the container with a small key, carefully unfolds the velvet liner,
reaches in. The ashes are grittier than he expected, more like comminuted s
than fireplace ash. He turns slightly until he feels the breeze at his back, then ta
a handful and wordlessly tosses it like an inept softball pitcher. Some drifts
the breeze but most of it falls to earth near his feet. He had created an imag
ashes caught in the polar winds, borne across hundreds of miles of ba
landscape, suffusing everything with the remains of the woman he once lo
Eternity.

Instead they lie at his feet.

"Patience," Demarais says, standing close and almost whispering. "Warm
like this, the breeze doesn't stay down for long."

Wilkes nods.

And he waits.

e smoke from Demarais's cigarette rises straight up, and the sun through the
cirrus feels warm.

en without warning the breeze kicks up again, barely moving the low
tation, then nudging the collar of Wilkes's jacket against his neck. Some of
aller grass begins to bend and he tosses another handful. Some of it falls, but
gh of it remains airborne for Wilkes to convince himself that it will never
earth. He throws more, always with the same motion, always in the same
tion. It's more ritual than ceremony, but it's right. And the breeze, as if in
ert, remains active until he draws near the bottom of the container and his tears
obscured his vision so much that he can barely see the ashes or their path. He
nothing, not aloud, not silently. He doesn't try to reassemble their twenty years
ther in a few final moments, nor does he improvise some incantation: he
ly does what he thinks she wanted.

feels a hand on his shoulder.

m going to take that walk now," Demarais says. "Maybe give you a minute."

o, I'm good. Thanks."

o, you're not. Take some time, look at the place and fix it in your mind."

ilkes puts his hand on one of the rocks that constitute the *inuksuit*. If he forgets
ything else Inuit, every other word and phrase and custom and myth and
nan and hamlet, he cannot forget this. He feels the roughness of the top
ces and the almost glassy sheen of the sides. All of it is cold, as if it hasn't
ht up yet with the thaw, the season, the solstice. But though it looks out of
ace, it doesn't budge, even when he leans on it. And there's some lettering, a
ays b, something like a broken question mark, still another that resembles
-framed eyeglasses. They mean nothing to him, but they mean something
theless. Maybe he can ask Manitok when he gets back to Baker, or maybe the
ery is a good thing.

marais returns. "The box...."

s yours. A memento. Or give it to Olanna. Maybe she'll expand some day,
the earth gets so warm that everybody gets squeezed up near the Pole and
ation becomes the only option. She'll probably be about 500 years old, but,
ever know."

er spirit will still—"

n joking."

now. We should go now. The party will begin and there'll be plenty of drunks
TV's all day and through the night. And you want to get back."

Wilkes wipes his face with his sleeve and takes one more look at the spot.
"I'm ready."

"Your cell phone. Does it take pictures?"

"Yes.".

"Stand in front of that *inuksuit* and I'll take your picture."

"Really?"

"Memory is fickle. Someday you'll wonder if this ever happened, if you v actually here. The picture will help."

Demarais struggles with the phone but manages to snap a few photos w Wilkes stands expressionless, his face as stony as the structure behind him knows what Demarais is doing, that these photos are in no way intended Wilkes. They're for the boys, so that someday he can tell them the truth and have them grow up the way their mother did, enveloped by some giga destructive, calamitous lie.

"The solstice," Demarais says, handing Wilkes the phone. "Where do you v to observe it, here or back in Baker?"

"The sooner I get to Baker, the sooner I get home. I should be able to get a f this afternoon with everyone coming in. Where do you celebrate it?"

"I don't. Having a day without darkness means nothing to me. The consolation I take from it is the knowledge that the days will begin to get shor

"That's consolation?"

"I like the cold. I like the dark time. I like people being shut up in their ho and contemplating their lives. When the days are long and the weather is w there's no time for that."

"And the long nights...more time to dream?"

"That isn't such a good thing for me. If I could take back some of those drear but I didn't make your wife come here. I just knew something would happen.

"I don't think she knew either. All her luggage, it was salvaged and returnec month. She had packed for warm weather, nothing more."

"So. We should get back before the drinking starts. Maybe you should tonight. Jane will have people in the gallery and you would be welcome. Sh good cook."

"But you won't be there."

"No, and it will be different without Curt."

"No visions of him? No inkling of what happened?"

Demarais shakes his head. "I dream of him a lot, but he's dead, even in the dreams. A good man. A good spirit. Still, the solstice parties will go on."

"And Keira? Do you still dream of her?"

He shakes his head.

"I hope you will understand this when I tell you that I miss her. Those dreams always disturbed me, but I always thought I was meant to do something good. I was wrong. Now I don't know why.... Come, we should leave."

The drizzle had begun again while they were talking, and the ride back is damp and unpleasant. Wilkes asks him if they can stop at Jane's so that he can pay his respects, but though Demarais agrees, he won't go in. He and his ex may not be enemies, but Gus doesn't want to exacerbate her suffering in any way.

When Wilkes walks in, he finds Jane moving some small sculptured pieces onto a shelf near the window.

"More walkby traffic?" he says.

It takes her a moment to recognize him.

"You were here in the winter. You were looking for someone. Curt said—he said it didn't work out."

"It didn't. But Curt literally took care of me back in January," he says. "He waited with me, helped me get everything straightened out, the protocol and travel. I was alone up here. I could never have gotten through that myself."

"He was at his best when everything was at its worst. That's why I don't agonize over his death. I really miss him. Ben does too. But Curt himself, that plane going down. He handled it."

"They should rename the airport after him."

"In the end he was just a pilot. His picture is in the *Naujat* though, behind the bar. And you can order a Brantley now: two shots and a beer. He'd probably appreciate that more than some big memorial. You, though. Curt helped so many people who didn't come back to say so. I hope things work out for you—"

"Wilkes," he says. She's forgotten the name. "Martin Wilkes. And thank you. Everything takes time."

He asks about Ben, about business, about the weather; but as usual Jane is trying to get something done. Outside he finds Gus leaning against a signpost.

"Let me ask you something, Gus."

Demarais looks startled.

"I don't think you ever called me Gus—ever called me anything. This must be Nous."

"It is. The window boxes on your house. Why?"

"I plant grass there. When I lived in Colorado I had a lawn and I wasted an h
every week cutting it. Now I can mow it with clippers in ten minutes. I cut it on
La fête du Travail."

"What?"

"Labor Day. We usually get our first snow within a week or so. I cut the la
before it dies. Also, if you visit and I'm not home, there's a key in each wind
box."

"I'm surprised you lock up. You don't seem the type."

"Lots of crazy people out there. You have to be careful."

The rapprochement between Demarais and Wilkes has little effect on th
separation, which is abrupt and conventional. No parting words of wisdom fr
the old man, no final apology from Wilkes. Two hours after scattering Kei
ashes, Wilkes is on a plane to Baker Lake with yet another pilot.

The aircraft rises into a leaden sky that renders the bay gloomy and ominc
From altitude he sees a large supply ship, probably finishing its journey north fi
Moosonee, heedless of the small bergs and drift ice in its path. Maybe it wc
have been romantic, he thinks, to have watched the ashes drift out over the wa
but that's not what Keira wanted.

As if he ever knew.

When he gets back to Connecticut he'll square things with McNally, tell him l
it ended. Whatever truths are out there, he no longer needs to know. Whate
secrets her parents held all these years, and Wilkes knows there are some, they
take to their graves. They loved their daughter, and whatever they did came
out of rancor or spite, but some mistaken notion of protecting her. He will alw
blame them, but his anger will be tempered by the knowledge that, in sheltei
her, they did only what he should have done himself.

Besides, they're still the boys' grandparents, and Wilkes knows the perils
challenges of a single-parent household, though he has read often enough that
never the question of how many parents but of how effective that one remai
parent is. But he is starting off with a lie: every visit to the cemetery will be a si
and every mention of their mother will remind the boys of a headstone in a tran
setting and remind him of ashes caught in an Arctic breeze. The Inuit would kr
and on some level so does he, that a visit to some marble marker is never n
than symbolic, that a visit to the Viet Nam memorial is no less affecting th
visit to the local cemetery where the family member is actually interred. Wi

n live with that lie at least for a while, but he will come back. Next time he will
ng his sons.

At the airport in Baker Lake he scuffles about for a flight out, but there's nothing
ailable until the following evening. That means getting out of Churchill at some
godly hour and spending another day in Saskatoon or Winnipeg. He no longer
es which, for both require a phone call home to the Easons to enlist their help
taking care of the boys. As always, they acquiesce.

At the co-op he surprises Manitok yet again.

I didn't expect to see you today. Did you finish things?"

In some ways," he says. "Now I can't get a flight. How are the preparations
ng?"

Good I guess. A lot of what happens is improvised and a lot of it depends on
w drunk people are."

Demarais warned me about drunk drivers."

In Repulse maybe. Not here. If you start up a motor of any kind, even a
erator or an outboard, you get locked up. It doesn't undo all the bad behavior,
it keeps us alive. So you'll be here for it."

I'm not going to do a very good job of celebrating."

You miss your wife. And you've been looking for answers since January, almost
f a year, and now there are no more questions. Your quest will have to be
erent."

This wasn't a quest. A quest has to be more than that. Curing cancer, ending
ger, exploring the moon—"

Call it a focus then. It has to change."

But the answers aren't answers. Everything seems wrapped up in coincidence
chance and—"

e stops: his eyes are tearing up.

Twice in one day," he says. "I didn't cry at the wake, the funeral, not until this
rnoon."

You're mourning the part of you that sought answers. You'll need some time to
ist. But even people in mourning," she says with the hint of a smile, "need a
ak. Listen."

e can hear music through a tinny speaker, distorted and far away, a few notes
recognizable.

Summertime?"

he nods.

"You had to steal an American song for your Canadian festival?"

"We'll sing it in Nunavutian if it makes you feel better."

"That's not a word," he says, then cocks his head. "Is it?"

"You're getting better. It's only 7:00 or so. Go back to your room and—"

"I wasn't planning to stay tonight."

"So you have no place?"

"I can try the hotel."

"Not tonight. You'd never find a vacancy. Here," and she reaches into her jeans pocket and pulls out some keys. Take these, one block down, left, number seventeen, upstairs. This key opens my outside door; this one, the apartment."

"I can't do that."

"Yes, you can. I'll be here until nine. Make yourself at home, get some sleep. You won't be doing that later."

"I told you—"

"You're not going to do a very good job of celebrating. I got that part. So you try. If it doesn't work out, you have place to crash. Take it."

He lifts the keys from the counter.

"It's a red building. I see you're traveling light. If you need clothes—"

"You have clothes for me?"

"I was going to say I'll sell you some. I'm still running a business here. Believe me, if Curt Brantley were alive and you were flying out with him, you wouldn't be going tonight. He would celebrate, so take his place. I'll be someone you know. And Deidre. And Leo, right, from the gallery? You'll feel like a native."

"A nap sounds good. You have a landline at your place?"

"Help yourself. Call home."

"I need to make some plans too. Next time I'll have my kids with me."

"Next time? Seriously? I knew that eventually you'd fall in love with our little town."

"I don't hate it, not at all, but my kids—. They need to see, you know, where this happened. Here, and in Repulse."

"Of course. You'll stop here at the co-op, right, so that I can meet them?"

"They don't travel with a lot of cash. They won't make good customers."

"I can always sell them something, and maybe you can put a picture of them your wallet."

"You never asked to see one."

"You didn't have one, otherwise you would have shown me."

'll have one by then."

ome in August when it's warm and green. There won't be much for the boys
o, but you'll be surprised at how it looks. And then, by September the first
v...and we start over."

hat's what this—this friend in Repulse said. Brantley's brother-in-law. And the
time begins."

he what?"

emarais, the man in Repulse, he calls it that. I suppose there's no Inuit word
t since it's dark all the time."

aggarik."

aggarik. Easy. I can even pronounce it."

flips her keys in his hands and picks up his bag.

isten, Manitok, I don't want people to talk."

ecause there's a man at my place? I guess on any other day I'd worry, but
dy sleeps on the solstice and the only ones who sleep together are the ones
wind up drunk in the back seat of a car or wrapped in a comforter on the
h. I don't get into cars with men and I don't take my comforter to the beach.
dy will talk."

e music continues in the background, occasionally swelling, and there is a
pop-pop too, then another.

irecrackers. Someone is starting early."

ou know, if you strung some red white and blue bunting around town and
ed grilling some hot dogs, it'd be the Fourth of July."

hen call it that if it makes you feel more like celebrating."

nods. It's more concession than agreement. He turns toward the door just in
to see a person of unknown gender enter, dressed like a polar bear and wearing
e cape. Wilkes laughs, turns back toward Manitok.

e smiles. "Falling in love with our little town yet?"

hat probably won't happen, but like I said, I don't hate it. I just don't think I'd
to live and die here."

ou're safe today," she says, as her eyes follow the new customer. "You're
dy alive, and nobody dies on the solstice."

a wooded area on a bend in the road, a state highway sign pokes above some ready overgrown weeds.

Hampton.

It's Labor Day weekend and the verdure of summer has already lost its sheen, the golden greens of June vanquished by the suffocating heat of July and August. The crimsons and russets are still a month away, but they're coming; and for the Wilkes family, it will be the first autumn without...after the first summer without...and the first spring...and on...and on....

Today it's muted greens and September drizzle: an ugly day to end the summer and an ugly drive to intensify it. Ugly, but comparatively short. Since Keira died eight months before, Martin Wilkes has made three trips to Nunavut, the last one with Brett and James, enduring long flights and sparse accommodations and eating their vacation fund. In Repulse Bay, he showed them the *inukshuk* where he scattered the ashes, told them they could pick up some dirt and scatter it too. The disclosure produces no histrionics, no tears, no anger. There remains, Wilkes knows even now, a part of each boy that has been unable to excise the word suicide from his mind. If he can't convince himself, how does he convince them?

In his new role he has eviscerated his work schedule, at times alienating the execs and the clients. He has retained the housecleaner, but taken on everything else at home, has been especially wary of the boys, devouring articles on childhood behavior in the face of a parental loss. They've been okay, but he knows better than to trust appearances any more. Today he hopes to bring one chapter to an end, not with another flight to the Arctic, but with a much shorter, much easier trip, a ninety-minute drive to where it all began—or ended: Hampton. On a June afternoon thirty years before, a Keira Eason he didn't even know began a descent he could inhibit but never stop.

"Maple Drive," he says, but the boys are hardly paying attention. They are totally occupied with their music and games. Wilkes turns down the street, then pulls over, but before he can come to a full stop, a woman approaches the car: blue shorts, UConn t-shirt, sneakers. It's Saturday and she's been working in the garden cleaning up the yard or maybe guarding against suspicious cars.

He opens the passenger side window: her face fills the opening immediately.

"Can I help you?"

"Just showing my kids where their mother grew up. 75 Maple."

She looks in the back seat, acknowledges the boys. James waves hi, B
approaches, but falls just short of eye contact. They hear nothing. The won
seems nonplussed. If they're here to see their mother's childhood home, then wh
is their mother.

"She passed in February of this year," Wilkes says. "I just wanted them to se

"Sorry for your loss," the woman says. She still seems wary. Is this some n
scheme where a father and two sons case the neighborhood for vulnerable hor
to burglarize?

"It was in the eighties," he says. "I'm Martin Wilkes."

He turns around, gains the boys' attention, motions for them to remove
earbuds. Exasperation but obedience.

"Be polite and say hello."

They oblige. And wait. Their father has told them the where and the why of
journey. There was never an indication of human contact, of visiting.

The woman acknowledges them, opening up a little.

"We've only been here about ten years. The Olmsteads had it before us. Y
wife must have lived here before them."

"That seems about right. The Reeds," he says, switching topics awkwardly. '
they still live across the street?"

"I don't share names. Don't take this the wrong way, but we have a neighborh
watch program. Had some break-ins last year, so we're a little cautious."

"Once-bitten, I understood. I only ask because there was an accident in that ho
a long time ago. A child, their child, was killed. My wife would never talk at
it, and now, well someone dies and you try to give that person's life some sha
guess. I don't know if I'm making myself clear."

"The people in that house," the woman says, conceding a fact or two. "T
pretty much keep to themselves."

"We just took a chance," he says. He had been afraid to call the Reeds f
certain they wouldn't talk to him, that they needed no further reminders of the
they lost their daughter.

"I've heard stories about that," the woman says, "from people who have bee
town forever. But if the family had trouble in the past, then it's the past."

Wilkes knows that there was no past for Keira Eason, not after that party,
after Sylvy, but it's easier to acquiesce. She is much younger than Wilkes,
cautious neighbor. Newly married maybe, no family yet, her husband putte
around inside the house on a Saturday morning, or playing golf with friend

ybe grocery shopping for a wife who works all week. No sign of children, and ybe no empathy for what happened on this street a generation before. She seems out to tell him to move along, but instead wipes her hands on her oversized t-rt and smiles.

"You can park right here and cross the street. It's safe."

He turns the key and the car quiets. The woman from #75 walks back toward her rd as Wilkes leads the boys up the walkway to the Reeds' front door. He has etched out some things he will say, but the plan goes immediately awry when door swings open to reveal a child James's age, standing silently, staring at him.

Hi," Wilkes says. "I'm looking for your...father?" No, that can't be. Grandfather ybe. Shit.

The child runs back into the house and yells something indecipherable while lkes and the boys stand on the stoop waiting. Seconds later a man appears in the orway.

Sorry about that," he says, looking more amused than annoyed. "My grandson es to answer the door. Can I help you?"

I don't mean to disturb you," Wilkes says, and lays a hand on James's shoulder. ut my wife used to live across the street. She was friends with...Sylvy. Was that ur daughter? Are you Mr. Reed?"

Albert, yes." His expression changes little, but there are slight creases in his ehead, and though Wilkes may be imagining it or simply projecting, he seems er.

My wife was Keira Eason."

The Easons. I remember them. Two girls. They moved away and we never rd from them. Do you want to come in? The rain...."

No, thanks, it's just a drizzle. Their other daughter was Hayley. She's out in zona now. Keira's—gone."

Gone?"

She died last winter."

So young? She must have been—well Sylvy would have been 42—"

lbert Reed pulls a cigarette from a nearly empty pack, then notices Brett and es and puts it away.

come out here to smoke when the grandkids are visiting," he says. "I'm sorry ear about your wife. And leaving two kids like that. Tough."

eed is probably the same age as Wilkes's father-in-law. Sixty? Sixty-five? but ooks much older, much grayer, much more, for want of a better word, beaten.

And what would Wilkes himself look like thirty years from now if somethi
happened to his sons? What would he look like right now if that pilot had not pull
off a miracle that January afternoon so that instead of waiting in LaGuardia tl
day, he'd been standing by the Hudson waiting for the bodies of his family to
retrieved? Albert Reed has probably never recovered, and Wilkes has no right
be here making things worse.

"We should be going," he says, then hears a woman's voice.

"What is it honey?"

Reed answers without turning around.

"Remember the Easons across the street? Their little girl, Keira. She passe
few months back. This is their...her husband."

"Martin Wilkes," he says. Did he even introduce himself?

"Abby Reed," she says. "Keira? She would have been about Sylvy's age. Go
so young. And these are your boys?"

He proffers their names, but the Reeds, though polite, probably want only
know why they're standing at the front door on a dismal Saturday a lifetime af
their daughter died. He should leave, but he's come this far.

"I just wanted to say—Keira was there. She wasn't supposed to be, but she wa

"What do you mean?"

"At the party that day."

Nothing. No reaction. No response. No surprise. Like dropping a bomb tl
watching it fail to detonate, leaving Wilkes with the awkward silence he hims
created.

"I...we...just wanted you to know."

"We knew. Her sister told us," the woman says.

"Hayley?"

"Yes. One day she got off the school bus right there." Abby Reed points to
spot where Wilkes's car is parked. "She crossed the street and said her sister
at the party and she knew all about Sylvy."

"Did you tell the Easons?"

"Of course. They said Keira was so upset she couldn't even look at this ho
anymore. I think that's why they moved."

Specter of death, Mrs. Eason's term for it.

"So they admitted that Keira was there?"

"They said Hayley liked to make up stories. It didn't matter. Sylvy was gone

ilkes nods. "Boys, why don't you wait for me in the car." They watch the boys
s the street, then Wilkes turns back to the Reeds. "I'm sorry to have brought all
up."

t's fine. We like remembering her. She was...a handful. Keira must have told
."

he never talked about her."

eally?"

never knew anything until a few months ago."

ur daughter was tough," Abby Reed says, stepping around her husband.
erything is so clear, even after all this time. We invited Keira to the party but
Eason said she was doing something else that day. Maybe they thought Sylvia
a bad influence."

he was our first," the husband says. He remembers her with fondness despite
misbehaving or distress. "We were kind of feeling our way through, if you
v what I mean."

's hard these days, raising kids."

s wife shakes her head. "It's always hard. We weren't even going to have the
. She'd been disruptive in school and we didn't want to reward her, but—"

insisted," Reed says. "Fathers and daughters. That's just how it is. The thing
doesn't matter who was there. Something like that, there's no explanation. It
happens. Maybe you can tell the Easons we still think of them once in a while.
moved out of here so fast we hardly had a chance to say goodbye."

l do that."

eira went off to Brainard for a while, I remember. Then one day, I think it was
e winter, they were gone. Just like that. No goodbyes."

rainard?"

ver in Rhode Island. Not far."

ke I said, we never really talked much about that. What's Brainard?"

bert's wife puts a hand on her husband's shoulder, a signal of sorts that he's
dy said too much, but it's too late.

rainard?" Reed asks, evasive. Stalling.

ou said she went off to Brainard."

hat's just a kind of private school."

ut not a private school?"

ou'd have to look it up. For all I know it's not even open any more. You lose
."

"But when it was open?"
Albert Reed shakes his head.
"Kids go through tough times."
"I know that," Wilkes says, motioning toward his two boys. "What
Brainard?"
"Tell you what," Reed says. "It's only fifteen minutes from here. You could d
over and—"
"It's Saturday."
"They don't close on weekends, or at least they didn't used to."
"So it's a boarding school?"
"Like that."
Wilkes steps away from the door, he doesn't want the man to feel threatened
the cryptic responses are frustrating him.
"Mr. Reed, Keira's gone. I'm just beginning to understand that there
elements in her life that I knew nothing about. Is Brainard an institution of s
kind?"
Reed's wife moves closer to the door.
"It's a school for kids with social issues," she says. "Not criminals, just
know—."
There are several appropriate reactions to the disclosure, and Wilkes choose
most inappropriate: he laughs.
"I'm sorry," he says. "I know it's not funny, but that makes no sense."
"We thought it was the shock of the accident. Kids can react in different wa
"So Brainard is an asylum?"
"It's a school. Nice place, up on a little hill."
"On a little hill? And fenced off?"
"I don't remember. We don't go by there much."
"But I'll bet there's a big gate in front."
Reed vouches for his wife. He doesn't remember either.
"And it's close by?"
"I can point you in the right direction."
"I have GPS, but thank you for...talking about this."
"Your in-laws," Reed says, returning to his normal volume. "How are
doing?"
"They're retired, living in Greenwich."
"And Hayley. Do you ever see her?"

She's out west, not much for family ties."

Give them our best," Reed says. "And our sympathy. The years go by, Mr.
lkes. Nothing much we can do about it."

Vilkes has never had a problem recognizing words that signal the end of a
nversation, and within minutes they're driving away. He thinks about asking the
ys if they want to see Mommy's school, but a cordoned off building on a hill
ctically screams insanity. When he gets to Route 6 again, he takes the left, heads
st, away from Brainard and whatever meaningless thirty-year-old truths lie
re.

IcNally, he says to himself. The guy is too smart not to have unearthed this little
bit. And Clifton in his solarium who "liked" Keira. He must remember, must
e been told that Keira had been sent to Brainard. Back then, in that community,
phrase itself must have been damning.

ven so, a few months in a special school doesn't define a person as crazy,
balanced, insane. It doesn't make her anything other than what she was, or what
had been before last January when the guilt of all those years overwhelmed her
she chose not to fight it anymore.

Do you think Mommy ate at that McDonald's?" James asks as they follow the
d out of Hampton.

Probably, sure. We should too."

e isn't sure he can choke down any food at all, but he owes the boys a treat, one
will placate them before the long drive back.

At home, still early afternoon, the boys salvage what's left of a wasted Saturday
le Wilkes unloads the dishwasher from the night before—or two nights. He
sure. From his kitchen window he notices Millie Hendrickson in an
ppealing oversized t-shirt, yard work apparel, and he wonders whatever
ame of that photo McNally flashed in front of him back in January, the bikini
and the towel. These days he talks to her on occasion, but the conversation
ays centers on his new life and how he and the boys are adjusting. And if he
her the truth, that plenty of mornings he doesn't want to get out of bed, what
ld she do? He doesn't fantasize about Millie Hendrickson anymore, doesn't
asize about anyone but Keira. The essence of fantasy: it can never come true.

nny how McNally had Millie's photo that fast, he says to himself, suppressing
ile. The guy knew everything, probably knew about Brainard and didn't want
lly Keira's memory. It isn't the job of a PI to decide what information his client
ds, but Wilkes remembers that fortune cookie, the heart of gold, and can forgive

that little foible, maybe call him tomorrow, just to check in as he has d
infrequently. They'll talk about the Yankees, maybe, or the stock market, or may
some new debauched clients McNally is gouging. Wilkes will provide some det
about the trip to Nunavut and ask about Lynne because he does remember t
McNally has a wife and she has a name. Maybe he'll tell the PI about the night
spent at Manitok's, he on the couch alone because by 3:00 a.m. he had fai
miserably at staying up all night, and she hopscotching between taverns
galleries, warming herself after that midnight swim until she wound up, with
sleep, at the co-op the following day. Wilkes won't mention Brainard or the Ree
or anything else that defines the chapter in Keira's life he was never privy to.

When the phone rings he checks the caller ID. Eason. Greenwich.

Not much, he says to Keira's father. Just hanging out. No mention of
morning's trip. One day at some family dinner James will undoubtedly mention
fact that they saw mommy's old house and there'll be a moment or two
discomfort. But then, like everything else, the event will recede into a past
Wilkes never shared. Or maybe, and the thought makes him smile, the tuurngai
those cold and evil spirits—will come around some day when Demarais, exact
his revenge at last, offers them tea and tells them where they can find Ma
Wilkes.

But not today. The mist has been scoured out by the warm westerly breeze
ruffles the salvias and the bees moving in concert with them. No retribution fi
those cold and angry gods this Saturday afternoon. It's too warm for the tuurng
too warm for the Inuit, too warm for Demarais and Repulse and stone statues
every other frozen memory that haunts him. But he notices also the first hin
color on some of the maples and without warning it begins: another banal mus
about the passage of time, more sorrow, more remorse.

Remorse. McNally always called it a phony emotion. Maybe that's just
cynicism of a man too much involved in the sordid and unsavory, or maybe it'
honest assessment of a man unwilling to turn a blind eye. In a way the PI is
like Curtiss Brantley, someone who knows the odds and accepts them with
question. After all, it was Brantley who flew those unpredictable routes on his
terms, and who, whether he spiraled downward to a sudden death or felt his
gradually slip away on the desolate tundra, left no room for what-ifs, no capa
for remorse. Wilkes has not reached that point.

In the yard Brett tosses an undersized football to James. The younger boy mi
it, then retrieves it from a garden plot that has lain fallow this summer, its e

tent graced only by some perennials that didn't require Keira's tending. Maybe
xt season, Wilkes says to himself, he'll turn the soil, start over.
"Come and play," James says to him, hugging the football like an infant.
Wilkes holds up a finger, in a minute, then sits on the sun-baked concrete of the
ck stoop.
Without Keira this picture is incomplete, every picture is, but each day he is
ter, or maybe just more normal. In a moment or two he'll go inside and pour
nself a gin, he's made a conscious effort to cut back, but on days like this....
He squints at the late-afternoon cirrus as a gust rattles the screen door behind
n.

Acknowledgement

gratitude to the Chimney Crest Writers—David Fortier, Dawn Leger, Michele
ko, Frank DeFrancesco, Linda Lynch, and the others who have at various times
part of the group these past five years—for their honesty, encouragement, and
usiasm. Thanks to all my teaching colleagues, especially Walter Wilcox—now
some three decades—genuine friend, superb teacher, self-effacing mentor,
iant colleague, and lover of the English language despite all its vagaries—or
be because of them. My love of the language began with Walt. And finally
ks to all the students I met while teaching English at Plainville High School. I
supposed to be the educator, but the classroom was always, for me, an
ation.

Lefora Publishing

Our mission is to publish new literature, including fiction, poetry, memoir,
criticism, with a focus on contributions that best serve to enhance and repre
the intellectual life of the New England region.

> *Lefora Publishing* seeks to support a vibrant community of writers
> ...by stewarding writers through the editorial and marketing
> process, ...by working with emerging talent as well as seasoned
> writers,
> ...by sharing in the development of their careers,
> ...by hosting an online journal,
> ...by sponsoring writing contests,
> ...by offering speaking opportunities.
> and we will do each of these as we create the *Lefora Publishing*
> legacy.

The porcupine depicted in our logo represents the character of
Englanders; in fact, the porcupine is a mammal indigenous to the New Eng
states. Additionally, the quill has a long history as a writing implement comm
utilized by writers in New England and elsewhere.

For more information about *Lefora Publishing*, including author submis
guidelines, please visit our website at *www.leforapublishingllc.com.*